THE BRONZE
HORSEMEN

CHRYSALIS

ENJOY THE EARLY
YEARS OF THE
FAMILY SERVICE
AS THEY STRUGGLE
TO SURVIVE

FEB 2015

The Bronze Horsemen

The First People To Tame Horses

David Mallegol

Library of Congress Control Number:		2012919978
ISBN:	Hardcover	978-1-4797-3962-2
	Softcover	978-1-4797-3961-5
	Ebook	978-1-4797-3963-9

To order additional copies of this book, contact:
Xlibris Corporation
1-888-795-4274
www.Xlibris.com
Orders@Xlibris.com

DEDICATION

To the two women who made a difference in my life:

My mother, Ruth Nenninger Mallegol
and my wife, Irma Ildiko Mallegol

ACKNOWLEDGMENTS

Discover magazine article "The Dawn Riders by William Speed Weed"

Sandra L. Olsen PhD of the Carnegie Museum of Natural History for her many publications for the Botai people, which inspired me to write this historic novel

Gabriele Roden MD, for guidance as an author

Patrice Wilton, for guidance as an author

Robert Roden, West Palm Beach, for the artwork and design

Robert L. Bacon of "The Perfect Write," editor and adviser

Irma Ildiko Mallegol, for proofreading, patience, and editing

Agnes Sanchez, proofreading

Xlibris Publication Team

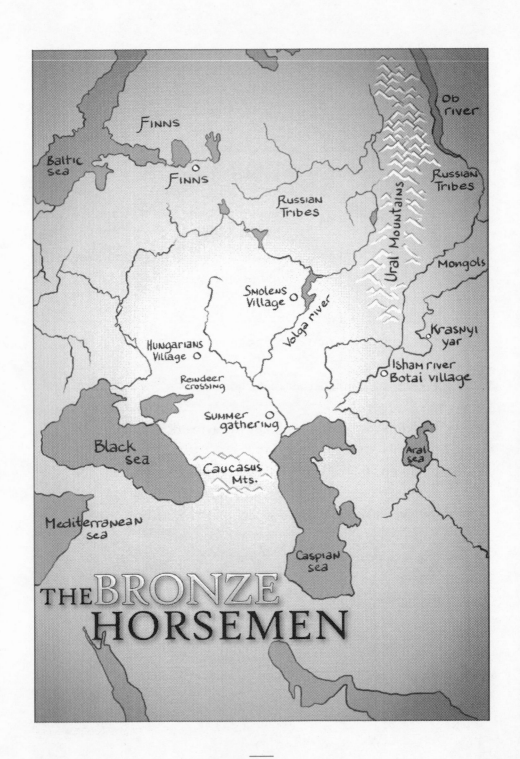

THE BRONZE HORSEMEN

Introduction

The Bronze Horsemen

SOMEWHERE, SOMEPLACE, SOMEONE captured a horse and rode it. This event changed the history of the human race for the next five thousand years. Recent archeological evidence as discovered by Sandra L. Olsen PhD of the Carnegie Museum, Pittsburgh, Pennsylvania, strongly suggests that the actual people who were first to ride a horse were the Botai (pronounced as [bow-tie]), a Caucasian tribe who lived in Southern Russia, or present-day Kazakhstan, where horses still play an important role in everyday life.

The Bronze Horsemen takes you back to the Bronze Age south of the Ural Mountains. Three small language-related clans of hunter-gatherers are driven from their lands by more powerful enemies from the north. Their enemies want their hunting territory that controls annual reindeer migration routes. The clans barely survive from one year to the next as their numbers are reduced by attacks from enemies, severe cold weather, and starvation. The clans can no longer fight off their enemies and leave their homeland. They move south where the clans form a new people, the Botai.

To add to their problems, an "accident" takes the life of their longtime leader, or as they call him, their Oldson. His death leads to new leadership when Bruno is elected. He and his childhood friend Daven change the lives of the people they lead. They are guided by a group of senior women who take part in major decisions. Slowly, the Botai fortunes change from those being hunted to extinction to the most respected and powerful hunters in the known world.

The Botai are the first people to capture, tame, and ride horses. They struggle to keep their secret from friends and enemies. Being mounted changes their mobility, methods of hunting, warfare, and how they obtain food. Distance is no longer a problem. They learn to defend their territory and improve their alliances. Their old enemies pay the price. Both men and women play major roles as they advance their society. In the real world, history notes the Botai were a dominant force for six hundred years, twice as long as the United States has been in existence.

Follow Bruno, Daven, Ildiko, and Diana as the Botai and their horses change the world. New ideas and new discoveries replace old ways. At the end, they use their advances against enemies who threaten their existence in a fight to the death. Just when they think war is over, problems face them again.

If you love horses, female and male heroes, winning and losing, and most of all revenge, I am sure you will enjoy this historic novel. I hope to have the second book, Adventures of the Bronze Horsemen, published within a year of the first one.

This is a book of fiction based on historical facts. I have created the characters, the problems, and the solutions. Any similarities to real characters, names, or persons is purely coincidental.

David Mallegol

TABLE OF CONTENTS

CHARACTERS

Botai:
Botai leader: Oldson (Leader or Chief)
Original Oldson: Sandar; wife Ruth, son Ander

Three Clans:
Horse Clan leader: Daven; first wife, Gertrude; second wife, Ildiko; children, Mikl and Marc

Bear Clan leader: Bruno; wife, Diana; twin sons, Jon and Flint; two daughters

Aurochs Clan leader: Janos; two wives, three sons Peter, Patrick and Tomas

Elder women: Ruth, Judy, Emma and Patts
Medicine woman: Patts

Hungarians:
First chief, Kraven; second chief, Rhoden

Horses and owners:
Gray Boy owned by Mikl

Dawn owned by Daven
Boomer owned by Bruno
Babe owned by Janos

Mongols leader: Temuge

CHAPTER 1

Eastern Europe: 3000 BC

I AM DAVEN, head of the Horse Clan and lead hunter for all of the Botai. Since you are interested, I am happy to tell you of my people and the adventures that take place during the next year, but first, here is what I remember about early life in my village.

Screams woke me and my father early one morning. It was dawn when the men with the red armbands attacked our village for the third time this year. Our villagers were in panic as they ran from their burning houses. I was afraid I might be killed when I came out and saw the Smolens leader. He was the same man who killed my mother on the last raid. I recognized the fresh scar that ran from his scalp across his right cheek to the point on his chin. It was my father who cut his face as they fought hand to hand with knives the last time we were attacked.

I was nine years old at the time and armed with a boy's bow. It was far from effective against two dozen hardened raiders. Still, I fired an arrow with a flint tip and struck the one with the scar on his face in his right shoulder. He laughed at the wound I inflicted and raised his hatchet to kill me, but a woman named Ruth pulled me away from the fight. We ran with the rest of the women and children, led by an elder named

---

Emma. My father killed two of those men with red armbands before he himself was killed that day.

My friend Bruno was ten years old and a big kid for his age. He fought alongside my father and grandfather and killed one raider and wounded two others as the marauders ran between our pit houses, setting more fires. When it was over, several of our homes were ruined and three more Horse Clan members were dead. A year ago, the Horse Clan had twenty-two people, but after the latest hit-and-run attack by the Smolens, there were just sixteen of us left, and only six men, including Bruno, who could fight. They did their damage and killing and retreated as fast as they came.

That night, Sandor, who we call the Oldson or chief, called our small band together. His features were rigid as stone, and he raised his arms to be sure he had our full attention. "The Smolens are too many and too powerful for us to fight. We have no choice if we are to survive. We must leave our homes and move." He waited for a response or an argument, but there was none. His people knew they had no choice.

Sandor spoke again. He nodded to his friend and companion, Tedd, and said, "Tedd has located a new land on the other side of the Ural Mountains. The new land has plenty of grain, a good supply of salt, fruits and berries, and horses to hunt. It will be hard work and a long trip. I see no other choice. The best thing about the new lands is that the Smolens will never find us." This brought smiles and a voice of approval.

Sandor, the Oldson said, "Tedd and I will attend the summer gathering. With any luck we will be able to convince our relatives in the Bear Clan and the Aurochs Clan to unite with us. They have also been under attack by the Smolens, and their numbers are reduced from last year, as ours are." Sandor glanced around at his audience. "If we continue to live here as an independent clan, we do not have enough hunters to defend ourselves. As leader of the Horse Clan, I will take you to a safer place on the other side of the mountains. That is my decision. We leave tomorrow, and we will not return. The trip will be difficult. I caution each of you to bring only what you can carry."

The announcement was a shock. No one wanted to leave our territory because of the crops we had planted and the plentiful animals to hunt, but everyone realized there was no choice. We left twenty years ago. The first winter was very hectic with building pit houses and hunting what we could before the harsh weather set in. We ate what we had been able to gather or kill in a relatively short time, and there was little meat for our stew pots. Luckily, the winter was mild and of short duration for once, and we made it to spring without losing anyone else.

That spring, the Bear Clan joined up with us in our new home, and the Aurochs Clan soon followed. Both had fought the Smolens during the winter and lost those battles to superior numbers. Like us, each clan had been reduced significantly from the preceding year. Abandoning their villages was also the only option left to them.

Our settlement was located on a branch of the Ob that ran north to an ocean some called the Arctic. We were south and east of the Ural Mountains, probably two hundred miles or so from the Smolens. South of our village were grasslands that ran from east to west for a thousand miles, maybe more. No one really knew. What we did know was that there were wild horses in those grasslands, and they would provide the meat we needed to survive.

Tedd liked this location for several reasons. Of greatest significance, there were freshwater and salt for meat preservation. Because our village was on a sharp bend in the river, the water ran faster here and remained unfrozen all winter. As an added advantage, our village was situated on high ground, so we were able to avoid spring floods. The area had adequate supplies of fruits and vegetables growing naturally in the area. No other people lived close to us, thus there was no longer a need to fight to hold our territory. With the dreaded Smolens out of the picture, we had no enemies and dangers other than an occasional bear or mountain lion that might roam too close. Of course, there were always wolves in the area if someone got careless.

The weather had already cooled as we approached the late summer. Horse hunts were a group effort involving all three clans. Two hunts did not meet our needs for a typical brutal winter, during which temperatures dropped to thirty or forty degrees below zero and stayed there for months at a time. We had already been successful with two hunts, and this would be our third. A fourth will follow.

Gathering peas, lentils, berries, mushrooms, and wheat has become part of everyday life in the fall for our women, but without horse meat, we would not survive the last two months of winter, those we used to call "the starving months." Before we learned to hunt horses effectively, we often saw the oldest and youngest of our people starve to death as winter wore on. I am told by Tedd and Emma, our oldest members that the total number of clan members has generally never increased. Starvation always held our population to a small group. Since the three clans joined together as one people, the hope is that we will develop better gathering and hunting methods, and our food supply will improve.

Our women already have good supplies of most of what we need, except for gooseberries, raspberries, and blueberries. Berries are essential to make pemmican, a combination of peas, berries, and horse meat packed into horse intestines and then smoked to preserve them. Pemmican is eaten as a cold meal on long horse hunts, like the one I am planning. It is a crucial staple since campfire smoke could be smelled from a long distance away by horses, alarming them and sending them deeper into the grasses where we would have no chance to hunt them.

In the Botai, as the three clans are called collectively, it is not unusual to have women included as hunters; actually, it is quite common. They have to pass the same tests as the men, except for lesser requirements with the spear and atlatl for which males have more natural shoulder strength. Our hunts this year have included three females along with four males who just came of age and passed the skills tests. Hunters, whether they are men or women, are the most respected clan members. As the lead hunter, I live for this time of year.

As I indicated in the beginning, the chief of a clan is called the

Oldson. He usually inherits his title as the oldest son of the past leader and takes over when his father passes away or steps down due to age or injury. Upon inheriting the title from his father, Sandor rarely uses his original name. Since the other clans joined us at our new location, their clan leaders deferred to Sandor, and he is chief over all three clans.

Normally the Oldson attends the hunters' meeting to offer advice and encouragement to the hunters, especially the newer ones, because if new hunters perform well during all four hunts, they become full clan members and can take a wife. Due to Sandor's advanced age of forty, he is no longer able to take part in the hunts himself.

Mostly he spends his time counseling people who have disputes, regardless of if it is a man and his wife or if it involves members from different clans. Many issues are trivial and could be settled without him. Since he can no longer hunt, he has time on his hands and has gotten involved with minor issues as well as major disagreements. The reason he did not attend the hunters meeting this time has nothing to do with handling disputes, or his age.

He severely cut his foot while going to the scat pit during a moonless night. The injured foot became infected and has not healed. In truth, it has gotten worse, and our clan is worried that he might not survive this injury. Sandor has been our respected and beloved leader for almost twenty years, ever since the Smolens killed his father and both my parents.

He takes his time with decisions, whether they are between individuals or something bigger that might affect two clans or the whole village. When he makes a judgment, it is final; and most often, the parties are satisfied. I do not envy his getting in the middle of family arguments and clan disputes. Being a hunter, I have no interest in settling petty arguments. I would only be comfortable deciding those issues that affect the Botai people as a whole. My hope, as with everyone else, is that he recovers by the time we return from this hunt.

Before we departed, I led the discussion regarding travel and the overnight camping rules. Bruno, head of the Bear Clan, and Janos, head of the Aurochs Clan, helped with the planning. Each took part, but it was my plan overall. When we hunt horses, we wear horsehide clothes and look like horses. Since human sweat gives off such a strong smell, we wash before we leave. My thinking is that it is better to smell like a horse if you are hunting one.

We also bring horse manure in sacks that are traditionally carried by the youngest hunters. This rite always draws minor complaints, but the young hunters become the experienced hunters in a year and do not have to carry manure for more than one season. As we travel, the manure ripens and smells worse. By the time we arrive at the hunt site, we all smell like horse droppings. It can get pretty bad. Yet just before the start of the hunt, to be certain all of our natural scents are masked, we rub manure on any exposed skin.

On the morning of the hunt, we ate an early meal and set out at daybreak. We have been walking and running for four hours, and my mind wanders to memories from the past. I will always remember learning so much of what I know about hunting and fishing from Tedd, who was actually my uncle and who was two years senior to the Oldson. At forty-two, he was considered ancient.

Uncle Tedd was the one person who always made time to teach me how to make bows and arrows and how to attach the feathers so the arrow would rotate while it was in flight. One time I decided to try a shortcut and made an arrow without feathers. But it did not fly for more than a few feet in a straight line or steady arc, so from then, on I followed his advice rather than question it.

Tedd showed me from which trees I could make the best bows and arrows. He also taught me how to chip flint arrowheads, but I was never the best at flint knapping, as he called it. I learned it was better to trade horse meat with the older men for better arrowheads. Tedd also showed me how to string a bow correctly and how to properly affix a leather strap on my left arm so the bowstring would not cut my arm as I practiced hour after hour.

My next learning experience was fishing, which was not all that dangerous compared to hunting… unless you cannot swim. So naturally, before I was allowed to fish, I had to learn to swim. Later he taught me camping skills and the importance of keeping one or more fires going at night. Because of their natural fear of fire, this would keep dangerous animals away. I remember Tedd saying, "It is far smarter to keep bears and mountain lions away than to have to fight them off in the dark." I never forgot that lesson.

The odd thing about Tedd was that he was never considered a good hunter, yet he was such a great teacher. Maybe it was because he was more interested in coming up with new ideas and showing others how to do things instead of practicing his skills to get better. I do not need new ideas. I need practice, so I do it continuously. I think that my son, Mikl, takes after my uncle more than me. The boy always has new ideas. When my father was alive, as strong a hunter and a fighter as he happened to be, he was always too busy to teach me. This seemed strange to me. However, my uncle always had time.

My mind came back to the task at hand, this hunt. At midday we stopped for a quick meal but never left the trail. I quickly ate my pemmican and motioned for everyone to move forward again.

Horses and deer can be hunted in two ways. The first way is what we call drive hunting. Several of us walk in a normal manner at a walking pace. We make just enough noise, talking in a normal tone to move the herd forward. We refer to these hunters as drivers. They push the game forward to what we call the lead line of hunters. Men in the lead line are a half mile or a mile in front of the drivers and remain hidden until the animals come to them.

The second way to hunt large game is called position hunting. With this type of hunting, a hunter in disguise stays well hidden from sight and waits for the animal to come to them, usually on a trail the animal uses regularly.

Position hunting is done by one or two hunters and offers a kill of a single animal. Driving horses or deer requires a large group of hunters but offers the chance to kill many animals. My plan for this hunt is to have five drivers and nine lead line hunters. Drivers are not usually in on the kill because the animals are being pushed forward and move away from them. Their work is to move the horses toward the lead line but not to fully alarm them. They also have to stay alert in case a horse turns back toward them in an effort to escape.

As the drivers move forward, they have to sound natural. When horses hear their voices, they move ahead of the sound. Too much noise alarms them, and they gallop from sight or reverse direction. To our right is the northern edge of the grasses where wolves prowl. Horses avoid the woods. To the left are open grasslands, which offer an escape if they run that way. Behind are the drivers and in front are the lead hunters. Our methods allow us to cover three of the four directions a horse can run.

We carry long bows and flint-tipped spears with atlatls for distance throwing. An atlatl attaches to the end of the spear like a hand and in effect makes the thrower's arm longer, adding distance and power to the throw. It takes practice and strength, but once the skill is perfected, a hunter can throw a spear almost twice as far as normal a person would. It is rare that a hunter has enough strength before the age of fourteen to master a spear and an atlatl, so fourteen years of age is the usual cutoff date for a young man to become a full hunter.

Bruno is a year older than I am and throws the atlatl spear farther and better than anyone who has ever challenged him. At the summer gatherings, he has been the best at it for as long as I can remember. Only one man, a big Hungarian called Kraven, gives him a challenge, yet he has never defeated Bruno in the atlatl throw or at any of the strength contests.

Kraven is not happy about losing to Bruno year after year, and we know he will be well prepared for next year's summer gathering contests. Bruno is just too strong. I am not a small man, but he towers over me and weighs a lot more than I weigh. We wrestle and challenge each other on just about everything. He always wins contests where strength is a factor.

I win when it comes to expertise with the bow. I practice more and rarely lose to anyone. When it comes to strength, without a doubt, Bruno is the strongest man I have ever known.

One time several years ago, we were hunting a bear and it turned on us. I struck it with my spear from a short distance, but the spear hit a shoulder bone and glanced off. The bear was wild with rage and almost reached me, roaring and snarling. The brown monster slashed at me with its massive claws as I tried to ready my second spear.

It was about to tear me apart when Bruno drove his spear deep into its chest and saved my life. Mortally wounded, it turned toward Bruno, and I rammed my second spear into its neck. Between the two of us and three other hunters, we finally killed it. We have many memories like that one and have been friends since we were kids. I think of him as my older brother, and I know he feels the same.

After a successful hunt, we remove any parts of the horse we cannot use for food. Little is wasted. We remove the head, lower legs, and large bones to lighten the load on the trip back. After butchering the meat, we always have a feast of the best parts: the tongue, the liver and heart, and special cuts of meat. We empty the intestines, but we save them for use in making pemmican for the next hunt.

If we kill one or two horses, we carry the horse meat back to the village packed in horsehide sacks. When we have better luck and kill several, we transport the whole animals by tying their feet together at the knees and slip a pole between the legs. Now the whole carcass can be lifted off the ground and placed on the shoulders of the carriers. We usually have two people in the front and two people at the back carrying the ends of the pole. Bruno never needs help on his end. He lifts the front of the pole and leads the way. We rotate positions and move the poles from one shoulder to the other as we walk. Due to the weight, the return trip always takes longer than the trip going out.

My hunters continue to walk all afternoon as the sun moves lower in the western sky. I remember another experience with my uncle.

When I was a boy, I asked my uncle Tedd how he could make a lariat that was fifty feet long when a horse was only about eight or nine feet long. It seemed impossible. He was just about to start making one and said, "Sit down, Daven, and watch. I will explain as I work." This could take all morning, and I wondered if I should have asked.

Tedd spread a tanned horse hide on a flat plot of ground and took out his sharp flint knife. He poked a hole in the middle of the hide and made a circle cut around the hole. Then he continued the circle around the first circle and kept slicing in a continuously larger and larger circle with the cuts never touching. Finally he reached the edge of the hide and stood up holding one end of the circle. The hide became a long piece of leather instead of a flat hide. It was still tangled in a circular design, but when Tedd stretched it out, it was about fifty feet long, just like he said it would be. He placed it in water and let it soak. The next day, he stretched the leather strap in the sun and held it down with a few rocks. When it dried, it was straight.

Our hunters have tried to capture live horses with their lariats, but we have always failed. We talk about it over fires during the winters. Getting a lariat over a horse's head has been done many times, but horses are so strong, they easily pull a hunter off his feet and drag him. When dragged even a short distance, a hunter's arms are cut by the grass, and they have to let go or be sliced to pieces. A few times there had been broken arms when a man was dragged over a hidden rock. This time we will try again. We always try.

Our travel so far had been over familiar trails. Main trails coming out of our village run north and south along the river and east and west along the edge of the grasslands. From these smaller trails, others split off in many directions. For the first day, we used our fast travel method of walking for one thousand paces and then running for one thousand paces. This gave us a much higher rate of speed than if we only had walked. We have done this for many years, and we could maintain this pace for a ten- or twelve-hour day for many days.

As we left the east-to-west trail, we entered five-foot-tall grass, and the walk became more difficult and much slower. This was where horses live. With plenty of water and grass for fodder, they thrived. Their natural enemies, including hunters like us, had difficulty hunting them due to their sense of smell, their eyesight, and their speed through the grasses. With these ideal conditions, the herds continued to grow. Wolves prowled the edges, picking off the old and weak just as we did years ago, but not anymore.

The four young men I mentioned have passed the skills tests and are ready to take a position in the lead line, where the kills are made most often. Skills tests are bow-and-arrow tests at fifty paces plus spear and atlatl throws. Lariat throws are included as part of their tests.

The most difficult skill test for a new hunter to pass is what I call the panic test. This test is where a hunter must launch four arrows into the air, before the first arrow hits the ground. I still practice this skill when teaching them. The beginning of the test is easy because the first arrow is already notched and ready, just like it would be on a hunt. The second arrow must be pulled from the quiver on the back of the hunter, notched, and fired with a full pull of the bow, as are the third and fourth arrows.

A mistake with any of the four arrows will cause the hunter to fail the test. If the hunter does not take a full pull of the bow, the arrow will not launch high enough and the first arrow will hit the ground before the fourth one is released. The hunter must concentrate on what he or she is doing and fight off the tendency to rush or panic. This test is designed to prepare them for hunting dangerous game.

At times, a stallion or a mare with a foal will run at a hunter in an attempt to escape. If a hunter panics and runs away, they can easily be trampled. The hunter must fight off his fear and continue to fire the second, third, and fourth arrows at a charging one-thousand-pound angry horse set on killing instead of being killed. I have felt that same fear many times and have seen experienced hunters drop to the ground in an attempt to hide or turn and run. When this happens, the horse usually becomes the killer, unless others in our group can take it down before it reaches the runner. Most of the time it all happens too quickly and the hunter is trampled. If a hunter is badly injured, they often do not survive the return trip because we have no medicine women on our hunts.

Among the four new hunters are Flint and Jon, twin sons of my good friend Bruno. Flint barely passed the four-arrow panic test. He did do well with the spear and atlatl and scored accurately with the long bow. I am concerned with his preparation, but Bruno assured me he is ready to prove himself.

Another new man is my son Mikl. He easily passed the long bow and panic tests, and he does well with the spear and atlatl due to his size and upper-body strength. Mikl was born in the third month of the year, so he is well past his fourteenth birthday and is bigger and stronger than I was at the same age. He only lacks practice. He is confident, maybe too confident.

The second twin son of Bruno is Jon, Mikl's best friend. He also passed the tests without problems. Although they are identical twins and born the same day, Jon was born before Flint by a few minutes, not that it makes any difference. The fourth new hunter is Joe, a member of the Aurochs Clan headed by Janos. Joe is physically the smallest of the fourteen hunters with me today. I comment on his size only because three of the hunters are women, yet Joe is still smallest.

One person who is taller and maybe stronger than Joe is his sister Agi. She is older than Joe by two years and has proven herself on many previous hunts. I have my doubts with Joe. He struggled during several skill tests. He gives in to panic and probably should have waited another year until he was fifteen. His mother pushed him because Agi already hunts and more likely because his father died while hunting horses years ago. Tomorrow will tell the story.

When a hunter proves himself, he can take a wife. Wives must always come from another clan, never from your own clan. Many times wives are from other groups of people with whom we trade at the summer gatherings. It is not as important for women to pass hunting tests because only a few of them have any desire to be hunters. Most women want to become wives and mothers and leave hunting to the men.

I am confident in my son Mikl as tomorrow approaches. I have to admit, I would like to see him practice with his weapons more than he does. Maybe he practices less because it comes too easily to him. He is good, but all of us can be better. I constantly work to perfect my hunting skills while he is usually looking at something new. He thrives on anything new.

As an example, last year he spent a lot of time on a new idea for a bow that did not seem to work. It was made of the same ash wood we make all our bows from, so it is not the wood itself. The piece he cut was from a tree that had a natural second curve at one end. His thinking was that if a bow normally has one long curve in the middle, an extra curve at the end should make it more powerful, similar to a bow with an atlatl at the end. He calls it a two-curve bow.

He finished the bow and practiced with it. When the extra curve of the bow was at the top, it drove the arrow into the ground. When the second curve was at the bottom, the arrow flew too far over the target. He was still working with it when we left for this hunt. Since the arrow could not be controlled, the bow seemed to be useless. The thing that made me wonder if it has any value was that when he shot an arrow at very close range, it drove the arrow farther into the target than any other bow.

All these thoughts run through my mind as we walk forward, pushing tall grass aside. The trail has become less distinct. I notice the manure on the ground has become fresh, a sure sign the herds are close. The sun has set as we arrived in one of our old campsites, one that we have used before, and we stopped for the evening.

This site is a good one with freshwater and open ground, offering us protection from possible predators. With a group this large, it is unlikely any predator would bother us. Just in case, I set two guards on opposite ends of the clearing. Tomorrow morning, we will move into position. It is not far now.

CHAPTER 2

The Oldson

THAT NIGHT, BRUNO, Janos, and I reviewed the hunt plan with the four new hunters. I drew the plan on the ground with a stick and identified the lead line of nine hunters with the four new men spaced between experienced hunters. There are five drivers plus two young men who are not yet of age.

One of these young men is Peter, the oldest son of Janos; the second is Patrick, his next son. Both of them have good skills; but Peter, at thirteen years of age, is exceptional. Both of them have served eagerly as drivers in the past and helped carry horse meat and weapons back to the village. By doing so, they have gained valuable experience well before their fourteenth birthday.

As we finished our meal, Janos got up to review the final plan with his Aurochs Clan members, especially Joe. Joe just turned fourteen years old. He has no father to guide him, and Janos is taking extra time with him in preparation for his first hunt.

Many years ago when Joe was a young boy, his father was killed on a horse hunt similar to this one. Joe's father was on the lead line when his first arrow hit a mare protecting her two-month-old colt. His arrow struck the shoulder bone of the mare and glanced off. His second arrow missed the mare entirely. Two arrows were shot with no results, and the horse was coming at him.

My position was off to the right. When I saw what was happening with Joe's father, I shot an arrow from a distance. I hit the horse in the flank, a good shot for such a long distance. However, my arrow was not a killing blow. It wounded the mare and distracted the horse from its charge momentarily. Joe's father hesitated instead of notching his third arrow. The horse was injured and turned toward him. He panicked and ran. In one fast motion, the horse ran over the hunter. It turned around, reared above him, and came down with its right hoof striking his head and crushing his skull. It all happened in an instant. I killed the horse, but it was too late to save the hunter. I will never forget seeing his crushed skull with his brains spilling on the ground.

We buried Joe's father in a clearing at the edge of the grasslands along with his hunting bow and an arrow. We never reuse the bow owned by the hunter who died in a hunting accident. It was considered bad luck. Leaving a bow and arrow is a sign that the man buried here was a hunter, in case he was ever found again. Before leaving him behind, we built a stone marker for family members who might visit his grave in the future.

Our ceremonial woman was not with us, so I said a few words of praise over the grave. I asked the spirits to accept this hunter as a member of the Botai. Janos also spoke, mentioning his good deeds as a hunter and family man over the years. Janos swore to take care of his wife and children until they were old enough to be on their own. We lost a friend and valued clan member that day. Janos gained a second wife along with her children.

Joe's mother was devastated by her husband's death, but as is our custom, she was provided for by Janos, the head man of the clan. After a full moon has passed, considered a proper time, she became Janos's second wife. The wedding was performed by our ceremonial and medical healer, a woman named Patts.

Janos's new wife, Sarah, was younger by six years and she was attractive. She was much more interested in sex than his first wife. She soon became his favorite and was heavy with another child three months later. Several more children followed the first one.

Janos was a happy man. He has a second wife to help his first wife with their many children and one who does not resist his manly needs. At first she just needed a husband and played it just right. By the time six months went by, she fell in love with Janos. She loved his caring ways and his easy disposition. Joe's father had not been so easy. Besides, his first wife, Dasha, actually liked her and the help she brought to the house. As I said, Janos was a happy man, at least for now.

When Janos left our hunt discussion and walked out of hearing range, Bruno asked me, "Daven, do you think the Oldson will survive?"

I replied, "I hope he survives. My fear is that at his advanced age and with his condition worsening before we left, it is more hope than anything else. When we left the village, Oldson was sleeping most of the day and night and was overcome with fever and pain. As we both saw, he could no longer put any pressure on his infected leg. I fear for his life."

Bruno said, "If he does not make it, the person who caused his death will have to be punished. All three clans will have something to say, and most of it will not be good."

I knew Bruno was talking about my wife, Gertrude. She was a beautiful woman when I met her on the first day of a summer gathering many years ago. Every man looked at her before we were married. It seemed as though I had won a contest when she chose me, and we were married. Looking back, we were too young. We had a child right away. She gained weight while pregnant and never lost it. Gertrude blamed me and our son, Mikl, for ruining her beautiful body. Lately, she has gained more weight. Before we left on this hunt, she had another argument with several women, including Janos's second wife, about doing her share of the work with gathering winter supplies. The fun, exciting marriage I had at first never returned.

I have also been thinking of the Oldson's wife, Ruth, the same woman who saved me from being killed in the Smolens raids twenty years ago. Ruth raised me from when I was nine years old. She has been a wonderful help for many families with no grandmothers. Ruth is a mother to me. She will be distraught if her husband dies, as will we all. Ruth has one surviving son, named Ander, and three married daughters, so she will have family to lean on. But if our Oldson dies, her house will be empty.

My discussion with Bruno continued for a few more minutes although he was quieter than normal and seemed troubled. I sense there was something else on his mind, but what it was, I was not certain. Perhaps it was about Gertrude. He may speak more of it tomorrow.

The normal succession when an Oldson dies or steps down is for the oldest son to inherit the title and replace his father as the new leader. Sandor's first son was killed on a bear hunt long ago, and a second son is not considered to be part of the succession. Ander could not inherit the title of Oldson, even though he is well qualified.

When the Botai village grew too large for the available food supply, a new village was started. Ander, after much discussion with his father, was appointed as the Oldson of the new group with the consent of Janos, Bruno, and mine. Ander and Janos scouted for a new location and finally located a site one hundred miles away. It was two years ago that Ander and twenty-six of our group formed a new people located on a branch of the Krasnyi Yar River.

The land where the Yar village was settled was unoccupied by any other people. The location offered ample horse herds to hunt and high ground on a bend of a clear river. There is also an abundant supply of peas, fruits, tubers, and wheat. They did not have much flint, so they get it from us. In the future, they can trade for flint at summer gatherings. One new food supply was an abundant herd of wild sheep, not a favorite meat, but in ample supply.

Many of us had relatives and friends moving east with Ander, and we certainly wanted them to succeed; so Bruno, Janos, myself, and our clan members helped the Yar move to their new location. The trip was a slow four days. We had to carry supplies, including temporary tents, food, and weapons. Families and children made it a slow walk.

When we reached the new location, we stayed with them to help build pit houses, harvest grains for bread, and vegetables to get them started. We hunted horses with them and dried the meat before heading back home. The Yar village is far enough away, so we never need to hunt the same horse herds as they hunt.

Far to the east, hundreds of miles from Ander's settlement, are the people with the yellow skin, the short ones with slanted eyes. They do not have normal white skin like the Botai, the Kazakhs, or the Hungarians. They are part of some other people. I saw one of them a long time ago, and my father called them Mongols.

They herd sheep and goats, and at times they hunt horses. Friends to the north, we call the Russians who attend the summer gatherings, say these people raid their villages and take children as slaves. Some claim that they are cannibals.

We discussed the possibility that, as the Mongols grow in numbers, Ander could face competition for horses. For now, it is no problem and should not be one for a long time to come unless something changes. In my lifetime there are few changes.

None of us have any idea how many Mongols there might be, but we doubt there can be very many. We doubt their intelligence. We also wonder if they are too far inbred or have a poor diet; otherwise, why would they have yellow skin and be so short and have slanted eyes? These must be deformities from marrying their own clan members. Generally, they are thought to be inferior to the Botai.

Bruno and I drank the usual three cups of water to fill our bladders, which would wake us well before sunup. We got up from our meal and gave each other a bear hug as we headed off to sleep. I laid my head on my sleeping mat and covered myself. I was warm and comfortable, and I looked at the clear sky with so many stars. When I closed my eyes, I heard wolves howling in the distance and wind blowing through the grasses.

CHAPTER 3

Succession

AS WE ATE our breakfast on the second day of travel, Bruno approached with a greeting, "It is a great day for travel, but we need to get moving soon if we are to reach our position for tomorrow's hunt." It was a perfect crisp morning with beautiful blue skies, one that made for an easy day of travel.

I responded, "You are right, we need to move out." I called to the camp, "Get ready. We leave in one hour." I spoke to Bruno saying, "The walk today will be slower since the trails are gone. We will have to walk single file and rotate the lead because the first person in line will tire quickly. The lead man will be stamping down tall grass as we go."

Bruno agreed and said, "I will start in the lead and you can follow me. I think we should let the four new hunters take some of the lead too. It will make them feel equal to the older hunters, but the rotation is up to you, Daven."

"Good idea, Bruno, about the new men. My son, Mikl, will follow me and then your sons, Jon and Flint, will be next. After that, Janos can lead followed by his new man, Joe. Peter asked to lead for a time too even though he is not yet a full hunter. That young man shows a lot of promise. I can rotate the order after that. By taking the lead, new men will feel like they are part of the team."

Bruno nodded his head in agreement and said, "Peter certainly does show promise." We packed our supplies and weapons and got moving in single file.

We walked silently except for the swishing noise of parting the grass. As I walked, I thought about Oldson and his health problem. He left his pit house that night to urinate as all old men did. Someone, using the trail before him, left diarrhea on the trail leading out to the scat pits. Oldson walked the same trail, and unfortunately, he stepped on it. As he tried to move away, he brought his foot down hard on a flint shard and cut his foot. The cut drove the diarrhea into his flesh. He had a fever the next day. When we left, his foot was badly infected. He was being attended to by Patts, our medicine woman, and her assistant, Elizza.

If the Oldson dies, his oldest son becomes the new leader. If there is no oldest son to move up, the eldest and wisest women choose the next leader because our society is matriarchal. Our system prevents one family from becoming the ruling family. Other tribes have seen one son kill another to take control. Our way prevents the physically strongest from taking over by force. With the Botai system, the elder women select the next leader, and fights are avoided. After a death, seven days have to pass before an election is held. This allows time for discussion and for reason to prevail.

By tradition, the women can only vote for a man to lead. The reason for that is natural. Since hunting is so important to our survival, it is doubtful that many hunters would follow a woman on a hunt or in a fight against an enemy, even if the female is a good hunter. The elders can select their own clan leader, their husband, one of their own sons, or any other Botai member. Being an elder female usually means that their husband would be even older than they are and not be considered due to age. A clan leader is the most likely choice. The elder women have seen the clan leaders in action before and have a good feel on how they make decisions. They have a record from the past, which tells how they can be expected to perform in the future.

If the Oldson was dead and a vote was to be held, I needed to talk to the elders. I knew if he died, those women would be overwhelmed with everyone in the entire village telling them what to do and how to vote. It was better to think that the vote would not be needed and that the medical women has saved our Oldson.

I continued to walk forward, behind Bruno, and thought about the succession. The first of the four women was Ruth, wife of the current Oldson. Emma, the mother of Ruth, was the second elder. She was already an adult before we left our former location on the other side of the Ural Mountains. She was the eldest, yet she was still active and physically able to do her part while gathering and often sets the example for others. Then there was Judy, an older cousin of mine who was related to my mother who was killed by the Smolens. And of course, there was Patts, the medicine woman. All four of these women were seen as leaders among our people and were well respected.

As leader of the Horse Clan and lead hunter, I have a strong interest in who would be selected. I am sure I will be among those considered as will Bruno of the Bear Clan and Janos of the Aurochs Clan. They will select the right person, and I will help them with their decision.

CHAPTER 4

The Berry Pickers

LATE SUMMER IS the time of year when the four elder women lead the gathering process while the men perform the final horse hunts. Our activities are in preparation to gather adequate food supplies for the coming winter.

We Botai people do not grow anything ourselves. We hunt for meat and gather what grows in our area to fill our needs. Each year, our foods seem to grow back, offering us a never-ending supply. We return to the same locations where chickpeas and lentils grow and harvest what the natural plants provide.

White and red tubers grow where there is sufficient rain and sun. Wheat is an abundant staple used to make bread and comes in three varieties. Dark red wheat is the best tasting, and it provides a good source of protein in addition to what we get from horse meat. Two light types of wheat grow intermixed with the red variety.

There are apples to pick and dry for winter plus raspberries and gooseberries that grow along the edges of forests. Here, the plants get just the right mix of sun and shade each year to grow well. Blueberries are a late-summer harvest and grow in wet swampy areas near the river. Today, the women are harvesting blueberries.

Lately we have had a few problems. The apples trees are getting old and produce fewer apples and are smaller in size. As a result, the gathering teams have had to travel farther to find new apple trees. The second problem is that although wheat grows everywhere, it is mixed in with other grasses like hay, oats, and straw. As women gather, they cut off the wheat grains or the seeds and collect them in woven baskets. It seems that each year there is more straw and hay and less wheat. No one knows why. The annual gathering takes more time to produce the same supplies. If this continues for too many more years, gathering will have to include distant areas. Ruth also tells me there are fewer raspberries. Those plants are old and produce less.

The gathering process, like hunting, takes many weeks of hard work performed by teams of women, children, and older men who can no longer hunt.

This was where problems with Gertrude started. She told Ruth and Emma, "Since I am the wife of a clan leader and the lead hunter, I should not have to work. After all, my husband produces the horse meat you eat all year. That should more than compensate for me not working in the fields."

Ruth and Emma came to me with complaints regarding who was working and who was not. The "who was not working" part fell at my doorstep rather than the Oldson's because the problem lay with only one person, and that was my wife, Gertrude.

Three years ago, she started to become lazy and was not doing her fair share. The elder women spoke to her many times to no effect. I also spoke to her repeatedly, which led to another argument. She got worse instead of better, and now, she hardly did anything if she showed up to work at all. Her usual claim was that she was sick.

This year, the elders refused to be abused by Gertrude any longer. Gertrude was fatter and lazier than ever and more argumentative, not only with the other women, with me too. The gatherers have had enough of her last fall and were not about to let her get away without helping this year. They came to me as a group with their complaint. Ruth, with

Emma's backing said, "If she does not work, she will not share in the food supplies this winter." They have drawn a line in the sand.

Gertrude was my wife of fourteen years. When she was young, she was a beautiful woman. She had dark hair, brown eyes, and a beautiful figure. Of course, I fell for the beauty and the figure just as many men would. We were easily fooled, thanks to nature. I could not see the problems just below the surface. Our home was a happy one for the first few years, but it turned sour like a rotten apple. Nothing was good enough for her. She claimed, "The women are jealous, and they hate me because I am beautiful." She told me that I was a bad husband for at least a dozen reasons.

From the onset of her pregnancy with Mikl, Gertrude cursed me. I ruined her body and her looks. It was my fault she got fat. After a while, she cursed men, women, being pregnant and the entire Botai village. She swore she would never have another child. Even as Patts tended to her while she gave birth, she cursed Patts too.

Instead of losing the baby weight after the birth, she ate everything she could put in her mouth. It went on year after year. She stopped taking care of the pit house and hardly cooked anything, except what she made for herself. That too became an argument.

When Mikl was ten years of age, he heard his mother say, "He is not my son, he is yours." Later that day, Mikl asked me why his mother did not love him like other mothers loved their children. I had no explanation other than "Your mother has lost her mind." I may have been close to the truth. Gertrude left Mikl with Ruth whenever I was on a hunt. It was about that time when Mikl started living with Ruth on a full-time basis.

Not one other wife in the village behaved the way she did. Children were seen as a blessing and were valued by every family. Not by Gertrude. Most men would have gotten rid of a woman like Gertrude and taken a new wife. If I divorced her, not one man in the village would take her, not even as a second wife. If she died during the winter, I worried that

Mikl might blame me for causing her death, so I put up with the situation as best I could.

In all this time there has only been one other woman that interested me, a Hungarian woman who I met two years ago at the summer gathering. She was full of fun and excitement and had interests of her own. The best part was that she was not married and was interested in me. We spent a lot of time together, and the more I got to know her, the more I liked her. After three days, I hated to leave her and thought about her constantly for the next eleven months until the next gathering.

The second year, I was overwhelmed with Ildiko. I let others do the trading while I spent every minute with her. We talked about everything including our values, family, and children. By the end of the day, we shared my bed. I was happier than I had been in years. Ildiko felt the same as I did; it was magic. We were in love.

The only problem was that Ildiko was determined not to be a second wife. I told Ildiko, "I would divorce Gertrude the day we reach the Botai village." Unfortunately, she had heard this promise once before from a man who wanted to be with her. When it came the time for the marriage ceremony to be held, he had not divorced his first wife, and Ildiko walked away.

She told me, "Daven, I love you and want to marry you. My worry is that if I come with you all the way to the Botai village and you do not have the heart to divorce your wife, who seems to be losing her mind, I could not come back to my village until winter passed. That would be six months. I would have no family or friends and would have to accept being a second wife. If you have no love left for her, why do you stay with her?"

She had a point. I should have divorced Gertrude long ago. As the gathering came to the last day, the thought of leaving Ildiko was heartbreaking for me and for her. I even thought about moving to her village with Mikl, but that was impossible. We hugged until it was time to go. I promised I would be unmarried the next time she saw me. I had to rid myself of Gertrude.

When I left for this hunt, it was time to gather blueberries at the village as the women always did. Gertrude had not helped gather wheat or apples claiming she was too sick to work. Instead, she slept and ate what she could steal from the central supplies while the rest of the village labored. Ruth, Emma, and Judy presented the facts to me. They were angry with Gertrude. Stealing was a serious offense.

Blueberries were the last food to be gathered. The work was done in teams of two people, except for Gertrude. She worked alone because no one wanted to be her partner. Everyone filled two large baskets, one in the morning and one in the afternoon.

Gertrude gorged herself all morning on the blueberries she picked. She ate ten berries for every one she put in her basket. By noon, her basket was still almost empty. Instead of working harder to make up for the time lost, she went to sleep. That afternoon, she woke up feeling sick to her stomach.

Her first basket held no more than a few handfuls of berries. She crept to where she knew other women worked. When their backs were turned, she poured berries from their baskets into hers, hoping it would not be noticed. When she returned with just one basket, she claimed, "My area was stripped of berries. It must have been cleaned out by a family of bears." The others saw that their baskets were not quite full as before and knew she was lying.

By the stains in her hands and on the front of her wrap, everyone could see she had gorged herself on berries all day and turned in only the few she could not eat. She stole what she had from the other workers. Gertrude ignored their glares. They had no proof. She left saying, "I feel sick." This time she ate too many berries even for her. Every woman was angry with Gertrude. They worked too hard and shared for the last time. It was over.

Even the newest wives yelled at her, "We will not share anything with you, you lazy slob. You are on your own this winter."

Ruth made it clear. "As much as your husband is respected, you are despised. You will have to gather what you can for winter. Expect nothing from our shared supplies." Scolding turned to yelling and then to screaming. They were angry. Ruth said, "I will file a complaint with the Oldson. The women demand that you be put out of the village." Not one person took her side. She would not get one piece of fruit or a single vegetable this winter. Gertrude had nothing to say, instead, she laughed at them as she waddled off in the direction of her pit house. She was easy to hate.

The night after the confrontation, there was no moon. Bruno and I spent the time preparing for this horse hunt, and Mikl stayed with Ruth as usual. Despite the turmoil, I slept at my own pit house, alone in my own bed. Gertrude groaned and complained about her stomach hurting.

I woke during the night when I heard Gertrude moaning that her stomach hurt. She had severe cramps. She struggled to get out of her sleeping rack and headed off to the village scat pits. This time, she really was sick. She barely made it out of the pit house when her bowels let loose on the trail. She left the disgusting mess where it fell and came back inside to sleep.

An hour later it happened, the Oldson arose to use the scat pit. As with every old man, he had to urinate several times every night. In the dark, he slipped in the mess Gertrude left behind. As he tried to step out of it, he placed his foot down on a flint shard and cut his foot.

I got out of bed at the sound of the Oldson yelling in pain and saw Bruno. He had also responded to the noise. I wondered if Bruno saw Gertrude and what happened.

Everyone knew the rule. If an adult member of the Botai caused the death of another member, they would be expelled from the village.

The rule applied to anyone over the age of ten. The length of time for expulsion depended on the facts and how the death happened. There was no minimum or maximum time for expulsion; however, there were cases where the expulsion was permanent, and this sounded like one of those cases.

CHAPTER 5

The Horse Hunt

AFTER A SECOND full day of travel, we reached the area for hunt. The men who led the group were tired after tamping a path through tall grass for so many hours. The followers had a much easier walk, but they were tired too. As we reached the campsite, I saw fresh horse manure everywhere, and I noticed strands of horse hair caught on the few stunted trees that survived here. We were close to one or two herds. Our location was probably eighty miles west of our village on the northern edge of the grassland.

Wild horses have roamed these grasses for years. Fodder was plentiful and not used by any other grazing animals. This grass was coarse and tough. It seemed that other grazing animals did not use it as food because they could not digest it or maybe they simply did not like its taste. With these perfect conditions, and without predators, horses flourished.

In order to be successful at hunting any animal, you have to know its habits. We have been hunting horses for generations, but only lately have we had enough men to be effective.

Horses are social animals and live in family groups. The typical group is headed by a stallion although we have seen herds headed by mature mares. One stallion will have numerous mares and foals. Young stallions stay with the group until they are two or three years old. At that age, the lead stallion drives them off even though they are his offspring. They are not allowed to stay to become possible challengers to their father. The young males form groups of three or four and roam the grasslands until they are fully mature at five or six years of age when they are ready to challenge for a herd of their own.

Our objective on a horse hunt is to take the biggest horses since they provide the most meat. A year ago, we watched as a young stallion fought an older horse for his herd. After a bloody battle, with repeated bites and kicks, the younger horse won because of his stamina. Finally, the older horse loped off to the river to nurse his wounds. The younger horse, also badly injured, watched his defeated rival leave. While the winner watched his defeated rival, we let our arrows fly. We killed him and three more mares.

That afternoon, while we butchered the meat, we saw the old stallion return to reclaim the remainder of his herd. Tomorrow, I hope for some more good luck like we had that day. After another cold camp of the usual evening meal of pemmican, we drank as much water as possible, knowing it would wake us up early and dozed off to sleep.

I woke before sunrise. Bruno and Janos stirred when I got up. We soon woke the others who were part of the lead line and ate a light meal. After eating, we prepared our bows, disguised our smell with manure, and headed off to get behind the sleeping herd. We were in place hours before the drivers and the herds woke up. The morning was crisp, the sun rose, and we waited.

An hour or so later, I heard a stallion whinny. Then more sounds came from a herd moving toward us, ahead of the drivers. I was tense. I remember what it was like for me on my first hunt, and I was thinking of Mikl today, on his first hunt. All four of the new men were my concern. Hopefully, they were ready.

I caught a glimpse of the herd and felt the excitement. I wondered if the horses could hear me breathe or if they could smell me. I checked my arrow as the stallion and three mares came into view. They were too far away for a good shot just yet. I trained my men to be sure the target is close enough for a killing shot. An early shot that did little damage could panic the herd. We waited. The stallion came closer and neighed, calling to his herd. I could see him clearly. His eyes were wary, and he had a wild look on his face. He pranced with his tail arced in the air. He could not see us, but as the noise followed behind him, he sensed that something was wrong.

With the distance being ideal, Bruno and I stood up and released our arrows at the same time. I struck the stallion, and Bruno hit one of the mares. Janos let his arrow fly at the same stallion that I hit on my first shot. I notched another arrow and scored another hit on the male. I hoped for an early kill, but it did not come so easily today. The big horse was not down even with three arrows in his hide. It turned away from me looking for an escape.

At the same time, Mikl fired his first arrow and struck one of the mares. He notched a second arrow and scored a second well-placed hit in its neck. The mare screamed in pain, staggered backward and sideways, and crashed to the ground. Mikl ran to it and drove his spear home. He made the first kill of the day and it is a solo, which is a great day for a young man on his first hunt.

Mikl looked at the dead mare on the ground and thanked the horse spirits for the meat. Right near the mare, he saw a beautiful yearling foal, a gray male that was with its mother. The young horse seemed unsure what to do, and to our surprise, the foal stayed by its mother's side, twitching and moving nervously. It nudged its mother near it's teats as Mikl reloaded his bow. He held off shooting the young horse because it was small and would not offer much in the way of food.

He reached for his lariat instead and quickly threw it over the colt's head. The horse, feeling the lariat on its neck, jumped away from Mikl with nervousness and fear. I threw my lariat and caught its front hoof. Mikl and I were on different sides of the young horse with two lariats in place. The horse was confused and afraid and pulled at both lariats. Being so young, it was not strong enough to get away from two men with the use of only three legs. It lost its balance and fell to the ground. I came around to Mikl's side so it could not get up. I secured a third lariat on another leg, and we had the horse. We were excited. We finally captured a horse, a small horse, but still a live horse and a young stallion at that!

While Mikl and I captured his foal, Bruno and his son Jon sent their arrows at another mare. Jon missed his first shot and notched his next arrow while staring straight ahead at the confused animal. Bruno's arrow hit the horse, and blood ran down its neck. Jon added another arrow to the kill. Bruno yelled, "There is another foal here," and he threw his lariat over its head. As strong as he is, Bruno was jerked off balance and pulled to the ground. He yelled for help, but we were too busy to help him. Bruno was left to battle the colt. It was an even match between a bull of a man and a foal that was too young to overcome its opponent's strength.

After a few minutes, the foal tired and could not pull Bruno any farther. Jon got his lariat on the young horse's rear feet and jerked it sideways. The small horse lost its balance and stumbled to the ground. Bruno tied the first lariat to the second and the yearling could not stand up. What excitement! Bruno and Jon stood up, raised their arms over their heads, and roared in celebration. After so many attempts and so many injuries, we had captured two foals on the same day. We also had two kills, but the wounded stallion was on a wild rampage.

The bloody stallion stomped the ground, snorted, and ran at Joe. Joe stared at the charging horse. Janos ran to help Joe, but he was too far away to have a good shot. When Joe missed his first shot, he should have re-notched a second arrow and fired again. Instead, he froze in place, unsure and scared. Joe was in a panic, just as I feared. Too late; he fumbled as he tried to notch another arrow. At the last second, Joe dropped his bow and ran. Even with the wounds, the horse was much too fast.

Joe dove to the ground in terror, but he was run over. Janos fired another arrow, the fifth to hit the horse, and this time the arrow found an artery in its neck. It staggered and finally fell to the ground. Joe's chest was crushed, and he was in terrible agony. His left arm below the elbow was splintered with both bones showing through his skin. He was bleeding badly and writhed in pain from so many broken ribs. Joe rolled on his side in agony and lost consciousness. He died that afternoon. It was eerily quiet. No one spoke a word. Losing a man that day stunned us.

As head of the Aurochs Clan, Janos performed a death ceremony. We buried Joe near the edge of the grass and built a stone marker to identify his grave. Since he died as a hunter, we placed his bow and one arrow in the grave with him, as was the custom. He died for the same reason his father died, because he panicked. Maybe Joe was too young to join us this year; maybe I should have refused to bring him. But had he kept his fear under control, he would have been still alive. When panic prevails, a hunter often pays the ultimate price: his life.

Several of us helped Mikl and Bruno with their foals. The horses were tied with so many lariats that they looked more like bundles of hide rather than horses. The other hunters were preparing to butcher the horses we had killed. With three large horses to slaughter, we faced a lot of hard work before we began the journey for home.

I noticed that Mikl's foal nervously attempted to nurse from its mother even though it was dead. It was afraid, being in the presence of human hunters and looked to its mother for comfort. Maybe it was her smell that calmed the colt. Mikl said, "It might help if I removed some of the mother's hide to calm the gray foal on the trip back." He cut away the udders and surrounding skin and tucked it in his carrying bag.

Butchering was started as soon as the two colts were tied to heavy brush and hobbled. First we gutted the horses and removed their heads and heaviest bones to lighten the load. We started a fire and roasted our dinner, the first hot meal in two days. Freshly killed horse flesh was delicious. As usual, the choice parts being the heart, the tongue, and the liver were eaten first. We shared these cuts with the group and talked of the hunt. Every hunter was still excited by the success we had today, but stunned by Joe's death.

By the time we finished eating, each of us was as full as we could possibly be. We knew the return trip would be long and hard, so we left as soon as we finished butchering. Bruno, Janos, and I wanted to use the remaining hours of the day to get moving. We cut off the hooves and ankle bones below the knees and tied their legs together. Then we slid a pole through the upper part of their legs and carried the horses upside down. Two hunters lifted each end of a pole, and we set off.

On the return trip, we were tracked by wolves. They quickly found the discarded parts of the horses we left behind and ate what they found. The wolf pack was hardly satisfied with bones, skin, horse heads, and hoofs. They smelled fresh meat and the two young horses we led along the trail. If they had a chance, they would attack and kill the foals, so we had to be alert, especially at night. I felt as though we were being hunted.

This hunt would be talked about all winter and for many more winters to come. It was the first time we caught not one but two live horses. No one except perhaps Mikl had a specific plan how these horses would be used. We normally butchered and ate every horse we killed in the past. It was not unexpected when I heard two hunters say, "It will be a pleasure to have fresh horse meat in the coldest months of winter." Two other hunters smiled in agreement.

The two captured horses actually belonged to Mikl and Bruno since they were the ones to bring them down. Maybe there was a better use for horses other than to just eat them? Maybe they could carry supplies or weapons on the next hunt? The question I had was, Could they be trained to do anything? I do have to admit, my first thought was the same as the other hunters, fatten them up and butcher them when our meat supply ran low this winter.

The return trip was difficult as they always were. Each hunter had to carry the equivalent of about one hundred pounds of meat, and it was a long distance back to the village. In addition, we had two foals to bring with us. If it proved to be too difficult to carry all the meat, we would have to eat what we could and leave some of it behind. Releasing the foals was not an option. As we moved forward carrying the loads, the foals pulled at their leads. They fought us every step of the way. That day we had a problem with no solution, because no one had done this before. Our progress was minimal. At this rate, it might take a week to get home.

Mikl remembered that the foals were more at ease when they were together. Somehow these animals comforted each other. We tried placing them together at the rear of the line. That made the work of tamping down a path much harder, so we moved both of them in front where they helped trample the grass as they walked. It seemed to help, but they were still pulling back and away from their guides.

Trying different options to get them moving took a lot of time, and we barely moved more than a few miles. Even that short distance was a struggle. After a lot of effort and not much ground covered, we stopped. Mikl placed the skin he cut away from the udders on his back and led the gray horse out front. The idea worked. The foals smelled their mothers and followed the smell. They moved slowly with hobbles on their legs and hesitated at times, but at least they moved forward.

The walk through five-foot-tall grass was slow work even though we used the same path we made on the way coming here. It was still slow. Bruno carried his share of meat and took the lead from Mikl. He led the way as he always did with his foal right behind him. I knew there would be no stopping early with Bruno in front. Two hours after dark, Bruno called us to a halt.

The group was tired. We camped just off the edge of the grasslands. That night we had a fire for cooking and for protection from prowling wolves that followed us at a distance. We made a fire and ate roasted horse meat again, saving our pemmican for the noontime meal the next day. I placed one man on each side of the camp as guards and changed the guard every three hours. My concern was the wolves.

CHAPTER 6

The Wolves

I WAS CERTAIN wolves followed us, but we felt safe with a large group of hunters. When we returned from previous horse hunts, we have been tracked, never attacked. This time, we had two foals that must have smelled like an easy meal. We decided to haul wood from the edge of the forest and build four fires, one at each corner of the camp. With fires glowing brightly all night, I expected to keep the wolves at bay. The problem was, having fires made the foals nervous, and we had to keep them inside of the camp for protection. These foals had never been near humans or fires before and certainly not wolves.

Mikl and I tied the young horses to strong ground brush in case wolves came too close. We pounded two stakes into the turf and attached thick leather straps to further hold each horse. If wolves appeared, the horses would not be able to run. I felt uneasy as I looked out over the grass. Nothing moved, but I was sure they were there.

After a meal of roasted horse meat, Janos and I assigned guard duty that rotated every three hours. I decided to use four guards, one at each corner near the camp fires. As part of the guard, one clan leader would participate with each shift. We could not take chances with these foals; they were too valuable. I reminded each guard not to look at the flames because it would take away their vision when they looked into the darkness. Janos and his clan volunteered for the first watch.

As I dozed off, I heard wolves howling, and they were not too far away. Sometime later, Janos sent one of his men to wake me for the second watch. We had eight men on guard at this point with the shift change. Janos warned me, "I have seen eyes circling the camp all night. So far there have been no problems." I was alarmed. This was a typical approach for wolves. They circle their prey, look for a weakness, and attack in mass when they find one. I woke Bruno and the rest of the hunters. I told Mikl and three men to guard the horses and placed the rest of the men around the camp. This was a serious threat.

Years ago, I designed a double-thickness leather guard for a hunter's left arm in case of a wolf attack. When strapped in place, the arm is protected from the wrist to your elbow. If a wolf attacks, the best defense is to block them with the left arm and crush their head with an axe held in the right hand. If the wolf got its jaws on the guard, its teeth could not penetrate the heavy leather. It was far better to kill them with an arrow if one can. With their dark coloring and quick movements, they were not an easy target at night.

After an hour, the wolves became bolder and closed the distance around the camp. I heard their low growling and saw their faster movements by watching their eyes. I yelled instructions. "If you have a shot, take it. Do not hold back." Flint and Jon had shots and let their two arrows fly. There were no cries of pain, so I knew those arrows missed the target. Minutes passed without anyone having another decent shot. We watched their eyes dart from left to right. They were in groups of two and three. It was certain they wanted the horses.

Somehow, the foals, even at their young age, knew wolves were their enemies. They were excited with their wide-open eyes. They snorted and stomped nervously, moving from side to side. If they were not staked, they would have run in panic and would have very quickly been taken down by the pack. I sensed their fear. They knew they were not safe, and I knew it too.

One of the wolves probed our defense with a quick move and retreated. This was a typical test of our will. Would we let them have the prey, or would we fight? Guttural growls came closer, and their eyes were down low as though they were in a crouching position and ready to leap. I was sure they would attack. Flashing eyes moved in every direction.

The leader got close enough for me to see it clearly, and I took a quick shot. The movement was so fast that I missed my shot and renotched a second arrow. Janos took a shot, and we heard howl, a report of an injury. If that was the leader, they might back off, but they were hungry and desperate. I yelled again, "Fire at them if you have a shot! Be ready to use your hatchets when they come at us. They will attack."

Jon let an arrow fly and struck another wolf. I could tell from the yelp that we had hit two of them. Mikl was guarding the horses when the pack leader leaped through the air at his throat. Mikl blocked the charge with his left arm. The snarling leader clamped his jaws on the leather armguard. Mikl smashed the animal's head with his hatchet, killing it on the spot. Training and practice paid off.

I yelled, "Is anyone injured?"

Mile and Jon responded at the same time. "We are okay." Just then a second and a third wolf charged across the camp, heading for the horses. Another big black one, that had to weigh over a hundred pounds, ran at Bruno; and the other two went for a foal. More wolves poured in right behind them, and the fight was on.

I hit one with my hatchet, chopping into its shoulder when I missed its head. It was seriously wounded when it hit the ground. With one more blow, I opened its skull. Another chop finished it off. Two other hunters fired arrows at close range. They killed one wolf and wounded the other. Bruno and three other men moved toward Mikl and Jon to defend the foals. Mikl killed another with his ax, and I struck one with my mine as it ran past me. I felt bones break. Three wolves were injured, several were dead, and the pack retreated with heavy losses as quickly as they came.

No one was injured, except Mikl who had a bruised left arm, and we still had our foals. The pack limped off, missing several members with more wounded. It all happened very fast, and it quieted down just as fast. As the wolves backed off, we could hear two of their injured members howling in pain. An hour later, only one howled. In most wolf attacks, the prey gets killed. This time, the wolf pack underestimated their foe; and this time, they lost the battle.

The original guard of four men must have looked beatable. I took over on guard duty with three other men. We rekindled the fires. I saw a few more glowing wolf eyes that night, but the attack was finished. I stayed on guard for four more hours and hardly got any sleep at all.

As usual, Bruno woke us early. "Wake up, everyone, it is time to get out of bed and get moving." The camp slowly stirred to life. I was groggy and tired. Although there were no wolves in sight that morning, I knew they were not that far away. We had a light breakfast. The foals were more nervous than the day before and harder to control. Even with the skins of their mothers on the backs of Bruno and Mikl, they were harder to control. We left quickly that morning.

As I walked with my end of the carrying pole on my shoulder, I thought, maybe people could own a horse. After all, we own our pit houses, our weapons, and maybe even our children, but we have never owned animals and certainly not a horse.

No one owned the grassland or the water in the river. These were part of nature and belonged to everyone. The territory we hunt belonged to every member of the Botai people. We all owned our tamed wolves. They earned their keep by guarding the village and were fed by everyone. People did have their favorites and fed them more, but they seemed to belong to everyone, not to one person alone. I still wonder if it makes sense to own a horse and what a horse could possibly do to be worth the work of raising them.

Mikl led his foal as he walked in front of me. He talked to me loud enough to carry on a conversation as we traveled. He said, "Jon and I are men now that the horse hunt is behind us." He told me, "When we return to the village, we want to stay at the pit houses where we have always lived since neither of us has a wife in mind." Jon walked with us, and he voiced his agreement. I thought for a minute, most young men already have a wife in mind by the time they pass their hunting test. These two were an exception. Either they were not ready for a wife, or more likely, they have not met the right person.

I called back, "That should work just fine."

Mikl has lived with Ruth for most of the last five or six years to avoid his mother. Staying with Ruth for another year or two would not be a problem. He could help with repairs to her pit house if our Oldson was gone when we get back. Jon can remain where he was, at his parents' home.

Mikl continued the conversation, "Father, no one is going to eat my colt even if the winter is a full six months long. I will keep my horse in a pit house of its own and teach it to work for me. In a year, everyone will want a horse, wait and see."

I asked Mikl, "What do you mean when you said working for you?" If we were not going to eat these horses, I wondered what he had in mind.

Jon and Bruno listened to our conversation. Mikl replied, "Horses are a lot bigger and stronger than we are. If we had a few full-sized horses, we could train them to carry the meat back from hunts like this one. The return trip from a hunt could be faster and easier. Just think if hunters only had to carry their weapons right now instead of all this weight. Life would be better, my father."

This son of mine always has new ideas. Maybe he was right this time, maybe a horse could be taught to do something useful and then again, maybe not. If not, the horse will be of full size in another six months and would make a nice meal at some point. We walked on. Both of us were in thought as we struggled with our back-breaking loads.

I said nothing further. I never thought of horses as being good for anything other than food. Would a horse work for a man? Mikl interrupted my thoughts by saying, "Father, I have an idea. If we tied a pole to each side of a horse and attached a leather carrying platform across the drag poles, we could place some of the horse meat on the platform. It would lighten the load off the hunters."

With a questioning look on my face, I replied, "It might work. For now we have to keep moving. When we reach home, you can try your idea." There was no doubt my load was heavy. If there was a way to train horses to carry some of it, I would be grateful. I trudged forward and wondered if horses had any intelligence at all. Could they learn anything, could they be trained? Maybe, but I doubted it.

I know I was stuck in my old ways. I said to Mikl, "The foals are still nervous from the wolf attack last night. We cannot add to their fear by placing poles on their sides right now. We have one more camp tonight. You can experiment with your horse when we reach the village."

Mikl agreed, "I can wait to show you, my father." The old ways were never good enough for that son of mine. He always thinks there is a better way to do everything. I think of doing what I do now and practice more so I could do it better than I did it yesterday. Mikl thinks of something we have done and proceeds to try to find a better way to do it. One of us needs to change.

Later that day, Mikl talked about the new bow with the second curve he and Tedd were working on before we left for this hunt. He had another idea how to make that bow work and wanted to try it when we get back. I reminded him, "When we get back, we will be busy for weeks building pit houses for these two horses. Otherwise, they might freeze to death over winter. Forget about the new bow. These horses are enough to worry about." He had no more ideas, not right now.

We walked until we came to an old campsite. This one was much easier to defend with open space and pits for fires. We ate the last of our pemmican and added some fresh horse meat to the meal. Tomorrow, we will reach the village and find out if the Oldson is still with us. I hope he is healthy.

The same wolves prowled the edges of our camp. This time, they kept their distance. None were killed because none got close enough to be a threat to us or "our horses." The whole idea still seemed strange to me.

I thought about how the village would be in an uproar when we arrive with two live foals. After all these years of trying to capture one, we finally did it. Hopefully, the Oldson can join the celebration. Mikl might have a tough time convincing the Botai that we have to build houses for them and carry food and water to them all winter instead of eating them. To his advantage, one horse belonged to Bruno. If Bruno decided the horses will not be used for food, there will be no further discussion, and the pit houses will be built.

Very likely, some of our people would think we had been in the sun too long or lost our minds when we tell them we have to build houses for horses. Bruno has not added anything to our conversation. He has not agreed or disagreed. I did see him nod in agreement when Mikl spoke of having horses carry meat back on a future hunt. Anything that might help with hunting was definitely of interest to me.

In the ten days we have been gone, the weather has become cooler. Leaves have turned color and started falling. If we were to have enough meat to last through winter, I needed to complete one more horse hunt.

Hunting is a pleasure. I welcome the planning, the action and excitement, and the time away. It gives me space from Gertrude and the problems she brings every day. I do not look forward to seeing her. Then again, she cannot be any worse than she was before I left. It is just not possible.

CHAPTER 7

Return to the Village

BEFORE WE BROKE camp the final morning, we built up the fire and threw green grass on it to make plenty of smoke. Hopefully, with a light wind blowing in the direction of the village, someone might see the smoke and send help to carry the meat. Smoke drifted throughout the camp as it rose above our heads, and once again, the foals became nervous and harder to control. They whinnied and pawed the ground and twisted their heads from side to side sensing fire. Mikl and Bruno stroked them by hand and tried to calm them down with soft words, yet they reared and pulled at their guide straps.

Mikl had another idea. He took the extra leather bags we used to carry meat and filled them with dirt. He tied the bags so that one hung on each side of both his foal. The extra weight used up some of their nervous energy and seemed to calm them. It has been a rough journey for these two young horses. They have had to deal with humans taking them from their herd, fires at the nighttime camps, attacking wolves, and now smoke. The weighted bags helped.

I cautioned Mikl, "Your horse might be too young to carry very much weight. You might want to lighten those bags a bit."

Mikl agreed to my suggestion and removed a third of the weight, and it worked well. His horse was older and larger and weighed a bit more than Bruno's horse, so he left a bit more dirt in its bags. His response was "Good idea, Father." I thought getting them used to having something on their backs might help with the "dragging poles" idea Mikl had suggested earlier.

We walked the worn path that ran along the edge of the grasslands from east to west. It led to the Ishim River. The Ishim flowed into a larger river called the Ob. Our village was set on high ground well above where they joined. During the coldest months, both rivers were iced up except on the sharp bend where we were located. The Ob River, unlike the Volga on the other side of the Ural Mountains, ran north where it emptied into a vast salty sea that seemed to have no end.

After breakfast, each hunter lifted his end of the long poles holding the slaughtered horses, and we started off once again. This was the third and last day of the return trip. The work was hard. Janos called out to me, "Either this horse is the heaviest I have ever carried, or I am getting old." I just grunted a response in return. I was thinking about Mikl's idea of training horses to work for us. Maybe they could lighten the load someday, maybe not. Hunting, without all the work on the return, was a pleasant thought.

In a few hours, I smelled water and soon after that I saw a group of ten people waiting for us where the east and west paths met the Ishim River. They saw the smoke we made this morning and waited for us to arrive. What a relief to see friendly faces after all these days being away.

The villagers were excited to see us and even more excited to see the horses. They were in awe and had a thousand questions about the hunt and how we captured these two foals. All of them asked questions at the same time, and it was a bit chaotic. We told the story several times. With all the excitement, we had to tell the same tale over and over again. Everyone was asking questions, wanting attention, and talking at the same time. They were impressed because it had never been done before. The capture of two horses was beyond belief. It was amazing.

Women's comments generally were "These two horses are small and will not provide much to eat, but they will fatten up by the end of winter." In celebration, they said, "We will have fresh meat when we need it most." Smiles and excitement were everywhere except on the faces of Mikl and Bruno. With all the emotions, no one noticed that Joe was missing.

At that point, Bruno, yelled in his loud, forceful voice, "No one is eating these horses, not now and not during the winter, not ever." The group hushed and became abnormally quiet.

One woman asked, "If these horses are not for eating, what are they for? Horses are good for one thing, to feed the village." There was a murmur of agreement within the crowd.

"Horses will be trained to work for the Botai. Do not even think about eating them. We have plenty of meat from our hunt. We will eat that." No one asked any more questions about eating the horses for now, but they wanted to know what Bruno had in mind. What could he possibly be talking about?

A woman asked, "What do you mean when you say, 'they will work for us'?" With over twenty people talking at the same time, it was noisy and hard to hear or to be heard.

Bruno had the same reply. "Horses are powerful animals. They will be trained to carry heavy loads like the one we carry right now." There were no further challenges to Bruno's statement.

Someone from the Aurochs Clan asked, "Where is Joe?" I also heard someone else tell us that the Oldson died shortly after we left for the hunt. Again, everyone was talking at once and asking questions at the same time. Did I hear that right? Was Oldson gone?

I asked, "What happened with the Oldson?"

Of course, everyone answered at the same time again, and we got very few details. The same woman described the bad news. She said, "His death was terrible, his leg turned black, and he became unconscious and died." That was all the explanation we got for now. In the next breath, she asked, "Who will lead the Botai people. He has no son to take over. Who would be the Oldson?" She was afraid of the coming change.

Janos spoke up with reassuring words. "If what you say is true, that the Oldson has passed to the spirits, the elder women will select a new leader. Everything will work out logically. The next leader will probably come from one of the three clan leaders who you already know. Do not worry, the elders will choose the best candidate. We have been through this before, and there is no need for panic." Janos worded it well. The crowd quieted, and we headed for home.

It was a relief to have help with the heavy load of meat. We retold the story of the hunt and of Joe's death all over again and how he was trampled. We tried to cover up how Joe panicked, but not every hunter told the same story; and eventually, the truth came out. Fear had overcome him. He panicked and paid the price. Without anyone saying it, Joe died the same way his father had died.

As we walked the final leg of the journey, most everyone stared at the young horses. They wanted a closer look and cautiously touched them. The presence of so many more people had the horses on edge, and the male colt kicked with his back feet a few times, which made the curious villagers a lot more cautious. Before today, most of them had only seen horses at a distance or those that we brought back from a hunt for food. These were women, not hunters of large animals.

Bruno and I talked as we walked. The talk was of the death of Oldson and the need for a new leader. Bruno asked, "Daven, what do you think? Who will be selected to lead?"

I told him, "I already had my mind made up. I know who I would select if I were one of the elders. It has to be one of the clan leaders. No one else has enough experience." I did not say who my choice was, and oddly, Bruno did not ask. He was thinking. I would make my recommendation to the matriarchs as soon as we returned.

I knew all four of the elder women very well. I have spent much of my time at Ruth's pit house helping her and her husband with house repairs and chores, eating her good cooking, and avoiding my wife, Gertrude. Ruth raised me when my parents were killed by the Smolens and now she helped me raise Mikl. Ruth and Sandor were parents to me. She and Mikl and I are very close, like a mother, son, and grandson.

There were three other elder women who would help Ruth choose the next Oldson. I was the Horse Clan leader and my elder woman was Judy, a distant cousin to me. She would listen to my advice on the coming vote. If I could convince Ruth to take my advice too, I had two of the four votes I needed. Choosing the next leader would go in the direction I wanted if I could convince one more elder. In case of a tie, Ruth, being the wife of the last Oldson, would have the final vote.

After a half day of walking, we reached the village, and the excitement started all over again. We retold the stories of the captures and of Joe's death. Mikl and Bruno and I tried to protect the young horses from the crowd as best we could. It was easy to understand the excitement and the amazing sight of two live colts when we arrived. It was an incredible feat that many thought was impossible after so many failures.

Bruno and Mikl watered the horses at the river and tied them securely to trees after hobbling their feet. They left plenty of room for them to graze. The horses were calmer now even with the noise and people and the tamed wolves sniffing at them constantly. They were hungry and grazed noisily. We gave the horse meat from the hunt to the women for smoking. One more hunt, and we would be ready for the winter.

I visited Ruth's pit house, and she told me the details of Oldson's agonizing death. In return, I told her the story of the hunt, the capture of the horses, and the truth of how Joe died. The capture of the foals was the biggest event in our village in a long time, but the death of her husband Sandor was just as important.

Ruth described how his leg swelled to twice its normal size and turned black from a massive infection. After many days of terrible suffering and no sleep, Patts, the medicine woman, gave him a hallucinating drink made from wild mushrooms. When he passed out, they made four incisions in his leg to drain the infection. The leg oozed a grayish fluid that smelled like rotting flesh. After many days of severe pain, he passed away. I felt her sorrow and her loss. She wept the entire time she told the story. Ruth lost a great husband, and we lost our longtime leader.

Our discussion soon led to the need to name our next Oldson. Custom called for a new leader to be elected in seven days, and four of those days were gone. Ruth said, "The new leader has to be someone experienced. He has to be one of the three clan leaders. We need a strong hunter and a family man who can understand women's needs as well as those of men." I let her speak without interruption.

Ruth talked further. "The next leader must be someone with good judgment, one that can put the needs of the entire village before just one clan." I nodded in agreement. I told her of my choice, and she was surprised. She said, "I was thinking about you, Daven, not Bruno, but I will consider your suggestion before making up my mind." After more persuasion, I finally convinced her. She would support my choice, Bruno.

Before I left her, Ruth was concerned when she said, "Not one of the villagers came forth with any information as to who left the diarrhea on the trail that night. Someone must have seen something. Maybe they were afraid to accuse the guilty person." Ruth was perplexed at the lack of information. She wanted facts. She was right the first time, someone did know. In fact two people knew what happened; but both of them, being Bruno and myself, were away on the hunt, and we just learned today that Oldson died. I knew I had to talk to Bruno. Without any doubt, he saw something that night just as I did. I decided to hold off until after the selection of the new Oldson.

As expected, the elder females of each clan were getting plenty of advice on whom to choose. I had to meet with the other voters as soon as possible to influence their vote. Clan leaders were considered to be important men and had a larger say in big decisions. Although in this election, they had no vote. Certainly their opinions carried more weight and their voices were heard more than other clan members, but they had no direct vote. Bruno, Janos, and I led our clans and worked well together. One of us was the natural choice.

Bruno and his wife, Diana, were busy with his horse. Diana was a natural with animals. She seemed to understand them and had the best ideas on how to handle horses and took the lead along with Mikl. Janos was at home trying to decide which of his two wives would get his attention first while his many sons and daughters welcomed him with affection.

When I reached my pit house, it was filthy as usual and it smelled almost like something died there. The clay cooking pot was dry and crusty, and the fire was out. At first, I did not see Gertrude; but as my eyes adjusted to the darkness, I saw that she was the huge lump snoring under the furs, sleeping off her last meal. Like the last few years, she left the pit house in a mess, and no food was ready. I was sick of her lack of care about anything, including me. I had put off making a decision on her. Now the decision was overdue.

CHAPTER 8

The Election

SINCE THERE WAS nothing to eat at my pit house, I went to Ruth's home that evening and stayed until the next morning. As the wife of the Oldson, she knew every detail of what was going on with the village but kept the issues to herself. She was never a source for gossip. Ruth did offer advice to her husband on personal decisions, especially those involving women. The biggest reason it was so comfortable to visit her was because she was such a loving, warm person. On top of that, she always had a stew pot brewing. For the last three years, her house felt more like home than my own.

Over breakfast, Mikl talked about nothing other than his horse. He had so many ideas that he could not stop talking. He was bursting with energy. One idea was to dig a single large pit house for two horses instead of building one house for each horse. His reasoning was that horses are social animals. He claimed, "They will be more comfortable being together, just as they were on the trail." I remember they did not do as well when they were separated. I agreed. The house has to be dug deeper than usual and would need a higher roof than those we built for ourselves. It would have no fireplace and needed to be very tight so that the horses' body heat alone would be good enough to keep them warm throughout the winter.

Bruno asked for help from every man not involved with smoking horse meat or gathering berries and apples. Women, older men, and children all were assigned to work in groups gathering those winter supplies. Our hunters had only one day of rest since our return from the trail when Bruno told them they were needed again. Everyone was working at something, everyone except Gertrude. She was eating. I assumed the food was stolen from central supplies because there was nothing in our house. Others knew she stole food and voiced their anger openly.

When Bruno called for help, he got it. There was a big group of hunters waiting for him that morning. All of them wore their new scruffy beards they started to grow as of yesterday. They waited to go to work with their spades and flint axes on hand. When Bruno arrived, they started digging.

A second group cut large poles for the support walls and smaller beams for the roof. Bruno stressed the urgency. He and I knew we had to get in one more hunt before it snowed. He explained, "We have about six or seven days to get this job done before we leave on the final hunt. He looked at the men and smiled when he said, "I like those new beards. They look great."

When we leave for the final hunt of the year, it is traditional for every hunter to grow a winter beard. Mine was already coming in with its usual reddish brown color. Beards in summer are too itchy and hot to wear, but with winter weather approaching, a beard helps protect our face from icy winds, so we all grow one. Young hunters take a lot of good-natured kidding with their first try at growing a beard. It does not look like much at fourteen years of age.

Mikl selected the location for the horse pit house and led the hard work of digging. This house had to be large enough for two horses to lie down and sleep. We have seen horses take naps while standing for short periods of time, and we have also seen them sleep while lying down.

None of us thought they could be on their feet all winter, so the pit house had to be larger than normal. It would have two doors, one at each end that could be closed off in the cold. Another feature would be a trough for feeding and watering. A fenced-in exercise and training yard would be built next to the house when it was done. The exercise yard was called a corral.

Mikl already had numerous ideas on how to tame horses. He told Bruno, "Diana and I will take the lead training both horses." He asked Bruno to name a team to help. Bruno asked me to oversee the project. Of Bruno's twin sons, only Jon joined us. I was disappointed that his second son, Flint, showed no interest. I was not sure if Mikl had any idea how to tame a horse, but I thought, *we shall see*.

Bruno told me, "I am happy to have Mikl and Diana try their hands at taming these horses, mainly because Mikl had the idea of placing weight in the leather sacks to quiet them on the return trip. That idea worked very well. Maybe his other ideas will work too."

Mikl was eating an apple he grabbed when he left breakfast. His gray horse smelled the apple, and to his surprise, his horse took a bite out of it while he held it. Mikl reacted with surprise and jumped back with half of the apple still in his hand. He looked at his fingers. To his pleasure, they were all still there. He approached his young horse again, and it stretched for the apple. This time, Mikl gently patted the horse's nose and talked to it before he let the horse have the rest of the apple. Apples would be a great help with training.

Mikl came back to Ruth's house all excited and grabbed another apple, not saying anything when he took it. He did the same thing with Bruno's horse. He stood back and looked at the two of them and thought that making a friend of a horse was possible. Mikl wanted a bond with these animals instead of a confrontation. With his patience, he would work to get it.

My one concern today was meeting with the elder women before they voted on the new leader. I had already talked with Judy, the elder of my clan. She heard me out but said that if I had not asked her to vote for

Bruno, she would have voted for me. She said, "Daven, you are a hunter, and you have leadership. The hunters will follow you anywhere. They believe in you. However, if you want Bruno to have my vote, he shall have it." The next was Emma.

I asked Ruth to come with me to meet with her mother, Emma. While we walked, Ruth said, "I have seen many clan leaders and many changes over the years. Emma and I were there when the three clans merged. We saw them come together and form the Botai. That merger changed our fortunes."

I listened to this wise woman as she talked. "I am thrilled that we are the first people to own horses. Bruno is right, horses will change our lives. They will lighten the burden of women, and allow mothers more time for their children. Just think," she continued, "Maybe horses could carry our firewood from the forest instead of us hauling it the way we do now." She was enthusiastic, as always. We approached Emma's house.

Ruth announced our visit when we reached her door, and Emma called for us to come in. She had three cups of hot sassafras tea waiting. I wondered if she was that good of a host or if she knew we were coming. As we sat and talked, I told her my ideas of who would make the best leader. That person was Bruno, not me. The coming vote was not just about leadership, it was about judgment, good decisions, and being a family man.

Emma said, "Hunters respect other hunters. The experience of being a clan leader is a must and will help the man who becomes the Oldson." She sounded like Ruth when she said, "The next person must lead all of the Botai, not just his clan. Daven, you would be my first choice, but Bruno, head of the Bear Clan, and Janos, head of the Aurochs Clan, also deserved consideration."

I told Emma as I told Ruth, "I do not want the position." I had some convincing to do. I told her, "I am here to ask you to select Bruno as the next Oldson." I reminded her, "My real love is that of being a hunter. My best efforts should be used to help feed the village." I told Emma, "My family experience was not a good example for anyone to follow especially with a wife like Gertrude, a wife I cannot control through reasoning, pleading, or threats."

Emma was quick to agree. "Something has to be done about Gertrude, but it has to wait until the new Oldson is chosen."

I assured Emma. "I would be honored to serve if the elders chose me, but Bruno is the best choice, and I will support him on every decision." I knew Bruno would deal with Gertrude far better than I ever did. I told Emma, "Bruno wants the position badly, and I am working to see him get it." It was only a small lie, one she could easily forgive when she found out that I made that part up.

Emma agreed to vote for Bruno, so I had three of the four votes I needed. Out of respect, we visited Patts and asked for her vote too because I wanted the vote to be unanimous. Patts was also our ceremonial leader and lead medicine woman. Without question, she was well liked and respected, as was her assistant, Elizza.

Patts greeted us outside of Janos's pit house where she was visiting as a medicine healer. She said, "It would be better to talk outside of Janos's house because his mother is not a happy woman. Janos's mother disapproves of him having two wives especially with the second wife being so young. The old mother said she understood the circumstances and the need of having to provide for his second wife, Sarah, and that she would not complain. As fast as she said she would not complain, she went on to do exactly that, complain some more." Patts shook her head.

We walked away as the old woman vented her displeasure with her son. Here was a mother who felt left out and overwhelmed with work. Janos was a clan leader, a seasoned and respected hunter and loved his two wives and many children. He had two daughters who were a year or two away from marrying age and three sons, Peter, Patrick, and Thomas. Peter would be a full hunter before winter as would his brother Patrick who was just nine months younger. Both have served on horse hunts and are already hunting small game. Both have excellent skills with their bows. There were several younger children and two more on the way. With so many children, the work never stopped.

The old mother went on and on as we walked away. She just needed attention and appreciation, but so did everyone else who lived there. This would make a perfect social problem for my friend Bruno when he wins the election! I could see the old grandmother at his door, complaining about her workload and lack of sleep.

The old mother finally went back inside, which allowed me to get back to the reason why we called on Patts: the election. I pushed with the conversation telling Patts all the reasons why Bruno made the best choice for the Oldson. Patts replied in a strong voice, saying, "Daven, you would make a great choice since you are a clan leader and the lead hunter. The men, the hunters follow you." I feared a possible split of the four votes with me being elected as a compromise.

I assured Patts. "I am a true hunter and love it. I do not want the Oldson position and the issues that come with the title. I would not do as good a job at hunting if I had to settle disputes." I insisted, "Bruno is the better choice."

I told another small lie when I said, "Bruno sent me to ask for your vote. He is the best candidate, and I am backing him as my friend." I said to Patts, "Think of me as a hunter, and only as a hunter." She seemed surprised to hear me say what I did and finally agreed to vote for Bruno. I promised to support Bruno in everything he did if he was elected. I had all four votes going my way. I hoped they would.

As we returned from our visits, Ruth told me, "The other women will not go against me." She said, "I would rather gently persuade them as we did than argue. Bruno will be an excellent man for the job as long as he has you to back him up if that is what you want." I assured her it was. I was glad Bruno was too busy building the horse pit house to notice that I was missing while I worked to have him become the next Oldson. Maybe I was being selfish, but I knew my problem with Gertrude was over. Bruno would handle that issue the first day as Oldson.

The final vote was delayed until the next day. Too many people were overwhelmed with work smoking horse meat for winter or off in the fields gathering the last winter supplies. The announcement was far too important to make at the end of the day when everyone was exhausted. My hunters were still tired from the return trip and now were building a double-sized pit house. To my surprise, even Flint joined with the work. Gertrude was nowhere to be found. Two women told me they saw her leaving the village and returning several times. Now she was missing again.

Gertrude and I were at the point where we hardly talked. There was nothing to talk about. Nothing would change her. She was always right, and everyone else was always wrong according to her. She told me she hated me. In reality, she hated herself. She said she had no feelings for Mikl or me and that she has no friends. There was not one person she could turn to for support, including me. I should have divorced her a long time ago, but I did not have the heart to put her out. With nowhere to go, she would starve, and Mikl would blame me.

The village was hard at work. Once we had the floor dug, Mikl led his horse with hobbles on its legs into the pit with an apple in his hand. To my surprise, the horse calmly followed him. It needed to be dug deeper, so we went back to work.

We were ready for another measurement, and Diana and Mikl returned with Bruno's horse. We were amazed at his control. Our second fitting told us it had to be deeper. Finally, by the middle of the day, the digging was finished. We placed the poles into the ground to support the roof when the matriarchs approached, and we stopped our work. The women who smoked meat stopped their work too. There was a decision.

Ruth raised her arm in the air and called for everyone's attention. The rest of the village gathered from what they were doing and joined the crowd. Ruth had the center position with the three other elders at her side.

She asked Patts for a prayer to bless the occasion. Once the blessing was finished, Ruth said, "There is a unanimous decision among the elders. We have a new Oldson." Everyone hushed their voices in anticipation. She thanked her deceased husband, Sandor, for all that he did in his years as Oldson. He moved us here and, along with Tedd and their wives, established our homes. He would not be forgotten.

Ruth waited for everyone to look at her. She made eye contact with the clan leaders and focused on Bruno. Then she announced and pointed at him. She said, "The new Oldson is Bruno, the leader of the Bear Clan." It was Bruno! I thanked the spirits for their help.

The crowd roared their approval. I grabbed Bruno in a big bear hug, and we jumped up and down like kids. Everyone crowded around to offer their congratulations, including his twin sons, Jon and Flint, plus his two daughters and his wife, Diana. It was a happy day in the Botai village. Bruno's problems were just beginning, and mine were about to come to an end. I was delighted.

CHAPTER 9

New Leader, New Rules

AFTER THE ANNOUNCEMENT, we finished the work with Bruno in charge. The men saw him in a different way, as the leader. A large double-sized pit house for two horses was taking shape. Tall poles for the walls were placed close to each other in deep holes. The holes were filled with small rocks and wet mud. When the mud dried, the poles would be held firmly in place. The spaces between the support poles were filled with mud on both the inside and outside, a building process that would later be known as wattle and daub. With higher side walls, the ceiling was well above the horses' heads. Even if a horse reared, it would not hit the roof.

Grass thatching was the last step. Long grasses were piled on top of the ceiling beams and attached with twine so rain ran off instead of leaking through to muddy the floor. Everyone was tired. We stopped to talk and admire our work, done in such a short period of time. Even the trench, used to drain rainwater, was almost finished. Tomorrow would see the final touches.

The group was on a rest break when Bruno called out to everyone. "There will be a meeting tomorrow right after breakfast. I need the clan leaders, their wives, and the four eldest women to attend. Everyone is welcome. We will meet in front of my pit house to review the rules by which we all will live." And he said, "There will be new ways of doing things."

Bruno said to me, "Daven, walk with me for a while, there are a few things I need to talk to you about." I wondered what Bruno wanted. After we were out of hearing range of the others, he said, "Most people were at least somewhat surprised that I was selected as the new Oldson, but you were not among them. How did you know I was elected? Even I did not know. Instead, I was certain the elders would choose you to lead."

I expected Bruno to ask me this question. I replied, "I was not surprised because I helped them make their decision." Bruno faced me with a questioning look on his face.

He asked, "What do you mean?"

I explained, "I have had Ruth's ear for a long time. She is like a mother to me and a grandmother to Mikl. And I admit, I persuaded my own clan elder, Judy, to vote for you. After all, she is my cousin, and I knew she would take my advice. With just Ruth and Judy, I had half the votes I needed to elect you."

I continued, "Patts and Emma took some convincing. I told them I was fully supporting you. I said I was the best hunter, but you were the best leader. I also added a small lie and told them you really wanted the Oldson title."

Bruno smiled and thought about my comments when he said, "The best hunter? That was also a small lie! Who captured the first horse?"

I was quick to respond, "It was Mikl, with my help, you just copied what we did!" We both enjoyed a hearty laugh for several minutes.

Bruno said, "Well, thanks for your support, I think."

Then he asked, "Seriously, Daven, why did you not take the position yourself? I would have supported you, just as you will support me. You are a hunter and a family man just as I am. I am at a loss as to how to run this group. It has always been Sandor who was the Oldson as was his father before him. He made all those family and social decisions, many of which I have no idea how to advise people."

Bruno verbalized his concerns. "All that husband-wife and within-clan squabbling is annoying. I am not sure how to deal with it and complete our hunts on time. From now on, I am just another hunter. Daven, you always run the hunts anyway, so I guess I do not have to worry about them. Officially, they are yours. I am more interested in working with Mikl and Diana with training my horse than I am in getting involved with meaningless disputes."

"Speaking of horses," he said, "I am going to call my horse by a name. Having a name will make the colt seem like she is more a part of the Botai rather than something anyone should consider to be a meal. It will give her an identity. We captured her at dawn and that will be her name, Dawn. One other thing, in the long run, I will need a stallion to handle my size and weight. Since you are now in charge of hunts, I need you to get one for me." He looked at me, pleased with himself and smiled; it was his first order as Oldson.

With that, I said, "You make me laugh. Today you were elected Oldson and your mind is right where mine would be, on training your horse and the next hunt rather than family disputes. Bruno, your comments are exactly why I did not want to be elected to lead the Botai. My judgment is sound when it comes to a hunt, but I cannot even get my own lazy-assed wife to contribute anything. She does not even cook food for me. I need to get her out of my life, yet I struggle to do it. I doubt anyone would listen to me on a family matter. I have no trouble making a decision when it comes to a matter within my clan or for a hunt, but not with my marriage. My hesitation may have cost me a chance with Ildiko, the Hungarian woman I want to be with. In comparison, your marriage runs smoothly. Bruno, you are the best man for the Oldson position, not me."

Bruno stopped walking and turned toward me. He was animated when he said, "What do you suggest? Should I rule as Oldson did, getting involved in all the small issues and never going on hunts with you? That will not work for me. Husbands and wives should make compromises between themselves, not get the leader involved."

We talked as we walked. I said, "No, Bruno, family disputes are not for you, in fact, they should not even be heard by the Oldson. When Sandor became Oldson, he was about the same age we are now. As he got older and could no longer hunt, he occupied his time by becoming more available and more involved with small issues. Many of those he should have avoided, but with not much else to do, it gave him a purpose in life. It was a reason to be needed. If I were you, I would set the new rules tomorrow morning. Let the clan leaders run their clans and husbands and wives run their families. Janos's family is a perfect example. He leads his clan very well and is a great partner on a hunt, but I ask you, do you want to get between him and his two wives and his mother? I doubt it. I would not go near it."

Bruno was quiet for some time. Then he said, "Daven, I appreciate your advice. I will use it when I talk to the village tomorrow morning." Bruno hesitated to get his thoughts together before he spoke again. "Let me change the subject. What did you see the night when Oldson was injured?"

This subject was something I wanted to talk about. I replied, "I woke up when Gertrude groaned saying she has stomach cramps as she left the pit house. I stayed in bed when Gertrude went outside. I did not actually see what she did. Then I heard the Oldson yell in pain when he cut his foot in the dark, and I went to the door of my house. When I did that, Gertrude rushed past me as she returned to her bed. Her entry was more than a brush. She pushed me out of the way."

"I felt something wet on my leg and wiped at it with my hand thinking it might be blood. Luckily, I smelled my hand instead of tasting it for blood. The smell told me it was diarrhea and it was loaded with blueberries. I thought, or maybe I hoped, she would clean up the mess the next morning. Although knowing her, she would be more likely to leave it where it was and deny any involvement."

I continued, "The next day when we left on the hunt, I thought the Oldson would get better and that the whole issue would be forgotten, except for the diarrhea mess on the trail. That needed to be cleaned up.

There is no doubt in my mind Gertrude caused the Oldson's death. On top of that, she fights with everyone and does not even come close to doing her fair share of work. By now everyone knows she steals food while others work hard to gather it. Women hate her. She has to pay for what she did."

I said to Bruno, "I know the rules of the Botai. There are no beatings or whippings allowed as punishments. I also know that when one person causes a severe injury or the death of another member, it is punished by being expelled. Causing the death of the Botai leader has never happened before. It is your decision. Whatever you decide, you will have no argument from me. I will divorce her no matter what your decision. Bruno, you are a brother to me. Gertrude is useless and no wife to me or mother to our son. I should have divorced her two years ago when she became selfish. I am not getting any younger, and in a few more years, I will be too old for any woman to look in my direction." I asked him, "What did you think, what did you see?"

Bruno responded, "I saw what happened. I was outside my pit house in the dark late that night thinking about the next day's hunt. Having four new hunters worried me, and I could not sleep. I saw Gertrude come out of your pit house. She was in no hurry and walked slowly. As fat as she is, I could not mistake her for anyone else. Even with no moon, I could see her in the glow from the fires. I watched as she took the trail that led toward the scat pits. Then to my surprise, she looked around to see if anyone was looking. When she saw no one, she squatted on the trail and let her bowels erupt like a thunderstorm. Daven, what I saw was no accident, no accident at all. Another person saw some of this, so there are three witnesses, including you and me."

Bruno continued, "My first thought was to demand that Gertrude clean up the mess and to make her do it in front of everyone as punishment. Right after that, Sandor came out of his pit house, probably to urinate as we all do at night, and he stepped in what she left behind and cut his foot. I also thought the whole issue would have been dropped after she cleaned it up. As we both know, it did not work out that way."

Bruno shared his thoughts further. "At the meeting in the morning, I will review new rules with everyone. After that, I will meet with the matriarchs to make a decision on Gertrude. I have to warn you, Daven, the punishment must be severe, just as it should be for a crime like this or the village will feel that I am soft on rules when friends are involved."

I nodded my agreement. "Bruno, you cannot afford to play favorites. You will make the right decision. A death of another member is a serious problem. You have enough evidence on the guilty party. I will fully support your decision." We bear-hugged and patted each other on the back and walked back to the village. With Gertrude nowhere in sight, I went to Ruth's pit house for dinner and saw that Mikl was already eating. It has been like this for a long time.

Bruno began the morning meeting promptly after breakfast with almost every adult present. All three heads of the clans and their wives were attending plus the elder females. I noticed Bruno's son Jon standing behind him. Jon took advantage of every opportunity to learn. His twin brother, Flint, was missing.

As the meeting started, it dawned on me; Jon was the oldest son by a few minutes, and it did make a difference. I could see that Jon was being trained to succeed Bruno someday and that Flint was backing out of the situation, just as he had been doing for quite a while.

By inviting the elders as named guests and including them on his first major decision, Bruno set up a unique group of people just below himself. These members would share his authority and provide advice in areas where he sought help. It set them apart. Unlike older ways, his advisors were not just clan leaders. Bruno added women to his circle of advisors.

Bruno spoke in no uncertain terms. "As the newly elected Oldson, I have three areas to discuss. I see my role as being responsible for the safety, welfare, and growth of the entire Botai people. As the Oldson of the Botai, I will limit my involvement to issues between clans or those that affect the entire village. My role is not to get involved with anything below that level.

"Within each clan, the clan leader, with input from the eldest female, will make decisions that affect that clan. Disputes between husband and wife should be decided by the husband and wife themselves. If there is no agreement, the clan leader and the eldest female will hear the dispute and make a final decision. Be warned. It is better to settle an argument between a man and his wife because the eldest female might be more likely to side with the wife. Settle it between yourselves before bringing any marital issue to anyone else." Bruno set a new tone. It would be different than when Sandor was the leader.

"My second topic is simple to understand. We are a people who work together and share in the results, whether they are good or bad. When we hunt horses in the fall, every hunter works for the good of the entire people, and the meat is shared among all three clans. We will continue to do that. We will continue to leave hunters behind for protection of the village. What is new is that those hunters who stay behind are expected to not only provide protection, they will take part in the work of gathering."

"Right now, we have a problem where some people are not contributing as much as they should or not contributing at all." Bruno paused as he scanned the audience. He took time to allow them to consider what each of them had contributed. Without naming anyone, everyone must have thought, *Did I do my share?*

"From here on, everyone must contribute at whatever level they can. Elderly women who can no longer help in the field can sew clothing or make boots and coats for hunters who need them. Elderly men can contribute by making flint points for arrows and spears. They can also make atlatls and bows and arrows. They will do so without being asked to help."

Bruno remarked, "Young people over the age of ten are expected to gather with our women and to help with cut wood for the cold months. And now, they are expected to help feed and water the horses. Even our oldest man, Tedd, is working with Mikl on a new type of bow and helping tame the horses. Mark my words, horses can be tamed. We tamed the wolves that help guard out village, and we will do the same with these horses.

"Each clan leader will be sure his members help as best they are able. Those people who do not perform will no longer be allowed to share in our winter supplies.

"Let me be clear. If you do not contribute, you will not share in the food." He paused for emphasis before saying, "If you are finished with your work, ask your clan leader what else needs to be done. Do not come to me.

"There is no change for children under ten years of age." He smiled when he said, "Children will continue to be children. Hopefully, they will be well-behaved children."

"Owning horses is new to all of us. There are already some complaints that the horses should not belong to any one person but to everyone. Others say we should fatten these horses up and eat them in the late months of winter.

"I have made a decision. The male horse belongs to Mikl and the second horse, the female named Dawn, belongs to me. You may ask why Mikl and I own the first two horses. You should not think of just two men owning two horses, you should think of many people owning them. You should think of owning one yourself.

"These are only the first two horses. We will capture more of them on every hunt. When we do, the next horses go to the clan leaders and then to hunters and trainers. Eventually, every member of the Botai, including women, can own a horse of their own as long as they train it and care for it. Listen to me on this point, these horses will not be eaten, not now and not ever. Think in a new direction, as an owner.

"This year we need to work harder than ever to gather enough food for ourselves and for the horses. As soon as the pit houses are finished, we will leave for the last hunt of the year. We need extra supplies of apples, hay, oats, and grass to feed our horses during winter. Your efforts will pay off soon when horses start to work for you."

People stirred. They had a few questions, and several talked among themselves. The horse issue was all new, and everyone was interested. Hunters were surprised at Bruno's announcement because in the past, those who stayed back only had to guard the village, which was a pretty easy job, now they will have to help with gathering. Women certainly appreciated this help, and it raised their status to just below that of a hunter. Bruno also promised horses to women as well as men. Women loved their new Oldson and felt more valued than in the past.

Someone asked an innocent question, "What can we do with horses other than eat them?" Someone else asked, "Should I have to go hungry so a horse can eat when I could eat the horse?" These were natural questions, not really grumbling. No one had much to say about not contributing with gathering because the only problem that anyone knew of was with Gertrude, and she was not seen at the meeting.

Bruno spoke again and put the questions to rest. "As I said before, I believe horses can be trained to work. Hunting trips will be easier if horses carry the meat back to the village instead of us having to haul it. A full-grown horse can carry the load of three or four men. When our women and elder men gather wood, horses will carry it back to the village for them." The crowd voiced their agreement. To me, it sounded like Mikl speaking, instead of Bruno.

Bruno let the crowd calm down before stating. "The five unused pit houses, those that were left behind when Ander departed, belong to the entire village. Do not use them for parts and pieces. We will need them to house horses if we are lucky enough to capture them on the final hunt next week, and there might be enough time to build new ones with winter coming." No one objected.

Bruno raised his arms and waited for everyone's attention. He said, "I have one final topic." This was the one everyone wanted to hear the most. "My final issue today is the death of Oldson." There was a lot of indistinct whispered talk. Bruno told them what he observed and what he learned from other witnesses, but carefully avoided their names. He summed it up by saying, "Without any doubt, it was Gertrude who caused the death of the Oldson."

The crowd shouted their anger with her. She was hated anyway. Women were the first to yell, "Expel her, whip her, throw her out, she steals food."

I glanced around and saw Gertrude hiding behind Bruno's pit house, listening in on the meeting. Of course she was eating while she watched. It looked to me like horse meat, and it appeared to be bloody and uncooked.

Bruno asked the elder women, "Please stay to discuss the penalty for Gertrude." The meeting was finished, and the group left with many of them still screaming for Gertrude to be punished.

I was impressed with the forceful directions Bruno gave to everyone. Clearly, we all had a purpose. Each person had to do their part to help the village flourish. Ruth, Emma, and Janos commented to me, they were also impressed with Bruno and his first village gathering.

The female elders followed Bruno to his house to discuss Gertrude's penalty. There was no doubt. She was responsible and would be expelled. The only question remaining was the length of expulsion. When Bruno asked for their advice, his alliance with the elders was stronger than it ever was in the past.

CHAPTER 10

The Verdict

AFTER THE MEETING, I returned to my house to pick up some tools to work on the pit house. We needed to push to complete it so we could get to the final horse hunt.

Standing in the door of my pit house was Gertrude. She cried, "I would have removed the diarrhea from the trail in the morning, but I was too sick that night. I did not mean to harm the Oldson. I was sick." She was always sick and always lied. "It was not my fault, it was an accident." I have heard all this before. She forced some tears and whined.

She went on and on about how the rest of the women were jealous of her looks. "They hated me from the beginning," she complained. It was a pathetic performance. She said, "I always loved you and Mikl. If only I could be given a second chance to make it all better between the three of us." Her act was anything but convincing. I laughed at her and shook my head saying no.

Gertrude pleaded with me through her forced tears saying, "I want to stay with you, I love you. I will cook for our family and gladly have more children. Please talk to Bruno for me. He is your friend, he will listen to you. I do not want to leave the Botai, I have nowhere to go."

I watched her performance and had seen it all before. It was so well rehearsed. She got on her knees, "Please save me, Daven."

I turned away just as she had done to me and her son all these years. I replied, "You no longer matter, not to me, not to anyone. It is too late. I have no feelings for you, none at all. If anything, I am like the rest of the village, tired of your act. I do not care about you or what happens to you. You ruined what we had a long time ago. In my mind, you no longer exist."

The more I looked at her, the more I found her disgusting. She cared for only one person and that was herself. I told her those words exactly. It felt good to say them after holding back all this time. I wondered why it took me so long to get those words out. Maybe I held back for Mikl's sake, but Mikl did not care about her anymore either. He had moved on with his life. Now, I would move on with mine.

I said, "It is true, no one likes you and that you have no friends. That is your fault, and looking at you lately, being beautiful has nothing to do with it. You have no love for anyone and contribute nothing. You snub your nose at the women when they get angry with you for your selfish ways. You think you are better than everyone else and have laughed at them in the past. Now they will have the last laugh. The entire village is anxiously waiting for your verdict.

"If you are ever allowed to come back, it will not be to this house. I will not take you back, and I do not know anyone else who would take you in. Think about the wolves when they find you, when the cold winds bite at your fat body, or when food runs out and you have no one to steal from. Then think about what we had years ago and how you ruined it. Gertrude, I hope you enjoy your travels."

She whined and cried. "It is almost the tenth month of the year, and it will snow soon. There will be nothing for me to eat and no house to keep me warm. I do not know how to hunt. I could die of the cold. Mikl will hate you if I die of starvation." I smiled. I have heard that threat before.

I said, "Oh, poor Gertrude. You are far too beautiful to freeze to death or for wolves to have you for dinner. As far as starving, you can live a year or two off all that fat you have accumulated. Tell death how you are right and the whole village is wrong. Maybe death will listen. I cannot hear you anymore."

I grabbed my tools and turned to leave the house. As I left, I picked up the jar with the sands we poured together when we married. I showed it to her and said, "I might as well get this over with right now." I carried the marriage jar outside and poured the sand on the ground and announced to anyone within earshot, "I divorce the evil woman known as Gertrude." I smashed the jar, and it felt wonderful.

Those neighbors who heard me cheered and applauded." Someone yelled, "What took you so long?" Finally, I was free of her.

I joined Mikl and the rest of the group finishing the horse pit house. The final grasses were being laid on the roof. It was already a foot thick with more grass being added. The drains for rain and snow runoff were finished, and the two doors were in place. It was surprising how much can be accomplished in a short time when a group worked together.

Mikl approached me and said, "I hear my mother's verdict is coming and the decision would be banishment." I said nothing. He knew his mother caused her own problems and that she was hated by everyone. He said, "To tell you the truth, I am tired of hearing about her from everyone I talk to. Even my best friend Jon said she was hated by every woman in the Botai and many of the men too." Mikl had heard it too often. She was a troublemaker, but now that she caused Oldson's death, she would be punished by banishment.

I said to Mikl, "The only remaining question is how long she would be gone." I added, "It could be forever." Mikl had little sympathy for her, but she was still his mother. It was a good thing for him to have horses to take his mind off the continued problems with his mother. He had to find ways to feed and water horses all winter and how to remove all that horse manure coming his way. I was glad for the horses and the problems they brought. Mikl would be too busy to feel sorry for his mother.

At noon, Bruno called for a gathering at his pit house. I knew the verdict was set. It was unanimous and final. The entire village gathered and listened as if there was a great joyous event about to happen, and in a way, it was. Even children were there. Bruno had Ruth with him as were Emma, Judy, and Patts. Bruno spoke. "I told you earlier today that Gertrude was responsible for Oldson's death. There is no argument or misunderstanding. It is a fact. I was one of the witnesses who observed what she did, and two others saw what I saw.

"The Oldson's death was not an accident. It was done in a reckless manner and done without regard to anyone else. We are treating this incident as if it were done on purpose. Gertrude took the life of Sandor." Bruno was definite in his tone. His face showed his authority.

"Never before has any Botai member been responsible for the death of our leader. This person is Gertrude. She has not done her share of work either. Gertrude has not contributed this year or last year and did little or nothing the year before that." The group shouted their agreement and nodded yes. She was the type of person who was not wanted in this village.

"If our rules allowed whipping, it would be done, but our punishments do not allow beatings. The rules allow banning the offender from the village. Because of continuing problems with Gertrude over many years and because she is responsible for the death of Oldson, her punishment is that of being banned. Gertrude is banned forever. She will leave us today although many people of this village feel she should be beaten. It is my decision that she will not be harmed, but she cannot return. She no longer exists."

At first, people were quiet, maybe in shock that she would be gone for good. They wondered after all this time would she finally be gone. Then Gertrude cursed everyone just as she had done many times in the past. "It was the women's fault!" she yelled. It was always everyone's fault, everyone except her. "You hated me from the first day of my marriage. You were jealous of me because I was beautiful and the rest of you are ugly. I am not to blame, you are." She turned and left with nothing in her hands, not even food. She walked away, sobbing. This time, the tears were real. She was in deep trouble, all of it brought on by her.

While everyone stared, she walked south along the river. People jeered and yelled insults at her. "You are not beautiful, you are fat and ugly." Others yelled, "You are lazy and disgusting. Do not come back. We hope you starve. There will be extra food for everyone this year with you gone. You smell like the scat pit itself." Gertrude was right on one thing, they did hate her.

We watched her leave. No one saw her when she was out of sight and changed direction to the east. Along the way, she picked up her hidden sacks filled with food and warm clothing and an extra pair of winter boots. All these supplies had been hidden over several weeks.

When the commotion was over, Mikl and I walked toward his horse staked near Dawn for grazing. The two horses comforted each other. Mikl told me, "Father, I have chosen a name for my young stallion based on his color. I will call him Gray Boy." He went on to tell me of his ideas on how to train horses. We talked about horses and his ideas. We already talked too long and suffered too much over his mother. She was my poor choice of a marriage partner. At last, I thought, it is finally over.

That night, I started to clean my pit house to rid myself of the bad memories and the filth she left behind. I noticed one spear and atlatl, my short bow and a quiver of arrows, were missing.

CHAPTER 11

Ildiko

MY NAME IS Ildiko. Six months ago, my uncle traded me to the meanest man I have ever known. I will tell you what happened.

As a young girl growing up in my Hungarian village, I followed my mother and my aunt and took part in all the things they did every day. We made clothes, shoes, belts, and boots, and we cooked meals. We made bread and prepared stew for dinner. When the men returned from the spring hunts, we smoked reindeer. In the fall, everyone helped with smoking and drying horse meat. Women gathered most of the supplies to prepare for winter. We harvested fruits including apples, pears, berries, and vegetables such as peas and lentils. We collected oats and wheat for bread and dug tubers.

When gathering was done, just when the weather turned cold, women and children collected nuts before snow covered them. Men repaired the houses, hunted, and cut firewood. This work was part of everyday life. What women enjoyed most while they worked was the social part; they loved to gossip. They talked when they started work early in the morning and continued until night when they returned to their pit houses.

For me, the social part was not very interesting. I really did not care whose husband was the best looking, the smartest, the strongest, or the best hunter. To me, it did not matter whose husband was the best sex partner or who had the biggest penis. It was silly and a lot of bragging, but my mother and my aunts thrived on it.

For me, other interests were more challenging than what my mother did. I liked my brothers' activities better than what my mother did day after day. I helped and did what was expected of me, but in my spare time, I learned how to make snares and how to use a bow and arrow. I hunted small game like rabbits, ptarmigan, and beaver. As I improved, I hunted deer with my brothers. That made me different from other Hungarian women because they rarely hunted.

When I made my first bows and arrows, they were pretty much useless, but I kept trying. After ten attempts at making a bow, it still did not work. My brothers laughed at me as I tried time after time to make a bow as good as theirs. When they laughed, it made me work all that much harder until finally, I was able to make as good a bow. Mine was smaller than theirs because they were taller than I am, and a bow has to fit the person using it.

My first arrows were worse than my first bows. I tried over and over, but time after time, my arrows just did not work. My oldest brother, Gabor, offered advice on how long the arrow should be in comparison to the bow and where to place the feathers on the arrows. My reply was always the same. "I can do it," and I went my own way. I remember thinking, "If they could do it, so could I." They said that I was stubborn.

I often wondered why there were feathers on an arrow in the first place. No one told me the purpose of the feathers was to make the arrow rotate as it flew through the air. Rotation allows an arrow to travel in a straight line and at a high speed without wobbling. Since I did not know what purpose the feathers served, I just glued them on the shaft. Even though the feathers were in a perfectly straight line, my arrows still did not fly.

I tried placing them in a different location on the shaft with no luck. To make matters worse, the feathers cut my left hand the first time I shot that arrow. I placed the feathers farther forward just to see how that might work, but my arrows fell to the ground just a few feet in front of me.

After a while, my brothers gave up and stopped telling me what to do or how to do it. Maybe this was because I always refused their help. After a summer of trying, they left me alone with my frustration. They watched and laughed, making jokes at my beginner attempts, and I was mad at them for weeks at a time. Sometimes brothers, even my youngest brother George who was my favorite, were useless.

Later that summer, I watched in silence as an old hunter made his arrows, and I saw what I was doing wrong. The feathers did not go on the arrow in a straight line at all. They were placed at a slight angle. My arrow-making problem was solved, no thanks to my brothers. I was still annoyed with them with their know-it-all, big-brother attitudes.

Once I learned how to make arrows from the old man, I showed my brothers what I had made. I shot one at the target we used for practice, and the arrow flew straight, as it should. I hit the target right in the middle. I was quite proud of my efforts. They just laughed and asked, "Who showed you how to make them?"

I said, "I made my own arrows. I told you, I did not need your advice."

Another thing I did that women did not do was swim. I loved it and could always beat my brothers. I swam all summer and into the fall until water temperatures cooled. Not many women or men in the Hungarian village could swim.

I remember one beautiful day in the fall. I stayed later than usual, lying on a rock in the sun to dry off. As I lay there, I watched a raccoon searching for food on the opposite bank. He was at the edge of the river where the earthen bank sloped down to the water. The masked bundle of fur used his tiny paws to turn small rocks over and found things to eat.

I was on higher ground than he was. I could see him, but he did not see me, probably because I did not move and was not at its eye level. Maybe the coon did see me, but since I was on the opposite shore, I was no threat to him. He just went on with his hunting, ignoring me as if he did not see.

Late in the day, I noticed four wolves stalking the smaller animal. After waiting quite some time for the raccoon to come out of the water, one of the wolves leaped off the bank and tried to grab the coon in his jaws, but he moved aside and swam a few feet farther into the river. He stayed just ahead of his attacker. The wolf swam after it, looking for an easy meal. The raccoon swam out into the river, just out of reach. It was obvious the coon was the better swimmer.

When the wolf was in deep, fast-moving water and well over his head, the raccoon turned around and swam toward the wolf. The coon had no trouble grabbing the wolf's hair and climbed onto its back, using claws that closely resembled a person's hands. With the weight of the coon on his back, the wolf was in trouble. He went under. In panic, the wolf splashed with his paws and turned back toward the riverbank, keeping his nose just above the waterline. The hunter became the hunted.

The raccoon easily clawed his way from the wolf's back to his head as the wolf slapped at the water with his paws and struggled to breathe. He tried desperately to reach the bank, but it was too far away. The other wolves watched hungrily from the riverbank while their leader went under and the raccoon went under with him. The weight of the raccoon on his head was too much. The wolf surfaced once more, gasping and struggling for air before it drowned. The rest of the wolf pack turned and left in defeat. There would be no easy meal this time.

The drowned wolf's carcass floated down the river with the raccoon riding on top of it. Eventually, he let go and swam back to shore. The raccoon shook off water and went right back to work at the edge of the river looking for food once again. I was fascinated. The smaller and weaker animal easily won the battle because he was the better swimmer. I walked back to the village thinking about what I saw that day. It was something I would never forget.

My oldest brother, Gabor, had already taken a wife. My second brother, Zalan, was not married but had his own pit house, and George, my youngest brother, lived with him. They looked at me as just a little sister. My oldest brother's wife was pregnant, and I would be an aunt soon. I was feeling old. Seventeen was old. Most women my age were already married and had children.

Two years ago, I started hunting with them for small game. We used position hunting where we waited just off a well-used animal trail and stayed hidden and quiet until game arrived. When an animal came along, we let our arrows fly. It took the four of us to carry back a full-sized deer. Being female, I have never been allowed to go on horse hunts. Horse hunts were considered to be too dangerous for women. That was one of the reasons I say being female was not as much fun as being a male.

At age twelve, my body started changing. Boys were friendlier, and for some reason, they paid more attention to me. I did not think I would change like that when I was a young girl. It just seemed to me that mothers were different than fathers and that it would always be this way. I would always be a kid with three brothers and a family and never thought about becoming a woman or a mother. Being my mother's daughter was fine with me.

At sixteen, my legs are longer and stronger, and they are shapely. The most embarrassing thing was when my breasts grew and my hips got rounder; my rear end changed in shape, and even my face changed. The most horrible thing was when I grew hair in places that never had hair before. I wondered why this was happening. It looked awful. I thought that no young man would want me now. I was wrong, the more my body changed, the more they showed interest.

I looked at my face in the river when I went swimming. I thought I was pretty. Instead of a child, I saw a young woman. I had to admit my body was curvy and looked nice. Several young men and some of the married men must have thought I looked good too because I could feel them looking at me. One man looked at me too often. His name was Kraven. He was a huge man, the oldest son of a clan leader, and he had a bad reputation. People feared him. I feared him too.

Most of my girlfriends by age thirteen or fourteen were already married. They talked to me about their lives. Marriage was allowed for women the month after they had their first blood. My married friends had a far different life than I did. Now at age seventeen, I wondered if I waited too long. Maybe I should have taken one of the marriage offers I had and became someone's wife. It was just that none of them were really right for me. I refused to get married just to be married. Now, after I refused the offers, there were not many unmarried men left, and most of them were younger than I was. I did not have a lot of choices.

Maybe I waited too long, but some men think they own you once you are married. My girlfriends complain to me that all they did was cook, gather foods, and take care of their children. They were expected to do whatever was necessary to manage their pit houses.

Men had a hard life too. They hunted, built pit houses, and worked to cut and gather firewood. They did face a more dangerous life than women, especially on horse and bear hunts, but their lives were more interesting. Women of the village did what was expected of them and behaved as they were expected to behave. The Hungarian way of life was about men and what they wanted.

I met Daven of the Botai at a summer gathering, and I was fascinated by him. He was a handsome man and a clan leader, but he was married. I hated the thought of being a second wife, and as much as I wanted to be with him, I turned down his marriage proposal last summer. I felt sick and cried when he left. I was miserable for weeks, and I missed him desperately. I still think about him every day. I know I made a mistake. I should have gone with him as a second wife.

Second wives are not as well respected as first wives. Men wanted second wives for sex and to help their first wives with the pit house and her children. Even first wives wanted a second wife for their help. As the first wife got older, she had less interest in sex and a lot of children to look after. Mostly, she needed help. If the second wife had a few more children, it would not make much difference. I did not want to be a second wife.

I thought about going to Daven's village, but it was a long distance from my village. It would take twenty-five or thirty days to walk that far, and it was far too dangerous for a woman to travel alone. It was not realistic. Instead, I hoped to see him this summer at the next gathering. I could not forget Daven. I made up my mind; if he still wanted me this year, I will marry him and become his second wife. It would be far better to be with the man I love than to be alone for the rest of my years. No one wants to be alone and without children when they get old, and seventeen is old.

I knew of the Botai people because several women from our village were traded to them as wives, and they had good lives. I learned much of this from Ruth, the first Hungarian woman to be traded to the Botai. She became the wife of their chief or their Oldson as they call them.

Daven has a son who is near my age. His name is Mikl. I met him and liked him, so it did not appear that I was heading into some hidden problem. This year, Mikl would be fourteen. Most likely, he would come to the gathering to look for a wife, if he did not already have one from home. With just one child, the work of being a second wife did not seem to be the same problem most second wives face. I wondered why Daven needed his first wife if he wanted me and had no children at home. He hardly spoke of his first wife, just some of his people.

A few weeks ago, on an early fall hunt, our chief took part as one of the drivers. The hunt was going as expected with the drivers moving the herd forward to a line of waiting hunters. A mare with a yearling colt hid in tall grass. The two horses were near a natural spring where the ground was below the level of the grass surrounding them. They had good cover and were well hidden.

The mare and her colt stayed in place until the drivers were almost on top of them. At the last minute, the mare bolted and ran full speed straight at the drivers to escape. The yearling was on her heels. No one saw them coming. The chief and another driver were knocked to the ground by the mare. They were battered and sore, and the chief's knee was bent at an angle that was not normal. It was badly dislocated, and he was in severe pain. It was impossible for the old chief to stand or put any weight on the knee.

The men did not know how to get his knee joint back in place. They were hunters, not healers. They tried to twist the leg from side to side with two men pulling on it and two men holding him down, but it did not go back in place.

They made a second try. One hunter placed his foot at the base of the leg with the other foot on the chief's hip bone. He pulled on the bad leg while the chief was held down. The chief screamed in pain and begged them to stop. All the attempts failed, so it was decided to carry him back to the village where the medicine women would know what to do.

He was laid on a leather horse hide stretched between two poles and carried home in the sling by four men. The ride in the sling was rough from what I heard; his pain was unbearable. He moaned in agony all the way back to the village. The healers, both women, gave him a strong tea loaded with mushrooms to make him sleep. Once the chief was unconscious, the healers maneuvered his knee back into place, but he was never the same. He could barely walk even with a crutch. He knew his time had come and resigned as chief. When that happened, my problems started.

CHAPTER 12

Kraven

AFTER THREE WEEKS, the old chief could hardly put any weight on the knee. He struggled to walk and still needed his crutch. Two medicine women administered pain medications and worked with him every day trying to get his knee to function again, but after weeks of trying, he realized that he would never be the same. If he could not walk, he could not hunt. He knew he was too old to lead and decided to step down for good. There would be an election for a new chief with the votes coming from the four clan leaders.

At about the same time the chief stepped back from overall leadership to lead his old Aurochs clan, the leader of the Mammoth Clan also decided to step aside and let his son Kraven inherit the Mammoth Clan. Kraven finally had a clan, but he wanted more. He wanted to be chief of all the Hungarians, not just head of his own clan, and the title was open.

Kraven was sure that with four clans, the vote would be split. He felt certain he had two votes for him and two against him. If that happened, the tie breaker would go to the oldest hunter, my uncle Lorand. The old chief would support Kraven, and Kraven would vote for himself. Voting against him would be Rhoden of the Eagle Clan and Karoli, leader of the Bear Clan. Kraven needed my uncle's vote to break the tie.

My uncle Lorand married my mother soon after my real father was killed in a bear hunt accident many years ago. That was the custom. When a hunter died, a brother was expected to marry the widow and provide for her and her children. Lorand was a good hunter and provided for his inherited family very well. Now he was in a position as the senior hunter where his vote was needed by both sides to decide the tie. Lorand usually sided with Rhoden, so Kraven's chances to become the overall chief looked slim. Most people expected Rhoden to become the next chief and rightfully so. He was respected and experienced, and he had good judgment.

Because of Kraven's ignorant behavior, my uncle often talked about him over meals at our pit house saying, "Kraven would never make a good chief. Perhaps he would be able to lead a clan, but even that was a question." My uncle was not his friend, and he somewhat feared Kraven because he was a bully, mean, and unpredictable. He was also the biggest and strongest man of the Hungarians, and he let everyone know it, not just the men, women too.

He did annoying things like slapping smaller men on the back of their head so hard it made them dizzy, sometimes knocking them off their feet. Then he laughed at the man and yelled at him, "Do not be a girl, be like me, be ready at all times." He was famous for punching someone in the stomach while they were not looking and mocking them for not being ready. He laughed as they gasped for breath. He chided them, "You have to be tough, like me." He was the only one who thought he was funny.

People hated him for his nasty habit of punching others when they were not looking. He pointed and laughed as they winced in pain. At times he did similar stupid things to women as well. One of his favorite tricks was to trip a woman when she carried a heavy load. Every time he punched a man or embarrassed a woman, he made another enemy, and he lost respect. People called him a stupid ass behind his back, but never to his face.

On horse hunts, Kraven often claimed that a kill was his when his arrow or spear only added to the kill, not the fatal blow. Then he claimed one of the choice pieces of the evening meal, saying in a commanding voice, "The right is mine," as he grabbed the tongue and tore into it like a starving animal and did not offer to share it with anyone. He left the uneaten scraps behind as an insult to the hunter who actually deserved the best parts. No man challenged him on his boasts because he was bigger and stronger than everyone else. He was intimidating. Only the big hunter from the Botai, the one called Bruno, beat him at strength contests as we all saw at the summer gatherings. Kraven hated Bruno.

Kraven bragged constantly. It was the norm for him. I have heard him, more than once, tell everyone that he was the best hunter, the strongest man anywhere, and that he had the biggest penis of any man. There were times when he would take out his huge member and stroke it or wave around in his hand in front of women and men. He told married and single women, "If you want a big son, maybe you should try my big penis. I would be happy to help you get what you want!" He laughed and said, "You will have a son even bigger than I am. Come and get it, ladies." Then he would laugh very loud as if it was a huge joke. It was a joke for him, but a crude insult to everyone else.

There were rumors that two married women took Kraven up on his boast. Both of these women had several children who looked like him with big frames for their age, but no one was sure. The husbands assumed the children were theirs. It was the type of gossip my mother loved.

Kraven's two wives did not care what he did. If they did care, there was nothing they could do about him anyway. His wives were used to his size by now, but there was a lot of screaming when he took his second wife. She was my aunt, the sister of my birth father. It was her first marriage and she had suffered all the pitfalls of being a second wife. Her life was one I did not want.

Kraven did annoying stupid things that people resented, but not things that were bad enough to cause someone to kill him with an arrow in the back during the confusion of a hunt. Kraven pushed the limit and tested your patience, but he held back just a bit. Everyone was intimidated by him, everyone except Rhoden.

The election was coming, and Kraven needed the tie-breaking vote. He desperately wanted the title of chief of all the Hungarian people. Rhoden, the Eagle Clan leader, stood in his way for all the right reasons. My uncle was the most senior hunter and held the vote that would beat him or confirm him. On most votes of any kind, Lorand sided with Rhoden.

Every young man strives to be a hunter and then becomes the lead hunter for their clan. A few men become experts in flint knapping, carving, or making bows and arrows, but most want to be hunters. When a hunter becomes well established, he might seek to be a clan leader. A few achieve their goal. One of the clan leaders becomes the chief.

My uncle was overlooked more than once. It was not because he lacked leadership or because he was not a good hunter, but because deals were made when a clan leader was appointed by the chief. The appointments in the past went to someone else. My uncle was an honorable man, and until now, he did not get involved with men who wanted control when they did not deserve it.

Kraven came to my uncle Lorand that morning with a deal. The temptation was too great not to listen to, even though he did not like Kraven. At age thirty-three, Lorand was old, and he knew it. This was probably his last chance, so he decided to talk. He reasoned to my mother, "There is no harm is listening to what Kraven has to say."

Kraven wanted two things and offered one in return. He wanted me as his third wife, and he wanted the title of chief. In exchange, Kraven offered my uncle the clan leadership of his Mammoth Clan when he became the overall chief. That night, I overheard my uncle telling my mother of the proposed deal. His judgment was clouded by his greed.

My uncle said to my mother, "Ildiko is already old at seventeen. She has had many marriage offers from young men from good families who wanted her. Any one of those marriage partners might have given me a good alliance and a clan leadership position. Since she has refused them all, no one will ask for her in marriage ever again. Men, especially young men, hate rejection."

He went on and on trying to convince my mother. "Ildiko might never find a husband even at the next summer gathering. Not one man of the other three clans was good enough for her. She only has eyes for the Botai, the one called Daven, and he is already married. So I ask you, wife, what difference does it make if I give her to Kraven as a third wife or if she marries the Botai as a second wife? Either way, she will be married. If she does pick the Botai hunter next summer, she will leave us, and we will not see her again. By giving her to Kraven, it will be better for her and for me. And we will at least know our grandchildren."

My mother was visibly upset and pleaded for me. "No one deserves to be the third wife of a mean bastard like Kraven, especially not my daughter. Ildiko may be a bit stubborn, but she is a good person. She does not make trouble with anyone. She is smart and helps me with gathering and every other chore."

"If something happened to you as it did to my first husband, she would provide for me. Ildiko can hunt. The boys are not as caring as Ildiko and my oldest son, Gabor, has his own family to worry about. Ildiko deserves better than the likes of that piece of horse dung, Kraven. It will get you what you want, but it will make her life horrible." She cried in sorrow at the thought of such a trade. My uncle would not listen. In the Hungarian people, women never had the final word. They could plead and beg, but men made the important decisions.

The next day, after another argument over breakfast, my uncle went back to Kraven and talked to him about the deal. I did not know the details of what was discussed, but when my uncle came back home, I went to him and I begged him not to give me to a monster like Kraven. For the first time I can remember, he turned his back on me and waved his hand as though he was saying, "Go away."

That afternoon when the vote was made, Rhoden had two votes

and Kraven had two votes as expected. It came down to my uncle, who had the final vote. Kraven said, "The vote is tied. Ties are broken by the senior hunter." Kraven looked at Lorand and asked him, "How do you vote, hunter?"

My uncle called out, "I vote for Kraven."

Rhoden was shocked. His mouth was open. He was certain, as were most people, that Lorand was on his side. He told Rhoden that he had his vote just two days ago. Rhoden was defeated. Kraven rose from his seat and strutted in front of us smiling. His father raised his arm in victory and yelled with enthusiasm, "Kraven is the chief." There was no cheer, no chant, and no celebration.

I went to my mother and hugged her as we both cried, but my mother could not help. It was too late. My uncle would get the clan leader title. I could not look at him. My brothers loved me, but they could do nothing for me. My fate was decided. My worst fear was being a second wife, now I was a third wife. I could not think straight.

CHAPTER 13

The Third Wife

AFTER THE VOTE, Kraven announced a feast and a celebration. Everyone was invited with food served from the winter storage supplies. During the meal, three men played music while couples danced and drank blackberry wine. Kraven made a speech where he thanked his father for his leadership over many years. His father waved to the crowd from a sitting position because his knee was still not right. Kraven told the crowd that the stocks of horse meat were full and the women had done a good job gathering. He wanted people to believe that everything was wonderful, including the election.

He introduced my uncle as the new clan leader and motioned for him to join Kraven at the center of the gathering. Lorand deserved to be a clan leader based on his merits, but he never got it. In his mind, all that did not matter now, he had his title. My uncle said a few words and quickly left the platform to Kraven.

Kraven became himself once again. He bragged, "The Hungarian people will continue to prosper and gain in numbers. We will be the largest tribe anyone has known, and we will win every contest at the next summer gathering. I will personally defeat the Botai hunter at both strength contests." He waited for applause, but there was little.

He continued, "Every new Hungarian hunter will find a wife. Women will know we are the best, and they will want to join us." He was back to boasting rather than setting goals or giving direction. After the first few minutes, only his father and his old clan were listening.

Kraven called in a loud voice, "I need your attention for one more important announcement." He waited for their attention. "As chief of the Hungarians, I will take a third wife." The crowd was stunned. No one else had a third wife; it was unheard of. Even second wives were unusual and mostly occurred when a hunter died and the widow needed someone to provide for her.

"Ildiko, the unmarried daughter of the new clan leader, Lorand, is my choice." He could not resist the boast, but this time it did not get him any honor; it did the opposite. Every adult was silent. Rhoden and the entire Eagle Clan was disgusted. No one offered congratulations. They were in shock. Now everyone knew how Kraven got the extra vote that made him the chief. Lorand traded the vote and his wife's daughter for the clan leader title. It was the talk of the village, and it was wrong. Rhoden stood up and his people stood with him. They turned their backs on Kraven and left the feast in silence.

The next day, Kraven appeared at the door to our house. In a loud voice, he demanded, "I want to see my new wife." I hid in the sleeping area, terrified. When I did not come out, he told my uncle, "Deliver her to me by midday and no later." He stared at my uncle, daring him to go back on the deal and repeated what he said in a very angry voice, "Midday, no later." My uncle nodded yes.

Kraven's demand was loud enough to be heard by anyone in the area. He was in his glory. When he left our pit house, he saw several people who were at their doors, listening to Kraven and his demands. They knew what was in store for me, forced sex and rape if I refused him. As a third wife, my only purpose was for sex. Nothing mattered except what Kraven wanted.

My mother tried to comfort me as I cried. She yelled at my uncle, "Your new title is a joke. Your huge ego has gotten the best of you. You know what Kraven will do to Ildiko. He will rape her until he gets tired of her and then he will rape her again. You are as horrible as he is. You are a dog. So what if you are clan leader? It means nothing. No one is impressed with you because they know you gave my daughter to that beast to get your stupid title. You have lost respect, not gained it. I hate you." She cried as she hugged me tightly to her.

I never heard my mother yell at my uncle, nor had she yelled at anyone else in the entire village in such a voice. The neighbors were outside their pit houses listening, but my uncle ignored all of them. He yelled at them, "Shut up and go back inside your houses." At noon, my uncle dragged me from our house crying, pleading, and fighting to get loose. He pushed me to the door of Kraven's pit house and walked away. He yelled, "She is yours!"

When I stumbled in the door, there was no medicine woman to bless the marriage, and there was no ceremony. Kraven growled at everyone, "Get out of the house and take all your kids with you. Come back in two hours and be ready to make me a meal." His two wives grabbed the brood of children and left. They knew Kraven wanted to have sex with me.

My father's sister, Kraven's second wife, whispered to me, "Use some bear grease on your crotch, it will hurt less. It will still hurt, but you will not bleed as badly."

I took her advice. With all the commotion going on and the two women gathering up their children, Kraven continued to yell orders. I was crying as I slid my fingers through the bear grease pot and rubbed a good bit on myself down there. As the wives and their brood left, Kraven blocked the door and rubbed his crotch. He was ready and bulging with a vicious look of desire on his face. I could hardly push a thin finger of my own inside myself, and even then it was tight. How could he push his huge penis in me without me being torn apart? I screamed in horror.

He smiled and then he laughed a hearty laugh. He threw off his pants and stalked toward me with his penis in his hand. I tried to run past him to escape, but he grabbed me with one hand and held his manhood in the other. I twisted and kicked him to no effect as he easily held me by the arm. His grip was like the jaw of an animal. I bit his hand. Blood ran on his skin. He yelled and let go of his erection for a minute. I tried to kick him in the groin, but he blocked my kick and laughed at my attempt to hurt him. Then I felt his massive hand strike me across the face with a heavy blow. I was dizzy and nauseous. I thought I might get sick and fell to the floor as everything became foggy. I was on my hands and knees, not sure where I was.

He lifted me off the floor and threw me on my back on the sleeping rack and mounted me from the front as I lay there thinking I might get sick. He stroked himself again, and my head started to clear. His big hand was on my throat when he rammed his erection into me. It was like a pole, and he was rough. The pain was terrible. I thought he was ripping me apart, and I cried out, but he had no pity. He just had his desire, and there was nothing I could do about it.

I was overcome with grief after Kraven raped me, and I stayed in bed sobbing for hours. I could not eat anything the rest of the day. I wondered how my uncle could care for me so little to give me to such a monster. I hated him for it.

The women and children came back in another hour or so, and my aunt tried to comfort me. They prepared a meal as they were told. Kraven was out of the pit house strutting around the village, bragging how he had just planted his seed and would keep planting his seed in his new wife every day until she has another son for him. He grabbed his crotch as he talked. People tried to avoid him, but that was hard to do with Kraven.

That night, he had sex with me again. He was just as rough as the first time, but it hurt more because I was still bleeding from the attack earlier that day. The next morning, before I was awake, he grabbed me again. This time I had no chance to get any more bear grease before he was on top of me. I was being torn apart. He had sex with me for six days in a row, and on some days, it was twice. Days became weeks. My life was terrible.

I was down in spirits and cried too often. There was no doubt I was feeling sorry for myself. I hardly ate anything and felt weak. I had not seen my mother or my brothers since my uncle dropped me here. I did not hunt or go swimming. I hardly did anything except sleep and be his sex slave. I was ashamed and wondered how could a woman be treated so badly and no one said anything. The whole village ignored what Kraven was doing because the rules allowed it.

The first wife ignored what was happening to me. If it was not happening to me, it was happening to my aunt. Kraven went to his first wife last. She was the first to bear his children and the oldest, and he cared about her. She had his first son and then many more sons and daughters. She told me, "He loves me, Ildiko, that is why you are here."

My aunt, Kraven's second wife, told me, "He will eventually slow down, but it might be several more weeks before he loses interest in taking you every day. It was that way with me, and then it finally slowed down." She also told me, "Use a mixture of two parts water and one part gooseberry juice to wash your vagina inside to prevent infection and to block yourself from getting pregnant." And she added, "Stop feeling sorry for yourself. Get out of the house and get active again. Get moving. Go see your mother. And by the way, she stopped to see you last week, but Kraven told her to go away. He told your mother, 'Ildiko is a married woman now. She does not need you. She has me to take care of her.'"

I decided my aunt was right. I had to get out of the house, but when I went to see my mother, she was not home. A neighbor told me she was at my brother's house. The neighbor also told me that she has been to see me several times, but Kraven chased her away. After many tries, she did not return. I found my mother at my oldest brother's house. She hugged me and said she loved me. We held each other for a long time. I talked and she listened, but there was little she could do. Men had the right to trade their females.

I returned to the only place I could go, back to Kraven's pit house. My aunt said, "Look, Ildiko, none of this is your fault. It is just the way your life will be as part of this house. It will always be the same." She reminded me again. "Use the gooseberry juice, or you will be pregnant in a month."

I whispered to her, "When I urinate, there is blood, and it burns."

She whispered back to me, "Get to the medicine woman and ask for what is called silphium. Gooseberry juice will not cure that." I followed her advice. I walked to the medicine woman right away and got some silphium. While I was out of the pit house briefly, I felt free. I knew I could not accept this as my way of life and I could not get pregnant by this bastard.

The next day, Kraven grabbed me again. I tried to pull away, but his strength was too much. He slapped me on the side of my head with the back of his hand, which made me see stars. He slapped me again and again. I tasted blood in my mouth and one eye swelled and closed. If I did not have sex willingly with him, I would get another beating. It was one or the other and sometimes both. He laughed and slapped me again gloating, "You will come to love me, third wife."

At this point, my aunt got on the floor on her hands and knees and said, "I need sex too." She spread her legs apart and said in a husky voice, "Kraven, my husband, you will not have to fight with me for sex. I want you right now." He was excited seeing her in that position, asking for him to come to her. I knew my aunt was offering herself in an attempt to protect me.

Kraven mounted her from behind and looked at me when he said, "You, third wife, will have to wait until tomorrow."

I ran from the pit house out into the village. As I looked around, it was obvious to me that people were doing all the usual things in the normal manner. Other than a few stares, no one paid much attention to me as I walked. What was happening to me was expected behavior. I saw women cooking meals, making clothes, and tanning hides. Two hunters were making arrows, and a flint knapper was busy making arrow heads. Life was normal for them. It was not normal for me, but no one was concerned.

I was in shock over what happened in just a matter of weeks. I decided to head to the river for a swim when I saw Rhoden and his wife, Gaby. I said hello and they returned my greeting. They looked at me with pity, but they could do nothing for me. Rhoden was a clan leader, Kraven was the chief. Rhoden could not offer me a sanctuary. That was my uncle's job, at which he failed miserably. I sensed that Rhoden was on my side. When I reached the river, I saw my friend, the furry critter with the masked face, at the edge of the water. He was going about his business searching for food. He was in his element with the water close at hand.

My heart was not in the swim, but it felt good to be in the water and to get some exercise other than fighting off Kraven. I was depressed, my insides ached, and I still bled. As I swam across the river and back again. I felt renewed and sat in the sun to dry. I could not accept what my aunt said, that this was the way my life would always be. I watched the raccoon as my mind wandered off, searching for a solution to my problem. I thought about how so many other women who did not take their first or second marriage offers and wound up being traded to an older man by their fathers as a second wife. For them, there was nowhere to go and no one to run to. I had to find a way out. If I ran away, Kraven would find me and punish anyone who showed me kindness or tried to protect me. There had to be a way out.

On the way back to the village, I met my youngest brother, George, who was practicing with his bow. He asked me to join him. He was as friendly as always and full of encouragement, but after talking with him, there was little he could do to help me. If he challenged Kraven, he had no chance, and he would be challenging the Hungarian way of life. The chief was in total command, and women were of secondary importance. If someone challenged Kraven, there was little doubt they would be killed. I took a few more shots with the bow and arrow and scored well, but my heart was not in it. My brother said, "The whole village knows from his bragging that Kraven was beating you into submission. I wish I could do something, but I have no way to help." I had no reply.

I thought about running away. I asked myself, "Where could I go?" If I went to the Botai and begged for a place to stay, they might give me a home, but it could cause a war between these longtime allies when

Kraven found out where I was. I had to find a way to deal with this by myself. With nowhere to go, I headed back to the dreaded pit house.

That night, Kraven fell asleep early, and I slept in a separate bed. My mind was full of fear, and sleep did not come to me for a long time. He snored almost to the point that the house shook. In the morning, he was on top of me before I was awake. I had no chance to get away and just lay there while he rammed away at my aching body. While he grunted and dripped sweat, I wondered if I should just cut his throat and take the consequences. It was an option. I knew the punishment would be severe. Most likely, I would be whipped, maybe killed. There had to be a better solution.

My life continued with more beatings and more rapes. It became months of horror, and I was losing the battle. I realized it was a matter of time until he broke bones or I was so badly beaten that I would no longer care about anything, including my own life. I have seen other women give up and never return to normal. No one helped them, and no one would help me. I came to the conclusion that somehow I had to kill him without being blamed. I thought of my little friend, the raccoon. He was smaller and weaker, but he beat his predator. I had to beat this one. The question was how.

Kraven finally mounted his first wife and had sex with her in front of the children, his second wife, and in front of me. He roared, "It will be your turn tomorrow, wife number three, and leave the bear grease off. I want you to be tight and ripe." He roared at what he thought was funny.

To his surprise I said, "I am ready to be your wife. This time I want it to be without an audience. I am tired of the beatings, I am yours."

Kraven did not have his usual smart response. He only said, "So you are finally ready to be a wife. It is about time, my hands are sore from beating you into submission." He laughed again and said, "You pick the place, blue eyes, I will bring the cock." All the while he talked to me, he continued to ram his first wife. He grunted and snorted and let out a roar when he climaxed. The children laughed as he rolled off her, totally naked on the floor and with his eyes closed in pleasure.

The next day, I approached him as he ate breakfast before he could throw me into bed and jump on top of me. I asked him sweetly, "Please meet me at the river downstream from where everyone swims. I do not want villagers watching, I want to be alone with you, Kraven." His smile was one of satisfaction.

I left the pit house and hurried to the river where I waited quietly. When I heard someone approaching, I waded into the water up to my waist. It was Kraven. He was rubbing his crotch.

When he approached me, I smiled and backed just a little deeper into the river. The water was warm and clear, and the sky was a beautiful blue color, a perfect day for swimming. Kraven looked at me with lust in his eyes as I removed my top and let my breasts come free, enticing him even more. They were full and round and floated in the water. It must have been a beautiful sight to the always-horny Kraven. He looked at me and licked his lips.

I smiled back and taunted him into coming to me. I said, "Bring your manhood to me and let me feel it." He felt the sandy river bottom with his feet and waded in up to his waist. I knew he could not swim. He was cautious as he moved deeper into the water, but he wanted me. His eyes were fixed on my nipples. I smiled sweetly and said, "I am willing and ready to have you, but I want you to call me, First Wife from now on. Admit it, my husband, you want me for sex more than you want your other wives. Why not call me First Wife?" It was a distraction. I ordered him, "Come and take what you want." He lusted for me and moved deeper into the river as I slowly moved backward.

Again, I taunted him again saying, "You are going to enjoy me this time. I need you after having no attention for the last three days." Again, he moved toward me. I said, "I want you to touch me. Come and feel what I have for you under the water." He was up to his neck and breathing rapidly in excitement as he reached his hand out for me. I said, "A real man would give me his loudest roar. Come and take me husband."

Kraven took a big breath and yelled out, "I want your body, First Wife." I smiled at him.

With that, he grabbed for me, not knowing the water was deeper than he expected. I was treading water using just my legs. Being a nonswimmer, he had no idea that someone could tread water. He was in over his head. I pulled him to me, and the current pulled us gently toward the middle and down the river.

I lured him with a smile on my face. Kraven must have thought I was starting to love him. He was pleased with my willing attitude and took his mind off the river. He lost track of where he was. Suddenly, he had a look of panic on his face when he realized he could not touch bottom. He did not know what I was doing when I grabbed his hair and pulled him to me.

He tried to touch bottom, but the water was too deep and the current too strong. We were being pulled gently down the river. His breathing was hard and rapid, and he panicked as he struggled to breathe. I swam with ease. I took a deep breath and climbed onto his back with one hand grabbing hold of his hair. Kraven went under.

He was frantic and struggled like a madman when I climbed onto his head, holding his hair, and locked my other arm tightly around his head. He and I were in a fight to the death. He struggled to punch at me and struck my face as he had done so many times before. I was willing to take a few more punches, even to risk death to win this fight. Nothing else mattered to me. Kraven gagged and kicked. At the end, he begged, "Help me. Please, help me!"

In his frantic struggle, he pulled me down with him. We both stayed under the surface for a long time, but I expected it. The big roar he let out when he yelled the part about wanting my body was his worst mistake. By doing that, he exhaled all his air. Kraven thrashed wildly under the surface and gasped for air but filled his lungs with water instead. He punched me under the water with little effect. He tried to choke me, but the water was my friend, not his. I was the smaller weak animal, and Kraven was the wolf.

I felt his body twitch and jerk time after time. Then he went limp. I rode his body down the river holding his head under water for miles. I had to be certain the beatings and rapes were over. Kraven never came to the surface again. Feeling his lifeless body under me gave me great pleasure. There was no more movement, not even a twitch. He was dead. I let the body of what used to be the meanest bastard from here to the Ural Mountains float away, and I swam to the shore. I watched for him to surface, but I never saw him again.

I walked back to where we entered the river. I took my time, drying in the sun. No one saw me. I waited for several more hours before returning to the village. By now, the body would be far downstream and most likely would never be found. I waited another hour before I returned to the village. I went to the pit house of Rhoden where Gaby greeted me. I asked politely if I could speak to Rhoden. Gaby told me, "Rhoden is busy with a married couple who needed counseling."

I calmly replied, "Thank you, Gaby. I am in no hurry. Let him finish his work, and I will wait here." She could tell I was swimming and brought me a cup of hot mint tea. I waited without saying a word as to why I was there.

When Rhoden was free, he greeted me warmly with Gaby at his side. I explained how Kraven drowned and pretended that it all took place just a short time ago. I tried to act as if I was excited over the ordeal, but I was hardly sincere, and Rhoden knew it. Rhoden was no friend of Kraven and accepted my explanation. He almost smiled at one point as I told the tale. He had a look of satisfaction on his face.

Rhoden calmly asked me to repeat the whole story of how it happened. I told the same story as I told the first time. Kraven went in the water over his head just to prove anyone can swim. He said, "It is no big deal." I said, "He went under the surface when he got in too deep. I was too small and weak to try to save him. I yelled advice from the shore, but it did not help. Kraven was gone."

Rhoden did not seem at all concerned. After telling the same story twice, I realized Rhoden was helping me set it straight in my mind. Rhoden asked his wife, "Gaby, please make some more mint tea for Ildiko, it will give her comfort." We sat drinking tea and talking for at least another hour before Rhoden called for two of his youngest and least experienced men to come to his pit house for an assignment. When the boys arrived, Rhoden sent them to search for Kraven's body. I heard him as he purposely directed them to the wrong location, far upstream.

I was still at Rhoden's house when the boys returned hours later. They had nothing to report. They did not find a body, and by now it was dark. They were told to stop searching any more today and to look again tomorrow morning.

It was dark when Rhoden, Gaby, and I went out of his pit house. He called his clan together to make the announcement. Rhoden stood near a fire when he said, "Kraven is dead. He drowned trying to swim across the river." People were surprised because he was young and strong, but there were no tears. Those who dared to think he was truly gone smiled. The two women who were rumored to have had children by him were among those who smiled. Their secret was safe. The next day, Rhoden informed the rest of the village.

Rhoden knew I was a hunter and that I was familiar with weapons. He knew there was a possibility that I would cut his throat or put an arrow through him. The bruises on my face were obvious, but the earlier beatings I suffered were well known by everyone because Kraven bragged about beating me. Rhoden did not ask me for further details. He did not want the body to be found. If it was found and if I had cut his throat, there would be a problem. Rhoden was satisfied to let the river have him.

After Rhoden's announcement, everywhere I went, people asked me questions. They wanted to know. "How did it happen? How could a man like Kraven drown? Was he really dead?" It must have seemed impossible.

I told the same story that I unknowingly rehearsed with Rhoden. Each time I told it, I gave less detail. "Kraven drowned trying to show me that swimming was not a big deal. He told me over and over, 'Anyone can swim.'" Knowing what a bragger he was, the story was easy to believe.

The next day, my uncle approached me and asked, "Will you move back home with your mother and me? We would love to have you come back. It would be the same again, like it was before this all happened."

I looked into his eyes and said, "I have no home, and I have no uncle, and you have no adopted daughter." I turned my back on him as several people watched. My mother was not with my uncle. I wondered where she was. That night, I slept at my brother Zalan's house. He and George were unmarried and had extra beds.

While we relaxed, my brothers told me they were preparing to take a journey to do some exploring as many young men do. They planned to leave in a few days and to be back before winter, but they had no destination in mind. They just wanted to travel for a few days. I told them, "I have the perfect destination in mind." And we made plans to leave in two days. Since I was going with George, Zalan decided to stay behind and help our mother prepare for winter.

Kraven's body was never found, so after seven days, according to custom, a vote was called to elect a new chief. All four clan leaders voted for the new chief, Rhoden. The only thing that was not corrected was that my uncle still had his clan leader title. Rhoden appointed my oldest brother, Gabor, to head his old Eagle Clan. He also named twenty-year-old Toth to be the lead hunter. Toth, a huge man, followed Rhoden everywhere.

Rhoden and his wife Gaby were well respected and liked. I visited them the day before George and I left. I congratulated him on being elected and told him, "I am disappointed and angry because of the way our laws allow men to treat women. These rules left me to be brutalized by Kraven. People listened, and they watched with concern, but they could do nothing because of the old laws." He did not disagree.

I faced Rhoden and said in my firmest voice, "No man should be allowed to give away a female member of his family. Women must have the right to decide what they want to do with their lives. I want to live in a place that values men and women, not just men." Rhoden let me voice my feelings.

I asked him a question, "Now that you are chief, will this be allowed to happen again? If it will, women will leave this tribe, and it will start at the next gathering when I return with the Botai. Women will gladly become second wives and take their children with them to join another tribe."

Rhoden was jarred by the thought. He knew I was right. Men had too much power, and women had very little. Rhoden gave me his word. "The old rules will change now that I am the chief. I will declare the changes this week at my first clan leaders' meeting. If your uncle disagrees, I will demand his resignation. I guarantee it will be done." He wanted me to think it over before I left. "Please stay with the tribe. I need you to encourage other women. The old rules will change."

I already made up my mind and spoke in a determined voice. "Rhoden, it is too late for me. I have been deeply shamed, and everyone knows it. No one will respect me if I stay here, and certainly no man will want to marry me. My brother George and I leave tomorrow morning for the Botai village. If I have to, I will beg them on my knees for a home for the winter."

I was calmer now and took a deep breath. "The Botai people treat their wives and daughters with respect. You have lost two good people. If the ways do not change, you will lose many more women. After a while, there will be none left to abuse." Rhoden knew I was right; there were rumblings everywhere. Women were angry and demanded change. Rhoden had to act.

I said good-bye and left. It was not Rhoden's fault; he had inherited the problem. I made my point because he was the one person who could do something about the "custom" of men ruling over their wives and daughters.

I walked to my old house and called out for my mother. She did not answer, only my uncle appeared at the door. His head was hanging, and he looked disheveled. He asked me to come in the pit house. I refused. I hated him for what he had done to me. After the beatings and rapes I endured, I was tempted to slice him across the face with my flint blade.

I felt the blade in my hand under my tunic. I wanted to hurt him as he had hurt me, but I held off.

The torture he subjected me to was fresh on my mind, and my eyes blazed with anger. Lorand came toward me as I again felt my blade in my pocket. I yelled at him, "Go back inside, I have nothing to say to you. Anyone who was willing to trade his daughter for a title should have to bend over while Kraven shoves his manhood up his ass. Get out of my sight, you pig." He was shamed. He said nothing as he turned and went back inside with his neighbors watching. This time, he said nothing to them.

Several women gathered behind me and yelled their agreement, "Give it to him, Ildiko. Men like Lorand are scum." They knew how he got his precious clan leader title.

I screamed, "You would let me be raped and beaten, and you did nothing. Send my mother out to me, you rotten pig." I had my blade ready. I wanted to stab him in his crotch.

His voice cracked. Tears welled in his eyes and ran down his cheeks as he meekly replied, "Your mother left me. She moved in with your oldest brother, Gabor."

I scolded him in a loud voice to be sure everyone heard what I said, "Good for her, you do not deserve a wife or a daughter." Several neighbors, including some men, cheered me as I walked to my oldest brother's pit house to see my mother.

We hugged when I saw her, and I told her I loved her. I said, "George and I are leaving. You will not see me again until the next summer gathering." She cried. Two of her children were leaving because of her husband. I warned her, "Mother, do not to take my uncle back again. He does not value women, and he will not value you." She promised to stay away from him. I doubted she would leave him for good because up until this happened, he was an honorable man.

The next morning, Rhoden came to George and Zalan's pit house and pleaded with me once again. "Please stay with us for the winter. Give me some time to make changes before leaving."

Rhoden said, "Your words are true. Women in every clan are demanding better treatment. Young women talk of leaving at the summer gathering. I fear that we could lose a generation if you leave now. I will make the changes we talked about, but I need you to stay here and be a symbol of the change. Besides, the distance is great between our villages. Winter is only a few weeks away, and the trip is far too dangerous to leave now."

I explained, "I am determined. I would rather die trying to get there than to stay here where my uncle holds a clan leader title and where men treat women like the animals they own. A woman is no better off than a goat and can be traded just as easily. This is not the life I want." George let me do the talking. It was my issue. It was also an issue for every woman in the village. I had that conversation twenty-five days ago when we left the Hungarian village.

The trip was long, tiring, and many times we were hungry. Luckily, snow came late this year. We left with our bows and arrows, our winter clothes, boots, and a good supply of food. We hunted small game along the way and gathered what we could. We traveled near the steppes close to the grass line, but in order to avoid wolves, we never walked in the woods. Since we were both wearing wolf hair coats, our scent was not easily detected by them. Other than being hungry and tired, the trip went well. I was thankful George came with me for safety and for company. As a brother, he was a great friend and would make a perfect husband for some lucky Botai woman.

From where we stood, George and I could see smoke off in the distance from the village. I said to George, "The Botai must be smoking horse meat for winter." The trail being so close to their village was well worn and easy to follow.

An hour later, we heard the Botai wolves howling to warn the village that something or someone was approaching. The big hunter named Bruno and several others greeted us. I searched for the one face I wanted to see, but I was disappointed. Daven was not there.

CHAPTER 14

The Plea

ILDIKO

I RECOGNIZED BRUNO, the Bear Clan leader, and several other men and women from last year's summer gathering. Wolves were part of the greeting party and circled around us, smelling our coats and furs. It was awkward for a short time as the villagers looked at us, and we looked at them. I was sure they wondered what we were doing here.

I broke the silence when I greeted the crowd, "Hello, Bruno and the people of the Botai, I am Ildiko of the Hungarians, and this is my brother George. We have traveled twenty-five days to come to your village. I am seeking Daven and ask to speak to your leader, the Oldson, to ask permission to stay in your village for the winter." I smiled and waited for a response. I could not find Daven in the crowd.

Bruno replied, "I am the Oldson. Our previous leader passed to the spirits several weeks ago. I welcome you as friends. Put your bows at rest and join us in the village. We will prepare food for you and a place for you to rest. Please follow me."

It was a formal welcome by Bruno, one with reservations. Visitors are rare at any time of year, but with winter just a few weeks away, I was sure they questioned why we were at their village after traveling such a long distance.

Bruno became our host as we walked toward the village. I could smell horse meat smoking for winter food reserves. Wolves continued to circle around us and smell us as we walked. I felt a nose nudge me from behind. It pushed me forward.

I saw many pit houses and one very large pit house, twice the size of a normal one. I thought that perhaps the Botai used pit houses for more than one family. This one had a pole fence connected to it in the shape of a circle. I wondered if the enclosure was used to hold misbehaved children. Being a guest, I did not dare to ask. I heard one villager refer to it as a corral. I did not know that word in the Botai language. George and I followed Bruno.

Many people we did not know greeted George and me as we entered the village. Ruth, who I have not seen for years, was one of the first to approach and greeted us. I saw a handsome young man who I later learned was Jon, one of Bruno's twin sons. Diana, wife of Bruno, also greeted us. Daven and his son, Mikl, were not in sight. I was thinking how I could best explain why we left the Hungarian people and journeyed here. The truth was the only approach I could take, with some of the details being left for another time.

As we entered the main village area, I saw an older man, someone called Tedd, working on a strange-looking bow. He had cut off the tips of a normal bow and was fitting odd pieces at both ends. I wondered what use it could possibly have. The bow did not look like anything I ever saw before. Bruno led us to Ruth's house and said, "Rest here, eat, and wait for me to return. I will bring my clan leaders for discussion of your visit." I knew I would see Daven, and my heart beat faster.

Ruth's cooking pot was steaming with a hot horse meat and vegetable stew, and it smelled good. My mouth watered at the aroma. George and I have been hungry since the day we left our village. Ruth spoke to us in the Hungarian language. She knew the language from when she was a young girl and lived back there with her parents.

She told us, "I moved to the Botai when I was a young woman of fourteen years of age to marry my husband, Sandor. We were married for our entire adult lives until he passed to the spirits a few days ago." Ruth had tears in her eyes, but she made us comfortable. We drank hot sassafras tea, and she served us from the stew pot. It felt good to sit and rest our weary legs after so long of a trip. The stew was wonderful. Ruth asked about old friends she knew, two of whom were my mother and my aunt.

I responded and talked about my mother. "They are fine and in good health. My aunt lost her husband recently. His name was Kraven. He died while swimming." I hesitated longer than I should have. Then I said, "Her husband was difficult. A few days after he died, she told me that she is happier without him." That required an explanation at a later time.

DAVEN

Bruno burst into the horse pit house where Diana, Jon, Mikl, and I were busy training and feeding the horses. Bruno yelled, "Daven, my friend, I have a very nice surprise for you." He had my attention. "A beautiful Hungarian woman just walked into our village and asked for you by name. She has blue eyes, long legs, and she is the same woman you were so in love with last summer. She is the one you talked about all the way back and every day since we have been home. You just got rid of that nasty wife of yours, and this beauty walks into your life. How do you get so lucky? The spirits must love you!"

I looked at Bruno in question and my face flushed because I knew exactly who he was talking about. I had not forgotten her. Not for one day. I thought, *Bruno must be kidding me*. I looked at him in surprise and asked, "Who is this woman you are talking about or are you making a joke with me? If it is a joke, it is a good one, but Mikl and I have a lot of work to get done here. Our horses eat more than we thought they would at such a young age." I added, "I only know one blue-eyed Hungarian woman who would interest me, and her name is Ildiko."

Bruno replied, "It is not a joke, and she is a beauty. It is Ildiko and her brother George. They have journeyed all the way from their village to come here, and, my friend, she did ask for you! They asked for a place to stay for the winter." Bruno continued, "I am wondering why two young people would take such a journey at this time of year. Could they possibly know about our horses and might they have come to see what we are doing? I am not ready to share our good fortune with anyone just yet. I need you to help me greet them and learn why they are here. They have already seen the corral but not the horses, so our secret is safe for now. Daven, drop your training and come with me."

"Mikl and Diana, please do your best to keep the horses as calm and quiet as possible so they will not be heard." I walked with Bruno. We picked up Janos on the way and asked him to join us in questioning the visitors.

We entered Ruth's pit house where our guests were eating. Ruth, being Hungarian by birth, was the first to welcome young women into the Botai as new wives of hunters. Hungarian women have married Botai hunters and Hungarian men have married Botai women for many generations. The exchanges from the Botai to the Hungarians were always with the Botai woman's full consent. They make their own choice for a mate. It has not always been that way for the Hungarian women.

As Bruno, Janos, and I entered Ruth's pit house, Ildiko stood and smiled warmly when she saw me. Her eyes were on me and mine on her as she greeted me first. I felt the warmth of her hand and held it longer than I would have with a stranger. She then greeted Janos and said hello in Hungarian and repeated the welcome in our Botai language. Her brother, George, did the same. I remembered her well from last summer, and was I brimming with excitement to see her here. It really was Ildiko.

I remembered when we met each other at the summer gathering two years ago. The attraction was strong. Last year, we saw each other again, and we fell in love. We spent a lot of time together and got to know each other much better. We shared ideas and talked about what was important to each of us and the differences between the two villages especially when it came to how women were respected among the Botai.

Ildiko was amazed to learn that elder women, at times, selected the Botai leader and also that they were wives, mothers, and hunters. Our love for each other was obvious on both our parts. The problem for Ildiko was that I was married and Ildiko was not willing to be a second wife. We did share sleeping mats the last night we were together, but she held on to her heart. She just could not accept being a second wife. I barely mentioned my problems with Gertrude, so Ildiko knew little of my situation. I did not want to sound like I was making excuses, so the story went unsaid.

Parting last summer was hard. I wanted Ildiko to return with me and be my wife. In the end, she held to her beliefs and stayed behind. As soon as I left, I longed to see her again. I made up my mind to divorce Gertrude, something I should have done long before the last gathering.

Bruno took charge of the meeting when he asked, "What explanation do you have for coming here?" George let Ildiko answer the question even though he was her older brother. It was her story.

She told the story of how her uncle wanted a clan leader title so badly that he traded her to the madman called Kraven. Ildiko told how Kraven brutalized her, beat her for months, and how no one in the village came to her help. The group listened with stern faces, wondering how this was allowed even by a husband. Beatings were not allowed with the Botai, even for the worst offenses.

George added a few comments saying, "Ildiko was bruised and battered about her face every time I saw her, but the rules prevented me from doing anything."

Finally, Ildiko said, "It was my good fortune that Kraven died while he was showing off trying to swim across the river a month ago. When I left, his body was not yet found. After being treated so badly and embarrassed before everyone, I had no choice but to leave. Thankfully,

George offered to come with me for my safety. We left behind two of my brothers and my mother."

There was silence for a moment after she told the story. Janos was thinking like a clan leader and asked Ildiko, "Who is in charge of the Hungarians now?"

Ildiko replied, "A new election was held seven days later after Kraven died, and a good man named Rhoden was elected." The three men nodded in agreement; they knew Rhoden and liked his ways. "Rhoden promised to change the old customs where women were used by the men in their families to gain power."

Bruno changed the topic when he spoke. "I welcome you to our village. If you chose to live with us, you must agree to stay for three years. The reason you must stay is because we have some secrets we do not share with anyone, even with our friends. As members of our people, you will soon learn these things. Perhaps our new ideas will be shared with your people next year, but not yet. I will give you a few minutes to think about my offer. We will give you some time to talk privately with your brother." As he said it, Bruno stood up and we followed his lead to leave them alone, thinking they might want to discuss the offer in private.

Ildiko was on her feet at the same time we rose and spoke immediately. She had a broad smile as she said, "I do not need a few minutes. I want to thank you for your kindness and gladly accept your generous offer. I am a Botai and very happy to be with you."

George said, "I am also happy to be a member of your people, or should I say my people now. I will gladly stay for three years, hopefully for the rest of my life."

We all sat down again, and Ruth served more tea. We talked about Rhoden, the new leader of the Hungarians, the travel coming here, and the man called Kraven. I sat next to Ildiko and our hands touched accidentally while everyone talked. I felt the electricity of her nearness. Both of us had the same feelings and the same desire from a few months ago. I said, "You and George will need a pit house. Mine will be available for a week or so while we are on the final horse hunt of the season. We have to leave in two days, so it is available."

I could see by the look on her face that Ildiko was puzzled. She most likely wondered how my pit house was available. I was certain she thought Gertrude was still there, but she held off asking any questions until there was a better time. Hopefully, we could be alone soon.

George said enthusiastically, "I have hunted horses many times and would love to join the hunt if that is permitted."

Bruno responded, "You can join us if you can pass the same skill tests every hunter must pass." Bruno went on to explain the tests and what was involved.

George spoke to Bruno. "I have never tried the four-arrow panic test, but I am eager to try it. The other tests are already familiar and should be no problem."

Ildiko said, "I have had enough testing over the last few months with Kraven as a husband and during the long trip. I need time to meet the women of the village and to gather needs for the winter if I can use Daven's house." She said, "Perhaps, Daven's wife has already completed her gathering chores, but I doubt she gathered enough food for me too." Ildiko laughed and we all laughed too. With Gertrude gone, we laughed for different reasons.

There was so much Ildiko wanted to ask Daven, but she needed privacy. Bruno asked George to come to the practice area with his bow and arrows and see how he did with the tests. George was a good-sized, strong young man of about nineteen years of age and felt confident with his bow and atlatl skills. He ate the rest of his meal and followed Bruno to the test area.

Everyone was talking as Ildiko's hand touched mine, not by accident this time. It felt good, very good. I remembered what Bruno expressed earlier, "How did you get so lucky." The discussion broke up when George and Bruno left for the practice area. Ruth stayed at her house, and Janos had both of his wives looking for him. That left Ildiko and me to walk to my pit house alone.

Ildiko told me, "I have the same feelings, the same love for you I had last summer. I have journeyed to the Botai to accept your offer. I will be happy to be your second wife. I hope you still want me."

I stopped and looked at her beautiful face and said, "I have the same feelings for you, Ildiko. I love you too, but I do not need a second wife." She had a look of surprise and disappointment on her face, and her mouth was open until I said, "I am divorced, and Gertrude is gone for good, banished from the Botai. What I need is a first wife, a real wife who loves me, one who wants to have my children and share my life."

She smiled from ear to ear and said, "Oh yes, Daven, that is exactly what I want." We hugged.

I told Ildiko the full story. Gertrude was banned for good, and I had divorced her before she left. She was not coming back. Ildiko was overjoyed. She would not be a third wife or even a second wife. She had her wish and would not have to share her house with another woman. I told her how Gertrude caused the death of the Oldson, of her selfish behaviors, how she stole food, and of the verdict by Bruno with input from the female elders.

"Whatever you do here, the women will love you even if you do almost nothing. Gertrude was hated by everyone. Thankfully, they still like me and will welcome you as my new wife. So now you know why my pit house is available." I suggested, "We should take our time to get to know each other before we become man and wife. I hope, when you get to know me better, you will still want to be my wife. Now let me show you my house and all the work it needs. When you see how dirty it is, you might want to stay with Ruth!"

We continued talking. "There are five empty pit houses, and they are in rough shape because they have been unoccupied for many months. Two of the houses are being used to store hay, oats, straw, and apples and the other three are being used for winter storage of dried horse meat, so mine is the only one available."

Ildiko told me, "Daven, I like the way you think. I have never met a man who cared about what I need and want. It was always about what they wanted." I thought that was a nice compliment.

Ildiko asked me, "Why do the Botai women gather hay, oats, and barley and store them for winter? Oats and barley are edible, but there is no use for hay, unless the Botai have a recipe for hay. Was that what Bruno was talking about when he spoke of secrets he was not ready to share?" Then Ildiko and I heard a whinny sound, like that of a horse. She asked, "Was that a child mimicking the sound of a horse?" Just as she asked me that question, we approached my pit house and went inside. I almost laughed, but I made no reply to her questions.

Ildiko saw that the house was well made. It had a good roof of thick grass, and the walls were solid and without gaps, but the house smelled. Every crock pot was crusty and dry. The place was a mess, and there was nothing stored for the winter. The hay on the sleeping mats was old, and the floor mats were filthy.

There were no supplies for winter. By now, the ceiling of most pit houses had supplies of everything hanging from them, and there was always a stack of wood for cooking and heating. Here, there was nothing, except the awful smell of body odor. Ildiko's work was in front of her. She knew what to do to make it a home and welcomed the challenge. She smiled and said, "In a few days, I will make this into a perfect home for us."

I explained to Ildiko that Ruth would advise her where the central supplies were located. I told her she would find horse meat, wheat, and grains for bread, fruits, peas, and lentils. I was about to leave; I looked at her blue eyes and kissed her. She smelled wonderful and felt better than wonderful. It was a great day for me. I said to Ildiko, "I have to help Mikl with some chores for a few hours." I pointed to the area where I would be in case she needed me.

She started cleaning the place immediately, pulling sleeping furs toward the river for washing, and throwing out the old grasses on the beds. There was still so much to talk about, but right now, she knew it was time to clean up the mess Gertrude had left behind. As I left, Ildiko called to me, "Come back at dinnertime. I will have a hot stew ready for you, and bring Mikl if he has nowhere else to go."

I called back saying, "I will be back without a doubt. I have to help with the horses right now." She had a puzzled look on her face and ran out of the house to catch up to me and asked about what I said. I replied in a matter-of-fact voice, "We have horses, and we are training them to work for us."

Ildiko gasped with a look of surprise on her face. She asked, "Did I hear a horse before? Is it true... do the Botai have horses? Real, live horses?" She said, "Daven, you are teasing me."

"I am not teasing." I explained and told her the story of how we captured them. "The noise you heard earlier was real. You and George can see them tomorrow." That was it. I let her know what the secret was, but they would have known by tomorrow anyway.

Day after day, Mikl, Jon, and Diana trained our horses. Ildiko was fascinated as she watched them almost every day. She soon joined us and became part of the team. Progress was steady; sometimes it was better than expected. Repeated small rewards and praise got results. When one of the horses misbehaved, it was scolded and got no reward. When a horse greeted us or responded to a whistle, it was rewarded with gentle pats, a rub on the nose, or a piece of apple.

When the carrying sacks were placed on their backs, they were rewarded if they accepted the bags with no trouble. Both horses were hobbled when they were in the corral. If they got out and were not hobbled, all of us thought we would never see them again.

Mikl whistled every time he approached or when he wanted their attention. Diana did the same. She talked to them more than anyone else did. It was almost as if they could understand her, but that was not possible. A horse could not understand a command from a person, or could it?

Diana was better than anyone else at handling them, and it became clear that Dawn was her horse more than it was Bruno's. Gray Boy received most of Mikl's attention. It rained that afternoon, and the drain worked perfectly. Rainwater ran from the thatched roof and away from the pit house. We would have no trouble with a muddy floor and rotted hoofs this winter.

Diana realized we still had a potential problem. We had a good supply of food to be used once snow came, but it was only enough for two horses. Her concern was that if the final hunt produced another captured horse or maybe even two horses, supplies were not enough to last through the winter. We needed to build another double-sized pit house and gather additional supplies. Due to the amount of work, the group decided to approach Bruno to get help.

When the training group arrived at Bruno's pit house, he was close by with George practicing with their bows. When we found them, Diana complained to Bruno, "With your Oldson title, you are going to have to let someone else practice with new hunters. We have a more important problem, and my horses come first. Daven is the lead hunter. He can train new hunters even better than you can, my husband." A strong wife of the Botai had spoken, and Bruno took notice.

Diana pushed the horse issue, and Bruno agreed. That same day, he called the original crew to get busy with another double-sized horse pit house. After setting the direction, I met with Bruno and Janos to calculate the amount of horse meat we required for the winter. We need to kill a minimum of three more horses to be sure we had an adequate supply. I held the hunters' meeting that evening with the departure set for the next day. Snow was the worry, without doubt; it would come soon. The men left behind to guard the village were directed to finish the pit house for the horses we hoped to capture and then to join the gatherers with their efforts.

I led the hunt plan. This time, we would head directly south along the east bank of the river. The trails were well worn in that direction, so travel would be fast, at least for the first day. Since no one had hunted this location for many months, the herds would be unaware of hunters. I wondered if Bruno explained to George how fast we travel, but I did not worry about George. I had his sister Ildiko on my mind.

I explained the plan. Once we were far enough south, men who were drivers had to cross the river again and march several miles south. When they got behind the herd, they would recross the river and drive the horses north, back toward the lead line hunters. That way, the return to home would be shorter.

I reminded the group we needed to take three horses. Our second goal was to capture another horse, two if possible. Once we have enough meat, it was better to capture horses rather than to kill them. Everyone was reminded how we had success capturing horses last time. "We must get our lariats around their feet rather than their heads if we are to bring them down." No one had questions.

Throughout the discussions, George listened carefully. Occasionally, I saw him looking at Agi, one of our female hunters. She was tall, athletic, and unmarried. George was looking at a potential mate. In my mind, he certainly had the right woman. The group of fifteen left the meeting to prepare their travel supplies of pemmican, clothing, spears, bows, and their lariats.

Diana worked with Mikl, Ildiko, and Jon training horses well into the evening. The weighted sacks were on and off them several times each day. Rewards continued, and the horses were learning fast. Even though these two horses were young, Diana was confident that they might be of help sooner than anyone thought.

Mikl and I returned to our pit house so he could he meet Ildiko once again and for a dinner at home. Dinner at home sounded good to me. The house was looking and smelling like a new place. The crock pot was steaming and smelled great as we entered.

Mikl and Ildiko renewed their meeting from a year ago. They seemed happy to see each other once again. We ate and talked about horses. Ildiko wanted to hear every detail about them. It seemed as if we were never apart, and before we knew it, it was dark. Mikl excused himself to head to Ruth's house for the evening. Despite my best intentions to give Ildiko time to settle in, we could not resist each other. I stayed for the night.

The love we knew from last summer was stronger than ever. Unlike her past forced marriage, this time Ildiko experienced warm tender affection. I hated to leave on the hunt tomorrow. I would miss her over the next week while I was away.

Mikl and George ate at Ruth's house and talked of the final hunt. After the meal, George went to visit Agi, supposedly about the hunt tomorrow. "It would be a new experience to hunt with a woman," George said as he left. It was not new for Agi. She had hunted with men many times over the years. Talk about the hunt lasted for a few minutes, and then it turned to a talk about them and their future.

Chapter 15

The River Herd

OVER THE LAST two days of travel, Janos and I had plenty of time to talk with George about why we captured horses instead of killing them. We told him, "From here on, we expect to capture horses on every hunt." The whole idea was new to him, just as it was to us a few weeks ago.

George asked, "Why would you go to all the work of capturing horses, building houses for them, and gathering hay and oats for the winter when we could just kill a few more and smoke the meat? It would be a whole lot easier than raising horses. Horses seem to be as much work as children. The Hungarians gave up on the idea a long time ago."

I told George, "We are training horses to work for us. They can carry more weight than several men, and it is worth the effort. When Bruno took over as Oldson, he promised that every hunter would own a horse of their own and that eventually, our women would have one to lighten their workload. The promise would also apply to you next year, depending on our luck on this hunt."

George was deep in thought for a few minutes as we trudged forward. He said, "I never thought about lightening our loads or having horses work for hunters, I just thought about how much work they would be.

I can see I will have to open myself up to new ideas if I am to be a Botai."

Unfortunately, Bruno did not come with us on this final hunt because he has gotten too involved with family disputes, the same disputes he said he would avoid. This was the first winter horse hunt he has not attended in years. I would have liked to have his help, but this time, I had to leave without him.

Last night, we had a cold camp and our usual pemmican meal. Without a fire, we could not even make an herb tea to warm us. The next morning, it was bitter cold when five drivers crossed the river and continued south for the first half of the day. We stayed in place at the campsite. I planned the reverse drive to the north because I expected snow and wanted to make the return trip as short as possible.

We busied ourselves rubbing manure on any exposed skin from the bags carried by the newest hunters. George was among the new men even though he had many hunts under his belt, so he was a manure carrier this time. This practice was foreign to him and something the Hungarians did not do. They had no elder called Tedd to teach them the secret of hiding your scent.

I noticed that for the entire two-day march, Agi walked with George, and they talked the entire time. She teased him about his "manly" odor while he carried his bag of manure. I heard her tell him he might never marry if he always smelled so "strong." They were enjoying each other as they rubbed manure on their bodies. I sensed another wedding coming, besides the one I planned with Ildiko.

Our weapons were ready, and we were about to set up the lead line when we heard someone or something coming toward our camp. Not knowing what it might be, we set our guard to block an attack. We rarely saw people all year, so I suspected it might be a single horse. To our surprise, the intruder was Bruno, and we were glad to see him. Somehow, he made up the distance and joined us just in time. I needed his leadership and skills.

He said, "I ran all night to join you. I am not made for family disputes. I told the female elders to settle whatever comes up. If they cannot settle a dispute, it could wait for the clan leaders to return. I would not miss the final hunt when our very lives depend on bringing home the meat we need for winter. So here I am. Who has some nice fresh horse manure for their Oldson?"

Agi and George offered their bag and let him dip in for himself. Bruno rubbed it on saying, "This manure smells great compared to complaining wives talking about their husbands or some other nonsense. It seems to me that if someone was always there to listen, the stupid issues might never stop." An hour later, the hunters were in place, and the wait was not all that long.

The herd was large and headed by an older mare instead of a stallion. Earlier, I instructed the young hunters to wait for one of the clan leaders to fire the first arrow. This time, it was Janos who had the best shot with George shooting right after him. Two more hunters added arrows, and the lead mare went down. The herd was nervous from what happened but continued moving away from the noise coming behind them. They smelled nothing unusual and moved forward. When they came within range, we let our arrows fly and two more mares were hit, first by Jon, Mikl, and Bruno and then by several other hunters.

Mares, foals, and yearlings were running in every direction in groups of two or three, trying to find an escape. For them, it was life or death, and they would not give up easily. We needed meat from three horses, and we already had that, so our efforts changed to capture another horse if we could. Bows were lowered and lariats became the weapon of choice.

Mikl threw his lariat around a mare's rear hoof and held on to one leg. Jon threw another lariat and caught the head, but the mare continued to pull as it struggled to get away. Two more lariats missed the rearing horse. I threw mine and caught its other front foot. I pulled in the opposite direction away from Mikl, and we had the horse off balance. It soon fell to the ground. We tied its legs together, and after a struggle on the ground, it finally calmed down from exhaustion. I noticed Bruno's son Flint doing nothing to help.

We saw that the mare we had on the ground also had a foal. It was about ten to twelve months old. Bruno threw his lariat around the yearling's front leg. The lariat slipped down and caught it by the lower leg. The young horse backed away and pulled Bruno with it. Bruno, being almost as strong as the colt, held on and called for help. Three more hunters closed in with lariats, and we soon had the young horse off its feet. The mother looked at its offspring with eyes wide open snorting, twisting, and trying to rescue it to no avail. We not only had three horses for meat, we also had two horses to train and feed for the winter. As we celebrated our good fortune, snow started falling lightly. In an hour, it was coming down steadily.

We butchered the three horses and roasted the choice cuts for our traditional meal after a hunt. With no shelter, except for our hide blankets, we needed to move. We ate hurriedly and stuffed our back packs with meat. Poles were placed to carry the carcasses hanging upside down, and we set off toward home. Our loads were heavy as they always were. The trail along the river was well known and, at least for now, was not hard to follow. Snow continued to fall, and the trail turned white.

We walked late into the night in an attempt to cover as much ground as possible while the snow was light. It would take two more days to reach the village and maybe more if the snow got too deep. Our group traveled as far as we could before we made camp. Four of the youngest hunters lagged far behind from carrying their heavy loads. When we stopped, we set up tents and built fires using horse dung for fuel and what scraps of wood we could find. Our meal was cold due to the late hour, but there was no complaining from anyone.

Snow continued all night, and sleep was difficult. Horse hide blankets were barely enough for my exhausted hunters. We were tired and cold. Mikl and Jon worked with the two horses, covering them with large horse blankets that they tied in place. They were hobbled and staked out with both young men sleeping nearby in case there was a problem. It was unlikely wolves would venture this deep into the grassland, so we were not too concerned.

Janos and I rose early that morning, well before sunup, and made a smoky fire to signal the village that we were coming back. Even as we built the smoky fire, we knew the distance was probably too far for the smoke to be seen. The snow was heavier today than the day before.

Bruno called the group together. "Men, I know you are cold and tired. So am I, and so are your clan leaders. We cannot stay here or we will freeze to death. To save time, we will have to eat as we walk. We leave in a few minutes." He took the lead as he always did. George followed Bruno, and I followed them. Flint was at the back of the pack, behind the horses. Travel was difficult as the snow deepened today.

We stopped several times to rest and to change the lead for the trail breaker. Everyone took a turn leading at first, but the young hunters tired quickly. At the end of the day, the same five or six of us did most of the work in the lead. We ate as we walked. Every two hours, we stopped to let the back of the line catch up, and every time we stopped, the line of hunters was strung out over a longer distance. We waited so we would not lose anyone. As soon as the four new men and Agi caught up, we started again. The hunters suffered as the temperature dropped.

Bruno called for a break. I built a fire, and we roasted some of the horse meat. Wind and snow had slowed us to a crawl. Once the fire was going, I checked on the last four men and Agi. The men were in good spirits; they were tired and cold, but not about to give up. Agi was the worst off. She told us that her feet were numb. George and I changed her socks with an extra pair of dry ones I carried and encouraged her to stay close behind the leaders when we set out. I noticed that three of her toes were black and felt like ice when I touched them.

All of us felt the bitter cold because our boots were wet and the temperature was freezing. The one positive we had was that we knew where we were on the trail because the river was within sight. When the light of day disappeared, I called for a short rest. During this break, Mikl and I decided to move the horses from the rear of the line to the front. The change in position was to help pack the snow for the rest of us. It took constant prodding, but they kept moving.

During the break, Mikl had removed the meat Agi carried and packed it on the adult mare, and George took the rest of her load. She was having a difficult time walking in freezing conditions. Snow continued as we pushed off again.

That night, I slept under a blanket with Mikl. With the wind howling and the freezing temperatures, many of us hardly slept at all. Agi said she could no longer feel her toes, so George placed her feet under his tunic to warm them. They slept together that freezing night, but they slept in opposite directions. George did not complain even though all he had to hold were her feet.

We knew tomorrow would be another rough day, but we also knew that if we pushed hard, we might make the village by nightfall. The horses were staked to heavy brush for the night. They slept on the ground lying against each other, covered with their horse blankets. I thought those two horses had to be cold, especially the young one. If not for nursing from its mother and the hide blankets we tied around them, the storm might have killed one or both of them.

Bruno and I woke the camp at sunrise. We made a fire and ate what pemmican we had left as we readied ourselves for the grueling trip. My clothes and boots were already wet when I dressed, and I saw that many of the hunters were having a hard time just getting moving, Agi was among them. She had trouble standing because of her frozen feet. She could no longer carry anything, so I took her atlatl and distributed the rest of her weapons among the men. Mikl and Jon coaxed the horses and got them moving. As we left, we added plenty of wet grass to the fire to make it smoke, and we pushed off.

The snow driven by the wind was blinding. The line of returning hunters stretched out as we headed north. After three hours, Bruno raised his hand in the air and called a halt to the march. Snow was coming so hard that I could hardly see his hand in the air. Bruno yelled, "I see movement ahead." We waited.

To our relief, coming south on the trail was Diana leading Gray Boy. Walking behind her were seven other villagers. Mikl's horse was fitted with two poles along his sides with a wide leather platform stretched between the poles, the idea he talked about on the last hunt. Gray Boy's sides were protected by leather flaps that prevented the poles from scraping his sides. Tedd helped with the design, and the leather platform was sewn by Diana and Ildiko who worked through the night to complete it.

We placed Agi on the leather platform and Gray Boy pulled her home. The men and women who joined us carried half of the horse meat. We were thankful for the help. With lighter loads, we made faster progress especially with the return trail being blazed by Gray Boy, Diana, and the villagers. Without Diana and Gray Boy coming to our rescue and the horses leading the way, we might have had to stay another night. One more night in that storm might have been fatal to some of us.

Despite the blustery winter conditions, many of the villagers came to greet us. I saw the new pit house the men built while we were away. Thankfully, it was complete and stocked with fodder. Mikl and Jon led the new horses inside where Diana and Ildiko dried them off with soft hides.

Before we went into our own pit houses, Bruno called to Janos, me, and his son, Jon. Despite the weather and being exhausted, he said, "Daven and Janos, you are the owners of these two new horses. Daven, you will have the adult mare and, Janos, you will have the colt. As we saw today with Gray Boy, they will pay dividends. Without Gray Boy, Agi might not have survived the storm. Now, everyone knows how horses can be trained to work."

Ildiko was at my side as Bruno spoke. George and I carried Agi to her house while Janos and his two sons, Peter and Patrick, walked home with him. Flint, Bruno's second son, was not there. I thought how little interest he showed in anything lately. Once Agi was in her house, Ildiko and I headed home, arm in arm.

CHAPTER 16

The Woman with Eight Toes

SNOW FOLLOWED US home and continued until it was several feet deep. Skies stayed gray, and winds blew from the north. Another snowfall came a week later. Between storms, we gathered more hay, straw, oats, and firewood. Winter had arrived.

This was a time for finishing old projects and starting new ones. Hunters made new bows, arrows, and arrowheads. For men, carving was a favorite way to pass the time once the necessities were done. Figures were created from old mammoth ivory, wood, or soapstone and often made to resemble a beautiful woman or favorite animals such as bears, mountain lions, birds, and mammoths. This year was different. Without a doubt, the favorite figure to carve was a horse. There must have been a dozen carvings of Gray Boy and almost as many of Dawn.

For women, winter was a time to make new clothing, hats, and boots, mostly from horse or wolf hides. They also made bone buttons used to close winter coats and tunics. A slot was made in the leather garment, and the carved bone was pushed through the slot. Each button had a small hole in it to attach it to the garment.

With four captured horses, a small team volunteered to train them. They were my responsibility. I named my horse Star for the distinctive white markings on her face. She was being trained by Mikl, Jon, Diana, and Ildiko. They did most of the actual work while I used my position as the lead hunter to get them help when they needed it.

Janos loved owning a horse. It got him out of the house and away from his two wives. He was having a great time asking everyone for the perfect name. He asked half the village for help with a suggestion and finally decided on Babe, which was offered by Ruth, because it was the youngest of the four horses.

Janos's house was noisy and full of turmoil with all his children and now with both of his wives pregnant again. He needed something to do to occupy his time for the winter and came to me looking for a suggestion. He said, "Daven, I need a project, one that will keep me out of my pit house for a month at a time. My wives and all those kids are driving me crazy."

I suggested, "Tedd has an important project with the atlatl, but he seems to be stalled. He needs another pair of eyes to help find a solution to make the bow work. Perhaps you could help him get the project back on track."

Janos was delighted. He liked the idea and thanked me, saying, "It is just what I need." He headed off toward Tedd's pit house.

Hunters also made new atlatls during winter. This weapon was carved from wood and looked like an extension of a human arm with a hand at the end to hold the spear. When a spear was launched, the atlatl was sometimes dropped on the ground and lost in the grass. Some of them broke during use, so extras were always needed. Each hunter made his own atlatl so that it fit him perfectly. He added personal designs carved into the handle to identify the owner.

Winter was also a time for monthly feasts and telling stories from the past. Each feast marked the passing of another full moon. Monthly feasts not only marked time, they also provided a reason to gather with friends and family, sing the old songs, and dance to music provided by two stringed instruments called the kobyz and the dombra. The kobyz has two strings and the dombra has one; otherwise, they are very similar.

The Oldson and the clan leaders visited different pit houses each month, so everyone felt included.

At these monthly gatherings, everyone talked about the arrival of Ildiko and her brother George, the deaths of Sandor and Joe, and the capture of four horses. Gertrude, being banned for good, was a favorite gossip topic. Among the gatherers, she was never seen again, and many wondered if she was still alive or if she might have died in the first snowstorm. No one really cared if she survived, but they loved to talk about her. She was a bad memory and would soon be forgotten.

This winter, we have the best stories of all, those of horses. After so many years of trying and so many injured hunters, we captured not one horse, but four of them. Even Bruno, as strong as he is, was pulled off his feet when he got his lariat over a foal's head and could have suffered broken bones if his horse was not a young one.

Now, capturing horses seemed so simple; it made us all wonder why no one ever thought of pulling them down by their feet instead of their head. At the first monthly feast, Tedd reminded everyone, "Once someone finds a way to do something that has never been done before, people always say it was so simple and wonder why they never thought of doing it the new way. Everything is simple when you know how to do it."

When Tedd made his comments, Mikl asked him, "What progress have you made with the atlatl bow idea? Or are you just making firewood with all those discarded pieces?" Mikl laughed as did Tedd.

Tedd replied, "Janos and I are working on the new bow every day even when I just sit and stare at all my failed attempts, I am working. We are making progress. For example, as we sit here and eat, Janos and I are boiling wood for a new design that we have not tried before." Everyone who visited Tedd's pit house talked about how it was full of discarded bows, pieces of wood, and ruined atlatls cut at various lengths. Many of the junked pieces ended up as firewood. He continued with one new design after another, certain that he would eventually succeed.

After the meal, Tedd and Janos returned to his pit house to check on the wood they were boiling. To their dismay, the wood had boiled too long and it split at both ends. This accident led to more frustration, but also to another idea. They added an atlatl to each end of the bow instead of just the one end without the second curve. In the long run, the atlatl did not work. It was too stiff to be used as part of a bow.

Between them, Tedd and Janos designed another bow, one with three curves. There was one big curve in the middle, like all bows have, and two smaller curves, one at each end. With three curves, Ted reasoned, "The new three-curve bow should have more power than an old bow with one curve." The first one they made was a rough design made from discarded parts and pieces. When the weather cleared and the resin glue dried, they would test the crude design.

Mikl said, "Tedd, I wish I had extra time to work on the atlatl bow, but I do not. We have four horses that need to be fed, watered, and trained every day. The biggest problem we have other than feeding them is removing all the manure they drop. Maybe I should feed them less so they make less manure." Mikl and Jon smiled at his joke.

Mikl asked Bruno, "Where should Jon and I dump all the manure?"

Bruno responded in his loudest voice, "Now I have to decide where you should dump horse manure? I can see being the Oldson is a very important job!" The group roared with laughter.

Bruno continued, "Burn what you can for fuel instead of gathering extra firewood. As far as the remainder is concerned, as long as it is not dumped in the middle of the village, I am not too worried where you put it. If the snow is not too deep, you can spread it out under the apple trees. After that, the closest area to spread it is where the raspberries and gooseberries grow. You can think about the strawberry patch too since it is closer. Our women might be angry with you next year when they pick berries and smell what you left behind, but maybe by then they will forget who did it." The subject was dropped and the feast was enjoyed by all.

The next day, Mikl and Jon started spreading manure around the berry patches and under the fruit trees. When the snow got too deep to carry it that far, some was distributed among the strawberries. Eventually, they piled it up against the outer walls of the horse stable with plans to move it in the spring.

When we first captured horses, we worried that they might freeze to death with no fire pit to keep them warm, but we noticed that as we piled the manure against the walls, the inside was warmer. Manure acted as insulation, so that worry was gone. Once the outer stable walls were stacked with manure, Mikl and Jon piled it against the walls of my pit house, and it too became warmer than any other house in the entire village.

Winter was a time to keep an ample supply of firewood ready for cooking and heating. When snow stopped, women, children, and men who gathered worked as a group to maintain our supplies. Unlike Gertrude, Ildiko was always part of these workgroups. It did not take long for her to have a friend in every pit house. She often visited Agi and found her brother George there on a regular basis.

This year, for the first time, Diana and Mikl brought Gray Boy and Dawn to help bring back a heavy load of firewood. The gatherers watched as the horses easily pulled their leather platforms piled high with wood, and the workers carried the remainder on their backs. Gray Boy and Dawn completed three days of work in one day. The gatherers agreed no one would eat these horses. Instead, everyone wanted one of their own.

Winter was also a time for weddings and making babies. George and Agi were married at the first full moon celebration, and Ildiko and I were married at the second. Wedding ceremonies consisted of making vows to love and support each other through good times and bad until death took one of the partners. Both partners poured sand from two jars into one jar symbolizing their union as a married couple.

Ildiko ran our pit house. It has never been cleaner, and there was always food ready. What a pleasure to have a normal household. Best of all is that there is love and affection and a place for Mikl when he wants to visit. My life became the one I always wanted. Hopefully, I was being as good a husband as Ildiko was at being a wife. I often asked her. "What can I do to help?"

She responded each time with the same words, "You are doing just fine." She was a joy to be with. It seems we always have so much to talk about, except when I asked her about Kraven and what happened to him. She became quiet. There was something she was holding back; some part of the story was untold. Maybe it was not important. Because my life could not have been better, I dropped the subject. She would tell me when she was ready.

Mikl visited Ildiko and me regularly. He stayed for a meal and slept over occasionally, but he mostly lived at Ruth's house. When George first arrived, he also spent his nights at Ruth's and spent his days helping Agi recover from her frozen feet. The pain was so sharp and so intense that it was described by those who suffered from it as though they were bitten by an animal. The name, "frostbite" described it well. Despite her slow recovery, George and Agi expected a baby in eight months.

Mikl and Jon, who were best friends, had horses on their minds. They talked continually of training, feeding, watering, new ideas, and more training. Of course they talked about manure too. Mikl gave up on helping with the atlatl bow and rarely visited Tedd.

Patts was a woman we called the "spirit seeker." It was a title of affection and respect. Her calling in life was the same as her mother's before her; she was a medicine healer. She also presided over fertility rites, births, weddings, and funerals. She led the ceremony when Bruno became the new Oldson. She had a special place in our minds. If she or her assistant, Elizza, was not present at your wedding ceremony, it was said you were asking for bad luck. I made certain she was present when Ildiko and I married at the second full moon celebration.

George was giving the best care he possibly could give, but Agi did not easily recover fully from her frozen feet. Had she walked all the way back from the hunt, the damage would have been far worse. She had no feeling in her feet when she reached her pit house. It was not until she warmed her feet in front of the fire that she got some relief. First, the feeling in her right foot came back; but as the left foot warmed, the feeling was one of pain, and her toes were black in color.

Elizza used the strongest willow bark teas for pain and applied a new poultice to her foot every day. One by one, her toes recovered, except for the two smallest ones on her left foot. Those two stayed black. After two months, the two black toes rotted away, and the toe bones loosened from the rest of her foot.

In another month, the two black toes were fully decayed and had no feeling at all. Patts made her a mushroom tea that put her in a deep sleep and removed the toes with her flint knife. Agi finally healed. She was a pregnant woman with only eight toes. Her future as a hunter was in doubt, but her future as a wife and mother was certain. When she was ready, Janos, as her clan leader, would decide if she could hunt again.

Agi became the topic of gossip among the women. The question women asked was, "Since she only had eight toes, would her child have eight toes when it would be born?" Her left foot was the talk of the village all winter. After seven and a half months, she delivered prematurely, and the baby had all ten toes. Agi's biggest problem was that her milk was not ready because her child came too early. She tried making a soft mush with crushed peas and water, but the baby only wanted milk. It lost weight day after day and there were no other new mothers who could help with their milk.

During daily training, Diana watched the foal called Babe nursing from its mother. Diana asked me, "Daven, what would you think if I tasted the milk from Star? If the milk is sweet to the taste, perhaps Agi's baby will like it."

I was not sure what to say, but I replied, "A foal thrives on milk from its mother, maybe it is similar to a woman's milk. Give it a try." Diana slowly approached the mare. It was still somewhat skittish with people, but it was most comfortable with Diana.

Diana gently tugged at the mare's teats and tasted its milk from her wet hand. After sliding her tongue back and forth, she took a second taste and licked her lips. She looked at me with a smile and said, "It is sweet and tastes pretty good. It is a bit different, but good." I tasted it and agreed it was not bad at all. She collected a cupful and took it to Agi. If this worked, it would be a gift from the spirits, because most babies like Agi's daughter have died of starvation when they were born too early.

Diana approached Agi's house and heard the crying call of hunger from the child. She explained what she had in the cup and offered it to Agi. Agi tried to pour the milk in her daughter's mouth, but the child gagged and choked. George cut a small woven piece from an old dress and dipped it in the cup. Agi placed a corner of the cloth in her daughter's mouth and Sophia sucked on the wetness as any baby would. As soon as the milk was drained from the cloth, she cried for more and more. Her crying finally stopped when she had her fill of the milk, and the child survived.

We talked about the many babies in the past that died when they were born too soon. There were at least six more deliveries expected this winter. Now that we had milk from horses, none of them would starve. The elder women approved of the idea, and Patts blessed it.

It was winter. The women had time on their hands and continued to gossip. Agi purposely hid her baby daughter's left foot under a blanket when the first nosey woman visited. Some of the visitors were not close friends; they just wanted a look. Not seeing the foot, the woman left in frustration. The next day two others came, and Agi hid the left foot again. The biggest gossipers spread the rumor. They said, "I am sure of it, the child has only eight toes." Then they said, "The child has no toes at all." Finally, they claimed, "The child has no foot or has a deformed foot." The more they talked, the more Agi and Ildiko enjoyed the fun.

At the next monthly gathering, Agi casually took off her daughter's shoes and changed her socks while the women stared. Agi smiled at the biggest gossipers as she pulled the new socks on her daughter's foot. The rumor was over, and the gossipers looked silly.

Horse training became an everyday routine. Mikl and Diana placed the sacks on the backs of the horses while they were in what we now called stables. The name came naturally because the double pit house kept the horses stable through the winter. They were exercised in the corral with the weighted sacks in place. We placed different horses in the corral at different times so they got to know each other. We were convinced horses were as social as their owners.

Daily exercises were rewarded with small pieces of apple and praise by the trainers. It was all new to the horses and new to the trainers, so the process went slowly. Mikl and Diana whistled to them every time they approached, and day by day, they responded to the whistles and to their names. We wondered if it was possible for a horse to be smart enough to actually know its name. Maybe it was just the sound of a certain voice they recognized and responded to that. I thought, in order to recognize a voice or a signal like a whistle, horses had to possess some intelligence.

When we examined dried horse manure, it was mostly made of undigested hay and grass with a slightly pasty substance holding it together. When it was dry, it hardly smelled at all. As we entered the fifth and coldest month of winter, it was still comfortable inside the stable. With all the horse manure we spread near the apple trees and around the berry patches, we joked that we were the "horse manure team" instead of the "training team." As time went on, the village found out for themselves when they visited the stables; it was warm inside, and they asked for their house to be done next. One woman demanded "her fair share of the manure."

Diana worked for weeks to make leather netting in the shape of a horse's head. The netting had two long straps on each side of the horse's head. It was an attempt to make something to guide the horses other than a leash, which did not work very well. After several attempts, the netting became better fitted and more comfortable for Gray Boy and Dawn and helped them sense the direction in which they were expected to go. Training and exercise in the corral went on week after week, and all four horses learned to pull poles with a leather platform. Gray Boy and Dawn were a month ahead of the newer horses in training.

One morning, Mikl told his teammates that he wanted to see if Gray Boy would come to him when he whistled. No one thought it was a bad idea, so Mikl said, "I am going to try it." He let Gray Boy loose in the corral on his own and stood back. At first, the horse did not know he was free of the leash and the hobbles. He whinnied and trotted in a circle around the corral, feeling he had more freedom than ever.

After a short time, Gray Boy calmed down. Mikl whistled, and Gray Boy came to him at the fence. Gray Boy got his reward. To the excitement of the trainers, Gray Boy not only came to Mikl, but nudged him with his nose for his reward hidden in Mikl's hand. It was another small step forward. Dawn soon followed the same exercise, and it became part of the routine. No one dared try it outside the corral or Gray Boy might run off and never be seen again. We wondered if Gray Boy or Dawn remembered when they were free, roaming the grasses with the rest of the herd, or was that a lost memory by now?

Two weeks after the fourth full moon celebration, Mikl had another idea with training. He asked Jon, Ildiko, and Diana if they thought it would be possible for someone to hang from the roof rafters and gently lower themselves onto Gray Boy's back. Instead of the usual weighted bags, the horse would hold a person. The bags would be used to hold the rider's feet. Since Gray Boy was the tamest of the four horses, Mikl wanted to use him for the test. No one knew what would happen, but the idea of a rider sitting on Gray Boy was an exciting advance. The only question now was who would be the first to try?

It had to be someone who was lightweight, strong, and athletic enough to jump free in case the horse became frightened and bucked. It had to be someone other than a grown man because Gray Boy was too young to bear that much weight. Diana was agile and strong, but she is a big woman and as heavy as some of the younger men. Mikl, George, and Jon were much too heavy for Gray Boy at this age. The trainers left the corral and came to see me.

They approached my pit house and called to see if I was at home. "Daven, we have an idea and we need your help." They went on to explain their need. I thought back to the day not too long ago when someone wanted to eat these horses. Now the idea was to try to sit on a horse and, maybe in the coming weeks, to actually ride a horse. I used to think that little or nothing changed. This year, it seemed changes were becoming the way of life with the Botai. Lately, Mikl's ideas have been coming more often, and I have to admit, they were more exciting every time.

The group explained their plan, and I thought it might work. The roof was high enough for someone to be able to sit on the horse and still have enough room to be clear of the rafters. I wanted to check with Bruno and Janos to get their thoughts. This was not like asking where we should dump manure. If it was possible to ride a horse, it could be the most important discovery since we learned how to build pit houses well below the frost line. If it worked, it could change everything. If it did not work, someone could be thrown off and injured. The next person to see with this idea was Bruno. I asked George, who was now part of the Aurochs clan by marriage, to get Janos and Tedd. This was a major decision.

The full group including Bruno met in the stable since it would be the setting for the test. The idea was presented by Mikl with comments added by Jon, Diana, and Ildiko. Bruno listened and looked at Gray Boy and then at the ceiling. He thought his way through this dilemma before he spoke.

"I can see the potential in the idea. If a man could ride a horse, it would be a huge advantage and place the Botai ahead of every other people from one end of the grasses to the other. Distance would no longer be such a great a barrier to travel, and hunting would change for good."

He said, "The Botai have a total of sixty members since Ander left and the Oldson died. When Joe was killed, we lost a hunter. By our good fortune, George and Ildiko joined us. We also have to consider that Agi is a seasoned hunter and is currently injured. I know she is recovering quite well and might hunt again one day. However, counting all of our hunters, we have twenty-two with five of them being brand new this year. My point is that I cannot afford to spare even one hunter for this test. So it must be someone who is athletic, but not one of our hunters."

Bruno's words held the truth. It could not be a hunter in case of an injury. It could not be a man because of the weight and certainly not a child. Peter and Patrick, Janos's sons, were good choices, but they were not familiar with horses, and most women were ruled out due to their inexperience. That left one obvious choice.

I shuddered at the thought. She was agile and athletic, strong and smart, and could do it if it could be done at all. Bruno could not spare a hunter, but I could not spare Ildiko. Of course, as soon as her name was mentioned, as being the first person to sit on a horse and perhaps ride it, there was no stopping her. Ildiko's training started the next day. Her famous words were, "If anyone can do it, I can."

CHAPTER 17

The Bear Clan Leader

USUALLY, BY THE start of the fifth month of winter, we were bored and tired of being indoors. We longed to be outside of our houses and return to normal spring activities. This winter was different because of the horses and their training. Training was exciting to watch and made the late stages of winter pass by faster than any other year. Even though Bruno was clear about the succession pattern, everyone wanted to know who would get the next horse. Hunters and trainers came first, depending on seniority. Nonhunters followed them.

The same routine was followed day after day. After feeding, watering, and manure removal, training occupied the rest of the day. The four horses had gotten used to the smell of the trainers, their voices, and their touch. Two new members, Peter and Patrick, joined the team as helpers and became direct trainers after a month. As the winter neared its end, horses and humans got to know each other.

Allowing the weighted bags to be placed on their backs earned each horse a reward of an apple treat or a pat and a soothing voice. Each horse was exercised in the corral with hobbles in place. The hobbles were looser as time went on, and after a while, there were no hobbles used in the exercise yard at all.

My adult mare, Star, was the hardest to tame because she was older and probably remembered her days of freedom when she roamed with the herd. We assumed that the young horses did not remember that time of their lives very much, if they remembered it at all. The routine continued until it was time for the next step, and the next step would be a huge leap.

Today was another cold, crisp morning when the team approached the stable. Mikl and Diana whistled, and Gray Boy snorted his welcome and watched as the team entered his stable. I was sure he expected the usual weighted bags to be placed on his back, but this time, instead of placing the leather bags on him, Ildiko quietly climbed onto the overhead rafter and took a deep breath. She held fast to the leather strap attached to the overhead beam and lowered herself onto the horse's back and lightly sat on him. While she did this, she talked to Gray Boy in a soft voice.

Gray Boy was over a year old and as large as Star. Ildiko held fast to the overhead leather strap with her legs around the horse's back. Most of her weight was on him, but she held fast in case Gray Boy became overly excited and tried to buck her off. It was a tense training point.

At first, Gray Boy did not know that Ildiko was on his back. The weight was similar to the weighted sacks from every other day, and he did not react at all. Then he turned his head around and saw her. He snorted and stepped sideways. He had an odd look on his face as though to say, "What is she doing?" Ildiko pulled up on the leather strap and held herself clear of the big gray horse for a minute.

As soon as Gray Boy calmed down, she lowered her weight on his back again. The feel of Ildiko alarmed him the same as it did the first time. He turned his head and looked at her. His eyes were wide open as he twisted his head around to look at her again, this time from the other side. Ildiko pulled herself up on the leather strap again to lighten her weight, letting her legs dangle along his sides.

Diana was on the floor of the stable very close to Gray Boy's head the whole time, calming him with her voice and her reassuring manner. She was actually in a more dangerous position being on the stable floor than was Ildiko being on his back. She had a way with horses that no one else had. Gray Boy finally seemed to know there was no danger and allowed Ildiko to sit on him for the third time. This time, she stayed there.

Then Ildiko got off Gray Boy and jumped to the floor of the stable. The overhead strap hung free. Ildiko went to Gray Boy's face so he could see her and patted his nose and rubbed her face on his. The total time on his back was brief, but the test was a success. Ildiko offered Gray Boy a piece of apple as his reward. Diana, Mikl, and Jon praised him and the beautiful horse seemed to know that he had done something special.

The training process was one of affection and partnering with the horses rather than a violent confrontation. It was gentle and caring, and it worked well. When word spread around the village, both Ildiko and Diana became the talk of the Botai village. They had equally dangerous roles, but only one of them sat on the horse that day.

Mikl and Jon added two more new members to the team, one of whom was George and the other was Elizza, the medicine assistant. With Peter and Patrick the training team now had eight members. Elizza's first calling was healing, but she wanted to do more, and she wanted to ride a horse.

The new procedure of getting on Gray Boy's back was repeated day after day. Gray Boy accepted the new process after a few repetitions. Dawn followed the same steps as Gray Boy. The process was easier with her as she was less afraid of Ildiko and Diana and accepted a person on her back faster than Gray Boy. Star, being an adult mare, was the most difficult, and Babe was still too young to have any significant weight on his back.

Gray Boy was in the stable when Ildiko let herself down on his back several days later. He accepted her as before and let her stay there. Diana took the head netting she had designed and placed it on him with the long straps attached at the ends. Ildiko held the long end straps and waited for Gray Boy to calm before she gently tugged on the left strap. The horse turned his head to the left even though he was still in the stable. A few minutes later she gently pulled on the right strap, and he turned to the right. Everyone smiled at each other because the new netting idea worked perfectly.

Ildiko had her feet in the old-style weight bags, but these bags were too cumbersome to work very well. Diana suggested the bags be cut away from the back, which would open up a place for the rider to insert their feet. This would be an improvement of having to place their feet in closed bags. After a team discussion on the design, Diana went to work. She discarded the bags entirely. Instead, she made strong leather slots for the rider's feet with straps that were tied around the horse's body and neck so the footholds stayed in place.

The next step was for Ildiko to sit on Gray Boy's back in the corral instead of the stable. To do this, Ildiko got on Gray Boy's back while he was in the stable. From there, Mikl and Jon walked him from the stable into the attached corral with leashes in place on both sides.

Bruno had asked that everyone stay back from the training area for this trial so as to not scare the horse any more than necessary. They could watch from a distance. The entire village stared with their eyes and mouths wide open, expecting something bad to happen. It was hard for them to believe a woman was on the back of a horse. It was an incredible sight!

I watched too, fearing that Ildiko might be thrown off, but as I watched, she was not afraid at all. She was focused and confident with what she was doing. From the look on her face, she enjoyed every minute of it. Ildiko became the first person anyone knew of to sit on a horse.

Mikl and Jon removed the leashes from Gray Boy's head. Diana was in the corral and walking right next to the horse, talking to him the whole time. Then she stepped away. Ildiko worked the leather straps to turn left and right and then slowly and gently pulled back on both straps at the same time, and Gray Boy came to a stop. Gray Boy learned what each gentle pull meant, and he responded well. He learned so much and had done it so quickly that we all came to believe that horses were smarter than anyone ever thought they were.

With all the preparation and training, the event went off better than we could have hoped. After two more days of practice, Gray Boy walked around the corral with his rider and took direction from light pulls on the head strap. Diana was the next to ride Gray Boy in the corral the following day. The Botai women had new status, and they loved it.

Riding outside the corral was the next challenge. The question was, would the horses obey the same commands outside or would they bolt and run away with their riders hanging on for their lives? No one knew what would happen. It would be another few weeks until the snow and ice all melted before they would find out.

Bruno called for a discussion with me and the hunters. He asked me to talk about hunting plans for the spring, so I led the meeting. I started off by recognizing the old ways. Spring hunting has traditionally been a clan event to restock meat supplies after the long winter. It was a time for young hunters to gain experience and be recognized for their skills. In the past, small hunting parties filled their household needs. I said, "This year would be different. Our needs have changed. Our goal is to restock each clan with fresh meat as quickly as possible and, more importantly, to capture more horses. If we expect to meet the Oldson's promise of a horse for every hunter, we need to work as a group, the same way we worked in the fall hunts.

"We must hunt as a team instead of as individuals. I realize that group hunting takes something away from personal accomplishments, but overall, team hunting provides more meat in a shorter time. It allows us to capture and train horses faster. I will lead the first hunt in a few weeks, as soon as the weather allows." Bruno acknowledged the idea to hunt as a team and the hunters agreed.

Bruno changed the subject when he told the group, "Mikl and Diana have added two new team members, but they need several more trainers if we capture more horses. Our women will have to gather harder than ever to find supplies, not only for people, but also for the horses. Tell your wives that Gray Boy, Dawn, and Star will be able to help them with gathering. Diana will be the contact when they need what I call 'horse power' to help them." The hunters repeated the new word, "horse power," and they liked the sound of it.

I waited for attention before I continued the discussion, "The second topic is the spring bear hunt. Our supplies of bear grease will be gone soon, and before long, bears will emerge from their winter dens. We will depart for the hunt right before the last of the ice and snow melt. With any luck, we will have the new bow that Tedd and Janos are working on to help us. I ask the clan leaders to give me the names of those who will join me at the planning meeting." I thanked them and sat down to listen to what else Bruno had on his mind.

Bruno spoke, "The third topic today is naming the head man of the Bear Clan." Everyone sat up and paid attention. This was big news. "Up until now," Bruno said, "I have held both titles, that of Oldson and leader of the Bear Clan. By tradition, the title went to the oldest son. This time, I have twin sons born on the same day, just a few minutes apart, but I have made a decision."

Bruno wasted no time and left no doubt. He bluntly stated, "According to tradition, Jon was born first, and he will be my successor as head of the Bear Clan. Please join me in congratulating Jon." Applause rang out, and hunters shouted their approval of Jon. His brother, Flint, hung his head as if he knew it was coming.

I thought about the announcement. Jon has been much more active with horse training, hunting, and learned from his father on community issues. Jon worked to get better while Flint spent most of his time with his new young wife Suse. Rather than taking a lead on anything, Flint looked lazy and disinterested as compared to Jon. Janos's sons, Peter and Patrick, did much more than Flint, and they were not yet fourteen. In my mind, the decision was justified based on both leadership and tradition.

Flint's face reddened, and his temper rose. He felt that he was being pushed aside unfairly. This was his last chance to speak up. He challenged his father in front of everyone as he yelled out, "Name three physical contests with the winner becoming the leader of the Bear Clan instead of handing the position to your favorite son." It was a desperate attempt to save face.

Bruno raised his hand to block the outburst as soon as Flint made it. He said, "I have spoken. the Bear Clan leader has been named, and it is done. No further comments are needed." The group of hunters came forward to personally congratulate Jon on his new position. At the same time, Flint sulked as he left the meeting. In Flint's mind, they were no longer twin brothers, they were rivals.

CHAPTER 18

The Krasnyi Yar Village

TWO YEARS AGO Ander, son of the original Oldson, left the Botai and settled the village he named the Krasnyi Yar. Hunting and gathering at times was not enough to provide adequate supplies for the Botai village. When the river was frozen over, and we were without what we call "river food" such as fish, clams, and mussels, we ran short of food. In severe winters, we also ran out of fruits and horse meat. The Botai population had grown too large to survive by hunting and gathering alone, so the thought was to split off a group and start a second village.

Ander knew he would not succeed his father as Oldson because he was not the firstborn son. His older brother died many years ago at a young age, so he was not in line for succession. After numerous discussions with his father and the clan leaders, it was decided that Ander would be the best choice to lead a new village.

He had the full support of the Botai who were his friends and relatives and the loyalty of the people following him. We searched for a new location over many months and found a place far to the east where there were no other people and plenty of horse herds. Ander left with twenty-six people from three clans and relocated one hundred miles away.

The move took over a month before he was fully settled on high ground above the main channel of the Krasnyi Yar River. The location had similar favorable features to our own. It offered good hunting and a supply of salt plus several types of berries, apples, and pears. Adequate rainfall allowed the grasses to grow tall enough to support horse herds.

There was plenty of wheat, barley, and oats to make bread plus peas, lentils, and tubers. Chickpeas and radishes were a bit harder to find. The river offered mussels and fish plus clay for pots and jars. There were also herds of wild goats and enough deer to supplement hunting horses. Copper was in short supply, but copper has always been hard to find. Overall, the location was a good one.

The only negative to the location was that there were stories we heard from the Russians, who lived to the north, that there was a primitive tribe of yellow-skinned people living farther east called the Mongols. The stories told of slave raids and even of cannibalism. Since we never came into contact with these people, we dismissed the stories as exaggerations.

Ander, with our help, moved whole families including women and children, food, supplies, and weapons plus tents for temporary cover. The one-hundred-mile trip with families and children was a much slower process than if it was a hunting party. Many of their Botai relatives made the trip to help them move all their belongings and to get them well established before we returned to our village.

The one problem I observed was that Ander did not have strong clan leaders. Their men were solid and experienced hunters, but the men who followed were not top leaders when they were with the Botai. They needed people with ideas like Mikl and Tedd. They also lacked women like Diana, Ruth, or Ildiko and strong elders for guidance. Mostly, the villagers were good hardworking people. Unfortunately, Ander was the only true leader.

Those of us who helped with the move stayed to build pit houses, cut firewood, and gather winter supplies. We completed one horse hunt for them, which helped establish a hunting pattern for the future. Since the distance between our villages by foot was great, we have not seen them for quite some time.

Ander, as the Oldson of the Krasnyi Yar, had heard no news from the Botai since he left. He did not know his father had died or that Bruno was now the new Oldson. The usual time to see them would have been at the summer gathering, but they moved away just before the late gathering and did not attend this year's gathering. We expected them to attend this summer.

Before winter snows began, the Yar villagers stocked their pit houses with smoked horse meat and winter supplies of lentils, chickpeas, apples, vegetables, and wheat for bread. Red wheat grew very well there, better than it grew near us. It offered more protein than lighter wheat that was more abundant in our area.

When Gertrude was banned, she worked her way eastward. She considered joining the Hungarian village, but it was too far especially at this time of year, so she headed to the Krasnyi Yar village as her best option for survival. She moved very slowly and with great effort through deep snow. The trip took much longer than it should have. This was in part due to her lack of experience as a hunter and traveler and in part due to her being grossly overweight and out of condition for such a trip. Her biggest problem was finding food in winter.

There was no central supply where she could steal food and no foolish group of gatherers to replenish her needs. She stayed in caves at night and walked farther to the east only during the daytime to avoid predators. She foraged as she walked, but during winter, there was little if anything to find. Favored tubers often left telltale leaves sticking above the ground by which they could be identified. But at this time if the year, they were covered with snow and frozen hard in the ground when they were found. She tried her digging stick, but it was hardly effective in the frozen turf and it broke many times. Even a new digging stick was hard to find. As a result, Gertrude went hungry every day.

At night, she built a fire in front of her cave entrance to ward off wolves that came to attack her. Gertrude saw their eyes lurking outside the cave entrance for hours at a time. She had one bow and a good supply of arrows that she had stolen from me and from others. She dipped the arrows in poison and shot the wolves when they came to investigate the smell coming from her cave. When she heard a yelp, she knew the arrow struck a wolf. That animal would die a day or two later. Gertrude was careful never to move from her current cave until she found a dead wolf to chew on the way to the next cave.

Wolf meat tasted terrible. It was strong and gamey, dry and stringy. Even with the strong gamey taste and the meat being hard to chew, Gertrude ate almost anything. She savored the wolf entrails and roasted them on a stick over her fire. The best parts were the wolf's tongue and liver. The heart was better than the body muscle. She ate it all, including the ears and eyes.

Wolf meat was supplemented with an occasional apple she found, one that never ripened and still hung on a tree. The few she found were usually rotten and wormy, but she ate them too. She chewed raw wheat and barley grains that showed above the snow. Still, she was hungry all day and all night and lost a huge amount of weight over the first month of travel.

She washed herself when the rivers offered an unfrozen opening. She no longer needed the strong body odor smell to prevent her husband from wanting sex. He was gone for good. After two months of slow travel in deep snow and living in caves, she finally saw smoke. Gertrude knew Ander's village was not far away. She had survived.

As she approached the village, tame wolves howled to warn the Yar that someone or something was approaching. With so few people in the vast steppes area, enemies were not considered to be a problem. Since the attacks by the Smolens twenty years ago, the Botai and the Yar villages have not been bothered by much of anything. Occasionally, a disoriented bear waking from hibernation or a mountain lion might approach, but that was rare. Upon hearing the wolves, Ander and his hunters prepared for a predator.

They watched in disbelief as a bedraggled traveler covered in tattered hides from head to foot staggered into sight. It was a woman, and she looked nearly starved. Her clothes of horse and wolf hides were worn and filthy. She stumbled to the ground as the tame wolves pushed and smelled every part of her including her crotch. One wolf howled in her face while she was on the ground.

Ander ordered her to remove her hood, and she did as she was told. He recognized Gertrude and said, "I know you, you are Daven's wife, or most likely, his former wife by now." There was Gertrude, the lazy, selfish glutton at his feet on the ground. A problem from the past had arrived at his door. She was someone he did not need.

Some of the villagers, especially the women, knew who she was and remembered how she behaved in the past. Despite her reputation, two women helped her to her feet. At Ander's order, they guided her to the center of the village where she was fed. She ate ravenously without speaking and glanced around at the new village.

It was on high ground near a river and had six occupied pit houses. There were two large pit houses that did not seem to be occupied. The Yar consisted of thirty-one members instead of the twenty-six they had when they left almost two years ago. Several women were obviously pregnant, so the village appeared to be slowly growing in size. Gertrude consumed everything that she was offered and looked hopefully for more. Instead of more food, she was led to Ander's pit house for questioning. Two clan leaders, men she remembered from the Botai, attended as did their wives, but they said nothing. Ander was totally in charge.

She had lost almost half of her body weight over an eight-week period of time, and it showed. Skin hung from her arm bones, and her face sagged under her chin. The woman they remembered as being enormously fat was now thin and bony. The body fat was mostly gone, but stretched skin was hung over her belt.

Her cheeks and nose were black from frostbite, and her left nostril had rotted away, leaving the nasal passage exposed, covered only by a large oozing scab. The black scab gave the impression of a hole in her face instead of a nose. There were other dark frozen patches on her face and forehead, so it was not surprising that some villagers did not recognize her at first. She looked twice her age, but she was only twenty-eight years old.

Ander wondered what she was doing here so far from the Botai village. He pulled his two clan leaders off to one side and asked them, "What do you think might have happened to cause her to be here? It must have been a serious offense, far more serious than just her well-known laziness." They had no answers. One of them guessed that she might have stolen something or injured one of the clan members, but that was only a guess.

Ander confronted Gertrude. He told her, "We will hear your story. It is my decision to allow you to stay or to be put out." Ander had the wives of the clan leaders attend because women were often better judges of other women than men were. Men naturally felt sympathy toward women, whereas women did not feel that emotion. And these women were the ones Gertrude would have to work with on a daily basis if she stayed.

If Gertrude was allowed to stay, there would be no clan leader, no Daven whom she could hide behind. She would have no status. In addition, as Ander looked at her, there was no physical appeal to this woman at all. She looked terrible with her nose leaking a bloody slime. She had no sexual attraction, no beauty that any hunter could possibly find desirable as a second wife. Second wives were for sex, children, and help for the first wife. These women remembered her sworn oath never to have another child, and her laziness was well known. She had none of the qualities to be a second wife.

Gertrude sat on the edge of a sleeping enclosure and looked at Ander with her sorriest face. She thought her usual act would work. One thing she knew for certain was that she could not tell the truth of how she caused Ander's father's death. She also knew there were about seven or eight months until the next summer gathering and a few weeks of return travel. After that, Ander would know the truth, and she had to be long gone from his village or face the consequences. Today, she needed to buy some time to recover.

Gertrude began to tell her story of denial and jealousy. She had rehearsed it over and over while she traveled. Gertrude shed tears when she said, "None of the problems were my fault. Those women hated me because of my beauty, my pretty face, and my beautiful breasts. They were jealous that my husband was a clan leader, and they accused me of things that I did not do."

The sobs came again at the right moment. She cried, "I am a good wife, a good person, and I was a contributor to the village." Her cheeks were covered with tears, and the black hole in her face flowed with a grayish ooze that ran down her face.

Ander roared, "Stop with this nonsense. Stop the lies." He was not about to be fooled by her whining. Gertrude started to plead again, but Ander cut her off. He yelled, "Tell the truth and tell it once. Do not lie because I remember your behavior all too well. You offered nothing other than selfishness, arguments, and disruption when we knew you two years ago.

"My guess is that the women of the Botai got tired of you and your lazy ways, and they had you expelled from the village, but I suspect there is more to the story. If you were expelled from the Botai for good, there is a bigger reason, and I want to know that reason. I will know the truth in a few months when the summer gathering occurs, so if you lie to me now, you will pay a more severe price when I return. If the truth is as bad as I suspect it might be, I may create a new form of punishment other than banning you. I suspect that you could be the first person in memory to be beaten before they are put out.

"Tell your story, woman. If I believe you, I will let you stay. If I do not believe you, you will be put out of here tomorrow. This village does not need a troublemaker, and that is your reputation. If you leave here at this time of year, you will take your last walk to your death. Speak the truth, and do it now."

Gertrude was at a loss for words and unsure of what to say. The story she concocted and practiced for two months would not work. When she was young and pretty, she could always find a man in the audience who would believe her and take her side. He would offer protection from "the women and the rest of them." This time, Ander would hear none of her whining. She hesitated while Ander and the most important people of the village listened in judgment.

Finally, she sobbed once more and said, "You are right, I was selfish and I did not do my share. I did not understand how I was hurting myself until it was too late. I was put out of the village for a month. During the first two weeks, I lived in a cave with almost nothing to eat until I finally killed a wolf and ate it.

"While I was living in the cave, I had time to think. I knew I was not a bad person, but if I went back to the Botai, no one would forgive me. The women would not give me a second chance, and I decided that I had nothing to go back to. I still loved my husband and treated him as well as any wife could, but Daven divorced me when I left. He wants a younger woman. I could not even count on my only son to help me, so I decided to come here to ask you for a second chance.

"I was given a bow, a knife, a few supplies, and clothes when I left. Once I realized that no one wanted me back in the Botai, the only other place I could go was here with you. While I walked, I starved and nearly froze to death. I thought about how I acted and what I did to be put out. I will never do that again. I only ask you for a second chance, a place to live and work. I am truly sorry for my past behavior. I am a changed woman." The story sounded good even to Gertrude. She sat with her head bowed and waited hopefully for Ander's decision. She wondered, "Was my tale of woe good enough?"

She told a believable story and carefully avoided the truth. With so little time to prepare, the story and her body language was quite convincing. She told just enough of the facts to get through this test. Of course, she left out the evil parts of how she stole the clothes, weapons, and food, and how she cursed the village and they cursed her back as she left. She was trying to survive. Ander heard what he already assumed to be the truth, but something was missing, and he sensed it. He pushed her with further questions to learn what Gertrude was hiding, but he got nothing else. Ander told her to wait outside where the goats were held.

Ander asked the two clan leaders and their wives what they thought. They talked generally about what was obvious, her condition, her smell, and her nose that had rotted away. They were of little help. The wives expressed their distrust of Gertrude. They knew she brought trouble, arguments, and disruption, but none of them had any new thoughts other than what they heard and remembered, so they were of little help. The two male clan leaders did not speak.

Ander called Gertrude back inside his pit house. He stared at her and let her worry before he spoke. "You will be allowed to stay, but your past behavior speaks loudest. I am assigning these two women and two others who will be unknown to you to observe your behavior. You will be watched by everyone present and by every member of the village. If you steal food, clothing, or weapons you will be expelled immediately. We do not allow beatings, but for you, there might be an exception made depending on your behaviors. Be warned. We do as the Botai have always done, we expel those members who do not contribute."

Ander said, "We have no empty pit houses. There are three extra houses we use for our goats and supplies. You will bed down in the pit house with the goats, not in the supply houses. If you are seen in the supply houses, I will assume you are there to steal food, and your days with us will end. We have recently tamed these animals, and they provide an important meat source and milk for the village. With the goat milk, we make cheese. I tell you this so you know these animals have far more value to us than you do. It will be your job to care for them. You will feed and water them, care for them, and remove their manure outside the village."

"If any man wants to claim you as a second wife, it will be his choice to do so. You are free to accept or deny such an offer. If you do not become a second wife, you know your place in this village. You are one of the goat herders. Since it is winter, you must make your bed as best you can with what straw there is available. In spring, when the snow melts, you can find your own straw."

"For food, you can ask the women of the village. It is up to them what they want to share with you. I will not ask on your behalf. Do not expect generosity, expect to work hard and tend the goats. No one gets anything without contributing here. If this is not acceptable to you, you will leave tomorrow."

She had no choice. She accepted, bowed her head, and thanked Ander for his generosity. Gertrude was reduced to being a goat keeper, but she had a warm pit house to sleep in and a safe place for the rest of the winter. She had bought time just as she needed to do. As expected, no man claimed her as a second wife. No man wanted her for sex, and not one woman wanted her kind of help.

Two nights later, while the village was asleep, a female goat delivered a healthy male baby. Gertrude held her filthy winter horse hide coat over the baby goat's head to muffle any sounds it might make as she strangled it. She partially roasted the newborn goat over the small fire in her pit house and ate all she could that same night. Her drink was the mother goat's milk. The mother had no use for it now; her baby was dead. Raw goat meat tasted far better than wolf meat.

Gertrude wrapped the rest of the baby goat in a leather sack and hid it in a hole she had already dug just outside the village. The meat was soon frozen and available for tomorrow after she ate her regular food allotment.

That morning, she told the former woman goat herder, "The mother goat aborted the baby. It was born dead, and I left the bloody mess outside the village for the nighttime scavengers." Her explanation was good enough for the retired herder who did not want her old job back anyway. Her thought was, "Let Gertrude have the duties of feeding and manure removal, the animals were smelly and a lot of hard work."

Gertrude's explanation covered her trail in case anyone saw her burying the remainder of her meal last night, and no further questions were asked. She thought to herself, "How stupid and gullible these Krasnyi Yar are." Only Ander concerned her.

Gertrude had changed. Instead of being lazy and a thief, she was more cunning than ever.

CHAPTER 19

The Three-Curve Bow

THE SIXTH AND last monthly winter feast was held late in the day. This month, the entire village was invited to a single feast. Everyone anxiously attended because Bruno promised something special was to be announced. Horse meat was roasted; boiled peas, dried tubers, and lentils were served with dried elderberries for desert. Blueberry wine and music added to the air of celebration. Thanks to the hard work of our women and hunters, the village supplies held out until spring.

All seven babies born over the winter survived and were doing well. George and Agi's baby, Sophia, was the first to be fed horse milk from Star when she was born too early for her own mother's milk to be ready. Before we had horses, a premature baby like her would have died. Not one elder starved this year.

It was one of our best winters in memory. The final feast was unusual because it was held outside, thanks to the warm weather. Being held outdoors, it was ideal for the demonstration we had planned.

Bruno let it be known earlier in the week that there were several announcements coming and that I would discuss the annual bear hunt. It had to be done soon because warm weather was approaching, and hibernating bears would soon emerge from their deep sleep. Our chance to find them in their dens would be missed if we did not act soon.

He also let everyone know that he had a surprise for them. Most people guessed that it had something to do with horses. Part of the announcement did have to do with the horses, but the main topic was something else. As Bruno requested, Patts blessed the outdoor feast and the coming of spring. Her assistant, Elizza, blessed the bear hunt and the safe return of the men.

During the meal, Janos and Tedd left for a few minutes and returned with their arms full. They held long objects that were well hidden under large horse hides. Bruno knew what was coming. He raised his arms and asked for attention. The music stopped, and the crowd quieted down.

He said, "You are about to see an advance in how the Botai will hunt in the future. With this new idea, we will lead every other tribe from east to west." Bruno thanked Tedd and Janos for their months of hard work, and he asked Tedd to explain what the audience was about to see.

Tedd stood and walked to be alongside of Bruno. He looked at the crowd and said, "The advance you are about to see is the result of one man's great idea. It all started with Mikl. But Mikl became too busy with another new idea. He was busy training horses, so the project was turned over to me. I worked on it for weeks, but this time I was stumped. It must be that I am getting old." He smiled as the crowd appreciated his gentle humor.

"I struggled to find a way to create this weapon. After weeks of going nowhere with it, Daven asked Janos to aid me with the project. Even with Janos helping me, it was a lucky accident that moved us forward. Maybe we need more lucky accidents in this village." The crowd smiled in agreement.

At that moment, Tedd dumped a pile of broken wooden parts and pieces on the ground. "These are just a few of my many early attempts at making what we were calling an atlatl bow in the beginning. An atlatl bow was supposed to be a normal bow with an atlatl attached at each end for extra power. After all these failed attempts you see at my feet, it just did not work. Atlatls are too stiff to be part of a bow. Most of my failed attempts were used to keep me warm, in other words, they went into my fire and were burned." The crowd cheered.

Bruno and I knew that if Janos, being a clan leader, performed the actual demonstration, the new bow would have more impact than if Tedd did it. Tedd pointed to Janos and asked him to step forward with the next part of the demonstration.

Janos came to the center and waved to the crowd. He was a popular clan leader and well-respected hunter. He spoke with a smile on his face as he said, "I am going to take credit for the original idea and all the hard work that came before me." Janos laughed, and the crowd laughed with him. He then held up his old long bow, already strung, so the crowd could see it. The performance comparison was coming.

"In my hand, I am holding my old long bow. It is one I have used successfully on many hunts with good effect. What I want to show you today is a much more powerful bow when compared to what we have been hunting with for all these years." He took the new three-curve bow from under the horse hide and held it up high for all to see. It was not yet strung and looked very odd with its new shape. Janos strung the new bow and held them up for comparison. He gave the new bow to Tedd to hold.

He notched an arrow in his old familiar bow and pulled it back to full extension and let the arrow fly at a target already set up for this display. The crowd watched as the arrow penetrated about one third of the way into the target. Then Janos exchanged bows with Tedd. He held the new three-curve bow above his head for all to see.

Janos said, "This is the new bow. The middle part is actually an old long bow and similar to my old one. By accident, the wood was boiled too long, and the ends split. That was our lucky break. When that happened, new pieces of boiled wood were shaped and bent into these new curves. We attached them to the split ends of the old bow as you can see. When it was glued together, shaped, and polished, we had the first three-curve bow. It looked familiar in shape except for the new curves at each end.

Janos explained, "The new bow has almost two times the power of the old bow. But even with the extra power, it requires no more effort by the hunter than the normal bow. On top of that, not only can it shoot an arrow farther, it fires the arrow with more power, so the arrows have greater killing impact. One more feature is that it can fire arrows that are larger in size and weight with heavier points. These arrows are almost like shooting small spears."

He continued, "The only negative we see is that it takes more time and skill to make this new bow. Now let me show how well it works. Let us imagine that the target over there is the bear we will hunt in a few days. I want to remind you that the first arrow penetrated the bear one third of the way."

With that, Janos notched an arrow and pulled the three-curve bow back to full extension. He let the arrow fly, and it struck the same target right next to the first arrow. The difference was that the second arrow penetrated the target all the way up to the feathers. All at once, the crowd stood up and roared its approval. There was wild applause and cheering as Janos notched a second arrow and fired it into the same target. Again, it penetrated up to the feathers just as the first one did.

Every hunter and young man rushed forward to examine the bow and the target. They felt the wood and examined where the pieces were joined to the original bow. Several other hunters went to the target to examine the arrows and check how far they penetrated. It was quite a bit later when the crowd finally calmed down and returned to their seats.

When the initial excitement was over, Bruno and I joined Janos and Tedd at the center of the gathering in a grouping of clan leaders plus Tedd. Jon remained in his seat next to Mikl. He was new to clan leadership and hesitated to take credit for any of the accomplishment. Bruno motioned for Jon and Mikl to come forward, and they joined us in front of the villagers. Bruno held Mikl's right arm over his head and applauded for him. He had the original idea and deserved some of the credit.

Minutes later, Bruno asked for quiet in order to speak. "This new bow is called the three-curve bow, and it will make us the best hunters in the land." The crowd cheered again.

"There may come a time when enemies try to take our hunting grounds. It happened in the past when the Botai were three small wandering tribes and the Smolens pushed us out. Our land was taken by others who had too many hunters for us to fight them. This new weapon will prevent that from happening again." This caused another cheer that turned into a standing roar of approval. Bruno continued, "The clan leaders and I have decided that we will not share this new bow with anyone else at this time. However, it may be traded or shared with an ally if we need to settle a debt or firm up a relationship." Again, there were loud voices of approval.

"In the future, our hunts will be safer because we can kill at a greater distance. We have four bows ready for the bear hunt starting in two days." Bruno held both hands up and waited for attention once more.

He spoke, "Each of the three clan leaders will appoint two men or women to work with Tedd and Janos, so the knowledge of how to make these bows will be known by every clan. If more than two people want to join the team, that will be even better. I expect every hunter to have a three-curve bow in time for the first horse hunt of the spring, and I invite each of you to try these bows after this gathering. Every hunter must attend the planning meeting for the bear hunt whether they are staying back to guard the village or coming on the hunt." Bruno motioned to me as he spoke. "The planning meeting will be run by Daven as usual."

"The last announcement is that there will be a major horse training test coming as soon as the weather allows. For the safety of the team, the test will occur once the ice and snow are off the ground and therefore after the bear hunt. It will be held on the first warm day after our return. Ildiko will attempt to ride Gray Boy outside of the corral." There were gasps from the audience. Individual discussions broke out everywhere.

Most people wondered if it could be done at all. Would the horse break free and run off with Ildiko? Would Gray Boy run back to the grasslands? Would she be thrown off and injured or dragged to her death? Or would she become the first person anywhere to ride a horse? Everyone wondered what would happen. In another week or two, they would have their answer. This was exciting news.

The crowd quieted down after some time. Bruno continued, "Gray Boy will be hobbled and there will be two leashes, but as we all know, a full-grown horse can easily overpower two men holding leashes. The test will be dangerous for the rider, so we ask that you stay back and away from the corral area. Since it has never been done before, we are not sure what will happen. However, if we are to get full use from our horses, it is the next logical step and has to be tried. For the safety of the team, please keep your distance that day.

"Ildiko is our most experienced trainer on horseback, so she will be the first to try riding outside the corral. If the first test is successful, Diana will be next to ride. My turn is coming sometime in the future when I am certain it can actually be done and the rider can survive!"

There were more shouts and cheering. The cheering turned into a chant. "BRUNO! BRUNO! BRUNO!" That chant was drowned out by a new one. The voices who yelled out loudest now were those of our women. Their higher-pitched screams drowned out the men with their own chant. "ILDIKO, ILDIKO! ILDIKO!" And that chant became "DIANA! DIANA! DIANA!" and finally it became, "MIKL! MIKL! MIKL!" Blueberry wine brought out their rowdy behavior, and it was fun, the most fun celebration in many years.

Everyone, whether young or old, was celebrating, smiling, cheering, and anxious for Ildiko to ride Gray Boy. Once Bruno had their attention, he continued, "If it works, I can see the day where every hunter will ride to and from horse hunts. We will be the first to ride to the summer gathering, and in the long run, every man and every woman will have a horse to help them with their work." There was another round of shouts and cheering, this time by both men and women.

"Also, as we capture more horses this year, each hunter who wants a horse for their own must become the trainer for that horse. There will be no exceptions. Each of you must train your own horse. We will not do it for you." He thanked the crowd for their attention.

The whole village talked at the same time. There were a few questions that were answered by Bruno. Mothers and wives asked as many questions as the hunters. Major changes were coming to the Botai, and as always, there were a few doubters. I was one of them last year when we captured the first horse, but Mikl and Ildiko changed me. Both of them could readily see better ways of doing things. It was Ildiko who convinced me to open my mind and see new ways of doing things.

As I watched Bruno in action leading this final monthly celebration, I was certain he was the best man to be the Oldson. I backed the right person. Maybe I was a better hunter, but Bruno had leadership, and his Botai people loved him.

After the exciting gathering, I met with Jon, Bruno, and Janos to discuss the bear hunt. We would leave at sunup one day from tomorrow. Janos will not join me on this hunt because he and Tedd were leading the effort to make a full supply of three-curve bows in time for the first horse hunt this spring. Diana and Ildiko, along with two new training members, Peter and Patrick, would take part on this hunt to help haul the bear meat back after we butchered it.

We had four of the new three-curve bows for the bear hunt. I would be using one of them along with the new heavier arrows and larger points. The larger arrows had much more killing power. Like every other year, I was excited to be heading into the field to hunt bears again. Danger was the exciting part, and I felt it.

CHAPTER 20

The Bear Hunt

EVERY HUNTER PRACTICED with the new bows, and not one of them complained that they did not work as well as their old bows. Better yet, they praised them as being no harder to use and said the new bows had more power. One hunter after the other asked for one of their own. Mikl waited patiently to take his turn and watched his idea become a huge success. He had pride in himself for having the idea first but regretted not having had the time to finish the project.

Two hunters from each clan would stay back to protect the village and to help Janos and Tedd make the new three-curve bows. Trouble from animal predators was unlikely at this time of the year, but there was always the possibility of a mountain lion approaching especially with the prominent smell of horses throughout the village. Lately, for some reason, I have been concerned with our old enemies, the Smolens, so I regularly assigned one or two hunters to guard the trail coming from the eastern side of the Urals.

We planned to take two horses, Gray Boy and Dawn, with us to return with the bear meat on the dragging platforms. They would be led by Ildiko, Diana, and Mikl. Patrick and Peter will assist, and George could help out if they needed him.

Ildiko and Diana would stay well to the rear and out of danger when a den was found. Once a kill was made, they would assist us with butchering the meat and returning it to the village. For safety, two men would travel with them on each return trip. Ildiko was an accomplished hunter on her own, so if needed, there would be enough protection for safe travel back and forth.

If we killed four adult bears, most likely there would be a similar amount of cubs. That would give us enough meat and fat for grease for at least the first six months of the year. Bear meat was never a favorite. It is too greasy and less sweet than horse meat, but at this time of the year, it can substitute for horse meat for a few weeks. Claws, fur, and canine teeth were awarded to those who found the dens or had an outstanding day of hunting. Claws were prized as decorative pieces for hunters and brought good value during summer trading.

The hunters meeting was about to begin. Bruno, in his role as Oldson, addressed the hunters before he left me in charge. He opened the meeting saying, "We have lost two hunters this year. As you know, Joe was killed on the fall horse hunt and Agi is unavailable due to frostbite. The good news is that Agi will recover and can rejoin us when her foot is healed. We have also added five new hunters this year, and we were fortunate to have George join the Botai as an experienced hunter."

Bruno held their attention. "Bear hunts are dangerous. My biggest concern is for the five new men joining this hunt for their first time. I expect every one of you to listen well to Daven as he describes the plan. Every hunter must know his role." Bruno motioned for me to take over.

"The timing is right for the annual bear hunt. I see dandelions growing and buds appearing on willow and maple trees. If their favorite foods are sprouting, they will emerge soon. We need to find them before they leave their dens."

"We depart after breakfast tomorrow morning. There is no need to leave before sunup since our prey is sleeping and the time of departure is not important. Each of you must carry enough food for ten days of travel. If we have good luck, we will feast on bear meat along the way. If we have no luck, we will have to get by with what we carry. Water will be available from springs and streams along the way, so you only need to carry a one-day supply. Unlike in horse hunts, campfires will be allowed.

"From the village, we will head toward the lower hills of the Urals, but we will not hunt in the mountains. Remember that it will be colder as we gain elevation, so bring a warm blanket for the evenings." There were a few basic questions about travel and camp rules after which I got back to the hunt plan. "For the first time, our horses will help carry supplies both to and from the hunt. We, as hunters, will only carry our weapons, food, and water.

"No one should even think about trying to kill a bear by themselves. With this powerful animal, we need to work together as a team. We will hunt one bear at a time." No questions were asked, and there was no joking; this was a serious discussion for experienced and new hunters alike. Everyone knew a mistake could be fatal.

I continued the training, "My father described a bear's den as anywhere the bear spends the winter. A den can be a crevice or a space under a fallen tree or what looks like an oversized burrow. Bears often cover themselves with branches and vegetation, so they are often very well disguised and hard to find. You could find yourself walking right up to an occupied den that may not look like a den at all. You have to be alert every minute. As we search for our prey, we must have silence. There will be no talking or eating along the way, so eat as much as you want when we stop for our meals."

"We will be hunting an animal that has been sleeping for five or six months. Do not be fooled into thinking they are weak or easy prey. Bears are able to slow their bodily functions down so well while they hibernate that they hardly burn any energy at all, and they do not defecate while they sleep, so you probably will not be able to smell them. They will be hungry when they emerge, but even though they have not eaten anything in quite a while, they are just as powerful as any other bear once they are awake.

"If the sleeping bear is a female, it will have one or two cubs with it.

The cubs are not dangerous. The mother is the danger and will be our prime target. Unless you are under a full attack by a cub, do not worry about it until the mother has been killed. The cubs will be confused when they come out of the den and easy to kill once the mother is down.

"An adult female with a cub is more dangerous than a male. If we cannot get the bear to come out of its den with spears and noise, we will light a fire and smoke it out. When the bear comes out, we will have hunters on only two sides of the den. The other two sides will be left open. That will allow us to have full use of our bows without concern that anyone will be hit in a crossfire. If you have a shot, take it. Do not wait for a command as with horse hunts. Spears are used as backup weapons.

"The best killing area is the neck or the heart. If we can hit one of the large arteries in its neck, it will bleed to death, but with a bear, death comes slowly. If it attacks and rears on its hind legs, your best target is still its neck. If you aim for the heart from the side, you will probably hit ribs, and most likely, you will not do much damage. Kills are not quick like they are with deer or horses. Bears are tough. They are dangerous even with a dozen arrows in them. They fight to the death. They will kill us if we do not kill them, so you have to stay in your assigned position and follow directions. If you do that, this hunt will be successful."

I reviewed all the basics because of the new men joining us. "If the den is on a slope, the hunters on the right side will have the first shot. Once it is hit, most of the time a bear will turn to face its attacker, and its neck will be exposed. At that point, the hunters behind the den or on top of it will have the best chance to land a killing shot. Fire your arrows without panic and as rapidly as possible."

"A spear is often the best weapon for the final kill. If the bear charges you, jab your spear into its chest. Forget the neck because it is too easy to miss. If it rears, jab your spear into its belly or chest, it will slow down and probably slap at your weapon. When it slaps at the spear, it gives the other men a clear shot with their bows. If you have to use your spear, back from the bear toward the hunters on your team. Do not back up opposite the bear or you could get hit in a crossfire. Retreat slowly, but do not run.

"If it is a one-on-one situation with the bear coming on top of you, dig the back end of the spear into the ground and let the bear impale itself. It is terrifying, but you must keep your wits about you and know that the rest of us will be helping you with the kill. This is a hunt where you cannot afford to panic. If you turn and run, the bear will be on you in seconds and tear you apart before the rest of us can kill it. Running is not an option."

Questions continued for quite a while. Everyone wanted to be sure they knew exactly what was expected of them. I pointed out that Bruno or I or both of us will be the ones to face the bear if it was still in the den when we find it. I reminded them once more. "If you find a den, call me or Bruno or your clan leader. Do not, under any circumstances, try to take a bear on your own."

The next day, we left after breakfast. Our supplies were being hauled by the horses. By the time I digested my breakfast, we arrived at the first low hills, and we turned west. A half day later, we found our first den, and it was occupied. George spotted what looked like a cave and signaled me with his hand.

The den was hard to see because the entrance was filled with brush. I whispered and motioned for everyone to get in their assigned places. Once they were ready and their bows were notched, I pushed my spear hard into the shallow cave. I heard what sounded like a grunt or a growl and quickly stepped back from the entrance with my spear ready. All of us were tense, but nothing happened. We waited a short time. The bear did not come out.

I exchanged my bow with George so he had my new more powerful weapon, and I took his. I approached the entrance and jabbed my spear hard again at the same spot again where I struck it the first time. This time, I hit something hard like a rock. I did not hit the bear, it had moved. I yelled, "The bear is coming out," and waited in front of the entrance in a semicrouched position. I held the spear tightly in a defensive position.

Suddenly, it came charging out of the entrance and saw me. It roared with anger being woken a week or two before it was ready. I held my spear between myself, and the bear and jabbed at it without making contact. The sleepy bear hesitated to get its bearings, not having seen daylight in many months. I distracted it just enough to make it stop and look around.

Jon and Bruno shot their arrows first. Both of them were using the new and more powerful bows. I slowly backed away in a crouched position with my spear in front of me jabbing at the bear and saw their arrows slam into its neck. One bloody arrow from Bruno's bow went all the way through its neck and came part of the way out the other side. More arrows hit it from two sides. I continued backing toward the hunters on my right and jabbed as I retreated. I maneuvered slowly in a circular motion so the bear would follow me. I jabbed and retreated again and again. As it followed me, it faced the hunters and their deadly fire.

As soon as the bear was completely out in the entrance and in the open, the hunters on both sides of the den shot their arrows at close range and scored hard, direct hits. At least eight more arrows found the mark with Mikl and George scoring well. The new hunters followed their lead. Several hits were in the neck and back. Two or three arrows hit its head and shoulders and glanced off not doing much damage.

It was such close-up action that only one arrow missed the bear completely. That one was fired from behind the group behind me and on my right. I clearly saw that it was fired by Flint and that it went dangerously close to Jon's head. I was partially facing Flint and the hunters, and I thought that I was probably the only one who saw what happened. Everyone else was too involved with the kill and the excitement to notice. I wondered if it was an accident or a very poor shot by an experienced hunter, or was it done on purpose? Jon did not seem to notice the arrow pass his head.

Even with a dozen or more arrows in it and already bleeding badly, the bear was not done yet. It turned to the right with a snarl. Blood flowed from its neck as it swiped with its right claw at Bruno. I was so close I could feel the bear's spit hit my face. Bruno stepped back just in time. The swipe missed the mark but tore Bruno's shirt. Bruno jabbed with his spear to fend it off as more arrows from other men found their mark.

The plan was working to perfection except for me. I was on defense without my powerful bow. When it clawed at Bruno, I drove my spear into its side, trying for the final kill. Arrows poured into it while the bear pawed at the spear and finally fell to the ground groaning. The excitement was over. The bear had come out just as I said it would and charged at me. My spear and the hunters' arrows did the job. We made the kill without an injury to anyone. I knew the good results we had today would give the new hunters more confidence for the next bear.

Arrows from the three-curve bows were deadly. The impact was far greater than those from the old-style bows. It was clear to me that with these bows, we were a much more dangerous foe than we had been in the past. We found two cubs hiding inside the den and made short work of them.

Mikl whistled, and the horses started forward even before Diana and Ildiko were ready to move. All that training was paying off. That night, there was an air of celebration as we feasted on roast bear tongue, heart, and liver and talked excitedly about the hunt. Ildiko and Diana tasted the best parts of a bear for the first time because these cuts never made it back to the village. We butchered the meat and removed the heaviest bones including the head to save weight on the return trip. The large canine teeth were removed as were the fur and claws.

George was the man who found the bear's den, so after the hunt was complete, he was rewarded that evening with the middle claw from of the right front paw. He chose the right paw since the claws were just a little bit larger than those of the left paw. I thought that even bears must be right handed and left handed. The rest of its front claws were divided up among the group by the clan leaders.

Rear claws were of little value due to their shape and because everyone knew it was the front claws that could kill a hunter. Claws made beautiful necklaces and spoke of hunter's deeds for a long time into the future. Agi would be proud of George for being the man recognized for finding the den. We loaded the dragging platforms, and the travel team left for home. I let the group sleep late the next morning.

Since we were only four hours from the village, we knew the team would be back in time to help with the next bear kill. I assigned two of the new hunters to mark trees with their axes so that our trail would be easy for the horse team to follow as we continued our trek. Marking trees was a simple task. Knowing how young men get distracted, I thought two of them would do a better job marking the trees than one.

The second day, we had no luck finding another den. One or more might have been there, but if they were, we did not find them. The third day, we came upon a den that was no more than a hollowed out curve in a soft wall of dirt. The female bear must have been young when it made its winter home because the den was poorly made. She was covered with brush with branches, some with oak leaves still attached. This time, since we could see it, we never woke the bear. We took our assigned positions and killed it right where it was hibernating. It had one cub, and we took that too.

The third bear den was found by one of the new men of my Horse Clan. This one was a deep cave and well hidden. The entrance was low, not big enough for a hunter to enter while standing. Small tight dens are dangerous for hunters because to enter, you have to crawl inside, and crawling prevents effective use of any weapon other than a spear. Even a spear cannot be used very well from a crawling position.

Bruno and I looked in the cave. It was so dark, we could not see anything. We moved forward on our hands and knees for a better look. We could a smell bear inside, but we could not see it, so we backed out the same way we entered, on our hands and knees. The situation was dangerous. I motioned for the group to come together.

I spoke in a low voice, "We have to build a fire at the door. Once it is burning, we have to make smoke. Look for wet wood, moss, or grass, they smoke well. We will have to fan it to push the smoke into the cave. That should arouse the bear.

"There might be an opening in the top of the cave where smoke can escape. If we block that hole, the smoke will get thick and wake the bear." I sent two men to search for the hole. "Our hunting positions will be the same as we used for the first hunt. Now let us get to work before this sleeping bear wakes up." In ten minutes, we had a fire going and threw on the wet grass and rotten wood to make it smoke. We fanned the flames with horse hides and pushed the smoke into the cave.

Sure enough, smoke started coming out of several holes in the roof of the cave. The holes were blocked with chunks of rotted bark and more wet leaves. Now everyone got in position, and we waited cautiously. Finally, we heard growls. It was a mother waking her cubs. She was a huge older bear with two cubs and probably weighed close to five hundred pounds. All three bears staggered out of the cave in distress with the mother at the rear, pushing her cubs in front of her. They were barely awake and confused by the smoke.

I took the first shot at the mother with my three-curve bow. The bow felt strong in my hands. We rained arrows into the huge mother before she knew what was happening. Our arrows struck the mother in the neck so the huge black fur would be a valuable one without having holes in the body of the pelt. The cubs stayed near the mother looking for protection and were easy targets once the mother was killed. When all three were dead, the men cheered. This bear hunt was going well. We had taken three adult bears and five cubs. The best part of the hunt for me was that no one had been injured.

Ildiko, Mikl, and Diana returned from the village after the first hunt. This time they not only had Gray Boy and Dawn, they also brought my mare, Star, to help too. I whistled to let them know where to join us, and they were on their way. That night, we all ate well again, enjoying the organs and best cuts of meat along with vegetables brought back from the village. We had a lot to talk about with the success we had so far.

We harvested the bear meat and fur and discarded the heavy bones. Ildiko spent the night with me, and Diana slept with Bruno. Mikl ate dinner with me and Ildiko and suggested, "Next year, we might be able to ride horses to and from the hunt and drag the meat along on the platforms while we rode."

I replied, "Mikl, I hope you are right. It would be a great step forward if we can do that. I will take riding over walking any day, but it depends on what happens when we get back and Ildiko rides Gray Boy." It reminded us that if the snow was melted; the riding test was scheduled to happen when we returned from this hunt. All three of us felt the anticipation and talked about it further.

That morning, we loaded the horses for the return trip to the village. With three horses carrying the load, it would be an easy trip. We needed one more kill before it was over. I was concerned the men were becoming overconfident. Before we left that day, I called the group together and told them of my concern. "When a hunt goes as well as this one has, it is easy to get complacent and relax. We need to kill one more bear. Each one of us has to remain as vigilant as when we started out. I want no one to get injured. Be alert, and we all go home safely." Bruno spoke in agreement with my concern. We continued our search for the next den, traveling near the lower slope of the Ural Mountains. I thanked the first pair of men who marked the trail so far and assigned two new hunters to mark the trail from here.

By noon, we approached a cave we had hunted before. It was a favorite for us and for hibernating bears. We called it the Cave Bear cave. This name sounds a bit odd, but there is a reason for the name. This was where our grandfathers and theirs before them long ago found three complete skeletons from a type of huge bear called a Cave Bear that must have lived long ago. The name Cave Bear cave is still used. Since that time, others who we meet at the summer gatherings have described finding similar bones of these animals in other caves in their territories. We have never seen a live bear of this size, so we thought they must no longer exist.

Our grandfathers picked through the remains and took the front claws they found. Since they were so rare, these claws were the envy of every tribe. Those claws were huge compared to those of the bears we hunt today. Our grandfathers took the claws and made four Cave Bear claw necklaces. Today, one necklace is worn by each clan leader with the fourth one worn by the overall leader. The necklace for the Oldson has three claws whereas the clan leader necklaces have one or two claws, depending on seniority. We wear these necklaces for every important celebration including the winter monthly feasts and the summer gathering.

The old skeletons were still in the cave covered with debris and leaves and branches brought in by more recent hibernating bears year after year. We also saw old fire hearths once used for cooking, or so we thought some ancient people from the past must have used this cave as their home. Last year, we scratched through the debris, the leaves, and branches on the floor and found five more front claws that our ancestors missed. These were kept back in our village.

There were a few broken spears with blackened tips, but none of those spears had a stone point. The people of this time may not have made stone spearheads. There were also numerous drawings painted on the walls from long ago and dark smudges that must have been made by fires used as lights for the artist as he drew the pictures. There were also outlines of hands, perhaps of the hands of the painter or those of clan leaders or shaman.

When we found the painted drawings the first time, we returned to the Cave Bear cave with Tedd and Patts to hear what they thought of them. The return trip was during summer when we knew there would be no hibernating bears to deal with.

Ruth had heard about these drawings when she was a young girl and still living with her original people, the Hungarians. They thought the drawings tell a story of a people who lived here long ago perhaps when the great wall of ice covered much of this land. There were also drawings of mammoths with long curved tusks and animals with bodies the size of mammoths but with shorter legs. The mammoths appeared to be ten times the size of a horse.

One drawing was of a huge cat with long front teeth unlike any mountain lion of today, and other drawings showed winged creatures that no one has ever seen. Were these pictures made of real animals, or were they created from dreams perhaps induced by hallucinogenic mushroom teas? We still talked about it over campfires. Whatever the correct answer was, the cave was a perfect den for hibernating bears and still used to this day.

We were a short distance from the entrance when I stopped the hunters and called the group together. I reminded them, "Our approach will be to concentrate on the larger chamber, which goes straight ahead. Chances are that if the cave is occupied, the bear will be on that side due to it being larger in size."

Because it has been occupied by more than one bear in the past, I assigned four hunters, led by Flint, to stay to the rear where the chambers split. They would not take part in the kill. Their job was to protect the hunters who entered first. Bruno stood next to me when I said to Flint, "You and your three men will guard against the possibility of an attack from a second bear that might be in the right chamber." Flint agreed as he nodded yes. He knew his assignment.

Oiled torches were lit, and we entered. It took a few minutes for our eyes to adjust to the dim light. With the light from the flaming torches, I saw a huge sleeping bear straight ahead and motioned toward it for everyone to see. Luckily, there was no second bear sleeping in the same chamber, but the bear that we saw was more than enough to meet our needs. Since there were no cubs, I assumed it was probably a male.

Just as we were ready to fire our arrows, the bear stirred. My first thought was that it must have smelled the smoke from our torches or maybe it smelled us. Bruno fired first. Jon and I were right behind him, and the rest of the hunters released more than a dozen arrows before the bear had a chance to react.

Some of our arrows struck the bear, but in the dim light, it was hard to see the actual form of the bear because it was lying in a curled-up position among branches, leaves, and debris. Our first shots did not kill it, and more arrows were fired rapidly. The three-curve bows struck hard, doing a lot of damage before it could get to its feet. The wounded bear charged at us. Bruno and I had our spears ready. We struck from the front with spears driven into its chest and neck as the rest of the hunters continued to release their arrows. The bear roared in pain and anger and swung its paws as spears found their marks, wounding it further. Still it fought in a rage.

We had no room to back up when the bear came at us because Flint and his men crowded forward to watch the action. The lack of space left one man with no place to move. The wounded bear clawed him and threw him to the ground. A second man was too close to avoid another blow and had his leg ripped open. I crushed my spear into its chest as Bruno slammed his heavy copper axe on top of its head and bones splintered. It was over, but it was too close of a call.

The two hunters who went down were not too seriously injured. One had a bloody mess on his leg, and the other was clawed on his arm and shoulder. Neither wound was life threatening, but they were bruised and bloodied. Both of them were angry at being crowded by those watching from the rear. Bruno calmed the men and said that he would deal with the problem later. Those claw marks would serve as a reminder of a mistake made this day by Flint.

Just then, a second bear growled and rumbled forward from the right chamber. Flint and the hunters in the rear were out of position. Luckily, the second bear ran for the opening of the cave. I yelled at Flint, "Let it go! At best you could only wound it, and a wounded bear is a terror in the woods." We had no chance for a kill; it was better to let it escape. We already had a successful hunt.

I thought to myself, this was twice that Flint made mistakes. I would have to discuss it with Bruno when the time was right. Right now, it was time to butcher the bear meat and enjoy a good meal, but Flint was a serious concern. Anyone who did not follow instructions was a danger to the rest of us. I lost all confidence in him as did his fellow hunters.

Another problem came up when the horses did not come forward when I whistled. Mikl, Ildiko, Diana, and Janos's two sons were overdue. My concern was they had a problem or got lost. The trees were supposed to be marked, so they should not be lost. I sent two men back to find them.

We dragged the bear carcass to the entrance and began to butcher it. I was concerned about their safety and hated the thought of carrying all that bear meat back to the village as we did before we had horses. Just then I saw the two men I sent to search for them, and was Ildiko leading Star. Mikl, Diana, and the others were not far behind. I was relieved to see them, but they were late by several hours. When Bruno and I asked what happened, they told us they had lost their way twice due to a poorly marked trail. If not for the help from Peter and Patrick, they might have never found us.

At times, new hunters took an assignment lightly when they did not see its importance. The two men got careless. Bruno and I corrected that right after the evening meal. We called them in front of the group and pointed out what happened, and they admitted there were sloppy with their assignment. They were told to carry all the spears back in addition to their own weapons. In addition, no one was to talk to them until we reached the village. Embarrassment was their worst punishment.

Flint and his poor performance was still on my mind. He had to be dealt with. I heard one of them complain to the other that Flint made a worse mistake than they did, and he was not punished. I spoke to Bruno. He assured me that Flint would be dealt with, but not right now.

That night, Bruno and I had the unusual pleasure of sleeping with our wives only because they were with the horses and part of the hunt. I noticed that Ildiko's body was softer and her breasts fuller. Was it my imagination or was the light from the campfire making me more appreciative of her beauty? Or, I thought, was she pregnant? I asked Ildiko.

She replied, "I am fine, everything is fine." She immediately changed the topic to the excitement of the bear hunt. It was her first time on a hunt of this kind, and she was still excited. She marveled at how well my plan worked. She said, "Daven, you could hunt mammoths if they still lived today. Just think, one mammoth would give us all the meat we need for an entire winter." I smiled, but I thought she was too full of compliments and avoided my question.

I thought how cleverly she changed the subject. I had to ask her again when we got home. If she was pregnant, I wonder, why did she not tell me? Then I remembered her scheduled ride on Gray Boy in a few days. Of course, that was it. If she told me she was pregnant, I would try to talk her out of the ride, and she would not hear of that. Her mind was made up. She had to be the first person to ride a horse. I was sure I was right. Ildiko was ready to have her first child.

CHAPTER 21

Riding Gray Boy

WITH THE BEAR hunt completed, it took a week for everyone to get back to their daily routine. Snow still covered the ground, so the test with Ildiko riding Gray Boy was put off until the snow melted.

The first night, we ate fresh bear meat in a major feast for the entire village. The remainder of the meat was preserved by smoking and the grease was collected in pottery dishes for later use in cooking. Some of the grease was used to make candles with the wicks now being made of tightly braided horse hair instead of fine leather strips. Bear furs were tied on wooden racks and the flesh removed with bone scrapers. The hide side of the skin was treated with brains from previous hunts until it was soft to the touch. After a lot of hard work, the hides produced warm fur for heavy clothing or winter blankets.

Bear claws were used as a form of money and traded to others who did something in return. Five front claws from an adult bear were enough for a hunter's necklace. Claws from bear cubs were given to wives and daughters for jewelry, but boys had to earn their own claws.

Everyone who did something got something in return. The better you performed, the more claws you might receive from the clan leaders. Bruno was not part of the reward process because by tradition, rewards were left to the clan leaders. Jon was one of the three clan leaders and took his place with Janos and myself as we awarded hunters for their accomplishments. This leadership role set Jon apart from Flint once again.

For this hunt, Flint received no recognition. I told him why in front of the men. He left his fellow hunters unprotected from an attack to the rear when he did not hold his men in place and two men were injured. It was a serious error.

I did not mention the arrow that came much too close to his brother's head. This was not my issue. I had to talk to Bruno about it before I spoke of it in front of anyone else. In my mind, that shot was taken without regard for safety or it was done on purpose to let Jon and Bruno know of his anger. Since I was the only one who saw it, and since it did no harm, I decided to keep my comments to myself for now.

Flint did not deny his lack of attention to his assignment in the last cave, but he did not take criticism very well. Instead, he argued. He was an experienced hunter and should not have let the excitement of the kill with the first bear distract him from what he was supposed to do. He let us down. I felt we were lucky to escape with only minor injuries. Next time, a mistake like that could be fatal. He left the reward ceremony in shame.

The original reward system for women who gathered supplies did not work in the same way as it worked for hunters. There were no specific things of value to be distributed for good performance as there were with bear claws. Elder women and men worked together to bring in winter supplies. At the monthly feasts, Ruth, Emma, and my cousin Judy—the elder women—recognized the best gatherers by name, but that was all they received.

Bruno changed this older system. Now, the elder women would reward the best workers with an extra share of the only sweet food we have other than berries, that of honey. If someone did not work when they were considered able to work, they were openly criticized by the elder women. If they continued to be lazy and were criticized a second time, they would be put out of the village for one or more days. In rare cases, women have been put out for a week.

It was agreed by everyone that without a system of reward and punishment, lazy workers would get even lazier and the hard workers would slow down to the level of the laziest. Eventually, everyone would work slower, and supplies would run out.

Gertrude was a prime example. She did less and less over the last three years and ate more and more. In the end, she did almost nothing. She had to be punished. Being put out of the village for two or three nights was feared because nights alone were dangerous. Second offenders got longer banishments. Although usable caves in the area were well known, they were bare of the most basic essentials like bedding, firewood, or any stock of food. A week alone in a cave for a woman could mean death, especially if it occurred during winter.

Elsewhere in the village Janos, Tedd, and their bow team members made three-curve bows for every hunter, and those hunters soon made their own bows after careful instruction. Arrows were a known item and would not change significantly except that the new bows could shoot normal-size arrows and heavyweight arrows. Heavy arrows had more impact at close range like those we used in the bear hunt but did not carry as far as lighter arrows. For horse hunting, the new bows gave us far greater distance at which we could make a kill.

A hunter we call Dann the Carver was working on a large flat stone at the entrance to our village. He was cutting out a five-foot-tall image of a horse with a female rider on its back. The rider had long hair flowing behind her head and looked just like Ildiko. Dann said it was indeed Ildiko on the carving and asked me what I thought. I agreed. I said, "I loved it."

My only concern was that she had not yet ridden the horse. I hoped the carving would bring her luck, good luck. Bruno encouraged Dann to finish the carving before the first hunt of the year. "It will bring us good fortune," he predicted.

Horse training continued day after day despite the weather. Gray Boy, Dawn, and Star were becoming accustomed to the weight of a person on their back every day in the stable and at times in the corral. Babe, the colt of Star, was a bit too young to bear the weight of a trainer, but she was learning in the corral as were the other horses.

The trainers waited patiently for the day when the last of the snow and ice would be gone. That would be the day of the final test, riding Gray Boy outside of the corral. The horses became used to the smell and closeness of people, and all four of them learned to pull dragging platforms. We made progress even when the usual process was just being repeated.

On one warm sunny day, we left two horses in the corral as we ate our midday meal. While we talked, Gray Boy, now eighteen months old, started smelling Star from behind her. She encouraged him by keeping her rear quarters in position just in front of him and lifting her tail. I realized that my mare, Star, was in heat. Gray Boy mounted Star, and we watched as nature took over. I said to the others, "We will have our fifth horse in eleven months without having to capture it!" Star had just started her own family. I thought, maybe her memories of freedom in the grasslands were fading.

While we watched the horses, Ruth, Patts, Emma, and Judy passed by the corral with two other women of the gathering team. When they got to the berry patches, we saw Emma point at the horse manure the trainers spread among the plants. I thought there might be trouble coming. Instead she said, "That manure must have made the difference. Our blueberry and gooseberry plants look healthier than ever, but the bilberry plants without manure are growing at a slower rate like in other years." She said, "Tomorrow, we will spread manure around the rest of the berry plants." She also noticed that half of the strawberry plants with manure were growing faster than those without.

Ruth checked the apple and pear trees to see if they were ahead of schedule like the berries. If manure worked for berries, maybe the fruit trees also benefited. When they reached the apple trees some distance away, sure enough it looked like the fruit trees with manure were ahead of schedule too. They were fuller with new growth and had more early leaves.

There were also new trees sprouting where a few apples fell to the ground and were covered over by horse manure. The following day, the women returned as a group with their flint spades and replanted the new trees; now they were one full tree length away from the old ones, so there would be room for them to grow.

The women were excited and shared the news with the remaining members of the gathering team. The next day, they all walked out once again to see the results of their work and what they called the "manure miracle." When they were done, they came to the corral and told us exactly where to put the next loads of manure. That was new. No one ever wanted manure before; now it was in demand!

Weeks passed and the ground started to soften and thaw. Ice and snow remained only in shaded areas where the sun did not warm the ground. The group of trainers came to me at noon and said, "Daven, we feel that the time is right. The ground is soft and the snow is gone. Bruno said the trial would be held when weather allowed and after the next full moon. Not only is the moon gone, the snow and ice are gone too. Conditions are right, and we are ready to ride Gray Boy outside of the corral." Ildiko was the most excited of all.

I asked them, "How confident are you that the horses have had sufficient training to take this next step?" I was worried about Ildiko, not the training.

The answer was unanimous, but it was Ildiko who replied, "We are confident, and I am ready to ride." I knew she was ready, but I also wanted to have that talk with her to find out if she was healthy enough to do this. Diana provided a second option if Ildiko was pregnant.

My concerns were not their concerns. I doubt I could stop Ildiko for any reason short of a broken leg! She could be stubborn, especially when it came to a challenge of any kind. She would not give an inch.

She would find a way to win if there was one. I knew the horses were ready too. Mikl, as the leader, asked for my answer a second time. "We need your permission to ride Gray Boy outside of the corral tomorrow. If it goes well, Diana will ride him right after Ildiko." Mikl added, "The following day, Jon and I will ride him too." It all depended how well it went with Ildiko.

I agreed with the trainers. "I know you are ready. I am convinced you have done everything that can be done to prepare, and tomorrow morning will be the day. Before we move forward, we have to let Bruno know what we are doing." I was still not sure how safe it would be for a pregnant woman to dare to try ride a horse. We walked to Bruno's pit house, and Diana entered without an announcement since it was her house.

Bruno, in his role as Oldson, was busy with some type of boring dispute between two women of the same clan. I could hear each woman pleading her case over some nonsense. It was another unimportant argument. I did not envy Bruno. While we waited, I sent for Janos and Ruth so they could hear the plan. Bruno made a decision on the issue with the women, and his meeting was over. Both of the women left his house smiling. I thought, yes, he was the right man to be Oldson. I would rather wrestle a bear with bad breath than settle disputes like that one!

Tomorrow's plan was described by Mikl and Diana. It would start in the stable as usual, with Ildiko mounting Gray Boy from the rafters and the horse being hobbled. Leashes would be in place when Gray Boy was led to the corral by Mikl and Jon. Ildiko would test Gray Boy's reaction to the netting controls. If he responded well, Jon and Mikl would open the gate and let Ildiko walk him out. Once the horse and rider were outside of the corral, the outcome was uncertain, even with hobbles in place.

Bruno said, "I agree, if it all goes well, you can let Ildiko try riding Gray Boy outside the corral." Ildiko and Diana clapped and jumped with glee. They were ecstatic. Mikl and Jon hugged and thanked me, Bruno, and Janos for our trust in them. Tomorrow morning would be a long wait.

That night while Ildiko and I ate our evening meal, I asked if she was healthy enough to ride Gray Boy tomorrow. I did not mention the word "pregnant," thinking it would be a less offensive approach.

With that, Ildiko took a deep breath, sighed, and exhaled. She frowned at me. She began speaking slowly and deliberately with frustration in her voice. "Daven, pregnancy is not a health problem. It is normal, and it shows that I am healthy. Every mother before me has done it. I am healthy, and yes, I am pregnant. I have been pregnant for four months, but there is nothing wrong with me. Even when I went on the bear hunt and walked all those hours back and forth to the village, I was already pregnant. I would not have missed the bear hunt for anything, and I will not miss being the first person to ride a horse. So please stop asking and stop worrying."

Her stern lecture continued, "Having a baby will be a wonderful change for us, and you will be a wonderful father. Our baby will know horses, and best of all, he or she will know their mother was the first person on this earth to ride a horse. Now help me clean up so I can get some rest. Tomorrow is a big day."

I hardly got a word in, but at least I knew she was pregnant and I would be a father again after all these years. I was overjoyed. Even though I am the lead hunter of a powerful group of men and a clan leader, I was just scolded by a five-foot-six-inch beautiful, pregnant woman. I just love her and her spicy attitude.

By morning, the word was out. "Stay back and stay away from the corral." The villagers did stay back and away, but not all that far away, just far enough. The whole idea of a woman sitting on a horse was almost too much to imagine. Until last year, we had never even captured a horse, and today, Ildiko was going to try to ride one.

Bruno motioned the trainers forward. He only said, "You are ready." The group of them approached the stable and called Gray Boy with a whistle in the usual manner. Ildiko climbed on the rafter and lowered herself onto Gray Boy's back just like every other day. Diana put the bridle in place along with the footholds. Mikl and Jon walked Gray Boy into the corral with leashes and hobbles in place just as they had done so many times before. Gray Boy responded well to the netting. As Ildiko pulled left, he turned left, and then he turned right as directed. He was rewarded with a pat on his neck. Everything was the same.

Then it all changed. The leashes were removed, and Jon removed the section of fence we called the gate. Ildiko guided Gray Boy in a circle around the corral once more before she directed him out and through the gate. Once outside the corral, he reared slightly and snorted. Ildiko let him settle down before she gently kicked with her heels to let Gray Boy know he could go forward. To her delight, he did just that.

At first, he moved at a walking speed. She gently prodded him again with a light flick of the reins and a gentle kick of her heels, and he went to a trot. She had never ridden him at a fast pace, and it was a jarring up-and-down motion. She felt a slight pain in her lower stomach area and then in her groin, but she ignored the pain with the excitement of the ride. It took a few minutes for Ildiko to realize that the rider needed to keep pace with the horse rather than the opposite. The entire village including children and elders watched in fear expecting something bad to happen.

Off they went out of the village while everyone watched. When she pulled the reins, Gray Boy turned as he always did. When she pulled straight back on both reins, Gray Boy slowed and stopped. They were at the far edge of the village when she turned Gray Boy around and headed back. It could have not gone any better. Ildiko stopped Gray Boy in front of the trainers and the cheering crowd. Out of excitement, the villagers pushed right up to the corral fence.

Ildiko yelled to Mikl, "I am taking one more ride." No one said anything to disagree with her. She was in charge, not me, not Bruno, just her. She kicked her heels a little harder this time, and Gray Boy jumped forward with his two front feet off the ground. She gleamed with excitement, but felt another sharp pain. She ignored it. Instead, her smile was from ear to ear, and yelled out, "What a thrill!" They were out of the village in no time, and after a few minutes, they were out of sight. Ildiko rode back and stopped in front of everyone… she was still smiling.

Ildiko exclaimed, "I felt like I was flying, like a bird leaving its nest for the first time!" It was a feeling of total freedom for Gray Boy and for Ildiko. She yelled over and over, "What a thrill! What a thrill!" She yelled, "That was the most exciting thing I have ever done!" She was thrilled beyond imagination and talking fast as she described her ride. "The return trip was much too short." She unknowingly placed her hand on her stomach as she talked about the ride.

The first person to come to her was Diana. Ildiko jumped off and handed the reins to her. It was Diana's turn, but there was no way for Diana to get on the horse until she walked Gray Boy back to the corral so she could climb on using the fence. She was the second person of the Botai to ride a horse.

The crowded grew in size as everyone watched in disbelief. Diana followed the same route that Ildiko had taken and returned to stop right in front of everyone. The riders smiled broadly and talked of how exciting it was to ride a horse. Everyone cheered, including the trainers, me, Janos, and Bruno. That was when I saw that Ildiko was bleeding. I asked her to walk with me and Patts back to our house. She felt the wetness and looked down to see the reddish color. She winced in pain.

Ildiko was ordered to stay in bed and to do almost nothing except bathe and eat. Patts stayed the night and visited every day after that. Patts said, "If you stay in bed, you will have a healthy child, if not, you will lose the baby." Ildiko followed orders. Fortunately, the bleeding stopped after a week and Patts let her resume normal activities, but no more horseback riding until after the delivery. A close call was avoided. I did not say a word about "being healthy."

There were never so many proud feelings for any women in any clan. Before today, they were cheered at festivals for their hard work. Today, women were heroes, and it was all due to Ildiko and Diana. They were celebrated as were hunters when they had their best day. Bruno and I were proud of our wives and proud and of our sons, Mikl and Jon, who made all this happen. After today, there was no further doubt, everyone wanted a horse.

Diana rode a second time the next day, but this time she was on Dawn. Later, Mikl and Jon rode Star and Gray Boy alongside each other. They now had plenty of volunteers who wanted to join the training team. Dawn had a bit more difficulty following directions, but the ride was another success. All those long hours of training paid off. Each rider described their experience the same way. "It was like being a bird in flight, like a soaring eagle. It was flying without wings. The speed is hard to imagine. It is a fantastic experience like no other."

The next day, Diana mounted Star in the stable and headed out of the corral. Jon opened the gate, and Diana directed Star forward. This time, Star ran at a full gallop straight ahead. Diana held the reins and wondered if Star was running back to the grasslands and the freedom she once knew as an adult horse.

Diana let Star run for a while before she pulled back on both reins, but the netting slipped to the side, and the horse continued to run forward at top speed. They were out of the village and heading into higher grass before the horse tired and slowed down on her own. Diana never panicked. She just held the reins and rode it out. By jerking the face netting from side to side, she finally got it back in place and turned Star back to the village.

Diana knew the face netting needed to be better and started to work on it that same day. She had such a good way with the horses that they trusted her and let her do almost anything she wanted with them.

She gently plied Star's mouth open to look inside and examine her teeth to see if something was wrong. She looked for the reason that the netting slipped sideways. There was no soreness or any problem she could see, but Diana noticed a gap between the horse's front teeth used to bite off grass and the next set of teeth used to grind grass.

Diana thought that was unusual and perhaps just a flaw that only Star had. She called Mikl and they both examined Gray Boy's teeth and saw the same gap between his teeth. Jon and Ildiko joined Diana as they inspected Babe and Dawn. To their surprise, all four horses had the same natural gap between their teeth.

Diana thought that if a piece of soft thick leather ran between the sides of the face netting and through the gap in their teeth, the netting would not slip from side to side as it did when she pulled on the reins with Star. Diana added the new piece of leather to the netting, and it worked just as she thought it would. The face netting was more certain, and it never slipped again.

The trainers and their horses were the talk of the village. Bruno's promise of a horse for every hunter had everyone willing to work extra hard to reach the goal, and there was a new purpose for the village. The Botai were years ahead of everyone else. With horses, they could move from one location to another faster than anyone else could, and they could carry all their supplies at the same time. Travel that took a week before would now take only a day or two. Hunting will change. Our world was different, and it was better.

CHAPTER 22

Thrown to the Ground

BRUNO SENT ORDERS through his clan leaders to begin construction of new stables and corrals. Men and boys of every age were recruited. Now that the ground had thawed, we could start building more double stalls for future horses.

The workers included every male of age, but Flint barely did any work at all. He watched while some of us trained the horses and the rest of us worked. Jon noticed him standing there and asked if he wanted to join the trainers, but he waved his hand, dismissing the idea as if it was below him. He walked away without making a response. Flint did just enough that morning to seem to be doing something. Not much, just something. I mentioned to Jon and Mikl that if they asked Flint to join the team again in a day or two, he might drop his pride and admit that he was interested. I told them to be patient.

Since the horse training was going well, I thought I would take a minute to visit Tedd and Janos to see how the three-curve bow work was going. They were boiling, shaping, and drying wood. The final step was gluing it together with resin and wrapping the ends with fine strips of wet rawhide. When wet rawhide dried, it shrank and tightened the binding. I saw several bows in various stages of completion. They had several helpers from each clan, and all of them were working hard. I stayed for a while to encourage them and watched the interesting process. They assured me that every hunter would have a new bow before the first horse hunt.

I checked on the stone carver. Dann was creating the likeness of Ildiko riding Gray Boy on a huge stone that faced somewhat toward the sky and faced the village. That project did bring good luck and was moving along pretty well too. I wondered if the village could be peaceful and quiet for a month before the first horse hunt of the year. It seemed that there was so much excitement for so long that the winter went by faster than it usually did.

It was the right time to talk to Bruno. I still had my concerns with Flint. Lately, he seemed to be getting interested in the horses and their training and showed particular interested in Gray Boy. Gray Boy was a beautiful horse, the easiest to train and the easiest to ride. He took commands better than any other horse and worked whenever we needed him. Maybe I was wrong about the arrow that was too close to Jon's head, but I was not wrong about Flint being responsible for exposing the hunters on the last bear hunt and the injuries they were dealt. On top of that was his attitude. It was miserable. It was only in the last two weeks that I noticed any improvement. I wondered if he had he turned the corner? Was he on the way back? Still, I did not trust him.

As I approached Bruno's pit house, I heard loud voices. At first I thought it was Bruno trying to settle another dispute between a man and his wife or some other issue that would have had me looking for a cave to hide in for a month if I were the Oldson.

The usual practice when visiting another couple's pit house was to call out to them as you approached to see if the owner or another family member was home before entering. If no one was home, you did not enter. I listened as I approached and hesitated for a minute because I heard voices inside. What I heard was a heated family discussion. Bruno and Diana's two daughters were already outside talking with friends, so I knew the discussion was not about them. It was something else.

I clearly heard Bruno. His voice was stern, and I also heard Diana and Flint. Bruno said, "Son, I have seen you sulking since I named Jon as the Bear Clan leader. I also saw you with your head down when you were denied any reward in bear claws after the last hunt—"

Flint interrupted his father before he was finished talking. "It was not all my fault. There were three other hunters there, and everyone else was excited too. I did not think there was a second bear in the cave, and besides, we already had enough meat. We did not need to kill any more bears." He was arguing emotionally and in a loud voice. His words were all excuses for his poor behavior. If Flint was not Bruno's son, Bruno would have cut off his feeble argument and dismissed him immediately.

Bruno let Flint say what he wanted to say before stating firmly, "Flint, you are wrong, it was your fault. You were the senior hunter among the group of men guarding the rear of the cave, and it was your assignment. It does not matter what you thought about us having enough bear meat. The hunt plan was laid out, and all of us knew our roles. That includes me and you. Daven is the lead hunter in all cases. It is the job of everyone else including me and you to carry out the plan. You did not do your job. In another hunt, it could cost a hunter his life."

Diana said nothing. She knew Flint had not been himself since Jon became the Bear Clan leader and now wore the clan leader's necklace. Bruno continued in a raised voice. He was angry. "The clan leaders were right in not rewarding you with even one bear claw. If it was my call instead of theirs, I would not have given you one either. You will not receive claws because your father is the Oldson, you have to earn them." Flint tried to argue, but Bruno continued.

"Flint, we have another more important issue to discuss. I saw the arrow that you shot, the one that was far too close to Jon's head. I am sure it was to let me know that you were not happy with my decision.

"Jon never saw the arrow, but I saw it, and I am sure Daven saw it.

And I am sure some of the other hunters saw it too. I know what you are thinking, you should have been given the Bear Clan leadership and you are telling me that you are angry. You have not asked me why I named Jon instead of you, but you need to know."

Flint was quieter and calmer now, although he was still feeling sorry for himself. He shouted at his father, "You showed favoritism, not judgment, and the title went to Jon because Jon is your favorite son, not because he is better than me at anything." Bruno shook his head saying no. He took a deep breath and let it out in exasperation. He wanted Flint to settle down and listen before giving his reason why he picked Jon to lead the clan.

A minute had passed before he continued. "Flint, it is true that Jon was firstborn. Botai rules say he was entitled to the position by birthright alone. However, that is not why I named him. That was the reason I gave to the village and a reason that allowed you to save face. You could have explained to anyone who asked, that I did what the rules call for with the firstborn male son inheriting the title of clan leader. You could have said that the decision was made just the way it was always made. It would have been enough of a reason for anyone who asked. Now, since you have stirred the pot, I want you to hear my true thoughts.

"Over the last six months I have seen you withdraw from being a leader. You took little interest when we hunted horses. You stayed in the rear and let others lead, and you asked me if you could stay home and guard the village. That is hardly the role for an experienced hunter.

"You did not get involved with constructing the three-curve bows, and you have shown no interest at all in capturing or training horses. Lately, you have gone your own way and let the rest of the Botai men carry you. I do not blame your wife Suse since she has been working hard, gathering with the rest of the women. It is you, Flint. I need leaders, hunters, and hard workers. I do not need a lazy son who sits in the back and lets others do his work. Those are the reasons why I chose Jon.

"I warn you, if you do not change, and I mean change right now, you will be shown no favoritism as my son when it comes to a penalty.

If I do that, I am not being fair to the rest of the village. I did not show favoritism with Gertrude even though she was Daven's wife, and I will not do it with you. So you have a choice. You can be the man I knew for so long, or you will have to face the consequences."

Diana said nothing. She knew Bruno was right, both as a father and as the Oldson. Flint had become lazy and withdrawn. Bruno was the leader of the Botai, and Diana was a leading trainer and the second person to ride a horse. Jon has shown leadership on hunts and with the horses. Bruno is the Oldson. They expected more from their children, and she knew Flint was not doing his share. He certainly was not being a leader.

I sensed that the discussion was just about over, so I decided to leave. There was no need for me to talk to Bruno about the arrow. As I walked away, I thought that not only was Jon the leader of the Bear Clan, he was in direct line as the firstborn son to become the next Oldson when Bruno passes on to the spirits or gives up the position someday due to old age.

Flint sat on the sleeping bed of his parents with tears welling in his eyes. His face showed anger and jealousy. He wiped the tears away and left the house saying nothing to either his mother or father. He would tell his wife his version of the story, favoritism and more favoritism. He had to think of a way to get even. He had to do something. He was not sure what to do, but his anger was not about to go away.

He went to his own pit house and pleaded his case with his wife, Suse. She listened, and as always, she took his side. She loved him and did not know anything about what might have gone wrong on the bear hunt. She only knew what Flint told her. It was true, he was down in spirits after his brother was named Bear Clan leader. She had always believed what Flint claimed, that it was favoritism by his father, and she had no knowledge of the arrow incident.

Flint smiled and said, "I have a plan to show them, show them all." She listened to him, and she thought, Flint would calm down and come to his senses. He just needed time. Time would heal him. She was sure he would become his old self again in a few days. Suse loved him too much to see the truth. Flint was over the edge as was his plan.

The next morning, Flint met Mikl, Jon, and me at the corral. Diana and two more trainers joined us a little while later. Flint asked if he could become part of the horse training team. I thought that perhaps his father's words made him think or that he may have come to his senses after he talked to his wife. Sometimes, wives have a way of making their husbands see that there is more than one solution to a problem, especially when their husband was on the wrong side of the argument.

For the rest of the week, Flint took part in watering, feeding, and removing manure, all the usual startup duties for a new trainer. Soon his duties increased. He walked horses in the corral and put on hobbles and removed them. He brushed the horses when they were in the stall, and he watched as various riders took turns getting on their backs from the rafters of the stable. He did not just watch them, he studied them. So far, only the core team and two new members have ridden outside the corral. It annoyed Flint that Peter and Patrick, sons of a clan leader and younger than himself, were already riding horses, and he was not yet allowed to do the same thing.

We planned to take all four horses on the first horse hunt of the year. We intended to use them not only going to the hunt and on the way back but to ride them as we approached a herd. Wild horses have never seen a mounted rider, so they might not be alarmed and allow our approach as long as our scent would not be detected.

Occasionally, a wild horse will approach a herd, but unless it is a mare, the dominant stallion will chase off any other horses he might think are challengers. Approaching on horseback might make capturing mares and their foals easier and less dangerous as compared to trying to capture them on foot.

Flint became part of the team, and the horses began to know him. He was fitting in, and after several weeks, we thought he might take Ildiko's place as a rider until her pregnancy was complete. At this point. she was six months along and was only allowed to ride a horse at a walking pace.

Flint complained to Mikl and Diana that he had not yet ridden any of the horses. He said he was ready and commented that it did not look all that difficult. I thought I detected some anger in his voice and held off before moving his development any faster.

I took notice when I heard Flint say, "I will arrive early tomorrow morning and start the day with feeding and watering. The rest of the trainers can take a break with the early arrival time."

Jon commented to me, "Flint seems to have turned the corner. Why not let him prove himself and allow him to start the day tomorrow?" I saw the look on Mikl's face. He was not so sure, and neither was I. I sensed something, it was my nature.

It was a month after Flint shot the arrow so close to Jon's head. His anger about his brother having the clan leader title was still fresh in my mind. And I remember his behavior and tone of voice during the discussion with his father while I waited outside Bruno's pit house not that long ago. Something did not feel right. At Jon's request, I gave Flint permission to start the day, but when Mikl and I were alone, I asked him to arrive at the usual time the next day. "No, I said, we will arrive a bit earlier than usual." Mikl agreed; he must have had the same concern.

The next morning, as Mikl and I approached the training area, everything seemed normal at the first stable. I took a breath and relaxed. Maybe I needed to trust Flint more; maybe he had really changed. Maybe I was too suspicious. Maybe not.

We walked to the second stable that held Gray Boy and Dawn, and we saw him. Flint had Mikl's horse in the corral with the gate section already open. When Flint saw us approach, he hurriedly climbed on Gray Boy from the corral fence and slapped the long reins on Gray Boy's flank and rode off. Flint looked back and yelled, "I will show you, I will show them all." He rode out of the village toward the woods.

Instinctively, we ran behind Gray Boy. Mikl stopped, took a deep breath, and whistled. It was the familiar call, and Gray Boy knew the command. The whistle told him to come to Mikl. Gray Boy slammed his front hoofs to the ground and turned to the right very quickly. The fast turn slammed the inexperienced Flint to the ground.

By now, Peter and Patrick and several other villagers gathered around Flint lying on the ground. Gray Boy walked to Mikl who rubbed his nose and gave him a chunk of apple. Flint was on the ground, stunned and bruised from landing so hard. He just lay there for a while. Then we saw his wife, Suse, come out of the woods with two packs and Flint's bow and arrows. It was obvious, Flint was going to steal Gray Boy and leave the Botai to go somewhere else. At this point, more hunters and their wives arrived to see what was going on with all the commotion.

Everyone saw that Flint was caught trying to steal a horse. Thievery was a punishable crime, and Flint knew he had to face the consequences. He would be banned. It was only a matter of how long. Flint sat up and looked at the ground. His plan to steal Gray Boy, and to "get even" was a failure. He was marched back to the village by the hunters and brought to Bruno. Bruno told Flint to go to his pit house and wait there to be called.

Bruno met with the three clan leaders and the elders to decide Flint's fate. It was difficult because Bruno had to make a decision on his own son. He had warned Flint a month ago that he would not show any favoritism. The decision had to be similar to what would have happened to any other member of the Botai if the circumstances were the same.

For the first time, Bruno asked the three of us if anyone saw anything unusual on the bear hunt. Of course, I told what I saw. The arrow was much too close. Janos was unaware of the arrow incident because he stayed back to build the new bows, and the elders had no knowledge of the incident. Jon said he felt the breeze of the feathers pass his head, but he gave Flint the benefit of the doubt. He said, "Maybe Flint had a clear shot and the arrow was not all that close."

As I listened to the discussion, it seemed obvious. Flint took that shot on purpose. Bruno explained to the group that he had a serious discussion with Flint several weeks ago where he warned him that his ways had to change. Bruno said, "There will be no more second chances, and there is no question of his guilt. Flint tried to steal a horse. He also took a chance with that arrow, and he caused two hunters to be wounded. " I said nothing further. Bruno had said it all.

Bruno asked for suggestions for punishment. Since we did not whip anyone as some tribes did, the punishment would be banning. The elders recalled past banishments and suggested a period of two to four weeks. The most recent banning was that of Gertrude. She caused a death and was hated by all for not contributing. She also stole food, but it was not a factor. Before that, it was hard to remember the last banning of anyone for more than a day or two. I suggested, "He should be banned for three or four weeks, maybe more. He could have killed his brother, and horses are too valuable to treat this lightly."

Jon had no input. Flint was still his brother, and he loved him. He thought about all the good childhood memories and could not consider the thought of punishing his twin brother. He said, "I will leave it up to the three of you since he is my brother." Jon was learning that being a clan leader was not an easy job, especially when family was involved.

Before we made a decision, we questioned Suse to learn what role she had in this incident. We found that she had no role at all in his plan to steal Gray Boy. Flint only told her that they were leaving for a few weeks. She thought she was just going on a trip with Flint. He told her he was ready to ride and had permission to take Gray Boy for a few days of travel. We told Suse that Flint was to be banished and that she was free to go with him or stay here with the Botai for the term of his banishment. We brought Flint into the room to learn his fate.

Bruno spoke, "We all know that you tried to steal a horse and that you failed. Horses are the most valuable possession of the Botai people. The trainers have spent almost a year with these animals. They are our future. I am sure that if you had been successful in stealing that horse, we might never see you again since you were already packed to leave for good. If you had your way, by now you would be on your way to your next destination, wherever that might be.

"The clan leaders and I will let you go to that destination on your own, but you will go there without a horse. You are banned for one full month. You are not to be seen by anyone for that time. If you are seen, the ban will extend for a second month.

"If you return here, your status with the Botai will be that of a twelve-year-old boy. You will have the duties of an unproven youth. You will carry manure and work for the women until you become a man again. It is your choice to take your wife with you or leave her here. If you do not take her with you and you do not return to this village in one month, she will be free to divorce you one month later and marry any other man of her choice."

Flint was defiant. He scolded us as he said, "I will leave tomorrow morning. Do not expect to see me again. As of today, you have just one son and two daughters. The other son who was born too late to be of value to his father will exist only as a memory. The favorite son will be yours to worship as you have always done."

He showed his anger when he said, "Just as you threaten me, I threaten you. Do not expect me to keep your precious secrets of the three-curve bow and that of the horses. Those secrets will make me a valued and welcomed member to another people. Any other tribe can use another experienced hunter, especially someone like me who knows your secrets." Flint turned his back and left without another word. Bruno kept a straight face, but he felt sorrow over the parting. He and Diana hoped that time might heal this wound, and perhaps they would see Flint again at the summer gathering. Today's discussion was over.

Flint went to his pit house and gathered his weapons, extra clothes, and a large supply of food for the long trip to the east. He would travel lightly and would not take Suse with him. She would be a burden on the trip. She was just someone he would have to feed and take care of while he traveled. She would remarry soon enough, and he would easily find a replacement wife.

Flint wondered if Suse was barren since no children ever came. He did not care any longer. That was someone else's problem now. He knew he would bring great value to Ander's people as an experienced hunter, and every tribe needed hunters. There would be plenty of women who would love to be his mate. He was a handsome young man and had no worries about that.

He also knew the secrets of the Botai, the three-curve bow, and how horses were captured and trained. He would be warmly welcomed by Ander, and in his mind, he would lead a clan before the end of the year. He also knew that Ander's father was dead, how he died, and he knew who killed him. That might be of interest to Ander, but this news was not of much value since no one knew where Gertrude was or if she was still alive. He left early and never woke Suse.

CHAPTER 23

Green Stones

FLINT HAS BEEN gone for over three months with no sign that he was coming back. No one has seen him. Suse was without a husband and had no means to keep her pit house repaired. She had been operating without a man's help. Like every other house, the roof needed repairs from the winter snows as did the walls and floor. She gathered wood as best she could for cooking and heating, and she worked with the women as always, but she did not have a husband to help her with heavy work. Living alone was not for her, so she tied the door closed and moved in with Emma, the elder of the Aurochs Clan. Emma has been alone for many years since her husband passed away and welcomed the company.

As the weeks passed, Jon felt responsible for Suse as the former wife of his brother. He checked in on the two women to be sure they had enough firewood and horse meat for their stews. He also performed the necessary repairs on the thatched roof and filled the walls with clay where it had frozen and fallen out after the bitter winter.

Even though Suse was Jon's sister-in-law, the more he was around her, the more he realized that he hardly knew her. At first, other than a polite greeting, they barely talked about anything. The relationship was formal in the beginning. As he did the chores and helped the two women, Jon and Suse got to know of each other. They slowly became more comfortable with each other as a man and woman.

To his surprise, Jon learned that Suse believed everything Flint told her. She was blind to his faults, but little by little, she came to know what really happened with Flint. It was not Jon who was the favorite, and it was not Jon who told her the truth. It was Emma and Ruth and several other women with whom she worked while they gathered in the fields. Women, especially older women with marriage experience, knew what Flint was all about. He was all about himself. It took a while, but Suse started to see the truth, and what she heard was not good.

There were other people too who were Suse's friends, and they all told the same story. It was not favoritism, it was Flint. He was immature and lazy and lacked leadership. She came to understand that she was fooled by him. By now, she knew he did not care about her. He left her behind without even saying good-bye; he just disappeared.

When Flint left, he never intended to come back, yet she mourned his leaving. It was as if her husband had died. After feeling sad and lonely for weeks, she became angry and then became indifferent toward him. At two months, she did not care about Flint any further. She lost the love she had for him at one time and moved forward.

Her first thoughts were to attend the summer gathering with the Botai where she hoped she might find a new husband. That was in the beginning, when she mourned her loss. As she got to know Jon better, she thought about him more every day and less about finding someone at the gathering. Having Jon at her side, hopefully as her husband, was almost too much to wish for. She told herself many times that Jon was just being kind and fulfilling a family duty to provide for her. She should not expect too much beyond that.

Physically, Jon looked exactly the same as Flint, but that was where the similarity ended. Jon was a caring and warm man and had the qualities Flint lacked. She often thought to herself, *How did I marry the wrong brother?* One evening, she finally asked Emma. Emma responded, "You did not look hard enough, young lady."

Suse knew there were many tribes who attended the summer gathering. Many of the young men were there for the purpose of finding a wife, even a wife like her who could not have children. She thought it would be better to be a second wife than not having anyone to love her and provide for her the rest of her life.

Jon continued to visit her, always trying to be of help. Suse waited for his visits and tried to look her best when he did come. When he missed a few days, she made an excuse to go visit him. Still, in her mind, Jon was probably doing what was expected of him. She wondered if Bruno, as Oldson and as Flint's father, perhaps told Jon to provide for her until she remarried. Was he doing what custom called for or was he doing more than just being polite?

She hoped for more. Suse loved being around Jon and could talk to him for hours. Jon was always on her mind. When he stayed away for a day or two, she missed him. She wanted Jon to want her as she wanted him, but she told herself, she had to be realistic. He was doing what was proper, what he had to do.

Today, I visited Tedd to get his advice. While I was on the bear hunt, I was sure that I saw a few of the green stones people called copper. At that time I was too busy with the hunt and the safety of the men to think about it much more and hardly remembered the exact location of those stones. Copper is a workable metal that can be pounded into shape and sharpened to a point. It can also be pounded into thin pieces, polished, and made into beautiful necklaces and jewelry such as arm bands. It also made workable buttons to close jackets and tunics when winter winds howled. But it was rare and hard to find.

I described what I saw to Tedd and he told me, "From what you said, Daven, those stones were probably copper, especially if it looked greenish in color. It might be just green from mold or mildew, but it is certainly worth another look."

Tedd's advice was "If you can remembered where you saw the green stones, and if you think you can locate the spot again, why not ride back and see if it really was copper. If it is just a moldy rock, one hard hit from your stone ax will tell you the story. A stone will crack and copper will dent.

"If it is copper, collect what you can find and look below the leaves and debris for more." Tedd suggested, "Daven, take a spade and dig a few feet in the ground if the ground is soft. It is very likely there may be more copper than what shows on the surface." I decided I had to try to find it. Our craftsman could pound it into shape in exchange for a small portion of what I find. What was left over would make a great item for trading next summer.

Craftsmen made copper ax heads for hunters that were mounted on a handle about sixteen inches long. An ax like that made a deadly weapon for close combat even though it was soft compared to a flint ax. In the hands of a strong hunter, a copper ax could kill a wolf or even a mountain lion with a single blow to the head. Bruno killed a bear on the last hunt with one. The problem was that after one or two uses, a copper ax head had to be heated, reshaped, and sharpened with a whetstone due to its softness. At times, a copper ax works better than a stone axe for close fighting because of its heavier weight and smaller size.

Copper could not be used to make arrowheads for the same reason—it was too soft. What we really needed was a way to harden copper so it would be more useful for weapons or tools. We tried making knives of copper, but they bent after one use. No one had an answer on how to harden it, so we continued to use flint for our arrowheads and knives.

It was too early in the year to hunt horses, so I approached Mikl and told him that I was thinking of making an overnight trip to search for copper. I described what I saw and shared Tedd's advice. Mikl loved the idea. We were both anxious to get out of the village for a few days and decided to take our horses, Gray Boy and Star, and ride back to see if we could find the green stones. I told him that I had my doubts about finding the same location, but I wanted to go anyway.

When I mentioned the idea and my doubts to Mikl, he smiled and said, "Father, I know the way. You did not travel back and forth to the hunt as I did with the horses. And you forget, Father, that except for the last part of the hunt, your men marked the trail with their axes. Those marks are only a few months old and will be easy for us to follow."

I said, "I did forget. The trail was already marked. We should find the copper easily."

The trip would be two days and one night, but it was a chance for us to have some father-and-son time together. Alone time with Mikl has been hard to find, especially since he moved out of my pit house and with the arrival of the horses. He and Diana have been the key trainers and were very busy with most of the new ideas coming from them.

We packed our carrying bags with a good supply of pemmican for the overnight trip since we did not intend to hunt along the way. We carried our three-curve bows and arrows in case we needed them, and we packed two small flint shovels on Tedd's advice to search the area. Hopefully, we might find more copper just below the surface.

A year ago, this trip would have taken a week or more, and if we were lucky enough to find any copper, we would have had to carry the heavy load of metal back with us. Now, with horses and the dragging platforms, the whole trip was different. It took far less time and required far less labor on our part. Riding horses, instead of walking all that distance was a pleasure. I packed only the leather platforms knowing that we could easily cut new poles for the return trip.

By midafternoon, we arrived at the spot where I thought I saw the nuggets and searched the ground. Everything was covered with leaves and looked the same. We dismounted and looked closer. With both of us searching, we spotted a few green stones, and then we found more. There was more copper than we would need for years. We picked up what was lying on the ground. Then we got the shovels and dug below the surface, and just as Tedd advised, we found more copper than we could carry.

We packed the leather carrying platforms and left it close by for departure in the morning. When we were done, Mikl and I filled in the hole so the ground looked smooth and undisturbed to a passerby. I added several fallen limbs to disguise the find. After that, we marked the location with three small piles of rocks and cut two trees off at the height of my head so we could find the same spot again. The markers were discreet and hard to notice, unless you knew what you were looking for. There was no sense loading the horses with too much weight; we could always come back if we needed more.

The night was an easy one. We made a fire in front of our tent and ate a meal and talked of many things. It reminded me of a long time ago when Mikl was a young boy and we took overnight trips together like this one, to hunt or just to experience nature. Tonight, it seemed easy to talk with him like it was back then. Of course horses and their training were the number one topic.

Mikl asked what my plans were for the spring hunts. I told him, "We need to take two or three stallions to fill our food needs for the next month or so. After that, the goal is to capture mares that were pregnant so we can increase our numbers of horses. Each pregnant mare equaled two horses in the long run. There would be no foals this early in the year. Hopefully, foals born into captivity would be easier to train than full-grown horses like Star. Gray Boy was a good example. He was a young horse when we captured him, and he was the easiest horse to train. We need more like him."

I explained further, "Mares are pregnant at this time of year. They are slower and easier to catch now than at any other time. On the second hunt, there will be mares with early foals and still some pregnant females. So this year, the hunt plan will be different. Bruno wants our hunters to be fully mounted by the end of two years, so capturing horses is more important than killing extras for food reserves. We will take only what we need for food right now and capture all we can."

Mikl said that he liked the plan. He was quiet for a minute or so and changed the subject when he said, "Father, I have been thinking about taking a wife now that I am a full hunter, and I have wondered what it was like to be married to a woman like Ildiko." His wording was a nice compliment, not only toward Ildiko, but also to me. I was pleased.

I responded, "Marriage can be wonderful if you have the right woman, but it can be awful if you have the wrong woman. The right woman can make your life beautiful, enjoyable, and fun, but the wrong woman can make it an absolutely nightmare." He laughed at the old Botai saying.

Mikl asked, "Father, was Gertrude the wrong woman?"

I said, "I have to admit that yes, she was the wrong one, and it was my fault for picking her. When she was young, she was a beautiful woman, but that was all there was to her. In the long run, she was a bad choice for a wife and a worse choice for a mother. Ildiko is the opposite. She was the right choice." I said, "It was too bad that Ildiko was not your real mother because your experience of being a son would have been much different and much better. Plus, you would have had a few brothers and sisters to grow up with."

Mikl hesitated while we watched the fire. Then he said, "Father, I need you to help me find an 'Ildiko' woman for me at the summer gathering. I mean a good woman to be my wife."

I promised to do so and told him, "With the copper we found today, you will have something of value to trade, but you do not need copper to find the right wife. You are a handsome young man with ideas and just the type of man that women want. You are tall, strong, and an excellent hunter." I also told him, "Be confident when you look for the right person, because every father would be proud to have you take his daughter as a bride. Maybe we can even throw in a three-curve bow in return for the right woman!" We laughed.

The protective fire burned brightly. Sparks popped and made a cracking noise as we talked. One hunting trick I learned a long time ago was never to stare at flames because if you looked into the darkness right after looking at flames, you would not be able to see anything. It was as if you were blind for a few minutes until your eyes adjusted. Mikl reminded me of that advice again tonight. He loved to repeat things that I taught him as he grew up.

Before we drifted off to sleep, I said to Mikl, "My best advice is not to pick a woman on the very first day of the summer gathering. If you do, your choice will most likely be based on looks alone. Take your time and look beyond the surface. Men are easily tricked by a woman's beauty, just the way nature designed it all. Bees go to the most colorful flower when the sweetest flower, the one with the most nectar, might be right next to the prettiest one."

He replied, "I will be careful, Father. I will pick my flower the second day." I added a few pieces of wood to the fire, and we drifted off to sleep.

We returned with enough copper for the craftsmen to make new ax heads, and we had plenty left over for trade next summer. The craftsman cleaned the surface and pounded what we did not need into rounded ingots.

Mikl said that he had another idea. He thought copper might be used as part of the bridle to connect the sides of the netting instead of the leather pieces we used now. The village craftsmen went to work on Mikl's idea and made a ring.

Diana remade the netting and added the copper ring. The new idea worked better than the old leather connections. When it was all done, the craftsman was proud of what he made, but he commented, just as Tedd had said earlier, "We need a way to make copper stronger so we can make knives and arrowheads that do not bend." No one had that answer. Overall, the trip was great, and I felt as though I knew Mikl better than ever. It was like when he was a child and told me everything.

Mikl and I walked Gray Boy and Star to the corral to feed and water them where Diana and two trainers were hard at work. I saw Jon coming to help us with our horses, and to my surprise, Suse was walking at Jon's side. Mikl did not seem surprised to see them together. It made me think that friends know more about each other than their parents know at times.

Tomorrow, I needed to talk to Jon, Janos, and Bruno. The horse hunt had to happen soon, and my plans were already set. As I told Mikl, we needed a month's supply of meat, but we needed to increase our herd more than we needed meat reserves.

CHAPTER 24

The Mountain Lions

DAY AFTER DAY, the men and I worked hard building double-sized stables and corrals for the next horses we expected to capture. While I worked, I thought about our goal. We wanted to be the first mounted hunters in the world, or at least what we knew of the world.

We were sure the world was a lot larger than the grasslands and mountains we hunted, but how big it might possibly be was another question. To the north we knew that the Ob River emptied into a vast sea where the water was too salty to drink. The Volga River, on the west side of the Urals, ran south to another sea that looked like it might be as large as the salty sea in the north, but there the water was clear.

Grasslands extended to the east and to the west for many miles. Old oral stories said that if you traveled farther to the east, there was a desert so dry that nothing at all grew. It was called the Gobi Desert, which means "waterless place." From listening to others at summer gatherings, we knew people have explored beyond those areas. No one was sure just how large it all was.

I was more concerned with the problems of survival that we face today and year after year. I worried about hostile people who someday might try to take the land we considered to be ours. It happened before, so I know it could possibly happen again. This time we will be ready if they come our way, but our numbers are small.

At times, I wonder about the old village beyond the Urals. It was where I was born and lived with my parents until they were killed by the Smolens who finally drove our small clan out of the area. When we lived there, we never had more than about fifteen to twenty members of the Horse Clan. We depended on the annual reindeer migrations for our meat supply and gathered what grew in the area. We also hunted deer and horses. Back then, we had just a few hunters and had little success hunting horses. I also wondered how large the Smolens might have become by now and if they had outgrown the old village. If that happened, they could become a problem for us once again.

I knew if we were to be successful defending ourselves in the long run, we needed an advantage over them being a larger group than we were. We have to be able to fight and hunt with bows and arrows while we rode on horseback. To do that, we needed to capture more horses and build more stables to house them.

As soon as the work on the new pit houses—or as we call them now stables—were complete, I wanted to try shooting my bow while I rode Star. No one had tried it yet. I wondered if it could be done with any confidence because riding a horse was not a smooth experience. It was an up-and-down motion and not what a hunter wanted while shooting a bow.

During the midday meal, I talked with Jon and Mikl about the idea, and we decided it was something we had to try. The three of us were experts with our bows and the best riders other than Diana and Ildiko.

Diana was not a full hunter, although she was quite capable with a bow. Ildiko was a very good hunter, but a very pregnant woman right now. The three of us were the logical choices to try shooting from a running horse. I rode Star, Mikl rode his horse Gray Boy, and Jon rode Bruno's horse Dawn, although it seemed that Dawn was more Diana's horse by now. She worked with Dawn constantly and rode her far more than Bruno. He was always too busy with one disagreement after another. He called them "community affairs," which sounded a lot better than arguments.

We mounted up and rode in a straight line at a gallop toward a fixed target. We shot our bows as we closed on it. Our attempts were disappointing. We missed the target, and we missed badly. We tried again and again, but we missed again and again. After two hours, we were more frustrated, and we were getting worse the more we tried.

After so many attempts, the horses became tired, and I nearly fell off when I concentrated too hard, trying to be the first of us to hit a target. Jon did fall off, which gave us a good laugh and an excuse to stop for a while. With the horse hunt being just a few days away, this would not work. If we were hunting horses today instead of shooting at a stationary target, we would have returned home with nothing to eat. Hunting from horseback might be possible, but it would take a lot more practice. Another problem became obvious: the piece of leather we called a saddle needed to be improved, so we asked Diana for help.

She went to work at the suggestion. In a week, she improved both the footholds and the saddle. The saddle was now secured to the horse by two belts. One belt ran under the horse and buckled underneath. A second belt went around the horse's lower neck and attached to the first belt in front. This kept the saddle from sliding forward and backward and offered a nice improvement over what we had before.

With the new saddle and footholds, horse and rider became one, moving in a fluid up-and-down motion. We practiced shooting our bows again, and learned that shooting while riding at speed worked better if the shot was taken when the horse was at the top of its galloping motion. It seemed to be a matter of time and practice before we perfected the skill.

When I returned to my pit house, Ildiko complained, "Our supplies of meat are getting low, and what remains is getting slimy. It smelled as if it is going bad." I knew that when my wife complained of slimy meat, it was time to hunt. My hunt plan was designed around what I was sure would work. Horses would be used to assist the hunters going to the hunt and returning home in a similar manner to what we did on the bear hunt.

I told Bruno of the bow-and-arrow practice on horseback and how hard it was to fire an arrow with any accuracy. I told him, "I believe it will be possible, but for now, we have to use what we know has worked in the past. We have eighteen fully trained hunters. However, six of them have only limited experience with what they gained last year. There were only two fourteen-year-olds this spring, Peter and his brother Patrick, so the burden with beginners would be light.

Bruno and I agreed to keep the practice session on horseback to ourselves for now. When it was perfected, we would share our success with the village, not before. I did not need doubtful hunters; I needed confident ones. I knew that early failures often became successes with more practice, just as we saw with the three-curve bow.

As usual, I thought about keeping hunters back at the village for protection. I had several older men who could help plus Agi and Ildiko, but both of them were pregnant. There were six boys aged twelve and thirteen plus Tedd who could take part in an emergency, but no one to lead the group. There were also a couple of women who could use a bow. Because I was uncomfortable with such light protection, I asked George to stay back to be sure Agi and Ildiko had enough help in case of a problem. George agreed to stay behind.

In return, I promised to capture the next horse for George. Naturally, he was a bit disappointed in not joining us, but he also saw that he was needed to protect the village. Agi, Ildiko, and Tedd were not enough in numbers in case of an emergency. George also wanted to be sure Agi was not exposed to unnecessary danger, especially since she was expecting her baby soon.

Bruno agreed with the protection plan, but he was much more interested in our bow practice session on horseback. He asked for every detail and said, "I can see the possibility of mounted men hunting and traveling on horses in the future." He talked about the time when we might have to defend our people if it became necessary, saying, "We can never again be driven out of our lands as our parents were." I knew he was right. We were not relocating, not ever again.

After Bruno and I spoke, I walked back to check on Ildiko. I thought about how villages like ours grew too large for the available food supplies and how the original people expanded to new territory just as we did with Ander when he moved to his current location. When the Smolens took our old village from us, we only had a few people left. The pit houses we left were not large in number. Certainly, they were close to expansion by now if they had not done it already. It was a long-term concern, but not an immediate one. My thinking was that if we captured the horses we needed, we will be well on our way to being fully mounted. A fully mounted group of men were a lot harder to defeat than men on foot, so the hunt today was all that much more important.

Bruno told me to hold the hunters' meeting. Attendance was a must for every adult male whether they were going on the hunt or staying back to protect the village. The hunt would be held in three days. That allowed Janos and Tedd time to complete a three-curve bow for every man making the trip.

Before we left for the hunt, Bruno and I wanted to see the carving of the woman on the horse completed. If we left before it was finished, we thought it might be a bad omen, and I purposely delayed the hunt until three days after. Now it was complete, except for final polishing and details. For our purposes, it was finished. Although the rider was a clear likeness of Ildiko, it was missing something, but I was not sure what it was.

We held the meeting outdoors in front of the new monument, and I thanked Dann, who created the carving. He was also a hunter, and I dedicated this hunt to him. He stood up when I mentioned his name as the carver, and the group gave him a cheer. I also noticed that some of the men referred to him as Dann Carver instead of Dann the carver. Talk like that made me wonder if anyone talked about me as Daven the hunter or Daven Hunter when I was not present. I doubted whether this idea would ever be permanent because no one needed two names. One was enough.

As I described the plan to the men; it was familiar because it was an evolution of what we did on the bear hunt a few weeks earlier. We would head east at twenty-five miles at our usual fast pace. And as in the past, we would use drive hunting. Bathing before our departure was part of the process. Most times, I think unwashed people smelled a lot worse than horse manure.

The first day, my plan was to kill bachelor stallions to satisfy our overdue needs for fresh meat. The second day, we would continue east for another twenty-five miles, but no farther in order to avoid any contact with Ander's men who would be very likely hunting also at this time of year.

I made one more announcement. "There is no longer a need to carry manure with us because from this day forward, we will have horses with us, and they can supply fresh horse manure whenever we need it." That brought a cheer from the youngest hunters who were scheduled to carry the manure. "However," I said, "there is a catch. When new hunters join us for their first hunt, they will still have to carry a small bag of manure as part of our Botai tradition." The experienced hunters voiced their approval with a cheer. Tradition was important.

We left early that morning and arrived at our first camp in plenty of time. I woke well before sunup and saw that Mikl and Jon were stirring as was Bruno. I roused the others, and we got moving while the drivers were left to sleep. It was dark with clear skies with just enough starlight to see our way as we followed a faint path running along the edge of the grasslands. We went forward about three miles before spreading out in a single long line that penetrated deep into the grasslands. With the glow of daylight starting to show, we knew the drivers would be coming soon. An hour later, I heard the familiar whinnying sound of horses being pushed.

I saw a group of four horses as they trotted nervously, coming in our direction. They moved together and stopped to look in front and behind them. They smelled the air and stamped their hooves. There was something or someone approaching them from the rear, yet they sensed something in front of them too. The muffled noise of men talking in low tones was enough to push them on.

As soon as they got within range of our lead line, we stood up and used our three-curve bows. Three of the four horses were hit with several heavy arrows in the body and neck from a longer distance than was ever possible before today. The fourth horse made a sharp turn to the east and escaped. The dangers of last year's hunt were no longer a concern. We brought them down before they were close enough to do us any harm. Not one hunter was threatened today.

The plan worked so well that not even the drivers knew we made the kills until they came upon us and saw the downed horses. Both drivers and lead line hunters saw how the new bows offered a safer way to hunt. It was midafternoon when we finished butchering the meat. That night, we enjoyed our evening meal of the best cuts, and several hunters talked about how well Mikl's original idea worked. The new bow performed better than any bow we had used before. There would be no eating pemmican tonight. Tomorrow we would continue in an easterly direction for the second and more dangerous part of the hunt.

Back at the village, there was no air of celebration, there was terror. It started when our wolves howled as they smelled the mountain lion and her year-old cubs as they cautiously approached our village. The female was a huge adult that weighed well over two hundred pounds. She slowed her approach when the village came into view and she sniffed the air, first in one direction and then in the opposite one. She smelled the scent of horses even though they were no longer in the village. She was looking for an easy meal of perhaps a young foal or a pregnant mare that might be too slow to escape. The distinct smell beckoned her forward.

At the sound of the wolves howling, George quickly directed the defenses. He placed the two older and experienced bowmen plus Tedd and himself and four young boys in the first line of defense. This group was between the mountain lions and the village.

The second line of defense was made up of three women, two older men, and four boys, and it was right in front of the main entrance to the village. Ildiko and Agi were in the second line of defense. The defenders must have looked formidable as the three lions came to a halt. They continued to smell the air and look for horses. George gave orders, "Do not shoot any of the animals unless the female passed the walnut tree. If she passes that tree, we have to attack them before they attack us."

George shouted again, "Kill the big female first, but only if she passed the tree. The second must group hold your fire. You will defend the first group as they retreat to your line and renotch their second arrows. From there we will make a stand." George knew that if a fight could be avoided by holding off for a few more seconds, everyone would be safer. The bow practice against panic was never more important than it was right now. George wished everyone had a three-curve bow instead of just Tedd and himself.

The big female lion looked around in confusion. She saw people who were ready to fight, but she smelled horses. Her cubs waited for her lead. The smell was strong. However, there was no horse herd in sight. Instead it was a village with a dozen defenders.

George saw her hesitate. He took the opportunity to add to her confusion. He told the defenders to yell at the lions in their loudest voices, "Go back where you came from. We will kill you and your cubs. Go back! Go back." The rest of the defenders followed his lead. They yelled and stamped their feet to distract the lions while the wolves snarled and growled. It was a tense moment that felt like an hour before the lion recognized she was up against what looked like a superior foe with two lines of hunters and a pack of growling wolves. She retreated, and her cubs followed with not one arrow being fired. The group of old men and women breathed a sigh of relief while the boys celebrated.

George acknowledged the group. "You were brave, and you followed orders. You did a great job. If not for your help, those lions might have had their way. With your help, they left defeated to hunt somewhere else. Good job, boys." He especially acknowledged the young boys who felt as if they protected the village while their fathers were away on a hunt. The older villagers smiled, and the boys congratulated each other and beamed with pride.

George placed two guards all day and all night on opposite ends of the village until the main group of hunters returned. The incident gave the boys a chance to show the rest of the village how brave they were. They were heroes and had something important to boast about. That night over the campfire, George told them, "You are hunters just like your parents, and you saved the village. You should be proud of yourselves."

Back at the hunt, we packed the butchered meat on the carrying platforms and sent four horses loaded with meat and several hunters and trainers back to the village. Our path would be easy for them to follow from this camp to the next since we walked in a single line and intentionally packed down the old grass down as we went. It took the rest of the day to reach the second campsite.

Since we had enough meat already, I changed part of the plan. If a stallion approached the lead line of men, we would move aside and let it run past. We wanted the mares and the foals they would deliver in a month or two. The lead line would work in groups of three and stay hidden in the waist-high grass until a mare approached. Then they would suddenly stand up and surprise the mare. Two of each group of three hunters would use their lariats, and the third man would keep his bow ready to protect the other men if it was needed.

By that evening, Diana and her group reached the village. They unloaded the supply of horse meat for smoking and ate a meal. They heard the story of the mountain lions and how the boys helped George, Agi, and Ildiko protect the village. The older men and women smiled and let the boys tell the exciting tale.

Diana and her group returned to the hunt early the next morning. They brought a good supply of apples for the horses we expected to capture. Diana rode on horseback, but the rest of the returning team was not trained and had to travel on foot. After so many hours of walking, they learned a hard lesson on the value of being able to ride.

Grasses hid us well as we waited. By midmorning, we heard the herd approach. It was large, with a stallion, six mares, several foals, plus a couple of yearlings. We held our ground and stayed hidden. They stopped and looked to the rear where they heard the unfamiliar sound of voices off in the distance. I watched the stallion as it ran between Jon and Mikl. We let it go.

Just then, Bruno stood up in front of an approaching mare. It stopped in surprise. The light brown mare with the dark mane reared just as we thought it would, and Bruno landed his lariat on a front foot. Janos threw his lariat and landed his too. I waited until a mare was almost on top of me when I stood up quickly. I threw my lariat as did my two companion hunters.

There were horses everywhere. With so much action, I did not see a young female horse running past me, but Jon saw it and threw his lariat as did one of his hunt partners. We pulled on their feet and took them down. Being pregnant, they tired quickly. We caught four pregnant mares and one young stallion. It was already a great day. A two- or three-year-old stallion ran by me, and I yelled to the bowmen, "Kill it," which they did.

Bruno asked me, "Daven, why the change of mind? Why did you tell the men to kill that stallion?"

I laughed and replied, "After such a great day, we deserve to eat well tonight." He heartily agreed, and we did just that, we had a feast. We had five horses at home, if we counted Star and her coming foal. Today, we captured four mares and a young stallion. If we counted the mares and their foals, we have fourteen horses, and the year was still young.

By noon, we saw Diana riding into view. The rest of her party arrived on foot an hour later. On our return to the village, Bruno and I presented George with his first horse, a pregnant female. Agi would own the foal when it was born. Janos walked toward his pit house with his sons, Peter and Patrick. I heard him tell them that they would own their own horses with the next group we caught. With any luck, that would be very soon. Both already had riding skills as part of the training team. Now all they had to do was wait for their turn. These two young men were welcome additions as hunters, and there was no better bowman of any age than Peter.

Our hunts over the next four months produced the same success. We killed what we needed for food and captured five more stallions, eight adult mares, and ten young horses under a year of age. We had more horses than we had hunters by late summer with two hunts still in the plans. Bruno met his promise, and he did it a year early. Every hunter had a horse of his or her own. Two horses went to Ildiko and Diana as trainers, and Peter got his horse from his father on his fifteenth birthday as promised. The biggest surprise of all occurred at the next feast when three women were recognized for their hard work over the years. Bruno awarded Ruth, Emma, and Judy with a foal of their own.

CHAPTER 25

The Second Arrival

GERTRUDE HAD BEEN living with the Krasnyi Yar as a goat herder for about six months. In the beginning, Ander had several women watch her every day. She was smart. She did what was expected of her and stayed out of trouble. After a while, she became part of the village activities, and no one paid much attention to her. Her routine was her own. She was merely referred to as Gertrude, the goat woman. Gertrude used the lack of close scrutiny to her best advantage. Ander made a mistake when they underestimated her.

She kept to herself. In addition to the food she was given for the work she did, she killed a good portion of the male baby goats as soon as they were born and ate them. What she could not eat the first day, she hid in a clay pot that she buried just outside her pit house. She ate the rest always at night when the village was asleep. In a day or two, she was hungry again. Her behavior was never noticed because she worked at several distant locations, meeting with other herders where the animals from the two herds became mixed. When the two herders departed a distant location, they took an equal number of goats but kept the same lead animals.

While moving her herd from one location to the next, Gertrude trained four large female goats to carry sacks with supplies on their backs and to drag poles that attached to their sides. She loaded them with weight as they followed her from one grazing area to another. After months of this, they became used to the exercise. She knew she would have to leave the Yar village in a few months and these trained goats would help her carry clothes, supplies, food, and weapons when she left. Her plan was to eat them only as a last resort.

Gertrude wore an oversized, loose horse hide frock that hung down to her ankles to hide her swelling body. After several months, one woman noticed that over the last few months, Gertrude had steadily gained weight. Because of the hard work and limited food supply, it was unusual for Krasnyi Yar women to be heavy. Her neck was full, her face was fat, and her belly pushed forward on her loose-fitting frock. One woman, the wife of a clan leader, and a friend of hers accused Gertrude of stealing food and eating more than her fair share. The two women had no evidence of wrongdoing, but she never liked Gertrude from her days with the Botai.

Gertrude explained to the woman, "I have a digestion problem. I gain weight because there is something wrong with my stomach." She whined, looking for sympathy. "The digestion problem makes me get fat when a normal person eating the same food that I eat would not gain weight. My mother had the same problem. It is not my fault, and I cannot control it."

Gertrude went on with her plea. "You should feel sorry for me, not accuse me of stealing food. I am a sick woman." A third woman joined the first two. They argued with Gertrude and made accusations, pointed fingers, and scolded her, but they had no proof.

Gertrude forced a few tears when she said, "You are lucky you do not have this problem. It is the reason why my husband left me. He said I was too fat, and he told me that he wanted a younger woman with a slimmer body." Gertrude was a very convincing liar.

The three nosey women walked away in anger. They were sure they were right, that Gertrude was a thief, but they let the issue drop for now. As they left, they yelled back at her, "We will be watching you, thief."

Gertrude knew her time with the Krasnyi Yar was limited because as soon as Ander met with the Botai at the summer gathering, the truth of what she did would be known. Ander would learn that she was the person responsible for his father's death. In her mind, the incident was not her fault either; she had diarrhea that night. She was sick. It was not her fault. With the summer gathering still several months away, she felt safe, at least for now.

While she worked with her goats, she heard stories and rumors from other herders. They talked about many things, mostly gossip, but the most interesting rumor was that of a village farther to the east where another people lived. They were called Mongols. Their leader was called the Khan, just as the leader of the Yar and the Botai was called the Oldson.

She also heard that Mongols were odd looking, had yellow skin, and flat faces. They were short, fat, and most women said they were not intelligent, more like animals than people. No one knew much more. Gertrude knew that rumors were often exaggerated and, at times, totally false. She was not worried. She assumed these people looked about the same as every other white-skinned person she ever met. She still thought of herself as attractive and hoped there might be a man for her among these Mongols.

She planned to leave the village in late summer when many of the hunters, some of their wives, and several young people looking for wives or husbands attended the gathering. No one would know when she left. She planned to slip away unnoticed while she worked at a distant herding location and leave with a good-sized goat herd. The herd would supply her with meat and milk for as long as she needed, at least until she reached the next village. It did not matter to her whether she lived among the Yar or another group. Among Mongols, she would find a way to survive especially if she brought a large herd of goats with her.

Gertrude was confident she would be welcomed to join them and spend the rest of her days there.

Her departure plan changed completely when she heard the commotion the next morning. Someone new had arrived at the Yar village. Men and women alike rushed forward to see who the visitor was and what news they brought. Gertrude stayed at the rear of the crowd out of the way and watched. To her horror, she recognized him! It was Flint, the son of Bruno. Her first thought was that he must have been sent here with a report of what she did. Gertrude moved quickly and without panic. She had a plan for this day.

While Ander, the clan leaders, and the rest of the people greeted the newcomer, she made her way to the opposite side of the village and entered the pit house where the goats were held. These were her goats now. She quickly gathered her belongings, the food she had hidden away, plus water, blankets, and a tent. Her weapons were ready. At the last minute, she stole an extra quiver of arrows from a nearby pit house, and she was off. Most important of all, she made sure her four trained goats were among the herd she took as her own. The villagers were too excited with the visitor to notice that she was not among them.

Gertrude strapped on her special footwear she made just for this occasion. Her boots looked like normal women's boots, but on the bottom, there were goats hoofs attached to the sole in front and the heel in the back. When she walked, the boots left tracks that looked like any other goat wandering to or from the village. Tracks like these were everywhere, and a few more hardly made a difference. It would be very difficult if not impossible for even the best hunters and trackers to follow her trail.

She took thirty-two goats with her and left in a hurry carrying most of her supplies on her back. What she could not carry, she placed in sacks carried by the four large female goats. The load was heavy, but she would only have to carry the supplies for a two-day walk. While the rest of the village celebrated the arrival of the newcomer, she traveled over twenty miles that first day and continued to move forward through the first night without sleep.

Late the next morning, just before midday, Gertrude stopped her rapid pace and found the dragging poles she hid in the brush some time ago. She attached leather platforms to the poles made from discarded goat skins and loaded most of her supplies on them. She buried her goat-hoofed shoes in a hole and covered them with rocks and debris, for them to never be found. Her trained goats would do most of the work from here. The dragging poles left faint marks on the green grass. These light marks were gone when a light rain fell for an hour, which allowed the grass to flourish with new growth.

In the meantime, Flint was concerned with telling his story as to why he left the Botai. He thought about what he would say for many several days before he arrived. Like Gertrude, none of it was his fault. He left because of favoritism by his father toward his slightly older twin brother. He came to the Yar for a new start. The new village offered him a new chance to show his hunting skills. He also knew the secrets of the new three-curve bow and that the Botai had trained horses. Flint was confident of a warm welcome.

He told his story to Ander and his clan leaders and a few others in attendance. The fact that the Botai had captured and tamed horses was exciting news. It was so overwhelming that his reason for leaving was hardly discussed at all. The conversation stayed on the topic of horses for much of the morning. Ander wanted to know how it was done and what he and his men could do to follow their relatives' lead. They discussed traveling back to the old village before the summer gathering to learn more. This was the most exciting news of their lifetime.

After lunch, the discussion then turned to the second secret, that of the three-curve bow and how it was a much more powerful weapon than their older bows. Flint showed his own new bow as an example, but since he did not actually make it, he could not build one for Ander.

During the discussions, the fact that Bruno was the new Oldson and that Ander's father had passed away came up, but not that Gertrude was responsible for his father's death. Flint had no idea Gertrude lived with the Yar and never brought it up. Ander, hearing about his father's death, assumed it was due to natural causes. He would ask for more details when time allowed and with less people present.

Gertrude was not mentioned until two days later. The reason her name came up at all was because the woman who accused Gertrude of stealing food noticed that she was missing. Even then, it was assumed she was out of the village with her herding duties, as it was not unusual for herders to stay overnight for two or three days at distant grazing locations.

Two more days passed before the nosey woman alerted her husband. Because his wife was always gossiping about someone, he ignored her griping about Gertrude, and another day passed. Finally, he checked the goat pit house and noticed that the remaining goats were complaining after not being fed or milked for days. When the husband checked on the animals, the herd looked smaller than the usual. He thought that some of the goats might be missing, but no one knew for sure how many goats were in camp or how many were being grazed somewhere else. One thing was certain, Gertrude was nowhere in sight.

Gertrude traveled in an eastward direction, hardly stopping for anything and having no idea how far she would have to go before finding the people called Mongols. At the end of the third day, the wind abated, and she climbed a rise and looked for smoke on the horizon, but saw nothing. She thought the distance must be farther than rumored.

She talked to herself, saying, "It is time to kill one of the goats and have a decent meal. I deserve it. I hope those nosey nagging women have no meat to eat tonight." She looked at the herd and pointed at one goat in particular. She said out loud, "I will eat her favorite black-and-white goat, the one she fed with treats all the time. The one she called Sweetheart." Gertrude laughed at the thought. She ate Sweetheart' with lust until she could not swallow one more bite. The next day, she loaded her supplies and food on the dragging poles and walked toward the sunrise.

Gathering food along the way became more difficult as the land became dryer and more barren. Grass was shorter here compared to where the Botai lived, but still plentiful enough so the goats were well fed. As always, Gertrude was hungry. She found peas and lentils and a few berries along the way. She uprooted tubers with her digging stick as she walked and ate raw wheat and oat grains along the way. She thought about killing one more goat. That would give her a week of fresh meat and certainly take her to the next village. She tried to hold off killing another one but could not ignore her stomach rumbling for a good meal. That night, she feasted on Sweetheart's daughter.

As before, she stayed in caves at night with the goats. Where caves could not be found, she used her tent and lit a fire. She kept her bow ready in case wolves came to her fire. Over time, she got better with the bow, but she had a limited supply of arrows and could not make more. She had to be careful. She killed a wolf that came to her tent the fifth night of travel. Luckily, there was no pack, just a young male loner. The meat was gamey tasting and bitter, but she ate it as she did on her last trek. She was back to survival and to starvation. She had to hold off eating another goat. They were the only value she brought.

Flint settled in as a Krasnyi Yar resident. He shared a pit house with another bachelor, a younger man than he was. It was good to have the company of someone just to talk to, but he wanted a woman. He had his manly needs. He never thought about Suse unless he had the need for sex. Suse was old news.

Any woman of age would do just fine, but to his dismay, there were few to pick from because this was a smaller tribe compared to the Botai or the Hungarians. The few unmarried women were either too old or too young. The one female of age was from his clan, so she was of no use to him. It did not matter. He would easily find a woman at the summer gathering. His next wife, unlike Suse, would bear him many sons. Sons he would treat fairly and without favoritism.

Ander visited Flint a few days after his arrival, allowing him time to settle into his new location. Ander wanted to know how his mother was and how his father died. He also wanted to hear all the news he could get about the old village. He was a Botai at heart and missed his old friends and family. He wanted to know about his friends, Bruno, Janos, and his son Peter, and he asked about me when he said, "How is Daven?"

Flint told Ander about his friends and family. His mother, Ruth, was well and was involved with every clan. But his father died many months ago. Ander was saddened once again at hearing the bad news. When he heard about the death first time, Ander thought his father died of old age. Now Flint told him, "Your father died not of natural causes."

Flint told the whole story of the painful death and how Gertrude was responsible. Ander was stunned, and he was angry. He had given that woman a home. Now he knew the truth. Ander wanted to make her pay for what she did. He called his five most experienced hunters and trackers and ordered them to start searching for Gertrude.

The search started that same day. His men looked for Gertrude in ever-widening circles starting at one, two, and three miles distance from the village. The others searched in wider circles at five, ten, and fifteen miles. One by one, they returned with their reports. They found nothing unusual; in fact, they found nothing at all, no tracks, no campsites, and nothing discarded.

Ander sent them back out to search again, this time in the opposite direction with the last man looking for her in a circle at twenty miles. There had to be a clue somewhere, a torn piece of clothing, discarded items, a campfire, anything to tell him where she went. He asked his men, "How is it possible that you can only find tracks of goats?"

The same thing happened after three more days of searching. There were no unusual footprints or markings, and no campfire sites. All they saw were goat prints that led in every direction. They worked in pairs the next day circling the village once again, but found no sign of her. Somehow, a simple herder had eluded them.

CHAPTER 26

Suse and Davenson

WITH MANY NEW horses captured, the village was buzzing with horse training. We were experienced, having trained horses before, and we knew what worked best. Diana, Jon, Mikl, and I had major roles along with other members, Peter, Patrick, Elizza, and other newer people.

Ildiko was temporarily absent from the team because she was ready to deliver our first child. She was spending time at home with Ruth and Patts helping her. While we missed Ildiko, we had plenty of help because Bruno told everyone in the village that if they wanted a horse, they had to train, feed, and water their horse daily. If anyone did not do their part, the horse would be given to someone else. No one hesitated because everyone wanted a horse of their own.

Women wanted a horse to help lighten their workload, to have a chance to ride, and to provide milk after a mare delivered a colt. The milk was either drank fresh or made into a lightly alcoholic fermented drink called Koumiss. Koumiss was bitter and had a strong taste, but it was said to be very healthy especially during winter when our usual foods were unavailable. Koumiss was like other drinks that one might not like the first time they tasted them, but it got better each time they drank it.

Two of the pregnant mares we captured have already delivered their foals, and two more will deliver any day. When the first two horses were born, it made me think, these were the first horses born in our village. It was a wonderful thing to be able to watch these baby horses as they took their first steps so soon after being born. In a few days, they were able to run and kick their rear legs with delight. The ability to run at such a young age must be the reason horses survived when other animals died out. Foals followed their mothers everywhere, nursing at every opportunity.

On the next two hunts, we killed what we needed and captured more pregnant mares and a huge stallion about seven or eight years old. We tried our best to be as gentle as possible when we captured mares so as not to hurt the mother or the unborn baby. It was a two-day walk back to the village and one female delivered her foal the second day while we were on the trail. It was only a matter of minutes after the mother cleaned her baby that the foal stood up and followed its mother toward our village. The process fascinated us.

The big adult stallion we captured was another story. He was a real fighter and gave us problems from the time we took him to the ground. He fought us all the way. Getting him to move in any direction was not easy, but I was determined with this one because Bruno wanted a big horse to carry him. We doubled the bags he carried and loaded them with wet dirt to the very top, hoping to tire him out. He bucked them off, and we refitted them and tied them twice. His load of mud must have been equal to the weight of two men. The horse resisted and kicked at every chance. We shortened the hobbles on his legs and tied extra straps from the front to the back. He was not ready to give up his freedom as he complained with snorts and whinnies.

We placed two heavy lariats over his neck and tied the lariats to our lead horses. They put a steady pull on him from the front, but he resisted and pulled backward. We had to prod him from the rear with the blunt ends of our spears to get him moving while being careful not to get too close. One kick could kill a man, and this one kicked hard and often.

I thought this horse might never cooperate. He finally tired and gave ground stubbornly, but he stopped constantly and pulled in different directions, always resisting the lariats. The question among the men was, Could this big horse be trained after eight years of freedom? I was determined. This was the perfect stallion for Bruno. If we could not train him, he very likely might become the first horse to be eaten after being captured. We eventually reached home and placed him in an unused corral where his training began.

Mikl and I were busy training the new horses when our lead flint knapper, Dann, asked me if I could ride out to the flint quarry and bring back an additional supply of flint. In the past, we used the closest quarry for our needs, but over the years, all the workable rocks were used up. All that was left were huge rocks that could not be moved. Now with horses, we could reach the second and larger quarry. The round trip that once took a week or more on foot now took just two days.

Before I could consider the trip, I had to check on Ildiko to see if I could take the time away. My normal routine was to check on her twice a day with her nearing delivery. This time when I asked about the trip, she replied, "I am doing just fine." This was her usual response, but this time, Patts assured me that everything was normal.

Patts reminded me, "When Ildiko delivers her child, you will be of little help, so take the trip. We probably need the flint more than Ildiko needs you right now." I was relieved.

We left the next morning, rode at a steady easy pace, and reached our destination that night. Mikl gathered wood, and I made a campfire to ward off any unwanted nighttime visitors. After we set up camp and ate our meal, we lay by the fire on our sleeping mats and talked like we always did when we were away from the village. I said to Mikl, "You will have a brother or sister soon, maybe even by the time we return."

He remarked, "Father, you are a lucky man to be a father again. You will be able to teach your new son or daughter all the things you taught me when I was a young. This time, your job will be harder because there is so much more to learn with horses being part of our lives. Knowing Ildiko, your child will be the youngest Botai ever to ride a horse."

I agreed, saying, "I am sure you are right, Mikl, boy or girl, this child will be a horse rider like its mother, and perhaps be the best ever. When you start something difficult like riding a horse at a young age, it is easier to be good at it when you reach my age."

Mikl told me, "Father, I want to do the same as you have done. I want to marry and have children of my own and make you a grandfather. I want to improve my hunting skills, find new ways to do things, and someday be a clan leader." I smiled to myself in the dark as the glow of flames warmed my face. I was happy to hear he was thinking seriously of marriage and children.

Mikl said, "Father, I need your help at the summer gathering. I have been thinking about this since we talked a several weeks ago. I want to find a wife who has more to offer than good looks, more than just beauty, I want someone like Ildiko."

This conversation was familiar, like the one we had when we camped out when we gathered copper. I told him, "Your future wife will be looking for someone exactly like you. If she was a member of the Botai, you would already know her. In my mind, she is not here, but she may very well attend the summer gathering, looking for you."

He changed the subject. "My friend Jon is in love with Suse, but she is hesitant to tell others of their affection for each other because Flint might return at some point. Knowing Flint, he will make trouble even though he left Suse without a second thought for her."

I agreed and replied, "Flint could show up one of these days either at our village or at the summer gathering. My advice to Jon is that Suse should divorce herself from Flint in a formal way so everyone in the village would be aware that her previous marriage is over. After that, she can do whatever she wants to do without a second thought. Marriage and divorce are simple procedures with the Botai in case things did not work for either the man or the woman." The rules protected the children who stayed with the mother, as did the pit house because a man could build another.

Mikl asked about the divorce process, and I told him how it worked.

Mikl then told me a huge surprise when he said, "Even though Suse never got pregnant by Flint, she is pregnant now by his twin brother, Jon. I am surprised, because they are twins. I thought they were exact doubles of each other, but apparently not."

That was a jolt! Everyone thought it was always the woman who could not have a child. This situation changed that thinking. It seemed the problem could also be with the man. I took my time before I said anything and finally replied, "I am glad for both of them, but since Suse is pregnant, that makes the matter of divorce and marriage much more urgent."

Mikl replied, "I will talk to Jon as soon as we get back. He listens to sound advice." I thought about Suse being pregnant before I dozed off to sleep.

In the morning, we loaded the flint on our leather platforms and started for home. Gray Boy and Star dragged the load of flint with no problem, and we made our way back to the village by evening. I was exhausted from riding my horse all day when I reached my pit house. Ildiko was resting, and Ruth was staying for the night in case the baby came. I sat on the extra sleeping platform and talked with them for a while before drowsiness overcame me. I kissed my wife and said goodnight. Then I walked to Ruth's house, which was empty except for Mikl who was already asleep.

Several hours before daybreak, Ildiko's first scream woke me. Ruth got up and called for Patts, who arrived in a few minutes. The screaming went on every few minutes, and I hardly slept at all. It was hours before it stopped. When it stopped, I sat up with a start. It was too quiet, and I was worried. Then the screaming started again, this time it was a smaller voice with a higher pitch, the sound of a newborn. I hurried back to my house, and Ruth greeted me at the door with a smile.

She said, "It is a boy, and he has all his toes and fingers." Counting fingers and toes was what people did when a baby was born. It was supposed to be a sign that everything was normal, but in all this time, I had never heard of a baby with the wrong number of fingers or toes.

I was thrilled. I would have been just as thrilled if it was a girl. A girl like Ildiko was a beautiful thought and another boy, one like Mikl, was wonderful.

I entered and went to Ildiko's side and kissed her on the forehead. She said, "Our son, Marc, is ready to meet his father," and she uncovered his fuzzy head. He was beautiful with light brown hair and blue eyes just like his mother. I was overjoyed. Marc was her father's name and a perfect one for our son. As soon as I calmed down, I was overcome by exhaustion and sat on the sleeping bench next to her bed. I was still tired from the ride and from being awake all night. Fathers always wondered why children were born in the middle of the night instead of the middle of the day.

Ruth said. "Daven, you look terrible. Go back and get some sleep." I was glad to follow her orders. I kissed Ildiko once more and told her I would be back bright and early in the morning to see her. Despite Mikl's snoring, I slept like a bear for the first time in two days and made my appearance the next day much later than I planned. With the focus on Marc, no one noticed my late arrival.

Ildiko had no further problems that night and handled the delivery just as she did when she rode Gray Boy for the first time or walked all the way from her original home. She said it was normal, and I had to agree, she was right despite my worries. Since Marc arrived several months before the summer gathering, Ildiko would be able to travel with me and bring Marc.

Marc would be the youngest Botai to ever attend a summer gathering, and Ildiko would be the center of attraction for every woman from the Hungarian people. Somehow, she got away from Kraven and found happiness with me. What made her the center of attraction was that life for women at her old village had changed for the better. Kraven was gone, and the old ways where women were treated poorly were gone with him. Males would never rule over their female relatives again, not in the old ways. A lot of the change came from the new chief, Rhoden, but Ildiko was the person who set that change in motion.

Agi and her baby, Sophia, were the first to visit Ildiko the next day, and Ildiko was delighted to see them. They had so much in common and always had a lot to talk about especially since they both had new husbands and babies. They were a new type of woman who would lead the Botai in the future. They were the Ruth, Emma, and Patts of the next generation.

Many other women visited and brought small gifts of food or flowers. For me, it was a beautiful day. I had a second son. Now, I thought, it was time for a daughter. I would talk to Ildiko "when the time was right." I had enough sense to know the "right time" was not "right now"!

Later that morning, Mikl visited Ildiko to meet his new brother. He brought a gift of apple bread that Agi had made for him. He brought news. There was an announcement coming in the Bear Clan. Suse would divorce Flint today at noon, and Jon planned to ask her to marry him right after the divorce. We had to attend. As Ildiko and I walked the short distance to hear the news, I whispered the secret of Suse being pregnant by Jon. She was thrilled for Suse and assured me that she could keep a secret. Ruth carried Marc and said it was time for Ildiko to get out of bed anyway. A brief walk was just what she needed.

Mikl had another story to share. "Father, most of the village members refer to Marc as Daven's son and have already lengthened his last name to Davenson." I thought about what Mikl said. If my boy continued to be called Davenson, he would join Dann Carver as the second member of the Botai to have two names with the second name giving information about the person. In my mind, no one needed two names. One was always enough in the past, but things were changing everywhere. I had to agree, Marc Davenson did sound distinguished, like someone important.

Just after the midday meal, Jon, as the Bear Clan leader, went through the formality of announcing to his clan, "Flint was banned and has not returned. He has not been seen for over three months, and his past wife, Suse, wants a divorce." He said, "Suse, please come forward."

Suse stepped to the front, holding the wedding jar in her hands. She lifted the jar over her head and threw it to the ground where it promptly broke into pieces with the sand splayed on the ground. In her loudest voice, she exclaimed, "I divorce the man I was married to, the man named Flint, son of Bruno!"

The crowd cheered her announcement. Immediately after that, Jon got on one knee and asked in a loud voice, "Suse, will you marry me?"

She screamed out, "Yes, yes, yes, I will marry you, Jon!" She had a big smile on her face when the couple kissed and hugged. The Bear Clan yelled their approval. No one was surprised because Jon and Suse were seen together every day. There was no word of her pregnancy, that announcement could wait for a few months.

One thing that I noticed was that Patts was not present at the ceremony. In their rush to get married, they forgot to invite her. They did ask for her blessing later. I wondered if that mistake meant there might be trouble for them at some time in the future. If so, trouble would most likely come in the person of Flint, and it would come when it was least expected.

By the end of the week, life in my pit house had settled into a new routine that included three people instead of two. It seemed to be natural and worked very well. Life was good again. Ildiko was a devoted mother as well as a loving wife, and I was back to training horses and building houses for them and thinking about hunting.

My long-range plan consumed my thoughts. I wanted to be able to ride to a hunt and back home again all on horses. I wanted to capture more of them and increase our herd before the next winter. Once we had enough horses for our needs, we could breed our own, and the herd would expand in a natural way.

I talked to the other clan leaders with another new thought. Just as people could not marry within their own clans, we had to be careful not to allow interbreeding with horses. I proposed that we make three horse clans to prevent related horses from breeding too closely. The idea was agreed upon, and another change was made. This one came from me.

Chapter 27

The Confession

FOUR OF US continued to practice shooting our bows while riding on horseback. Our first attempt a few weeks earlier had been a failure, because I was too impatient and rushed the process. This time it would be deliberate and carefully done.

To start, we shot our bows while the horses walked. Even at a walking pace, the bowman had to release the reins to shoot. We learned to hold the reins with our knees. That way, it was easier to grab them once again after taking a shot. I fell off once as did Jon, but we were not injured. Mikl laughed at us and made sure we did not forget it. We practiced day after day, and we improved. After many days of practice, we finally mastered the new skill and could shoot our bows at a gallop. I kept Janos and Bruno informed of our progress.

Bruno set up a demonstration day a few weeks in advance. He wanted to display our progress to the village. The date, set in advance, gave us time for more practice. Bruno also needed the time to work with his new stallion he called Boomer. Bruno wanted to be able to introduce the demonstration on horseback, but Boomer, captured after so many years in the wild, needed a lot more training.

Bruno called for a feast to celebrate our spring hunting success. It was to be held on the first day of the next full moon. It gave us extra practice time. When the day arrived, he addressed the village, "The promise of a horse for every hunter has been met. And with your help, we did it a year earlier than I thought possible. With any luck, every adult, whether they are a hunter or a gatherer, will have a horse of their own by the end of this year. Next year, we expect to have a horse for every boy fourteen years or older. Girls can have a horse when they become of age or when they marry." The crowd cheered his announcement, knowing it actually was an advantage for girls since they occasionally married before age fourteen.

Bruno recognized Ildiko of the Horse Clan as being the first person to ride a horse and Diana of the Bear Clan as the key woman on the training team and the first person to deliver a baby horse. "Women are part of the Botai," he said, "as wives and as leaders." The crowd yelled their approval.

Bruno also thanked the elder women for their wisdom and leadership. "Our supplies lasted through what we once called the starving months of winter." He identified Ruth of the Horse Clan, Emma of the Aurochs Clan, and Judy of the Horse Clan as the leaders. They stood up, one by one, and acknowledged the cheers.

"Now," he told the gathering, "you will see another step forward for Botai hunters. Please stay seated right where you are and watch and enjoy this demonstration." Bruno whistled as the four of us rode into sight in front of the crowd.

Each of us made a coordinated motion at the exact same time as we took our hands off the reins and held our arms out to our sides for all to see. They could not see the reins tucked under our knees. Then we grabbed our bows from our backs, notched an arrow, and held it directly in front of us for a few several seconds so the crowd could see what we were doing.

We rode in a single file line and galloped forward. I was in the lead followed by Mikl, George, and Jon. One by one we passed the target and released our arrows, with each man striking it perfectly. We rode past the crowd, came to a halt, and turned back toward them. We heard their roar of approval. They were impressed and continued to cheer.

Bruno let the villagers savor the feast for several minutes as we stopped on our mounts alongside of him. Then he said, "I expect every hunter to finish their individual training with their horses and be able to shoot while riding by the end of this summer." He cautiously mounted Boomer and walked him at an easy pace in front of the crowd.

Boomer was nervous and still had a long way to go before he was fully tamed. He was a big horse and a handful to ride, but he was intelligent and strong enough to handle Bruno's size and weight. Bruno looked in command astride his big horse as it stomped the ground and snorted his annoyance at being ridden. I hoped Boomer behaved for a few more minutes, or we could all be embarrassed.

While mounted, Bruno requested of the crowd, "Please keep the secret of horses when we attend the next summer gathering, which is just a month away. We will take horses with us to help carry the supplies. After that, our horses will be kept out of sight." It was obvious. The future was right in front of us; it was here with the Botai. This was the best village in the world.

There would be one more horse hunt before the summer gathering. Peter would take a major role in the hunt. He easily passed his bow-and-arrow and atlatl skill tests although since the development of the powerful three-curve bow and their heavy arrows, the need for an atlatl was fading.

During his skill testing, I was amazed to watch Peter as he launched five arrows before the first one hit the ground in the panic test. I was very impressed because neither Bruno nor I or any other hunter could do this even when using the new bow. It had never been done before that day. I thought I miscounted the arrows and asked Peter to repeat the performance. He repeated it not once, but two more times. I was convinced. This young man had exceptional bow skills. I sensed that Peter would be a leader at an early age. He was certainly a welcome addition to my hunters.

The feast was over. Ildiko was quieter than usual tonight. I asked her if we should head home, which we did. The full moon glowed brightly as Ildiko and I walked back to our pit house. We heard the music played on stringed instruments in the background and our people singing the old Botai songs from the past.

Ildiko seemed tired, so I carried Marc as we headed back when she said to me, "Daven, I want to tell you something important. There are things you must know about me before we attend the summer gathering, and it might be best to share the story with Bruno as our leader. I need to tell you what happened with me and Kraven, and how I escaped from him."

I always thought there was more to the story and that Ildiko would tell me when she was ready. Whatever the problem, there had to be a solution. I walked to Bruno's pit house to get him. I had every confidence that he should know the full story. I called to him as I approached his house, and he came out to greet me. I told him, "I need you to help me and Ildiko. She has some information to tell us, which might create a problem for you and me at the next gathering. This time, my friend, it appears there is a real issue for you to solve."

Ildiko began her story as soon as Bruno arrived. "I was unmarried, a good daughter to my mother, and a hard worker. Other than my chores, I was free to do what I wanted until the old chief stepped down due to a serious injury while hunting. According to clan rules, his oldest son, Kraven, took over the lead of his father's clan. Kraven was not well liked because he was mean, crude, and a bully. He was feared by the men, except for Rhoden.

"Kraven was not satisfied being a clan leader. He was driven to become chief of all the Hungarian people, but he did not have the votes to get the title. Kraven came to my uncle, who was also my stepfather, and he offered him a deal. My uncle would get his long-coveted clan leader title. In exchange, my uncle had to vote for Kraven and give me to him as his third wife. My uncle made the deal, and my life became a horror.

"My uncle delivered me to Kraven the next day. He was already married with two wives and many children. Having three wives was unheard of before this happened. I knew he wanted me only for sex. Kraven was more brutal than I could ever imagine. I went through weeks of being beaten into submission and sexual terror.

"I was bruised and beaten daily and bleeding in my female part. I endured it as long as I could, and no one came to my aid. The rules allowed Kraven's behavior. No one said a word except for my mother. Everyone knew what was happening to me but did not help. After so many beatings and rapes, I came to realize that Kraven would eventually kill me if I did not do something. So I made a plan to kill him before he killed me." Bruno and I were almost in a trance listening to her fascinating story.

Ildiko continued with the tale. "I enticed Kraven into swimming with me in the river, knowing he could not swim. I told him I was ready to be the wife he wanted, but not in front of everyone else this time. He eagerly agreed to come to the river where he could have me willingly. I was in the water when he arrived, and he came after me wanting sex. Once he was in deep water, I swam to him and climbed onto his head. I pushed him under just as I saw a raccoon do to an attacking wolf. He panicked and pulled me under with him, but I expected it and held my breath. He was no match for me once we were in the water, and I drowned him.

"I stayed with him until there was no more life in him and watched as his body floated down the river, never to be seen again. If his body was found, I am sure it would appear to be a drowning, exactly as I said because, there were no wounds to be found. I followed my dream when I left with my brother the next day and came to you, Daven.

"That is the whole story. Rhoden was smiling when I told him the story and hardly searched for the body. I am sure he was delighted that Kraven was gone in a natural way, by drowning. I thought it would be best if you knew the story completely before we met the Hungarians this year. Rhoden is a wise and reasonable man. He changed the rules after

I left, so that a father, an uncle, or any male could no longer trade away his female relatives against their wishes."

Bruno and I were stunned at the amazing tale. We agreed Ildiko was innocent of any wrongdoing. She would have died if she did nothing. She defended herself when her people and their rules left her vulnerable to harm.

We both knew Rhoden and respected him. Kraven was unpredictable and a nasty problem for everyone with whom he had contact. The world was better off without him. Bruno said, "Rhoden will expect compensation for the loss of George, a senior hunter, and he might want something in return for Ildiko despite the reason why she left."

He was deep in thought. A few minutes passed when Bruno commented, "I have a deal in mind. The deal, if he takes it, will satisfy Rhoden, and it will make him a more respected leader in the minds of his people. I am confident he will take the exchange, and after it is done, we will have a better ally. Do not worry, my friends, it will all work out in our favor." Bruno stood and looked at Marc and said, "What a beautiful child. It is a good thing he looks like his mother." He chuckled and headed home.

CHAPTER 28

Hunters on Horseback

ILDIKO AND I spent a lot of time with Marc every day just watching him learn new things. It had been so long since Mikl was this age that I do not remember the little things he did as a child. I love the way Ildiko watched over Marc so protectively, never taking her eyes off of him. The simplest things like smiling in response to a new noise or someone coming to visit gave us pleasure. Ildiko often called him Marc Davenson as did the rest of the village.

Agi and her child, Sophia, visited with Ildiko and Marc almost every day. They had so much in common and so many things to talk about that they have become very close friends. Suse also visited quite often. I never remembered Suse being so alive, so animated and talkative as she was now. From Mikl's comments on our last overnight trip, I thought Suse must be in her third or fourth month of pregnancy by now, but no announcement had been made. I would ask Ildiko about that because women told each other about those things when men were not around.

In a few days, we planned to hunt for horse meat to feed the attendees of the summer gathering. Peter was on the front line in this trip with his brother, Patrick, taking part as one of the drivers. With good reason,

Peter was confident. He was not like Joe, a wobbly beginner we all doubted; this was Peter. There were no wobbles with this young man. According to tradition, he was expected to carry a small bag of horse manure as we all did in the past. That would not change.

This time, I planned to use the standard lead line of hunters but to drive the herd with men on foot and on horseback. Our goal was not to try to capture horses this time. I wanted every hunter to focus on the test of hunting on horseback. If it went well, hunts in the future would be different as they would be completed by mounted horsemen. This was a learning process.

I did not ask Bruno to ride with me as a hunter because he has not had enough time to work with his new horse, Boomer. So it will be Mikl and me who would be mounted with backup by Jon and George. Bruno did not question the plan. He would join the hunt as part of the drivers. Just riding Boomer to and from this hunt would add to his horse's training.

I set the hunters' meeting for two days. That would allow time for the hunt, butchering of the meat, and the return to the village where the meat would be smoked for the summer gathering, which would start two weeks later.

The location of the summer gathering was always the same as were the dates following the eighth full moon. The location was on high ground overlooking the mouth of the Volga River where it emptied into the Caspian Sea. Our friends, the Hungarians, traveled south and east. The Botai and the Krasnyi Yar traveled southwest. Two groups of Russians came from different northern areas east and west of the Urals. Their travel was mostly south. The gathering was centrally located so no group had to travel too long a distance. Since the Russians traveled the farthest, they sometimes attended every other year and were expected this year. Everyone had the same purpose in mind: to trade goods like salt and copper, furs, and new ideas. It started many generations ago as an opportunity for young men and women to find spouses.

At the hunters' meeting, one of the senior hunters from the Aurochs Clan walked up to Peter with a big grin and gave him a bag of ripe manure. Patrick stood to acknowledge the gift, holding it high over his head while the crowd enjoyed a good joke. His brother, Peter, laughed the hardest. Patrick bowed to the applause of the group, showing the manure. He opened the open bag, smelled it, and made a face as if it was awful. Then to everyone's surprise, he grabbed a handful of manure, squished it in his hand, and threw it to the crowd. The senior men howled at the fun. They ran from their seats to avoid being hit. The whole place was roaring with laughter. Patrick was as much fun to be around as was his brother.

We departed on schedule. Ildiko kissed me good-bye and called to me, "Be careful, Daven, Marc needs his father to raise him." I have to admit, I never thought about being injured before today. After two days of travel, we camped without a fire and settled in early. That night, I slept under a clear, star-filled sky. I wondered if we might all sleep late in the future and mount our horses to hunt. It all depended on how we did today.

For the first time in many years, I was not part of the lead line of hunters. I slept late with the drivers. The four of us rode on horseback walking alongside the drivers. An hour later, we spotted a herd in the distance. Being mounted, I could see over the grass. There was a good-sized herd of about ten or twelve horses off in the distance. We talked in low voices and walked forward. The four of us kept pace with the men on foot.

The lead stallion saw Gray Boy and Star. Instead of moving away, it behaved as if we were other stallions challenging him for his herd. He reared and stopped to accept the fight. As I suspected, the older horse did not seem to notice the riders and allowed us to approach. That was his mistake.

I was in the lead and crouched low behind Star's head, guiding her with my legs to the right side of the lead stallion. Star ran at an angle so that I came alongside the stallion, staying about fifteen feet away. I released my first arrow at his neck, but with the excitement, I missed my first shot, and the stallion closed in on me with its teeth bared. Star gave way running parallel to the stallion, staying far enough away to avoid being bitten. I notched my second arrow and hit the big brown horse at close range. It was a powerful blow to the neck. The big male screamed in surprise at the pain as blood ran down his neck. With his remaining strength, he tried to ram Star and knock us to the ground. Then the stallion tried to kick Star with its front hooves.

I was riding close but not within striking distance of its feet. The stallion circled to attack again when my second heavy arrow hit it in the chest. The power of the three-curve bow and the heavier arrows proved to be too much. He staggered forward in a last attempt to attack when my third arrow put him down. The drivers on foot were close enough to see the action.

Mikl on Gray Boy landed his first arrow when the other young stallion turned to meet his challenge. It was not a killing blow, and he missed his second shot. The other horse had no idea there was a hunter trying to kill him. No wild horse had ever seen a mounted hunter before today. The surprise was to our advantage. By now, the rest of the herd scattered in several directions, running in small groups of three or four.

The young stallion reversed its direction, away from Mikl, to try to get away. He might have escaped with only a wound, but when it turned back toward the drivers, Peter and Dann landed their arrows. Peter got off a second arrow that also found its mark. That young man can shoot! Janos hit it, and the horse went down.

Two more mares were taken including one killed by George and Jon both riding on horseback. We had all the meat we needed for the festival. The rest of the herd including mares, yearlings, and foals ran into the grasses and regrouped.

We butchered the meat and, as always, celebrated with a hearty meal that night. Every hunter was full of excitement and talked of the action well into the night. Each of them wanted to be riding a horse next time. We all talked about how surprised the stallions were when two horses with riders approached them. I was certain the men would practice and be ready before the end of the summer. Hunts would be different in the future.

I talked with Mikl as we roasted our dinner. We were joined by George and Jon. A few minutes later, Bruno and the clan leaders came to our campfire and ate dinner with us. I said, "I was very satisfied with today's results, but without all the practice we put in before the hunt, we might not be sitting here talking about our success."

Bruno agreed. "Every hunter, including me, has to get a lot better before we can be comfortable hunting from horseback. If we are not well trained, we could be thrown off and trampled, kicked, or torn apart. This is a whole new experience, and we have to improve our skills before we mount up again." There were no disagreements.

We divided the meat and loaded it among several dragging platforms and started for home. Two horses pulled our supplies. For the first time, I saw the return trip took less time than when we rode out. We only had to carry our bows and water sacks. This was quite a change from the past. Hunting would always be a dangerous job, but it was a lot less work now compared to what it was in the past.

CHAPTER 29
The Summer Gathering

IT WAS TWO weeks later when we left our village. The annual event covered five days with two of those days being used for travel. Of course, not everyone from our village attended. However, we had a larger group than usual this year. There were six new hunters, and four of them wanted to find wives, so they were attending for sure. There were two young women who also went on the trip because they wanted to find husbands or at least looked to see what choices were available.

It was not unusual for women to go to the gathering as a single person and come home with the same status. If they did find husbands, they have already promised to keep the secret of our horses and new bows for a three-year period. Bruno and I realized that for many reasons, our advances in weaponry were almost impossible to keep for very long. A new wife would share such things with her husband. It was just too exciting not to tell once she married into another people. Before it became common knowledge, Bruno wanted our people to be fully mounted and hunting on horseback well in advance of any other group. Naturally, he was more concerned with enemies gaining the secrets than he was with friends.

Mikl, now seventeen years of age, Ildiko, Marc, and I left for the gathering two days in advance because we wanted to get there early and pick the most central campsite for trading. Since our village was the closest to the gathering location, we always brought a large supply of horse meat for the evening festivals. Our second chore was to gather firewood. This had been a difficult work in the past, but with our horses, it would be a lot easier this year.

The first day, people arrived at different times, so they cooked for themselves and set up their campsites. Contests were held for three days with feasts each evening. The fifth and last day was one of departure.

As soon as we reached the gathering site, we cut logs and used our horses to drag a good supply of firewood into the camping area for everyone who needed it. We did not want our horses to be seen, so we found an open clearing with good grazing about a mile away and hid them out of sight and out of hearing range. As we staked and hobbled them, Mikl said, "Father, I remember your advice about a first-day wife. I will not even talk to a woman on the first day." As he walked off to wander about the campground, I wondered if he actually meant what he said.

When we returned from staking out the horses, some people had already arrived including one of the expected Russian groups. I also saw hunters from the Hungarians who arrived early to claim a good location, plus Moldovans and Kazakhs. The Krasnyi Yar and other Russian tribes were yet to appear. Among all these groups of people, it was the young women who left their villages and the hunters who stayed where they were born.

For parents, this was a time of happiness and sorrow in that their daughters might find a husband and leave to start their own families at a distant location. For many mothers and fathers, the summer gathering offered a once-in-a-year opportunity to visit their daughters and often to meet their grandchildren.

The gathering was a time for trading with the most sought-after item being salt. Every person attending the gathering, whether it was man or woman, had something to offer. Women traded woven hemp dresses, boots, pots, and foods plus buttons made of ivory, copper, and wood. Some women traded tanned furs and medicines. Men traded copper, weapons, carvings, and their daughters. I could see the day when horses would replace salt as the most desired trade, but not this year.

Salt was one thing every tribe needed. It was used for food preservation and flavoring. Fortunately, salt is plentiful near our village. The availability of salt, most likely from a dried-up lake from many years ago, was one of the reasons that the Botai village was located where it is.

This year, Bruno knew he had to settle a debt with the Hungarians. He had to compensate them for George who left them and came to the Botai. They would be less concerned with losing Ildiko because single women were allowed to marry and leave. Bruno and I carefully planned exactly how to make the trade for the new three-curve bow, not only to cover the debt, but to have our friends indebted to us.

Russians come from three different areas and brought beautiful soft white furs called ermine, which were rare and highly valued. The Russians were different. Instead of hunting and gathering what we needed, they grew crops and herd animals. Many of us wondered why the Russians worked so hard farming crops when there was plenty of food to be gathered right where it grew. The farm work did not seem to be worth the effort. As I said that, I remember that it was not long ago when we said the same thing about horses, until we tamed them. Horses were hard to find in the north where the Russians live, but they have learned to herd sheep and aurochs instead.

Every year, we brought slabs of grayish white salt. Each piece was about two to three inches thick and two to three feet in length. These slabs were always difficult to transport over any distance due to their weight and bulk, but with horses, the weight was no longer a problem. We also had copper and four black bear cub furs for trade with the larger furs being kept by us for bedding. Bruno had two of the rare cave bear claws we found on our last bear hunt, but these were not displayed for trade. Only the three Botai clan leaders and the Oldson are allowed to wear cave bear claws as part of their necklaces.

Bruno placed hunters on the two possible trails by which the Yar would arrive. He wanted to intercept them before they reached the gathering site. We had a plan for Ander that he would certainly want to hear.

In exchange for keeping the secret of our horses, we would teach them how to capture and train horses for themselves. We also had three horses back at our village, one for each clan leader that they could take with them on their way back. Before that happened, Ander and his men had to be trained to ride. The Yar were our relatives and friends, and we wanted them to be as capable as we were. In return for the horses, we asked them to keep the secret. Since we were giving them so much and expecting so little in return, we knew they would not refuse the offer.

The one concern was Flint. Bruno assumed it was likely he would be with the Yar and might attend to look for a wife. If he was with the Yar, he would have shared the knowledge of horses and the new bows to make him appear more valuable. That was not the biggest concern. Bruno worried that he might brag to others at the gathering to get revenge on his father. If Ander agreed to our plan and Flint did not keep his silence, he could be banned from the Yar village. If that happened, he had nowhere else to go, so Flint had little choice. However, Flint could be trouble even if he made the promise.

Later that day, word was sent that Ander and his group were seen five miles from our camp. He had eight people with him, and Flint was one of them. Bruno mounted his big stallion, Boomer, while Janos and I mounted Dawn and Star. Mikl was on Gray Boy, and we left at a slow trot.

When we saw Ander and his people ahead, we kicked our heels and headed right toward them at a full gallop. We were a bundle of dust and noise careening toward the tired group of unaware travelers approaching on foot. As we stormed into view, the Yar scattered into the brush, thinking a wild herd of horses was charging at them. We came to a thundering halt right in front of them and called a greeting of welcome. Bruno pulled back on both reins, which made Boomer rear high on his back legs. It was exactly the approach Bruno wanted, a surprise beyond belief. The Yar were stunned.

We dismounted with broad smiles. It still took a few minutes for Ander to recognize us and to understand what they were seeing. Some of them were crouching just off the trail in fear. After a while, they saw familiar faces and came forward cautiously to greet us in return. They stared at the horses. Some touched Gray Boy and Star, but they were wary of Boomer. It was obvious that several of them were in a state of shock that we actually rode these animals.

After greetings and hugs, Janos and Mikl rode back and took our two horses with them. Walking with the group would give us time to talk with Ander and the clan leaders. Bruno explained what he had in mind in exchange for keeping the secret. As expected, Ander anxiously agreed and could hardly believe his good fortune. Even though Ander had learned from Flint that we had tamed horses, the sight of us riding them must have been amazing. Ander was overwhelmed to know that he would own a horse of his own before the week was over, something he could only have dreamed about before today.

We arrived at the location where the horses were kept. Ander and his people saw the other horses we brought. They were healthy, tamed, and well cared for. He knew they had tremendous value. We explained how we brought our tents, weapons, food, slabs of salt and gathered firewood for the whole camp using them.

Flint said nothing, and Bruno said nothing to him. Flint saw his brother, Jon, working with the horses, but he did not see Suse. She was out of sight. Her pregnancy was past six months, and she was resting in a tent after the long journey. After not having any contact with Suse, I wondered if when Flint saw Suse, would he think he had some rights to her after all this time.

Ander called his people together into a group. They had all listened intently while we walked the trail from where we met them to where the horses were being kept. The discussion was between Bruno and Ander, and it was Bruno doing most of the talking and Ander doing most of the listening. Ander asked his people if everyone had heard what Bruno had to offer. Everyone voiced that they had heard saying yes in unison and nodded.

It was an outstanding offer of help from old friends for which Ander was grateful. He could see how our lives had changed in two short years since he left. Ander had just a few questions. He asked, "If possible, I would like to leave four of my group at this location so they can learn how you captured and trained your mounts. I want to get started today."

Bruno agreed except that Flint could not be one of the trainers. Bruno said, "Daven"—nodding in my direction—"will be your contact for hunting on horseback. Mikl, Jon, Diana, and Peter will be your contacts for training." Smaller groups formed to get started right away.

Ander asked each person in his group if they could keep this secret while they were at the gathering. If not, they were told to return to the Krasnyi Yar village immediately. Everyone agreed without hesitation. Ander pointed at Flint and asked him directly if he agreed so that his answer would be heard by all. When he was asked directly, Flint agreed, but without the enthusiasm the rest his people showed. If not for the fact that Flint wanted to find a wife, Ander would not have allowed him to attend at all. Everyone sensed the tension Flint brought with him.

The issue was decided. It was back to talk of news from the two villages with relatives and friends and making small talk. Finally, the four remaining members from Ander's group made their way to the summer gathering in order to get one of the better campsites. The four who stayed behind went with their trainers. Ander thanked his old friend Bruno for his generosity.

Then he turned to me and said, "Daven, I would like to talk to you on a personal matter if you have time." I agreed, and Ander told me the story of how Gertrude arrived at his village looking ragged, frostbitten, and starving. "She asked to be allowed to stay. Knowing her from the past and who she was, I was very interested to learn why she came to my village."

I told Ander about Gertrude's role in his father's death, adding, "I thought she was dead. I count my blessings that Bruno did what I should have done long ago, gotten rid of her. For me, it was easier to kill a bear then deal with her."

Ander told me, "No man wanted Gertrude when she arrived. She was skin and bones and looked terrible. Not one hunter wanted her as a second wife, and we had no extra pit houses for her when she arrived, so I offered her the house we used for our goats. I gave her a job, herding goats in return for sharing their living quarters."

Ander told his story, "I saw that frostbite had taken a serious toll on her face and that she lost half of her nose. She was unwashed and smelled as though she was diseased. Gertrude looked like an old woman. The last time I saw her was a day or two before Flint arrived. Now that I know the story, I know why she ran. Curiously, over the months she lived with us, she had gained considerable weight. I had people watching her to prevent her from stealing food, but they saw nothing unusual. She did her herding as assigned without causing any problems, so I let her stay."

Ander said, "If I knew what she had done to cause my father's death I would have banned her the same day she arrived with nothing, not even food. When she left, she took a good part of our goat herd and plenty of supplies." He said he was always wary of Gertrude and never liked her. She was someone that trouble followed. He wished his hunters had found her when they searched the surrounding area and still wondered how she got away without a trace.

Gertrude was cunning and certainly manipulative. She easily conned men. Looking back, I had to agree, both Ander and I had been conned. Bruno saw through her from the start; there was no fooling him.

Ander told me, "She escaped with about three dozen goats, maybe more. No one ever kept a close count of the animals worked by any herder. The only possible place left for her to go would be to the yellow ones with the slanted eyes. Since she looks different than they look, they might kill her on sight. However, if she had a herd of goats with her when she arrived, they might allow her to stay if she survived the journey. I guess we will never know. "

We talked for a bit longer before Ander left to join his people at the main gathering. As he walked out of sight, I wondered if Gertrude was still out there somewhere. I could not wait to tell the story to Ildiko. Women loved news like this. The story of Gertrude was disturbing. After thinking about the tale for some time, I found it interesting, but I really did not care if she was alive or dead. She was gone for good, but I thought that once before.

Chapter 30

Marinova

WHEN I GOT up that morning, I saw that many more people from distant areas had arrived overnight after long days of travel. Tents were erected, and traders were busy setting up displays of their trade goods. Janos and George were assigned to display our goods for the first day. Jon and I covered the second day with Mikl and Bruno handling the third day. With no specific assignments, the rest of us were free to walk the camp, look for trades, and greet old friends. By the third day, most deals were done, but often the biggest and most difficult trades were completed on the last day. Weddings were held the third day.

We displayed full-sized grayish white slabs of salt, green-colored copper ingots, and the four bear cub furs plus many smaller items offered by individuals. Bruno had the cave bear claws. Our salt slabs were so heavy that most women could hardly pick one up, so if a trade was made, they usually brought their husbands. Carvings and flint spear heads were shown along with full-length woven dresses our women made from grasses. Salt was our most sought-after item.

For the first time, a big woman from the Kazakh tribe had clay pots in different sizes that had a shiny finish on them instead of the raw clay pots we made. She or someone from her people discovered how to create what she called a "glazed finish." Ildiko was excited when she saw them and said, "Not only are the new pots much nicer to look at, they are easier to clean." We had plenty of salt to trade, and Ildiko wanted those new pots at any price.

After seeing them, she pleaded with me to come with her to see them. "Daven, the first person to trade with her will get those pots for the best price. They are beautiful, and they will not last long." I cannot get too excited over pots of any kind, so I did not think of them as being very valuable. She pulled me by the arm, and off we went.

We walked straight toward those pots. The big Kazakh woman needed salt because it was rare in her area. She could trade salt back at home for whatever else she needed and make more glazed pots on her own. Ours was her first trade of the day, so we made an easy exchange, glazed pots for a half slab of salt. Ildiko was delighted. We had plenty of salt, and the woman had more pots, so everyone was happy. Once a trade was agreed upon, the goods were exchanged immediately, so the woman followed us to our table to pick up her half slab of salt.

I asked the men to cut one full slab in half to finish the deal. When the woman saw the full-sized salt slabs she was astonished. She remarked, "No man from my tribe could have carried such a heavy weight over so long a distance." She asked, "How was it done? What man could carry such a load so far?"

I tried to look confident when I smiled and said, "Botai men are strong and durable. It was no problem bringing them here." She looked at me and at Janos and George standing behind the table. She smiled and made a comment, "Botai men are looking stronger and heavier than last year. You must be eating well."

She asked, "Did you have enough food during the starving months? Did anyone die this past winter from starvation?" I told her that one person died, but I did not mention it was from a hunting accident, and I did not mention the death of our leader. I did not want to tip her off as to why we were doing so well, especially if we were compared to twenty years ago. She was right. We were better fed and looking healthier this year and we had no shortage of food this winter.

The burly Kazakh woman left struggling to carry her half slab of salt to her tent. As soon as she left, Janos, George, and I cut all the full-sized salt slabs in half and hid the rest in the tent. The woman was right; without horses, there was no way possible for us to have transported so much salt for trade.

I thought she would gossip with her friends telling what she saw. I was right, as soon after she left, her friends came to our display of goods. They acted as though they were interested in trading, but they were really being nosey. When they looked, the slabs of salt were half the size of what they were a few minutes before and the supply was smaller.

Ildiko admired her set of shiny pots. Janos and George both made the same trade for their wives because they knew they would want them when they saw Ildiko's. When they got to the woman's table, her supply of glazed pots was going quickly, and the price soon doubled.

When Bruno and Diana returned to our tent and Diana saw the pots we traded for, she wanted a set too. Diana rushed to the Kazakh woman's table and saw that there was only one set left. Now the woman wanted a full slab of salt plus a copper ingot. Bruno was not happy that he had to pay more for the trade than we did, but he agreed to the deal. Now the woman demanded a woven dress when she confidently said, "I need the biggest dress you have." Diana had no choice and agreed to include the dress. As Diana and Bruno left her table, the big woman called out, "Next year I will bring more pots." Despite our best efforts to learn her secret of the glaze, she told us nothing, not even a hint of how they were made.

The Hungarians, headed by Rhoden and his lead hunter, Toth, approached our trading table and asked for Bruno. Bruno had left the area right after the trade for Diana's pots to look at the site where the strength contests were scheduled to be held later today. With Kraven out of the picture, Bruno was the heavy favorite in both of the strength contests. The first one was called the rock carry and second was a wrestling contest.

Standing behind Rhoden and Toth were Ildiko's uncle, Lorand, with her mother, Irma, and her oldest brother Gabor.

Ildiko was in the tent with Marc, admiring her new bowls, when she heard familiar voices and came out to see who were there. She was excited to see her mother and brother. She went to her mother and greeted her with a long hug. Gabor joined in on the hug. Mother and daughter were together again and excited to see each other. They all talked at the same time. Ildiko's mother asked to hold Marc. The baby, about four months of age, was in constant motion. Ildiko's mother enjoyed every moment holding and kissing her beautiful grandson. Irma asked about her daughter's journey, about George, and wanted to know everything about her life among the Botai. Ildiko told her mother that George was here too and that he had married and had a daughter. This was a true family reunion.

Her mother was proud to tell Ildiko that Gabor became the clan leader when her husband resigned the title. She said, "Your stepfather could not live with his guilt after trading you to Kraven and resigned." The truth was that her stepfather was depressed and miserable after her mother moved out of their pit house and lived with Gabor for almost four months and begged his wife to come home. Irma refused to come back. At one point, she poured the sand out of their clay marriage pot and broke the jar. She yelled at him, "I am never coming back."

Her mother said, "Lorand knew he was wrong. He never fully appreciated me until I left the house." Lorand, standing just a few feet away, was miserable without her. At the end of the first month, he pleaded for her forgiveness. Irma told him. "I will live with my son until you acknowledge what you did and find a way to make it right again."

After three months, he resigned as clan leader and asked his wife to come back. According to tradition the oldest son, Gabor, inherited the title. Rhoden agreed with the change. After four months, Irma finally forgave her husband, and Lorand moved back home. The condition was that he had to tell her daughter that he was wrong and how sorry he was for what he did. He had to beg her forgiveness. Now he waited behind his wife to do just that. A number of young Hungarian women who despised Lorand for what he did waited to hear the apology.

After waiting for an hour while Ildiko ignored him and talked with her mother and brother, Lorand stepped forward and tried to apologize, but Ildiko would hear none of his plea. She stopped him in midsentence when he tried to ask for her forgiveness.

She faced her uncle and screamed at him with hate. Her face was red and no more than a foot away when she yelled, "I no longer have an uncle and certainly no stepfather. My uncle is dead. I have a mother, three brothers, and a husband who loves me. I have a son and another child coming next spring. As for you, I never want to see you again." The wrong was too severe for her to forgive. It was a permanent scar the family had to bear as best they could.

There were eight young Hungarian women watching the confrontation. They watched the family argument, taking the side of Ildiko. They were angry with Lorand and they still hated Kraven and the old ways. They joined in, "You tell him, Ildiko. He deserves no daughter and no wife." They were as angry as if the horror of Kraven and the beatings and rapes were done to them instead of Ildiko. They yelled again, "If Ildiko was a son instead of a daughter, the trade would be unthinkable is that not true, Lorand? You are in the same group of horrible men with Kraven. Maybe a woman should do something similar to you. Maybe you need an arrow in the back some night." Ildiko was their heroine because she was the one who stood up to the old ways and forced the change. The group closed the space now and continued the confrontation. It was getting out of control when one woman spit at Lorand.

Rhoden wisely stepped forward between the two groups and asked the young women to leave the area. Her uncle walked off dejected, and Rhoden changed the subject, "Ildiko, you might want to know that Kraven's body was found a week after you and George left. It had washed many miles downstream and may never have been found except that it was caught between a fallen tree and some midstream rocks.

Most of his body was underwater when my hunters found his remains.

They examined him as best they could and found no knife wounds or spear marks just as you said. His face was partly eaten by scavengers as they tore away at what parts of his body were above water. His body was bloated, but there was no sign of violence. Our conclusion was that Kraven drowned." Hearing that was a relief to Ildiko and to me as her husband, but there was still the issue of compensation for losing a hunter like George.

The strength contests were held in the first day after everyone had arrived. There were two events as usual, with sixteen men from eight tribes entered. The first contest was one where a huge stone had to be picked up and placed on a stump. Then the stone was rolled off, and the man had to pick it up again and carry it to a second stump where the process was repeated with the stone being placed on the first stump once again. Two men competed against each other at the same time. Whoever moved the rock three times and did it the fastest was the winner of that round. The winner of each round moved forward until there were two men left.

The contest started an hour after lunch. Contestants were matched from different tribes so as not to compete against each other until later rounds. During early eliminations, Mikl and Bruno were in different groups as were George and Jon. All four Botai men won their first and second rounds, so there were just four men left, and they were all Botai. Bruno had always won before, so he was the most confident by far. After the third round, Jon and George were eliminated, and Mikl faced Bruno for the title as the "strongest man of the stones." Mikl was the underdog and the center of attention, because no one in recent memory had beaten Bruno, not even Kraven.

There were two groups of Russians, and they were cheering wildly for Mikl, the underdog. At the front of their group was a tall beautiful raven-haired woman. She was cheering the loudest. She saw only Mikl. He was tired after lifting those rocks so many times to get to the final round. He barely heard anyone in the crowd until the raven-haired beauty yelled his name with a heavy Russian accent. "Mikl! Mikl! Mikl!" she cheered, as did her fellow Russians. He turned to see who was calling his name with the odd accent. When he saw her, his eyes opened wide with delight as he wiped sweat from his face.

He was surprised this beautiful woman was cheering for him. His first thought was that it was not the first day of the gathering. That was yesterday, and we had arrived two days before that to gather firewood. Now instead of thinking how tired he was, he thought how much he wanted to beat Bruno. It was the last round and he was focused. He took a deep breath and a drink of water. Bruno was smiling and confident. Mikl knew very well that Bruno had not been beaten since the first year he entered these matches ten years ago. Diana and the Bear Clan cheered for Bruno while my Horse Clan and Ildiko yelled for Mikl.

For the final round, the rocks had to be moved three more times. The start would be when Rhoden blew his reed whistle. Bruno smiled and waved to the cheering crowd. He knew he was stronger than Mikl. Mikl was focused on the start whistle. Rhoden raised his hand to get the attention of the final two competitors, and after a short wait, he blew his whistle to start the competition.

Bruno was caught off guard, still waving to the crowd. He saw Rhoden's raised hand, but he was smiling at Diana and was thus unprepared. Maybe he was a little bit too confident. I was sure that in his mind, Mikl was just a young man and had little chance, but Mikl was alert and jumped into action from the start.

He picked up his rock and placed it on the first stump. The rock was pushed off the stump by one of the judges and onto the ground. Mikl lifted it to his shoulder and placed it on the second stump before Bruno was done with the first one. Mikl had the lead when his second rock hit the ground. When Bruno's second rock hit the ground, it rolled over, further slowing him. Mikl picked his rock up and moved with surprising speed to the final stump before Bruno could do anything to catch him. To everyone's surprise and delight, Mikl was the winner. He jumped in the air in celebration.

The crowd went wild. The underdog won! What an upset this was.

After ten years, someone had finally defeated the unbeatable Bruno. Mikl was the hero of the day even though Bruno was liked and respected by all. He lost because he was overconfident, and he knew it. Being the good sport that he was, Bruno clapped for the winner and held his arm in the air.

Overconfidence did not happen with the second strength contest, that of wrestling. Bruno pinned his first man without wasting any time. He moved forward each round as did the lead hunter of the Hungarians, Toth. In the final round, Bruno faced the big Hungarian and defeated him too. Bruno was the man being cheered this time. He was the best wrestler and received a leafy laurel headband just like Mikl for his earlier win.

When the contests were over, the Russian girl wasted no time coming to meet Mikl. She was very tall, had a beautiful smile and a perfect figure, especially for such a tall woman. Her name was Marinova. Mikl later learned that her real name was Marie and the "ova" part was added to all Russian women's names because it meant the daughter of her father. In her family, it meant, the daughter of Marin. They talked for hours as they walked the camp site. She had never married and came with her uncle Lazar this year in hopes of finding a husband. Mikl was very interested, but he was wary.

A woman this attractive must have serious reasons why she was not married. He wondered what the problem was. She was far too attractive not to be asked for in marriage. He later learned that she was considered too tall by her people's standards. Most men were three or four inches shorter than Marie was, so she was not chosen. That was not a problem for Mikl. She was just an inch taller than him, which suited him perfectly.

Ildiko and I met Marie after the strength matches when we went to congratulate Mikl. I winked as I said to Mikl, "Congratulations, my son." I hugged him and whispered in his ear, "We have been in camp for three days." Mikl smiled knowingly and nodded to me without making a comment. Marie smiled at me, not knowing what we were secretly saying to each other. She only knew a few words of Botai that she had learned from her uncle on the trip to the gathering.

We left them alone to get to know each other. Ildiko said to me, "If my guess is right, she will be coming home with us, my husband, so you need to catch one more horse."

I smiled and replied, "I like her, and we need a daughter-in-law. We have extra horses, and I can catch a few more if we give one away."

Marie told Mikl the main reason the Russians were at the gathering was not for her to find a husband. It was a far more serious reason than that. When they returned from the gathering two years ago, they learned that many more Russian farms were brutally attacked with all the farmers and their wives being killed in the attack. Some of the farmers were burned alive in their own houses, and it was not the first time this had happened.

Marie told him that twelve children were taken from these farms and never found, so it was assumed they were taken as captives or slaves. The surrounding farmers did their best to find the children, but they were farmers, not really hunters or trackers. The men looked for weeks, especially south of their village. It was assumed that the yellow ones committed the killings and kidnapped the children. Four of the children were Marie's cousins, and by now they would be about her age. The other eight were from surrounding farms. Their area was not the only one attached; it happened every spring.

Her people hoped there might be some knowledge of what happened to the children. Unfortunately, after talking to every attendee, no one had seen them. If anyone might know of them, it would be Ander's people because they lived farthest east and closest to the yellow people. Some said they were cannibals and might have eaten the children. Fear often caused rumors, but Ander's people knew nothing of them either.

That night, there was a feast with everyone invited. All the contestants in the strength contests were introduced with the winners being introduced last. Mikl got the most applause, even from Bruno, who stepped back to cheer him and acknowledge his victory.

Later that evening, Rhoden, Toth, and Ildiko's older brother approached the Botai feast table. Bruno greeted them. He opened the conversation saying, "I know we have things to discuss. I suggest that you meet us the next morning at the Botai trading tent." Bruno smiled in a friendly manner and assured Rhoden, "We will have no problem coming to an agreement for George and Ildiko." I knew what he was going to trade with Rhoden: it was the three-curve bow.

Bruno asked Rhoden to bring his best man with a bow and arrow. Rhoden quickly replied, "I will bring Toth, the man you defeated in wrestling. He will be happy to have another chance to compete with you at the next contest, whatever it would be." Toth, standing close enough to hear his leader's comments, smiled confidently. He did not know it would not be a contest between Bruno and Toth. Bruno had another plan in mind, one that would better make his point.

Once Rhoden and Toth left, Bruno asked Janos to be sure Peter met him early tomorrow morning for a bow-and-arrow contest. Peter would be the challenger to Toth, but it would not be with the standard bow and arrow that Rhoden and Toth expected. It would be Peter, a fourteen-year-old, and his three-curve bow against Toth, a giant of a man with a standard bow. I thought to myself, "Ildiko was worth every three-curve bow we had and all we could make."

The only problem that arose that evening was that Flint saw Jon with Suse. Flint had looked all day for a woman to be his wife, but as each woman got to know him, she backed away as fast as she could. They sensed that Flint only wanted a sex partner, not a wife. Flint stared angrily at Suse and Jon, but they ignored him. Then Flint noticed the curve of her belly. To his astonishment, she was pregnant! He asked himself how that could be when she produced no sons, no children at all during their marriage. Since he had not seen her in so many months, the child could not be his.

To his further astonishment, he learned that his brother had married his former wife, and she was pregnant by him. This was too much of an insult to let go. He boiled with rage. Flint had to do something. He would show his father, and he would do it before this gathering was over.

Chapter 31

A Debt Paid in Full

RHODEN CAME TO the Botai tent with Toth at his side just after breakfast. Bruno, Peter, and I were there to greet them. Bruno congratulated Toth on getting to the finals of the wrestling contest yesterday in his first year of competition. After a bit of friendly talk, Bruno brought up the business at hand, commenting, "The Botai and the Hungarians have been friends for many years. We have traded together, shared new ideas, and shared families through marriage. Today, we must clear up a debt we owe for George who, by the way, is an outstanding young man. Daven and I want to extend the friendship for another generation by fulfilling our debt."

Rhoden was concerned. He said in a stern voice, "Since the departure of Ildiko and her brother, the young women of my people have been talking about nothing but her departure for a better life in your village. If that continues, more women will leave. It is not the fault of the Botai, it is the fault of Kraven and the old ways. I have changed those unjust rules, but unfortunately, the anger continues." Without saying it, Rhoden and his clan leaders had a problem with their leadership image. To impress his people, he needed something from Bruno to show that he had made an outstanding trade for George.

He voiced his complaint further, "Bruno, the young man accompanying you, Peter, has already asked one of our Hungarian women to be his wife. The wedding ceremony is set for the third day of the festival. Many of my group wish them well and will attend the ceremony, and I hope you do too. A second Hungarian woman has accepted marriage with another Botai hunter, so two more of our women will be leaving to join the Botai."

He did say proudly, pointing to Toth, "One of your Botai women will marry Toth at the same ceremony, but a debt, a big debt, is owed for George." Rhoden said, "Ildiko is not the problem. Being a single woman, she had every right to find a new husband." In Rhoden's mind, Bruno owed something significant to the Hungarians. The problem was bigger than just George; Rhoden had lost stature.

"Since Ildiko left and told how well she was treated at her new home, every young Hungarian woman wants to find a Botai hunter to marry. It seems that even your food supply is better. Many in this summer camp have commented that the Botai look better fed than the rest of us.

"Ildiko tells everyone who listens that women are respected in your village and take part in major decisions. They actually pick the next leader at times." Rhoden was pushing for the debt for George to be righted. "With two more women leaving, I need to balance the scales."

Bruno agreed. "Balance is needed." He reminded Rhoden of what he himself had said just a minute ago. "Your problems came from Kraven, not from the Botai and not from you. It will take time to change people's thinking.

"I suggest that you form a council of senior women, one from each clan. You can assign them specific duties, things to decide on their own. It will give them respect. The issues they decide is not the important thing. It is the feeling of being included that they want. You might be surprised at their suggestions. They often have better ideas than I have. Rhoden, my friend, as you and I know, the old ways of men ruling their women do not work any longer." Rhoden thanked Bruno; he had a good point. Bruno asked the small party to walk with him to an area outside the gathering site for the next discussion. We headed in the direction of the targets that we had set up the night before.

The group consisted of Bruno, who was carrying his old-style single-curve bow, along with Toth carrying his bow. Peter joined the walk without carrying anything. I carried four new three-curve bows concealed under a large horse hide so the Hungarians could not see them. As we walked, Bruno and Rhoden talked of difficult social problems they dealt with over the last year. They also talked about hunting and winter food supplies. To Rhoden's surprise, Bruno commented that the Botai had no problems this winter with food supplies.

Rhoden asked about Ander and his new village, which seemed to be also doing well. "My women tell me that Ander's group has more children than ever."

Bruno said, "Ander left with twenty-six people from our village, and two years later, he has thirty-six, counting all the children. My son, Flint, is the latest addition, and he makes thirty-seven in total. Food for the Krasnyi Yar was adequate despite the long winter, and so far, they have not seen the yellow people of the east."

Rhoden replied, "Hunting was good, not great in my area. However, we still ran low on supplies in the starving winter months. Horse hunting was difficult because the herds have become more wary of our hunters and kept their distance. Since horses are harder to kill, we depend more on the annual antelope migration for meat. Two of my elderly people died of starvation last year." As always he said, "The oldest and the youngest suffered the most when food runs out."

Bruno said, "Rhoden, my friend, I may have just what you need." The targets came into view.

Toth, a bit edgy, asked, "What is the purpose of this long walk, certainly it is not just a bow-and-arrow contest? The annual bow contest is held later this afternoon."

Bruno responded, "It is a not a contest, it is much more than that, it is a demonstration. I ask for your patience. Please try to hit the targets with your arrows. We will do the same. When the practice is finished,

I promise that both you and Toth will have no further questions about why we came here."

Toth was annoyed as he looked at the three targets. He grunted an annoyed response saying, "I can hit the first two targets, but I doubt either of us can reach the third target. It is too far away for any bowman."

Rhoden agreed, saying, "I believe Toth is right, the third target may be beyond reach. Please give it a try."

Toth asked if he should go first or would it be Bruno. Bruno said "Toth, you shoot first, but it will be Peter shooting next, not Daven or me."

Toth asked angrily, "Is the purpose of this walk to insult the Hungarians?" This young man is half my weight and size. He may be a good bowman, but since he attended this gathering for the first time, he is no more than fourteen years old. He has no chance at all, especially at the third target. He may not even reach the second target."

Bruno patiently asked Toth once more, "Please shoot first." Toth scowled at Peter and then Bruno. He took his time and set himself in a balanced stance with his feet set wide apart as he drew his bow back and let the arrow fly at the closest target. He hit the target, and the arrow penetrated so that half of the arrow was still in the target.

He did the same with the second target, but the arrow arced more to cover the longer distance. The arrow struck, true; however, its power was spent, and it hardly penetrated. The third target came next. Despite three tries with plenty of arc, Toth's arrows fell short. "As I said, the distance is too far. No man can kill an animal at that distance." Toth stepped back. Rhoden and he were pleased with his effort.

Next it was Peter's turn. Bruno said to me, "Daven, please give Peter his bow."

At this point, I uncovered what I carried and handed Peter one of the new three-curve bows. Rhoden and Toth gaped, their eyes wide and their mouths open as they tried to comprehend what they were looking at. They asked at the same time, "What is that and how does it work?" As the lead hunter, Bruno asked me to explain the oddly shaped weapon.

I told them that after two years of work, we devised a new bow. It has not one curve, but three curves and that the bow increased the power by almost double of what the old bows have without it being any harder to use. They looked at it as if it was a precious secret, like how to make copper harder. Both men examined where the pieces were glued together in an attempt to understand how it was made. They asked numerous questions, but they still had their doubts that it was better than the tried and true bows we all used in the past.

Bruno said if they liked what the bow can do, they could have one for themselves. Bruno added, "Let my young hunter, Peter, who as you said, 'has no chance,' demonstrate what this weapon can do. If I am right, our Hungarian friends will be able to hunt better and have no more starving winters."

Peter stepped to the line and fired his first arrow, striking the target with ease and with force. It penetrated all the way to the feathers instead of halfway. Bruno let Toth and Rhoden study the shot for a few moments before Peter shot at the second target. The second arrow also struck true, but without the arc of the older-style bow used by Toth. The arrow penetrated more than halfway into the target right next to Toth's arrow. The comparison was obvious.

The third target was so far away that it seemed impossible for such a young man to be able hit it especially since Toth, who was Bruno's size and had almost as much strength, had not been able to reach it after three tries.

Peter took his time and let the arrow fly. Just as I instructed him, Peter overshot the target on purpose. They were amazed. It could not be! Peter's second attempt hit the target. The Hungarians could not believe what they saw. Peter casually remarked, "Sorry for the first miss. Sometimes I underestimate the distance with this new bow. Its power takes some getting used to." Toth and Rhoden could not speak. They did smile. The demonstration worked just as we planned.

At this point, Rhoden and Toth looked at Peter and applauded his performance and their appreciation of the new weapon. Toth asked to try it. With his strength and skill, he shot at the third target and struck it easily. "What a weapon! Of course we want one," smiled Toth.

Rhoden asked, "How many wives will it take to own this bow?" wondering what the Botai would want in trade this time.

Bruno told Toth, "The bow is yours to keep and the other three we carried here are for you to award to your best hunters. You only need to give one thing in return, and that is your word to keep the secret of this new weapon between ourselves. I do not want to share it with others at this time." Rhoden was all smiles and said, "You have our word, and all previous debts are more than balanced, including George and Ildiko!"

Bruno said, "Rhoden, I have one more gift for each of you to apologize for all the time between today's meeting and when George left the Hungarians. I would like to present each of you with an ancient Cave Bear claw for your necklaces."

Neither man had one when they arrived, so it would be noticed by all and would show that these two leaders had traded very well. They had made a very good exchange for just one hunter and an unmarried woman who could swim. Their people would be impressed.

Bruno told Rhoden, "Ander and the Krasnyi Yar already have the knowledge of the three-curve bow, but others will have to earn it. We are allies, so it comes to you first. I do not want to share it at this time. My clan leader, Janos, is waiting for you at our trading tent. He was one of two men who developed the new bow and will share the knowledge of how to make them with your best bow makers when we get back." Rhoden thanked Bruno. The debt was more than satisfied.

Peter left earlier than the rest of us, wanting to get back to his new lady. We took our time before returning. Toth and Rhoden examined the workmanship during the walk back. They could see the bow was made from several pieces of wood and glued together with resin and tied with rawhide. Bruno added one more caution, "In order to hold on to the secret, we cannot use the new bows in the bow-and-arrow contest scheduled for this afternoon." Rhoden and Toth replied at the same time, "Of course not!" They did not want to share the new weapon any more than we did. Janos worked with the men assigned by Rhoden for the rest of the day, explaining every step of the construction process including the good luck they had and the mistakes he and Tedd made along the way to the final product.

Bruno let the men discuss the bow and asked to talk to Toth. They walked out of hearing range when Bruno said, "I chose Peter for the demonstration because he is the best young bowman I have seen in many years. In my mind, Peter, although he is only fourteen as you said, is the favorite to win the bow-and-arrow contest for short distance. He is the first man we have ever seen to fire five arrows into the air before the first one landed. No one shoots as fast and as accurately as he does. The only way he can lose is if he makes a mistake."

That was quite a statement with so many experienced hunters in the contest. Bruno continued as he told Toth, "You, Jon, Mikl, and George will be right there with him, but even they will need a break to beat him." He cautioned Toth, "You might want to avoid competing against such a young man. It might be better for your image as the lead hunter of your people to shoot against him in the long-distance competition. I say it as a friend to avoid having such a young man beat a senior hunter, but I will leave the decision up to you." Bruno continued, "Neither Daven or I will enter the contest. We are leaving it to the young men."

Toth now saw Bruno as a friend instead of an opponent or a man from another tribe. Maybe Bruno was right. It would be embarrassing if a fourteen-year-old beat him, so he decided to take the advice. Toth said, "I will watch this contest with you and Daven and enter the long-distance event where strength is a factor. This should be fun."

As we arrived back at the gathering, I thought it was too bad that Tedd was not here to see the new appreciation of his bow. Mikl had the original idea and deserved some the credit along with Janos and Tedd, but he was too busy courting the Russian woman to care about bows right now. I filled him in on the demonstration and how well Peter performed later that evening. He was not surprised.

Peter was delighted to be in on the demonstration. It raised his status in the Botai and with the Hungarians. He had impressed both Bruno and me. Ander already knew of his skill. I knew he could have hit the third target on his first try, but he followed my instructions and overshot it. By overshooting, the bow was all that much more impressive. Following a plan like this one gave me the feeling that I could count on him when he was needed. He had tremendous potential. The Botai were well prepared for the next generation with Jon, George, and Mikl, and now with Peter and his brother just behind him. We had talent to lead the Botai when Bruno, Janos, and I became too old to lead.

CHAPTER 32

The Bellows

TRADING WENT FORWARD at full speed late the second day. Diana and Ildiko traded for the women's medicine called silphium. This medicine could cure female urinary pain. It was highly valued and only found west of the Hungarian village, so it had to be traded for each summer. Silphium was the one thing that Patts said she had to have, so we made sure to bring back a good supply. Diana traded copper and salt for the drug.

Mikl roamed the trading area with Marie, talking to everyone and looking for anything new. He came back holding hands with the Russian woman to tell me that there was something that fascinated him. Of course, if it was a new idea, it would be of interest to Mikl. He said one man from the Russians had a device that he called a bellows, but the man spoke only Russian, and he could not explain what he had to anyone, except Marie. Marie acted as an interpreter for Mikl. Since no one could understand him, Mikl was the only customer. Marie said the instrument could make fire so hot that it could melt copper.

Mikl was so excited that I told him to make a trade for it, whatever it was. If it was useful, we could copy it and make our own bellows. It was an easy trade because no one else could understand the Russian man.

Mikl traded raw copper and a half slab of salt for this new invention. The Russian included a supply of tin with the trade, but we had no idea what to do with tin. Mikl thanked him and took the new metal anyway. He said, "Why be impolite?"

The Russian could only say the word over and over again, "combination." Marie tried her best to interpret the word, but it had no similar word in the Botai language. Both traders were happy with their deal. Mikl was anxious to show Tedd what he had. He said to me, "Father, I understand the use of the bellows. It produces more heat than a fire normally gives off, but there must be a use for tin, or the man would not have carried it all this distance. Tedd might know what do with it. If not, they could experiment, or maybe Marie could explain it better with more time."

The second day called for two more contests. The first was swimming and the second was the bow–and-arrow target shooting for long and short distances. Both contests were open to men and women. Swimming was first. Each swimmer had to reach a small raft anchored in the river and return to shore. Since the water was cold, just four men and women entered.

Ildiko was one of the four contestants, as was Marie. Ildiko and Marie won their first round, so the winner would be one of them. At my whistle, the race was off, and the taller and younger Russian took the lead with her strong kick. Ildiko was a body length behind and kept the pace to the turn at the raft. Ildiko used the younger woman to her advantage, staying in her wake. Marie touched the boat first, but her turn was unpracticed. She came to a stop and had to regain momentum while Ildiko made a smooth turn underwater and took the lead.

Ildiko held a body length lead on the way back and touched the marker near the shore first and won the race. She was cheered by everyone, and she hugged her competitor, who most likely would be her daughter-in-law very soon.

The bow-and-arrow contest for short distance followed. Since everyone used a bow regularly, it was one of the most popular events every summer. Sixteen men and women entered from every group. The contestants were broken up into four groups with tribal members mixed about so that hunters from the same people would not compete against each other in the early rounds.

The rules were that you had to hit a target with five arrows at twenty-five paces. The winner was the one who landed five arrows first. Judges were me, Toth, and one of the Russians, plus Ander. Ander commented to me that he wanted to see how Peter fared against older and more experienced competition.

The hunters came to the line. Mikl and Jon were in separate groups. Flint was placed in the same group with Mikl, but he was separated from Jon for good reason. George was in another group with several men considered as favorites. Peter was in the fourth group against three hunters. He was unknown, except to those from the Botai, and even there he was only known as a new hunter. That all changed with this contest.

Peter fired off five arrows, all of which landed before the others in his group could shoot four arrows, and not all of the others hit the target. He was so fast; he seemed to be unbeatable. Only two winners from each group advanced to the next round, so there were now eight bowmen left. Toth whispered in my ear, "Bruno was right. Peter is magical when he has a bow in his hands." I nodded and smiled in agreement.

Mikl, George, Jon, Flint, and Peter were still in the contest, along with one Russian and two Hungarians. Flint was paired against Peter. From seven men and one woman, there would be four competitors left. In the second round, Peter did it again, and he did it with ease. He shot five arrows and hit the target before Flint notched his fifth arrow.

Flint looked like he was a man in slow motion. Peter rested the tip of his bow on the ground and watched Flint shoot his last arrow. Flint, in an angry voice, said, "Peter must be cheating somehow." He demanded to inspect Peter's quiver to see if some device had helped him get his arrows out so fast, but upon inspection, nothing was found. Flint was a bad loser.

There were four men left. They were the best of the best. The judges consulted for the final round. Toth stood next to Bruno and Rhoden and whispered to Bruno, "Your advice was good." Bruno nodded yes. He smiled and said, "It is not over yet, but Peter really is good, and this is just his first year."

The final four hunters lined up and notched their arrows. At my whistle, they fired their first arrow. Just as before, Peter landed the first arrow and notched his second before anyone else. He fired and hit the second and third arrows too. His fourth was on the way before anyone else's. Mikl was just a few seconds behind as was George.

The Hungarians were cheering for George even though he was now with the Botai. At heart, George was one of them, no matter where he lived. The pressure mounted with every shot, and Peter had the lead. As he pulled his fifth arrow from his quiver, he missed the notch for the arrow on the string and lost a few precious seconds. Mikl and George got their fifth arrow off just before Peter and all three hit the target almost at the same time. It sounded like *thump, thump, thump*, with maybe a second between each thump. The judges ruled that Mikl won, George was second, and Peter finished third. Jon finished a very close fourth. I was proud with all four finalists being Botai. Marie jumped up and down with joy. She was ecstatic.

As expected, Toth, who was wearing his new cave bear claw on his necklace for good luck, won the distance bow shooting with Jon coming in second and Mikl was third, but it was not that close. Toth won with time to spare. He had picked his fight well. Jon and Mikl were happy with their performances. Peter, being smaller in stature at age fourteen, did not compete in the long-distance contest. He was busy celebrating his strong finish in the first contest. He had his pretty Hungarian girl named, Jeanne, holding tightly to his arm. I said to Ildiko, "Peter will be unbeatable next year."

At the dinner feast that night, the Russians were happy because they had adopted Mikl as one of their own. He had won the short-bow contest and he had won the first strength contest against the mighty Bruno. The Hungarians were happy with George finishing second in the short bow contest. Peter and his Hungarian wife-to-be, Jeanne, celebrated his third-place finish. With all the various winners, Peter and Mikl were the men everyone talked about. Jon was happy finishing well. As long as he had Suse and a baby coming soon, he was a happy man. With the strong competition, he was congratulated by many for making the finals.

Flint was also happy, but in a negative way. He was gloating because Jon did not win any of the contests, but that was not enough for him.

CHAPTER 33

Day of Revenge

TWO CONTESTS REMAINED on this, the third day. The first was a running event and the second the tug of war. The foot race covered one thousand paces, long enough to be a combination of speed and endurance with twelve contestants entered in total. There were ten men and two women. Several men looked good in the warm ups, but no one tried too hard in warm ups. Jon and Suse and a few others stayed back to look after the horses. Since Flint had not been seen, Bruno and I were concerned that he might try to do something dumb.

The racers waited at the starting line. I was the starting judge this time. I raised my arm to let them know the race was about to begin, and as it often happens, one runner left too early. This time it was Marie's uncle, Lazar, who jumped, and he was set back three paces. Runners jogged around a bit to warm up again before they got back in place for the restart. Lazar looked confident even though he was penalized. He had long legs like Marie, an advantage in a long foot race. I raised my hand again and blew my whistle. They were off.

Peter took the early lead. If it was a short race, he would have a good chance, but this was a long-distance race. Mikl and George held their places in second and third, a few steps behind Peter, with Lazar trailing them. Peter slowed at the midway point and dropped off the lead. Mikl and George passed Peter with Lazar running a close third. If not for the setback at the start, Lazar would have been in the lead. With one hundred paces left, Lazar seemed to have found a second wind and passed Mikl. The Russians cheered wildly.

With the finish line approaching, George was still in front. Lazar kicked his long legs a bit harder, and he passed George making him the first to cross the line by just one stride. He raised his hands in the air and yelled something in his language that only Marie and the Russian groups understood.

Marie told Mikl that Lazar yelled, "This win is one for the children." The children he was thinking of were those they came to look for, those likely taken by the hated yellow-skinned people. Marie wiped tears from her eyes just thinking about them.

Mikl placed his arm around her shoulders to console Marie. "Eventually, we will find those children, or they will escape when they can. I would escape when conditions were right or die trying." Mikl hugged her.

Mikl did not say it, but he wondered if the children knew where they were or which way would take them home. He also wondered if they were still alive. Slaves were unknown among the various groups attending the summer gathering, but we all knew that if the children were taken by the Mongols or by the Smolens, they would be worked to death. When food supplies ran low, slaves got little food and often died of starvation. Mikl thought they might be too weak to escape, or they would have tried to get away by now. It was what he would do. Maybe they did try to escape and were killed trying. He let the thought go for now.

The final contest was held later that afternoon, and it was the biggest event of all, the tug of war. Five members from each clan teamed together to try to pull the other team into a muddy hole in the middle of the field. The losers, especially those at the front of the line, would be dragged into the watery mess. The two favorite teams were the Hungarians and the Botai, each with a very strong man in Toth and Bruno.

After the noon meal and before the final contest, there was a joint wedding ceremony for all new couples. Peter had chosen a petite Hungarian beauty with pretty blue eyes, who was the perfect bride for him. Mikl was arm in arm with Marie. Toth was also being married for the first time to one of the most attractive Botai women. Many more couples waited to take their vows, but Flint was not one of them. Flint was rejected by every woman he met, which added to his misery.

Janos called out to Toth in a teasing manner, "Toth, you will be so tired and muddy after the tug of war contest you might not make a good husband tonight. Maybe you should sit on the sidelines and save yourself for your wedding night." He laughed.

Someone else yelled, "If you enter the tug of war you will be too dirty for the marriage bed!" Toth took the teasing well. It was an enjoyable time for everyone. Toth laughed almost until he said his vows. Each couple brought their individual jars full of sand to be poured into a single jar, joining them together in marriage. The ceremony was performed by the Hungarian ceremonial woman since Patts did not attend. When their turn came, each couple spoke their own words to personalize their marriage vows.

Mothers and fathers were happy to see their daughters become wives, but they knew that it would be a year before they saw them again, hopefully with a grandchild next year. Because so many women changed tribes to marry their new husbands, language was not a problem. Most members spoke more than one language.

The Hungarian ceremonial woman spoke the formal words of marriage slowly and deliberately in two languages. She paused so everyone could interpret the wording, and then she asked each couple to pour their sands and be joined together. After saying their vows, each couple kissed and waved to the crowd of friends and relatives who politely applauded. Families were joined together on the third day of the gathering, as they were every year. Vows of friendship and promises of support if needed were renewed. Hungarians, Moldovans, Kazakhs, Botai, Russians, and for the first time, the Krasnyi Yar peoples were allied once again.

Bruno and Diana were the first to congratulate Toth and his new wife. Rhoden and Gaby were there as well. Ildiko and I hugged Mikl and Marie as our young son, Marc, crawled between our feet and pulled on our leggings for attention. Lazar and his band of Russian followers congratulated Marie with big hugs. He said, "Mikl, she is my Marie too, please take good care of her." Mikl, with a big smile on his face, promised to do so. The favorite niece, the one Lazar loved so much, was finally married to a good man who did not think she was too tall.

Marie spoke in Russian to her uncle Lazar, saying, "I will miss you." She thanked him for being her father as well as her uncle. Lazar asked all of us to look for the children over the next year. I told him that if we found them, we would bring them to the gathering next year.

Lazar guaranteed us he would be there again, not only to see Marie and Mikl, but to learn anything of the missing children. Lazar said, "I will never give up trying to find them."

What Lazar did not know was that one child would be there for sure, the unannounced child Marie was already carrying. If Lazar attended next year, he would know soon enough. George, Agi, and their daughter, Sophia, joined in on the fun, but Jon and Suse missed the marriage ceremony because they were tending to the horses, along with Diana and a few others at the concealed site.

Groups of men assembled for the final event, the tug of war. In the first round, Bruno and I and our team faced off with one of the newer Russian tribes. They had four men and one man's wife. Although the wife was as big as a man, it was a short contest. They had no chance at all. Bruno, Mikl, and I might have beaten them if there were just the three of us. The end came in less than a minute, with us laughing throughout.

It was pretty much the same story for the Hungarians with Toth and Rhoden anchoring the line. They turned their backs and pulled the other team into the mud with ease. Several more rounds were completed with the Botai and Hungarians looking the strongest.

Next up was Ander and his team from Krasnyi Yar. Flint was still missing, so they had to use a fifteen-year-old hunter instead. Still, they won their first round. Now Ander and his team came up against us. It was not much of a struggle. The same happened with the Hungarians, who won their second round easily. The best two teams, ours and that of the Hungarians, had one hour off before the championship took place. It was time to relax and enjoy the day.

There was plenty of good-natured boasting about who was going into the muddy hole. Bruno said, "It is rumored that mud makes your hair grow, but since I have never been in the mud, I am losing more hair every year." He laughed.

Toth responded, "Bruno, you will have plenty of hair next year. You are going in head first!" The comments went on and on for the full hour. I was concerned because Flint was still missing.

He was well hidden back where the Botai horses were being secretly held. He watched and waited as one after another of the Botai men and women who tended the horses returned to watch the final match in the tug of war. Diana stayed late. It was almost time for the start when she checked with Jon, asking, "Will it be okay with you if I return to watch the finals?"

Jon replied, "Certainly, Diana, all the horses are watered, and only Gray Boy needs to be fed, so there is hardly any work left to do. Go and cheer for Bruno and Daven and the Botai when they pull the Hungarians in the slop. It should be great fun."

Diana was excited. This was the last event, and she knew Bruno would lead his team in the finals. This was the one event that everyone remembered from year to year. Diana hurried to get back in time. Flint stayed in the woods and waited. He would make his move as soon as Diana was out of sight and sound.

He let a few more minutes pass to be sure she was gone. Gray Boy sensed Flint's presence and nervously moved sideways, throwing his head from side to side looking in every direction. Gray Boy snorted a warning. Horses have a good memory. Jon and Flint looked the same and probably smelled about the same to Gray Boy since they were identical twins. They were the same size, they had the same hair color, and were an even match when it came to strength, but they were totally different when it came to personalities. Gray Boy knew it was not the good son he smelled. It was the bad son.

Flint watched and waited as his anger, his madness, overcame him. He would right all the wrongs done to him. He would get even with his father for the favoritism and with his brother who was handed everything. Getting even was long overdue.

Jon washed Dawn as Suse left to gather extra hay for Gray Boy. He was the last horse to be fed. When Suse was out of sight, Flint made his move. He slipped out of the woods and came up behind Jon and smashed his head with the flat side his flint ax. It was a devastating blow even with the flat side of his ax. Flint cut Jon's scalp open and fractured his skull with one blow. Blood flowed as Jon fell forward, his face hitting the ground. Jon moaned and moved involuntarily, but he was unconscious. Flint would kill him before Suse returned and make his escape. No one would know anything. He would simply join Ander's group as they headed home.

Even though Jon was totally unconscious, Flint scolded him and cursed him. He angrily recalled about how he had suffered one humiliation after the other all because he was born a few minutes after his "favored brother." Those few minutes should not count for anything, but since they did, Flint was ready to deliver the final blow and change all that. Finally, he would have his vengeance.

He felt no remorse. His father, the famous Oldson of the Botai, would mourn the death of Jon and beg Flint to return. Flint was done talking. Suse might return. It was time for Jon to die. Flint stood over Jon, held his spear, and cursed his brother one final time.

Flint yelled, "It is time for you to die, my brother." His face was beet red, his pulse racing. Sweat ran down his forehead, and his eyes bulged with anger and hate. Flint had his spear in his right hand ready to throw it into the limp body on the ground. Just then, Suse returned with a basketful of hay. She screamed in horror at what she saw.

Flint panicked. He had to kill Jon fast. He pulled his spear back with his right arm in a throwing position while he gleamed at Suse out of the corner of his eye. As Flint hurriedly raised his spear, he struck Gray Boy with the blunt end of the spear, much too close to the horse's genitals. It cut the horse's flesh.

Gray Boy's natural reaction was to strike out at the source of pain. He kicked hard with both back legs and struck Flint. One hoof crushed his ribs. The other hoof hit Flint's head with tremendous power. It was over in an instant. The side of Flint's head was split wide open, and he collapsed on the ground right next to his brother. Gray Boy jumped and whinnied with terror. He kicked again in panic and pulled on his leash, but struck nothing this time. Both brothers lay face down, both badly injured.

Flint was barely conscious; his eyes were open but hardly focused, and he struggled to breathe. His chest was crushed in from the back. Rib bones pushed out of the front of his chest, and blood streamed from his head wound. He could not speak. Suse tried to revive Jon, but had no success. He bled profusely from his scalp wound. Suse had little medical knowledge and did not know what to do, so she ran for help. She knew there were medicine women at the gathering. It might be too late, but she had to try to save her husband.

Suse reached the gathering just as Toth and Rhoden climbed out of the mud hole. The Botai had won the tug of war, and the victory celebration was underway. None of this mattered. What mattered was getting help for Jon.

She ran to Bruno and cried in panic as she told him what had happened. Bruno quickly called out for the Hungarian medicine woman. She came forward immediately as did her assistant. Bruno did not ask Rhoden for permission for him to use his healers. This was no time for formalities. Bruno wished Patts was here; she was the best healer of all. Suse led the way back with many of the attendees following to see what had happened. Bruno and I knew that the secret of the horses was over. He would gladly give it up if he could save his sons. He loved both of them.

The Hungarian medicine women went to work, but the one attending Flint said there was nothing she could do to help him. Bones stuck through his chest, and one lung was exposed from the wound to his back. His head was split open, and his brain showed. He was beyond help. Flint labored to breathe as blood ran from his mouth. He suffered for a few more minutes, gasping for air, and died.

Jon was treated by both medicine women who used horse hair from Gray Boy's tail to sew his scalp to his remaining hair line. It was the first use of horse hair for stitches. It worked better than human hair used in the past because horse hair was longer and stronger. Jon drank a concentrated willow bark tea, which helped with the pain. He nodded off to sleep.

He regained partial consciousness after an hour before falling back to sleep again. He slept most of the rest of the afternoon after being given a strong mushroom tea. When he was awake, he asked where he was and what happened. He asked the same question at least five times. Jon had a fractured skull and a severe concussion. The medicine woman said, "He will get well, but many weeks will pass before a full recovery." Each time Jon woke up, he asked the same two questions, "Where am I?" and "What happened?"

Because of the incident with Flint, everyone saw to their surprise that the Botai had horses, and they all wanted to know how it was possible. Questions came from everyone. "How were they tamed? How did you do it?" Now the big Kazakh woman knew how the Botai brought so much salt for trade and how they gathered so much firewood in just one day. Women knew how Ildiko and Agi traveled so far and so easily with children only a few months old.

Hunters asked other questions. "How did the Botai manage to capture horses in the first place?" Everyone had tried to capture them so many times in the past, but they too were dragged, cut up, suffered broken bones, and had to let the horses go free.

The questions all led to a long discussion between the Botai clan leaders and the rest of the clan leaders. The hunters wanted information. Everyone asked something, and all of them yelled at the same time. Bruno finally called the questioning to a halt. The Botai would explain what they did and how they did it in the morning. There was a funeral to perform before they discussed the business of horses.

Flint was buried later that afternoon. His death ceremony was given by the same Hungarian medicine woman who tended to him. He died as a coward, not as a hunter, so his weapons were not buried with him. I said to Ildiko, "If Patts had blessed the marriage of Suse and Jon, perhaps this would never have happened. On second thought, Flint would have brought grief with him one way or another."

Bruno and I met with Janos, Mikl, Diana, and Ildiko to agree on what we would tell everyone. Jon was still sleeping from the mushroom potion and was in no condition to take part. Bruno asked the group, "How do we explain the horses? Do you suggest we describe how they were captured and how we use them?" He was looking for advice. After a few minutes with several possible explanations offered and considered, it was obvious that only the truth would get us back in everyone's good graces.

We decided to tell the basic story of the capture and how they worked for us although they were not fully tamed. After that, we would answer what questions we were asked, but no more than that.

I suggested, "We can explain that this was our first time using horses for anything. No one would know any different, because they have no experience and would not know what to ask. We can tell them that we were reluctant to tell anyone of them before they were fully trained to work. We did not want to look foolish if it failed. The Botai, being a proud people, did not want to look foolish." The group agreed with me. This would be the basic strategy.

The next day started with every hunter, every clan leader, and most of the women in attendance. The story of tamed horses was the most exciting tale in a lifetime. One woman was overheard saying, "It seems that horses can be used for more than just food."

At Bruno's direction, I began the meeting. I said, "We made many previous attempts to capture a horse, as you all have. All of our earlier attempts ended with failures just as yours did. We had the same injuries and the same disappointments." The crowd murmured their agreement. I waited for their attention when I explained, "We changed our tactics. We landed our lariats on their feet instead of their heads, and we had success."

I told the story of how we caught our first two horses and got them back to the village, using hobbles and weighted bags to tire them. I told how we prodded them from the rear and tempted them with apples, all to get them to move forward. "I credit much of it to my son, Mikl, who captured the first horse we now call Gray Boy." Mikl waved in recognition as Marie held tightly to his arm. I also told the story of the wolves trying to take away our success on the return trip and explained how we trained them to work pulling leather dragging platforms.

I assured the group. "Horses have more value than just as a food source, but they take a lot of work and patience to keep them. If you are not careful working with them, they can be dangerous, as we saw yesterday when Flint was killed." I talked about building double-sized deep pit houses for winter survival, watering and caring for them, and the benefits of manure. I said, "It may sound like a lot of hard work, and it is, but if we can capture them and train them to work, you can too." The crowd cheered.

I left out anything about riding horses. If I told them that a woman, Ildiko, was the first person to ride a horse, they would not have believed it. According to our discussion, that part of the tale was intentionally omitted. I asked for the women's attention at this point and said, "If the men want to take a short nap on the next subject, it will be okay with me." Of course that sparked more attention.

Everyone was listening intently when I said, "A horse that has recently delivered a foal can be milked, and the milk can be used to drink. We had an incident where a mother delivered a premature baby and did not have milk of her own for her newborn. We substituted the mare's milk for mother's milk and saved that child." The women gasped; could that be true? I asked Agi to stand, which she did. She held Sophia in her arms. I told the crowd, "The daughter Agi holds is the child who survived on horse milk." Women stood up and cheered. Everyone of them knew of a child who had died of this same problem, so this was amazing news.

One hunter asked, "Are horses worth all the work of building houses, feeding them, and watering them all winter when they can simply be hunted for food as needed?"

A woman in the crowd yelled back at him, "If a horse can save a baby, they are worth any amount of work, you fool!" Other women agreed as they sounded their approval and hooted at the man. The hunter who asked the question had nothing more to ask. He had his answer.

I let the noisy disapproval quiet down before I replied, "The hunter asks a good question. I have his answer. Hunter, you are right, horses are a lot of work. The decision to own one is up to you. Capture them and train them or kill and eat them, it is your choice. I can tell you this, when you have enough horses, you can breed your own herd. If you do that, you will never have another man or woman, whether it is an elder or a child, starve to death over winter. We know how they have helped us. Decide for yourselves." Again, the crowd roared their agreement.

A question was asked by Rhoden about training. I told him, "Training has to be a group effort. It is far too much work for one or two people. Our training was headed by Mikl, Jon, Diana, and Ildiko." This caused another outbreak of noise because women were named as half of the trainers.

I continued, "Training will continue for many weeks. It will take a lot of hard work to get where we are in the process, but if he, Rhoden, named a group to do the work, they will become leaders in a new area and will be admired by all." Questions quieted down after another hour of discussion. I could sense the determination by some and the doubt by others. The question in their minds was, "Could they do what the Botai have already done?"

Losing the secret of having tamed horses, the secret we tried so hard to keep, raised the status of the Botai. It was obvious, the Botai won contests of skill and strength, and we were ahead of everyone else with new ideas and new ways. Rhoden already knew of the three-curve bow and now he was more impressed than ever. He held the Botai and their leaders in awe. He said to Toth, "We will adopt their ways or lose ground to them."

Others knew the roles our women had performed as they answered training questions from the crowd. Ildiko and Diana were admired by all, especially by other women. We did not give details unless a question asked for specifics. Eventually, no more questions were asked. The hunters, clan leaders, and women walked around our horses. Some touched them and examined them up close, but they were careful when they got close, knowing the tremendous power of horses.

Rhoden and Toth came to me after the meeting. They told me they definitely would follow our lead with the horses. Toth asked, "Daven, my friend, would it be possible for me and three of my hunters to follow you home and learn more of what you did with horses?"

I responded, "I have to consult with Janos and Bruno before I can give an answer, but I think it is to your benefit to come with us." We met off to the side and quickly agreed that the Hungarians were a larger and more powerful group than the Botai. They are valuable allies. We might need them at some point.

Bruno said, "We need them more than they need us. Daven, tell Toth that as an act of friendship, he and Rhoden and their men should join us when we head back. We are happy to share our knowledge with them. It will allow me to create a real friendship with a leader like Rhoden. His people will see him in a different light after this week. And he will be in our debt for many years to come. The days of Kraven and mistrust are a thing of the past. This is an opportunity to build a friendship with a people who are stronger than we are."

I returned to talk to Toth and Rhoden. They anxiously waited for our reply. "Not only do we invite both of you and your hunters to come back with us, we also invite your wives to be our guests. They have as much to learn as do the hunters."

Rhoden thanked me and walked to Bruno to thank him. Bruno said, "Rhoden, as a gift of friendship, you will take four of our trained horses back with you."

Rhoden was astounded at the offer and good-naturedly said, "How many wives will this cost?

Bruno looked into Rhoden's eyes when he asked the question. He smiled as he clasped Rhoden by the shoulder and said, "Plenty, my friend, plenty. According to Daven, Hungarian women make excellent wives!"

We left the summer gathering with Ander and Toth and their people joining us on the return trip back to our village. We knew that the story of tamed horses would spread over a wide area. We hoped the word would be slow to reach the feared yellow people in the east or the Smolens to the north because we expected that those people would be the ones to bring trouble at some point in the future. If trouble came, we had friends who would help us.

Chapter 34

Peter and the Yar

BEFORE WE LEFT, Bruno and Diana and three men from his old clan built a stone monument at the northern edge of the gathering site to mark where we buried Flint. The gathering broke up that morning as travelers packed their trade goods and supplies for the walk home. It was the first time the event ended in such a sad manner. Usually, the departure day is one of celebration and time with family. This year was different.

The story of our horses was the talk of the week. It was a fascinating story. Janos was right; they listened, but they did not know what to ask to be able to do it themselves. I am sure next year, the Hungarians and the Krasnyi Yar will ride horses to this gathering, as will the Botai, but I am not sure about the others.

Jon was groggy and weak from the blow to his head and was unable to walk any distance, so we placed him on the hauling platform and headed for home. The other horses were loaded with our belongings and traded goods, including Mikl's new bellows, a supply of tin, and a good amount of silphium. In earlier years, we would have been carrying all this on our backs. Today, we carried only water and weapons.

We talked as we traveled. I told the Hungarians and the Yar, "The only way you can learn what we know is to do it yourselves. Why not stay with us until you know how to care for these animals? I suggest you join us on a hunt and see how we capture them." If they stayed with us, it meant they would not go home for weeks, but they could learn our ways. Both groups thought it was a great idea and readily agreed. They would return to their villages a few weeks later than expected, fully mounted, and well prepared to capture their own horses.

Ander asked to have a private conversation with Bruno, Janos, and me so we walked ahead just in front of the rest of the travelers. To Janos's surprise, Ander asked about Peter and his development. He wanted to know what role was in store for him over the next year or two with the Botai. Bruno asked me to reply on his development.

I spoke in regard to his skills. "Peter has the best bow-and-arrow skills for any man at his age I have ever tested. I have to admit even I am not able to shoot as well as he can. On the negative side, Peter is still a young man. Although he learns quickly, he lacks experience. He has just a few hunts under his belt, but on those hunts, he has done very well."

Ander knew how well Peter did during the bow demonstration with Toth and Rhoden and that he nearly won the short distance bow contest. I continued, "He is married now, so his skills and maturity are on target, similar to what you and I did at his age. The best thing about him is that he has tremendous potential."

Janos, Peter's father, was deep in thought as he listened and wondered why Ander inquired about his oldest son. Janos held back with his own questions until he learned more.

Ander changed the subject when he said, "When I began the new village, we struggled to survive that first year. Even with your help building our pit houses and the supplies you gave us, we barely made it through the first winter. Hard work and perseverance got us through, but it was a close call."

I recalled the people who went with Ander; there were eight full hunters and two young men twelve and thirteen years of age. Eight hunters were barely enough to hunt effectively. The Krasnyi Yar group was comprised of men and women who were best described as hard workers who followed orders well.

Ander continued saying, "My two clan leaders are good men, but I have no one to replace myself as head of the Horse Clan, so I continue to hold two positions. I need to develop someone to follow in my footsteps, someone who can lead a clan next year." He let his words hang in the air without an answer, but it was clear to me he was placing a request for Peter. Bruno had plenty of help with Janos and me plus Tedd and other senior men. Right behind us were Jon, Mikl, George, and Peter.

On the women's side we had Ruth, Diana, Emma, Judy, and Patts as senior women with Ildiko, Agi, Suse, and Elizza behind them. Marie would soon be part of our young female leaders. Ander lacked such a team. When he left our village, he took twenty-six people and now had thirty-six, but the new members were young children.

Ander explained his situation further. "When Flint arrived at my village, I guessed that he was looking for a new opportunity. I was willing to let his reasons for leaving the Botai village stay with him. I remembered Flint as a young man with huge potential and thought well of him. I was glad to see him. The fact that Jon was born first and would inherit the title of Oldson never came to my mind. I thought Flint would flourish in the new setting and take a leadership role rather than dwelling on problems from his past. As we all know, that did not happen."

Janos thought about Peter. He also thought about his second son, Patrick, and his third son, his two wives, both pregnant, and of his many other young children. It was an ideal opportunity for Peter. Janos would not hold him back. He also thought that now, with horses to ride, he could visit Peter more often than just once each year at the annual summer gathering. The one-hundred-mile trip could be made safely on horseback in two or three days.

Ander told Janos of the opportunity for his son. "Peter is impressive. I can see him leading a clan in a year or two. With experience, he could be my replacement in the future." When he said this, Ander looked at Janos, in effect asking for his father's permission once again. If he asked for Jon or Mikl, he would not be able to have one of them because they were too well established with the Botai. It had to be someone younger. George was not a possibility. He was older and set with his marriage to Agi, plus he just recently relocated from the Hungarians. Peter was the perfect fit. He had the right skills, the perfect age, and was full of potential.

Janos thought for another minute before he said, "I like the idea that my son could lead a clan and perhaps eventually lead the Krasnyi Yar. It would certainly be an honor. The opportunity is too great for me to act selfishly."

Janos talked as a clan leader when he said, "All of us want the Yar to succeed. You are our friends and relatives. If Peter stays with the Botai, it will be years before he can contend for a clan lead. If he goes to the Yar, he will be of immediate help with his energy and skills. His mother and I will miss him, but with horses to ride, we can visit him and his new wife more often. Ander, you may approach him when you think the time is right. It will be his choice."

During the gathering and on the return trip, Mikl and Marie continued to practice speaking her native Russian language and his language, that of the Botai. Both were quick learners. Mikl already knew how to say many of her words like *hello, friend, father, mother, cousin, follow me, food, water* and several more words and phrases. I wondered why he always wanted to learn something new. He would not need to know her Russian language now that Marie was coming to live with the Botai. She would learn our Botai language, but that was Mikl. He always wanted to understand the newest thing even if it was a language that he would probably never use.

When I think back, Mikl's ideas have been changing the lives of the Botai while I concentrated on being better at what I already knew. Even hunting has changed. Twenty years ago, we did not have enough hunters to be able to hunt horses very well. Now we hunt on horseback. Mikl saw the value in the three-curve bow before anyone else, and he was the first to capture and train a horse. He traded copper for the new bellows and a supply of tin, and now he was learning Russian. I guess he is right most of the time. I just had trouble giving up older, proven ways.

When we stopped to eat the noon meal, Mikl took out the bellows and examined it again. I approached him to also look at the bellows when to my surprise, he greeted me in Russian saying, "Hello, Father." I was confused and asked what he said. He explained that he said hello. Then he talked about the bellows and said, "I cannot wait to show it to Tedd. I still do not understand what Marie is trying to tell me about the metal called tin. It must be important or her uncle would not have brought it all the way from his home to trade." Mikl told me, "Marie said it was part of a plow, used in farming. But, Father, I still do not understand what she is talking about. What is a plow? Maybe Tedd will know what it can be used for." I loved him for his curiosity.

After two days, we approached our village. Jon walked for a half of an hour that morning after which he rested on the dragging platform, but he got off it and walked when we came into the village.

His scalp looked awful. It still oozed blood where it was sewn together with horse hair. Bruno sent Jon directly to Patts for her examination. They cut his hair away to better observe the wound and clean his scalp. Several more stitches were added, but three areas were left open to drain the blood. Next they placed a poultice on his head and bandaged it. He looked worse than when he arrived, but he had a better chance for full recovery now that we were home. Patts gave Jon strict instructions to do nothing other than eat and rest for the next two weeks, or his condition could become worse.

People greeted us with smiles and hugs, welcoming us home. They asked about the gathering and, "Who won the tug of war and the strength contests. Did Ildiko win at swimming? Who won the bow-and-arrow contests, and who won the wrestling match?" They wanted to know about those who attended and who got married. Any information on relatives and friends was always of high interest to those who stayed home.

Those of us returning were more subdued than normal. The villagers

311

sensed something was wrong, and we told them what happened with Flint and Jon and how we lost the secret of having tamed horses. They were shocked to hear that Flint tried to kill his brother and that Gray Boy killed Flint with one kick. In comparison, the contests were of little importance.

Bruno and Diana turned the conversation from the negative to the positive. Diana and Ildiko spoke of the new marriages for both men and women and introduced the new arrivals by name and identified to whom they were married to. Bruno introduced our guests for the next two weeks. Of course everyone already knew Ander and his team, but Toth, Rhoden, and his three men and their wives were new to everyone. Diana introduced Marie as Mikl's new bride and Jeanne as Peter's bride. She also introduced the other four new brides and said that Toth was one of the new husbands married to a Botai woman.

Marie appeared fascinating to the Botai women. She was taller than any woman in the Botai and taller than most of the men, but she was friendly and beautiful. She was the daughter of a Russian farmer, which was a new idea to all of us. She spoke a few words in broken Botai, words admiring the apple orchard and the berries. When she did that, she was immediately welcomed into the women's society of gatherers. Ruth and Emma said the women started the new plants. This was an opening for Marie because this was what her people did, they farmed.

She told as best she could how, at her farm in Russia, women and men worked together to move plants and seeds from distant locations closer to their homes. If the plants originally grew in partly shaded grounds or wet marshy lands, they replanted those plants in the same general conditions. Her people already knew about fertilizer and the need to water plants during the dry season. Mikl helped her tell her story.

Years ago, her people ate the biggest seeds and replanted the smaller seeds. That produced smaller and smaller plants each year. Her father reversed the process where they ate the smaller seeds and replanted the largest seeds. His idea worked, and crops became larger each year. It was a lesson they had learned the hard way.

Marie, over the following months, became part of the gatherers who led the way to farming among the Botai. Lentils, wheat, and beans would be farmed next year as well as gathered. The apple orchard was already started, and the berry patch would be expanded. Her Russian parents harvested fruits and vegetables instead of gathering only what nature provided. Marie taught the Botai that farming was a new way to have a more reliable food source. It would change the lives of the Botai.

Mikl saw that Marie was already welcome with her new people. He thought, "She is so unlike my mother." He had chosen his wife well. She was an "Ildiko" in a different way. She was not a hunter, she was a farmer. Mikl would teach her to ride a horse and learn Botai ways. He took the advice his father suggested: not to choose his woman on the first day. He repeated that advice to himself. "First-day wives are based on beauty alone. They are usually a mistake. Second- or third-day wives are much better." He would remember that advice for his children someday.

In his spare time, Mikl worked with Tedd on the bellows. Mikl explained that Lazar designed it after his own mouth. It sucked air in from the back and pushed it out of the front. The airflow made for a hotter flame, and copper became workable. Instead of pounding copper into shape as in the past, it could be melted and poured into wooden forms. The first thing they made was a copper ring to replace the leather one for Gray Boy's bridle.

Marie joined them as they worked. When Tedd asked her about tin, she said, "In my home, tin and copper were combined to make copper harder. This did not make sense to Tedd. Marie repeatedly tried to make them understand her. The problem was that the word *combined* could not be translated into the Botai language. She tried to show them what she meant by using hand gestures, but to no avail. With much frustration on everyone's part, the tin was set aside. Mikl said to Tedd, "Someday, we will find a use for it, just not today."

I unloaded our horses, and Ildiko opened our pit house. She was pregnant and tired from the long trip, yet she started a fire and cooked a meal for us. I helped get the trade goods unpacked and brought in some extra firewood. I wondered if the next child would be another son or perhaps a daughter this time. I had the next hunt on my mind as I worked. For Ander and Toth, it would be their first hunt of this type. They were not ready to hunt on horseback, but they would join us and learn.

The following morning, Ander, Peter, Toth, and their men joined the training team. They learned how to feed, house, train, and tame horses. Riding would follow once these basics were mastered. The pit house with its high roof rafters was explained first. Both men and women climbed up and used the rafters to sit on a horse for the first time. Sitting on a horse was a thrill. The biggest change for Toth and his men was to work side by side with the women. Diana, Mikl, George, and Ildiko were the trainers. Having women train men was new for the Hungarians.

When they learned that Ildiko was the first person to ride a horse, they were more impressed than ever. They saw that the typical male and female roles had blended since Bruno became Oldson. Many of the old ways that had been determined by sex alone were gone. Rhoden thought about Bruno's earlier advice. Every night, he met with the two women and his men to discuss new roles for women when they returned to their own village. Rhoden called it the women's council. The first thing they would decide would be the members of the horse training team.

The visitors joined us as we built a new double-sized pit house. We demonstrated how we whistled when we wanted our horses to respond and rewarded them each time with praise and apples. We showed them how to use leg hobbles and the bags we used to weigh down new captures to tire them and bring them under control. No details were omitted. They learned in a few days what it took a year for us to develop.

Soon the new people mounted up in the pit house and walked a horse in the corral for the first time. They used the reins and got the feel of being on a horse, a strange and exciting new experience. There were smiles from ear to ear at the thrill. Later each person took a turn in the saddle while Gray Boy, Star, and Babe were walked outside of the corral. We did not use Dawn since she was about to deliver her foal any day.

Gray Boy would be a father for the first time. The last training step was riding outside the corral at a walking pace and then at a gallop. The next day, they worked with the horses they would take back with them, the ones that would start their first herds.

Riding a horse at a gallop had the same effect it had on us. It was thrilling and dangerous at the same time. It would be a full two weeks, maybe more, before Ander and Toth and their people mastered riding. Next we demonstrated how we rode and shot arrows into a target. We warned them that this skill might take months to master, but it had to be learned if they were to hunt horses or fight an enemy while riding.

I planned the hunt for the following week, after Ander and Toth had time to practice being in the saddle. We took eight horses and fifteen hunters including all of Ander's men, Peter, and Toth's men, plus the four women who were in training. Ideally, all of them should have had more riding experience before they took this step, but the learning process was shortened due to time.

We traveled two days before we found a herd, and once again, the wild horses had no experience facing mounted hunters. The stallion allowed our horses to come forward without running away, seeing our approach as a challenge to take his herd.

We targeted yearling colts for capture because they were easier to train. As soon as a lariat was landed, we added a second or third line. With several lines on a colt, it was quickly taken to the ground. We loaded our captures with weighted bags as usual, attached the hobbles, and pulled them in the direction we wanted them to go. The young horses soon tired and followed us. Ander and Toth were amazed at how we had perfected the process in such a short time. The lead hunters brought down four adult horses for meat. We butchered them, ate well, and we talked into the evening.

After the evening meal, Ander approached Peter and asked him to take a walk with him when he said, "I have something I would like to discuss with you, Peter. Let us step away from the crowd." In a minute or two, they were soon out of hearing range.

Peter was too young to have been friends with Ander before he left, so he was on guard when Ander asked to speak to him. Peter wondered if he had offended Ander in some way or performed poorly on the hunt. Had he made a mistake? He was wary, thinking that some bad news was the topic for this discussion. The silence was obvious. Peter asked in a respectful manner, "Oldson, what do you have on your mind?"

Ander, in Peter's mind, had a similar status as his father or that of Bruno or Daven, so talking privately had an impact on him. He wondered why this conversation was one on one. *Why is this man, Ander, leader of another group outside our own, talking to me without a senior Botai member or my father being present?* It had to be something serious. Peter was concerned, very concerned. He could not think of a mistake, a misjudgment, or an offense on his part.

Ander stopped and faced Peter. Peter anticipated bad news. Instead of criticism, Ander spoke of the Krasnyi Yar and how they struggled and of the success they had so far. Peter wondered what was coming when Ander told him how impressed he was with his role in the three-curve bow demonstration, his hunting skills, and his performance at the gathering contests. Whoa, this was praise, not criticism. It sounded like good news.

Ander took a breath and said, "I need a man like you, Peter, and I need him badly. I need a leader who can take over my Horse Clan within a year. There is an opportunity for a man like you with the Yar." The approach and the offer was a big surprise, and it shocked Peter for a minute. He could hardly speak.

This was not just good news; it was an opportunity of a lifetime, almost beyond belief. A clan leader within a year or two! That would not happen in five years if he stayed with the Botai. It was unexpected, but it sounded exciting. He had questions, which were all answered by Ander except one, but Peter did not ask that question... could his brother join him the following year? That question was for another time. Peter said, "I am very excited to be considered. I am sure you can understand that I have to talk to my father and my wife before deciding."

Ander smiled and placed his hand on Peter's shoulder in a gesture of friendship. He replied, "You only need to talk to your wife. Your father and the Botai clan leaders are proud of you and pleased that I want you to join me. They see the opportunity for you, so the decision is yours, after you talk with your new wife, of course."

Peter was overwhelmed. He thanked Ander again as they walked back to camp. He had a hard time nodding off to sleep that night. He decided he would join the Yar when Ander left for home. He already knew Jeanne would go wherever he went. Hunters were the highest-ranked members of every people, even with the recent changes for women. Peter would become a member of the Yar in a few days, but in his heart, he would always be a Botai.

He told Ander the very next morning. "Ander, with my wife and me, you will have thirty-eight members instead of thirty-six." He smiled when he said, "I am a Yar! Next year, I promise you, we will drag Daven and Bruno into the mud!" Ander welcomed Peter with a bear hug.

Over the next two days, we captured eight new colts and two adult horses from two different herds by approaching on horseback and using the same techniques to bring them back to our village. We had replaced all the horses we promised our friends. The rest of the week was devoted to training and riding for Toth and Ander and their people.

We held a feast on the last night our visitors were with us and pledged our allegiance to each other. Bruno and Ander made a joint announcement, "Peter, son of Janos, and his wife would join the Krasnyi Yar." It was a surprise announcement and it caused a lot of excitement. Peter was congratulated by all and hugged by his younger brother Patrick. They had always been together until now and would miss each other. We celebrated and sang the old songs with the Yar joining us. We drank blueberry wine and danced to the music well into the night. Our visitors tasted koumiss for the first time. When they were told what it was, they could not believe they were drinking fermented horse milk.

In the morning, we stocked Ander and his group with food, three-curve bows, and several horses when they left for their village. Toth and

Rhoden stayed two more days to train further before he and his people departed in the opposite direction. Little did we know we would see Peter sooner than we expected. It would not be good news that brought him back.

CHAPTER 35

Threatened

WE RESUMED THE usual work at this time of the year. When leaves began to fall, it was time to prepare for the cold months. Ruth, Emma, and Judy led the women in early season gathering. Wheat was ready for harvesting. After wheat, they would gather hay and oats for our horses. Short flint blades were used to remove the heads of the wheat from the stalks and collected in woven grass baskets. Marie brought a new idea when she taught the rest of the women to replant a portion of the seeds by dropping them into holes made with our digging sticks. Vegetables were harvested including lentils and chick peas. Winter was ten weeks off.

Blueberries, raspberries, along with strawberries, were ripening. It would be a good year. When manure was spread last winter, it made a big difference. Some of the strawberries were covered with it, and some had none. The elders saw that the plants with manure were twice the size of those without it. This year, each plant would be covered. We would double the supply of fruit without adding new plants. Strawberry runners, growths from older plants that resemble vines, would start new plants. The strawberry patch would increase in a natural way once the women removed the weeds choking them.

Apples were larger and more plentiful this year too with the old trees producing more fruit than in the past. The new trees from last spring were coming along well. Some of them were relocated one tree length from the mother tree so they would have room to grow as they matured. Marie had plans to increase the apple orchard by saving seeds after the apples were eaten and replanting them next spring. The Botai were becoming farmers.

Tedd and Mikl worked with the bellows every day, melting copper and carving molds for every shape they needed. Dann joined them by providing his carving skills for the molds. With the bellows, copper was melted and poured into whatever shape was needed shaped whether it was something for a bridle or a cooking pan. Until now, making a copper pan by pounding it into shape was nearly impossible. Mikl and Tedd with their bellows made the difference.

Mikl had another new idea. He created a series of woven mats that rolled up when not in use and hung from the neck of his horse. His mats were of a similar design to what women used to make dresses, but his had four layers. When he unrolled the odd-looking mats, they looked clumsy and awkward, flapping in front of his mount. I had no idea what it was supposed to do and assumed it was to keep his horse warm during winter rides. I asked him what he was making. He responded, "I am working on an idea to protect Gray Boy." I thought I must be right. It was something to keep his horse warm.

After using the bellows for weeks, Mikl and Tedd decided to take it apart to see how it was made. Once they did that, they would build an even larger one. Bigger would be better and produce a hotter flame. In their minds, a hotter flame would heat copper faster. Making the new one was a challenge they could not resist. They worked on it every day. When Marie took her noontime break from gathering, she asked them, "Have you made any progress with the tin my uncle traded, Mikl?"

Tedd responded, "I am not sure how copper and tin are related, but over the next few weeks, I intend to figure it out." Tedd mentioned, "Perhaps tin might be used as a mold to pour copper into rather than using wood." This seemed unlikely because two metals would bind at least partially and ruin one or both. He promised to work with it during winter when he had more time. Right now, he said, "We are too busy making a new bellows that will be twice the size of the first one from Lazar to think about tin."

Elsewhere around the village, Dawn had her first foal, which added one more horse to our herd. Gray Boy had fathered his first colt, a male, and his line would be continued. As always, watching a colt take its first few wobbly steps was a total joy. If only humans could do that!

Agi and Ildiko had become closer as friends and visited each other daily. Both had young children, so there were always things to talk about. Even being at the midpoint of her second pregnancy, Ildiko gathered supplies along with Agi and the rest of the women. Both of them welcomed Marie as part of their circle of friends.

Jon was recovering from his injury, but it was taking longer than anyone thought it would. Suse had her hands full caring for him and her new child, but at least he was getting better. His scalp no longer oozed, and Patts finally stitched it close. However, everyone could see where his scalp was reattached to his hair. He would always have a permanent scar line where no hair grew.

He took his first horse ride two days ago. As the lead hunter, I was glad to see him back on his feet. I needed him. If he could not join us on hunts, it would be good to have him at the village for protection. Four new pit houses were ready for the recently married couples. Overall, our village was full of activity.

Then something happened. Peter and another hunter from the Yar village arrived back at the Botai enclave. They brought bad news. Peter saw me first and told me what happened. We went to Bruno with the information. He asked the other clan leaders to meet in council at his pit house just as soon as they could. It was an emergency.

Peter told the story. "While Ander and the Krasnyi Yar were away at the summer gathering, two of our young men were hunting deer in an area to the north and east of the village. They rarely hunted that far away, but being young, they saw this as a hunting trip and as an adventure. They were seen and attacked by a group of the ugly slant-eyed yellow people who were hunting in the same general area.

"The two Yar men were near the lower slopes of the mountains, just north of the grasslands. They were caught in the open and had little natural protection. The yellow people screamed like animals and chased them on foot mile after mile. One of the slant-eyed yellow men got within bow range and fired an arrow as a desperation shot to try to kill them from a long distance. The arrow sliced along the right side of one hunter and caused some bleeding, but it was not a killing blow.

"At first, the Yar hunters ran toward their village. After an hour of running desperately, they turned north again so as not to give away their home location. They never stopped running until night came over them. The cover of darkness allowed them to escape. The yellow people lost them and finally gave up the chase. The two Yar hunters finally made it home a few days later and told the story."

The attack was unprovoked and meant to kill the Yar hunters. The contact was serious because the yellow-skinned people now knew there were others in the area. Being discovered presented a serious danger. The yellow men would never stop looking for them until they were found. When they were found, the Yar, being smaller in numbers, would be slaughtered. We could not let that happen.

I spoke after Peter told what he knew of the run-in. "We know from what we learned at the summer gathering that the yellow-skinned people ventured north and raided Russian farmers and took their children as hostages. After hearing this story, my thought is that the yellow skins may think the two white hunters of the Yar were actually Russians looking for their stolen children."

Bruno said, "The yellow people look different from us. They will consider anyone unlike themselves as a threat. If this threat is not answered, they will eventually find the location of Ander's people. They will hunt Ander and our friends to the death. If they lack the strength in numbers, they will recruit others like themselves and attack. After they destroy Ander and his people, eventually they will come for us." Bruno asked me, "Daven, you have led many hunts, what do you think?"

I was ready with my response and said, "I agree with Bruno. These people are a dangerous threat to our future. The yellow ones will search until they find the Yar. If they act as they did in the past with the Russians, we can expect no mercy from them, and we should give no mercy. When they raided the Russians, they killed the adults, took their children, and destroyed their houses. In doing so, they burned some of them alive. We have to expect them to repeat what they have done in the past. It almost sounds as if it is a sport for them.

"In my opinion, if we attack them first, we have the element of surprise on our side. However, my friends, if we attack, we must kill every one of them and hide the fact that we did it, or others of their kind will come looking for us. The best hunter knows his prey and understands their habits, where they go and what they do. I think of these yellow skins like any other animal I have hunted, but right now, I know very little about them.

"We need to know their numbers, their locations, what they do, and where they go. I want to know what weapons they have, how many pit houses or tents they occupy, and whether they are mounted or not. I want to know if they have three-curve bows or even better weapons. I also want to know the access routes in and out of the village and where the next neighboring village is located. I do not want to underestimate them. They may have ten-year-old hunters or women who can kill us if we are not careful.

"To our advantage, they know nothing of us, and they will not know we are coming for them. If I was in their situation, I would be looking for the two men they chased. Their numbers will tell us if we need to ask our friends, the Hungarians, and maybe even the Russians to help us. If the other villages are not a threat, we may be able to wipe them out with the men we have within the Yar and the Botai."

When I started speaking, I said we would have to kill all of them. I fully believed this. If not, the survivors would gather more yellow people from neighboring villages and they would come for us. I dreaded experiencing a surprise attack like the ones the Smolens used to do that killed our families years ago. My greatest fear was that our wives and children could be enslaved, or worse. It has been twenty years since we had been at war. Now, I saw no other choice. We have to remember the Smolens attacked us when we were small individual clans and drove us out of our lands. This can never happen again.

I paused to take the measure of each of my fellow clansmen. "I have had a plan in mind for some time for a problem such as this, but have no doubt, it will be brutal and not for young hunters who could have a hard time living with what we must do."

Bruno spoke. He said, "Daven, please continue, like it or not, this discussion has to be heard."

I said, "My plan will keep the rest of the yellow skin people from ever knowing who destroyed their relatives. Others will come looking for their brothers after not hearing from them when the winter months have passed. They will never know who killed off an entire village and left no clues behind. We must be committed to kill every man, woman, and child, without exception. Not one child can be spared or taken for adoption, not one. If we do that, these same children will always look different. Eventually, they will learn the truth and bring revenge and death to us.

"I am making an assumption that the yellow ones are very confident in their ability to kill anyone who threatens them because they have successfully attacked the farmers to their north and have done it for years without paying a price. This time they must pay for their evil."

I asked Bruno and Janos, "Do you want to talk further right now or would you like to take a few hours to think about our options?" Bruno, Jon, and Janos wanted the time to clear their heads and think about what I said.

Before we went our own ways, Bruno asked, "Daven, how is it that you have this plan ready after just hearing of the attack on the Yar when I heard about it just a few hours ago?"

I replied, "My friend, I have been thinking about an attack from an outside tribe for years just in case it ever happened. It is my job, as lead hunter, to be prepared for every possibility. I remember what the Smolens did to the Horse Clan and later to the Bear and Aurochs Clans when you and I were children. If that happened again, the Botai might not survive as a people. I always thought it would be the Smolens who would grow in numbers and need more territory. I thought they would be the ones we would face, but it is the yellow ones we must fight. I fear the Smolens may still be a threat before our lives are over."

Bruno was deep in thought as we returned to our houses. He said, "I will see you in two hours." He entered his pit house, which was next to my own. Peter walked with his father to his house to visit his mother. We agreed to get back together in two hours. What we face was a life-and-death decision. It needed to be fully thought through. I talked to Ildiko, but not about this problem. She would learn of it soon enough. I wanted to enjoy her company, her warmth, and that of Marc. If we go forward, some of us might not return, but if my plan was followed, I am confident we will not lose too many men.

Two hours later, we got back together. This time, Jon, Mikl, George, and Peter joined us. Tedd, Emma, and Ruth attended, at the request of Bruno, because they were already adults the last time we were at war. Bruno described what happened to Ander's men and why Peter was back at our village. He told the group of the options. The news was bad, the solution grim. Bruno asked me, "Daven, what are the next steps?"

I responded, "Peter must return to the Krasnyi Yar village immediately. Report to Ander and tell him that we are coming in eight days. Mikl will return with Peter as a scout and equal to Peter. Ander will know of our commitment if I send my own son. Peter and Mikl will gather information and wait for us to arrive." I made it very clear, "I do not want Ander or anyone else to take any action before we arrive. When we have knowledge of them, we will know their vulnerabilities, and they will be easier to hunt."

I thought about previous horse hunts where I never wanted to completely wipe out a herd. It was better to take some of them but leave enough behind for them to regroup and grow once again. This situation was the opposite. I did not want them to regrow ever again. Nothing would be left of them to come back.

I turned to Peter and said, "There is one more issue. I want you to watch for white-skinned young people of your age who are very likely to be held as slaves. They will not be part of the normal village activities. They will be workers and guarded by Mongols. If you see them, do not make contact. Do not make contact even if they are being whipped or tortured. I will repeat myself… if they are whipped, tortured, or if one of them is killed before your eyes, you do not make contact. You and your scouts must not be detected."

Without saying a word, I knew Mikl understood what I said. Peter gave his word. "I will follow your direction." From his past performance, I had every confidence in him.

I turned to Mikl. I said, "My son, in this scouting assignment, Peter will be the leader. He is a Yar and will direct the Yar men Ander assigns to help. Until I arrive, you will report to Ander as will Peter." Mikl and Peter nodded in agreement.

Mikl was ready to leave with Peter. It was an exciting time. It was also a dangerous adventure. He said his good-byes to Marie and Ruth and bid farewell to me and Ildiko. The last person he talked to was Tedd, who was left with the half-finished bellows, the copper, and the tin. Mikl still wondered what to do with them. With luck, Tedd would find a use for them while he was away.

Marie had given up trying to explain it. She was too busy with her farming projects and her morning sickness to think about a bellows and a few metals. She kissed Mikl good-bye and told him she loved him. Her parting words were, "Come back to me, we need you." As he rode off, he thought about what she said, especially the word *we*. She was pregnant. He was off to face the most danger he had ever encountered.

Mikl rode with Peter. He had his new bow and supplies and his odd-looking woven mats rolled up under Gray Boy's neck. I could not imagine what useful purpose they would serve. If not new metals or the three-curve bow, it was the bellows. Now it was rolled-up mats. I asked myself, "What possible use could those mats have?"

CHAPTER 36

Inside the Mongol Village

AMONG THE YELLOW people, all the talk was about the two skinny white hunters the Mongol hunters had chased off a few weeks ago. They looked strange with their long bony legs and heavy beards. No healthy man should have so much hair. Their legs were so long that the Mongols thought they had been in-bred for too many generations. They looked deformed, like older versions of the prisoners they had taken over the years from the farms they raided. One chunky Mongol woman said to her friend, "The white-skinned ugly ones must have come to look for their children. Well, they can have their dead bodies back soon." They laughed, knowing the annual festival was coming shortly.

With winter approaching, the weakest slaves were always killed off at the end of the year. They hardly worked anymore and had outlived their usefulness. It took more effort to keep them working than what they produced in the fields. Hasar agreed he would talk to his older brother, Temuge, the Khan or king. These slaves were about used up.

As Hasar approached the ger, or the circular skin tent of his older brother, he thought about how Temuge became Khan here several years ago. Temuge ruled as all Khans did. He made all the decisions and was unquestioned by anyone, except perhaps by his second brother, Hasar.

His third brother, Hachun, had less privilege when compared to Hasar. If these two younger brothers questioned a decision by the Khan, it was done in a very careful manner and certainly not in a confrontational way. Neither one of them dared to raise a question in front of another clan member. Topics for "discussion" were allowed only when no one else is present.

When Temuge was a boy, he lived with his mother and father in a different Mongol village many miles east of here. On occasion, a distant relative, a Khan from another location, visited and told wild stories full of battles, conquests, and excitement. When Temuge came of age, he and his two younger brothers wanted to experience that excitement. They left their mother's village to join the distant relative to battle the ugly white northerners called Russians.

When they arrived at the new village, Temuge soon found out that two of his half-brothers, both a few years younger than he was, were already in the camp. When Temuge followed his distant relative into what was described as "battle," he discovered that it was more of a raid than a battle, and the raid was against unarmed farmers, not against fighters. It took little bravery as they burned farms and the people in them, but it was still exciting. The raids produced slaves and whatever else they could steal. It was the most exciting thing these Mongols did all year.

Over time, Temuge learned that his Khan was an absolute tyrant and not well liked or respected by his own men, but without doubt, the relative was feared. He was a dangerous man with a sword or a knife and had a temper to go with his fighting skills. The Khan ruled with impunity. No one dared challenge him on anything. He did whatever he wanted. If someone did not agree, they secretly left the village during the night with their family and whatever they could carry to look for another place to live.

Today, the Khan ordered a raid on another Mongol village. They were to kill the ruler of that village and take anything they could find of value. The relative wanted his sword and his light-skinned wife to settle an old grudge from when these two men were young boys. What he did not know was that the man he identified to be killed was an uncle to Temuge, someone who helped raise him as a boy. Temuge loved this uncle like a father.

The plan was simple. Kill the leader, take the younger women as second wives, and steal their herds of sheep and goats. The old women and their children would be left behind to fend for themselves. If anyone of his men wanted the old women, they were welcome to them. The Khan said, "By the time the children became adults, the raid would be forgotten." The sheep and goats and the older women were not important to Temuge, but killing his favorite uncle was another matter entirely. His face reddened, and his anger boiled.

While the plan was being described by the Khan, Temuge exploded in rage. He objected to killing the uncle, and he said so in front of the rest of the men. Temuge knew that speaking out against the Khan was an insult and a serious offense. It would not be ignored. No one challenged him without paying for it, usually with his life.

Temuge was smart. When he shouted his objection against the raid, he stepped toward the ruler instead of away from him. Temuge was so close he could smell the Khan's breath of goat's milk and onions from his morning meal. Temuge was so close, he could touch him without extending his arm. In this position, the Khan could not raise his sword, but Temuge could use his knife. The curved blade was already in his hand, and he used it expertly.

With one quick motion, Temuge slashed his bronze blade across the Khan's face, slicing it open and cutting across one of his eyes. The leader's cheek hung from his face, and his eye was split in two pieces. He howled in pain as blood gushed from the facial cut. The Khan was stunned. In no time, he was covered with his own blood. He could hardly see anything even with the good eye. The Mongol men, who did not like the Khan, backed away to watch Temuge and the Khan fight, knowing one would die. They laughed with delight and yelled in excitement at the surprising knife attack. They stood back instead of defending the hated Khan.

The knife slash was not a killing blow, but the Khan was badly injured. His vision was blurred, and his pain was severe. His legs wobbled, and he dropped his sword on the ground momentarily. He screamed in horror and held his face with both hands to stop the bleeding and cursed his attacker. Blood rushed down his face and dripped on the ground.

The Khan looked in his left hand where he held one half of his eye. In desperation, he tried to push the piece of the eye back into the socket. He staggered as the half of the eye fell out again. He felt the ground and reached for his sword. Temuge stomped on the Khan's hand with his boot and felt bones break. He smiled confidently as he grabbed the Khan by his greasy hair, pulled his head back, and cut his throat. The Khan bucked and choked several times and fell face forward. He was dead.

Temuge screamed, "I have killed this man who would kill my uncle. You will live a better life with me as your leader. I am your new Khan!"

Hasar was at his brother's side instantly and raised Temuge's arm high in the air and proclaimed, "Temuge is the rightful new Khan." His third brother, Hachun, stood with him and the two half-brothers quickly joined them. The five men, all with swords in their hands and ready to fight to the death, made a formidable presence.

The rest of the Khan's men did not challenge the brothers; instead, they cheered the new leader and pledged their allegiance to Temuge. They chanted, "Khan! Khan! Khan!" Temuge was better liked than the old ruler anyway. By now, the rest of the village had gathered to see what happened. The women joined their husbands cheering for the new leader as four white slaves were called to remove the dead body. "Let the wolves have their fill of this piece of goat dung," Temuge declared.

From that day forward, one head man from each ger reported directly to Temuge. There was no designated "second in command." Despite that, the rest of the village knew if there was a second in command, it was Hasar. What Temuge ordered was done, and there were no questions. Raids on the farmers were his to call. Orders might include raiding another Mongol village, stealing sheep or goats, kidnapping women, and at times they murdered another clan member if the Khan directed it. His authority was absolute.

There were eight families in this village with a total of sixty people. Each head man owned his wife, his children, his weapons, and his house. All of them were ruled by the Khan. Slaves and herds were also owned by the Khan, but shared by all. Of the sixty members, there were twenty-three men and boys of fighting age. Each man was armed with a bronze sword, a knife, and a bow, but they were not yet mounted.

It was Temuge who ordered the most recent raids on the Russian farms. He directed the kidnapping of the young people and the torture and killing of their parents and burning what was left behind. Some of the adults were burned alive while he taunted them to come out and save their children before he ate them! Of course, neither the Russians nor the Mongols understood the others' language.

Temuge claimed it was raiding that honed their fighting skills and eliminated boredom, but it was more of a massacre than a fight. The farmers were just that, farmers not fighters. However, the Mongol fighting skills were not what they once were. They got lazier as time went on because the slaves did most of the work and because they became herders of sheep and goats. Hunting was no longer necessary.

Raids were carried out at night and always by surprise, so the farmers had little chance to fight back even if they could. The farmers were not as skilled with bows and arrows as they once were. Instead, they hid in disguised cellars under their houses or under a shed. A few escaped that way being undetected, but most were found and killed for sport. The Mongols loved the sport.

It was exciting to raid the northerners who looked so odd with their pale white skin, strange wide open eyes, and full beards. They were so strange and different looking that it was easy to take no mercy on them. The ugly whites lived long distances apart from one farm to the next, so no help was available. They were easy prey. By the time the people from an adjoining farm saw smoke from last night's raid, it was too late. The raiders and the children were gone.

After stealing everything of value, including goats and sheep, the Mongols ate all they could and kidnapped children who were old enough to work. Younger children were of no use. They were killed off with their parents. Aurochs were too big to herd, so they were eaten or shot with arrows just to watch them die. It was great fun.

On the return trip, captives were blindfolded and walked in circles for a week or more while the main body of raiders returned in a more direct route. The captives were made to cross and recross the same rivers time after time. They traveled mostly at night to add to the slave's confusion. When they moved during the daytime, they went north. But over the long trip, they moved in a southerly direction. Slaves were allowed only water. A weaker captive was easier to control. By the time they reached the Mongol camp, they were completely confused and exhausted. When they arrived at the Mongol village, they were finally fed a solid meal.

To discourage them from trying to escape, they were made to watch their homes being burned. They heard the screams of death coming from inside. If they did escape, they had no idea where to go, no home, and no parents to return to. They worked all day and, at night, were locked in an enclosure made of poles and sticks. It resembled a cage. They were tied to a wall. If any one of them was found untied in the morning, they were all beaten bloody with sticks by the women. After weeks of captivity, they were without hope. They just tried to survive.

Temuge prohibited his men from having sex with the captives. He knew if sex was allowed, it would produce a group of half breeds, and half breeds might threaten his control. In his mind, the whites were human, but inferior and unintelligent compared to the Mongol race. Besides, they were so ugly, no man should want to have sex with them. The rule applied to everyone except of course, to himself. If one of his house slaves became pregnant, his medicine woman took care of the problem by giving the slave enough poisonous mushrooms to kill the baby. If the mother died in the process, it was not questioned.

New slaves were a curiosity at first, and the Mongol women enjoyed tormenting them. They were relieved that of most of the work of feeding the village was no longer theirs to do. The women only needed to attend to their massive herds of sheep and goats. These six new slaves would be added to the healthiest from last year's crop. Others who could hardly work anymore would be slaughtered as part of the coming winter festival. The slaves who screamed the most while tortured were the best. It was the highlight of the year.

Hasar announced himself at his brother's door. He pretended to be visiting on a social basis, but he still thought about the recent run-in with the two scrawny white men a few weeks ago. Hasar said, "Brother, those two men had to be Russians looking for their children. I am concerned that they escaped to the north. By now, I am sure they know where we live. Do you think they could mount an attack on us in an attempt to rescue our captives? My concern is renewed because one herder woman claims to have seen the same two men again today just outside our village."

Temuge snorted, "They are the least of my concerns. The whites do not fight, they hide. Those two are probably still running. They will never attack this camp or any other Mongol camp. Forget them, brother."

Temuge continued saying, "With winter approaching, my concern is food. It is time to hold the annual festival. We have enough food for ourselves. Schedule the festival to be held as soon as the fall gathering is complete. Pick those to be tortured from the weakest of the field workers. Of course, we will keep our house slaves to tend to us during winter."

Hasar saw that his brother was not concerned about the whites and laughed with Temuge as they drank their tea. He changed his approach and added a bit of bravado, saying, "The farmers might know where we live. I agree with you, I am not worried about an attack from such weaklings. They have no will to fight. They are not Mongols. I would slaughter them the day they arrive."

Temuge chortled, "I am sure the woman who said she saw the skinny whites was having a daydream. Women are foolish. By now those two are probably a hundred miles from here. Besides, it would be exciting if the Russians attacked. I would love it! We could kill them without having to travel all that distance to the north and keep a few as slaves. It would save us a lot of effort." They both enjoyed a hearty laugh.

On the way back to his own ger, Hasar passed the goat yard. He saw the bedraggled ugly white woman with half of a nose dressed in so many layers of filthy rags. She smelled bad. She had wandered here many months ago with a good-sized herd of goats that were mixed with the Mongol goats. It was a good thing to mix different animals to avoid inbreeding. She brought value as a herder. She was certainly ugly, but she knew how to herd and was useful. Without much concern, Temuge had let her stay.

Of course, the white woman had the status of a slave, a filthy Russian, Hasar presumed, but a good worker. She had no weapons except for a small flint blade and needed no guarding. If she did escape, she had nowhere to go, so why guard her? She was a good slave and ate little, yet she stayed fat and healthy. Hasar wondered how this woman could stay healthy with so little food when the other white slaves got weaker on the same amount of food.

The other thing that bothered Hasar was that her language seemed to be different from that of the rest of the slaves. Of course they all had to be Russians, there were no other people. She must be from a distant village, one where they had a different tongue than those in the farms we raided. Or more likely, they had no true language at all and just made sounds and grunts that made no sense. Temuge laughed at the notion of whites attacking them. Hasar would not worry either.

CHAPTER 37

The Plan of Attack

AS WE DEPARTED our village, I thought about how far we have come in one year. We headed west to confront an enemy with sixteen fighters. All of us were mounted, armed with three-curve bows and a copper ax at our sides. Pack horses followed behind with our food and supplies, tents, spears, and atlatls and many extra arrows tied in packs. We carried our bows, a full quiver, and water. I thought there might not be another force of a similar size anywhere in the world who could challenge us. Just the thunder of hoofs beneath us was awe-inspiring. We had powerful weapons, we're well trained and possessed mobility that no one else had. And we were disciplined hunters.

In two days, we arrived at Ander's village. The distance was covered easily and without incident. Bruno and I led our impressive group of mounted riders into the Krasnyi Yar village followed by Jon and Janos. It had been well over two years since we had seen some of these people, and many were related to the men in our group. It was a reunion we would have to repeat when the circumstances were more pleasant than this situation. Ander, Mikl, Peter, and the entire village came out to welcome us.

Ander greeted us. He told us, "My men have been scouting the enemy for five days. Mikl returned today and shared what he and Peter have observed so far. Peter stayed with his men to further scout the enemy." After greeting old friends and relatives, we gathered to discuss their observations. I thought of this enemy as if it had the cunning of a mountain lion and the viciousness of a wounded bear. There was no room for mistakes.

Mikl drew a map of the Mongol village on the ground. He identified the locations of the round tent-like houses called gers. Mikl said, "Peter and I can see light and shadows coming through the walls, which tells me two things. First is that these houses were skin-covered and easily penetrated by heavy arrows. The second was that the houses with lights at night were occupied by people instead of animals or supplies."

He added, "Most likely the slaves were kept in houses without light, which are one of these," as he pointed to his drawing. He identified the houses where people were seen entering and leaving and several others that were used for storage or to hold goats and sheep. Mikl said, "There appears to be a small herd of goats kept in camp at all times for food. The rest of the animals are grazed outside of the village at long distances away. These distant herds are controlled by just a few herders. They can be dealt with later."

I studied the drawing of the village. There were six large occupied circular homes. Three other tents hold supplies and one more had animals with a herder or elder who handled them. The last unlit house probably held slaves. I thought it was very likely that these were the children Lazar and the Russians were looking for last summer. The largest house, located in the middle of the village, seemed to be the central point in the village and very likely that of the leader's. Our scouts heard passing villagers refer to him as the Khan.

Mikl described what he observed. "We saw roughly a dozen captives, maybe more working the fields. They were taller, thinner, and white skinned, unlike any member of the Mongol tribe. The slaves work long hours and are always guarded. They have little clothing and looked severely undernourished, almost as if they might collapse and die at any time. They are distinctly different from the Mongols who are short and fat and have black hair."

Mikl was not sure if these slaves were male or female. He said, "They are certainly not children. These slaves might be the same ones Marie's uncle searched for, but they could also be some other young people who were enslaved from somewhere else. One thing is certain, they are slaves. Peter and I never got close enough to be able to tell much more about them."

Mikl mentioned one other odd observation. "There is one other tall person who lives with the goats and sheep. He pointed to the house where this herder lived. That one is dressed in layers of rags and seemed to be well fed. I am not sure if it is a tall Mongol or a slave. The herder is not guarded and has freedom to roam the village, so I assumed they are part of the village. It is odd that the person is as tall as we are. The person could be a threat."

I thought about the situation and gave an order. "This herder must be regarded as another Mongol until we know better. I think they might be an elder who no longer has any family but was probably good with animals. Even an old herder, whether it was a man or woman, has to be considered as dangerous as anyone one else. Kill that one at the first opportunity."

It was my intention to make the raid look as if wild horses that the Mongols have hunted for years finally took revenge and attacked them in return. If the Mongols were superstitious, as many primitive people were, the plan would work. After we killed them, we would smash their bodies and heads with horse hoofs I brought along just for that purpose. No face would be left intact, and every head must be smashed. Crushed bodies and heads would be the only evidence we would leave behind. There would be horse tracks from us everywhere. Nothing would be burned and no children adopted because horses could not do that. Once we rescued the slaves, Ander and Bruno could determine what to do with them.

I instructed the men. "On the morning of the attack, you must dip every one of your arrowheads in the hemlock poison Patts made for us." I hesitated and let them think about what I just said. "Not a single man woman or child will be allowed to escape. If they do not die from your arrow, they will die in a day or two from poison.

"Relatives of these people will wonder why they have not seen them after the winter months and will come looking for them. They will find this village, but all they will see are the smashed bodies and hoof marks of horses. We will remove every arrow and be careful not to break any, so no arrowhead will ever be found when the bodies decay or they are eaten by the winter scavengers. Let their friends think it was the same horses they hunted who took their revenge. Mongols coming here next year will never know who did this work. Remember, men, not one person escapes."

I continued with my observations. "The village is composed of ten houses. The occupants of each house are probably an extended family with men, women, children, and elders. I guessed there were about sixty to seventy members in total, perhaps a few more. With sixty members, I assume that there are twenty-five fighters, so our numbers will be about even with theirs." I asked Mikl if there were any other facts we should know.

Mikl reluctantly recalled, almost confessed, that one more issue needed to be discussed. He said, "Despite our best efforts to stay concealed, one of the female herders probably saw two of our scouts by chance, so they might be on guard against an attack."

I asked Mikl, "Did the Mongols chase the scouts or come looking for them?"

He replied, "No, no one came out. Not one hunter came out." He said, "I thought that was odd since they chased the two Yar men a few weeks before and followed them for miles." I had an idea, which altered my attack plan.

Mikl added one more important fact. "Peter and I saw that the Mongol men are armed with long swords. These swords are held in scabbards by a belt at their sides. When these swords are seen at a distance, they glint in the sun and are a different color than copper. I saw one of the men kill a sheep with a single blow without bending the blade. They are unlike anything I have seen before. They are as long as a man's arm if not longer. If the Mongols get close to us, they have a deadly advantage over us since we have no weapons to match these."

I listened to what Mikl said and thought that the swords must be made of a new type of metal to be so long and yet strong enough not to bend. I wanted to examine these weapons when the fight was done. Their bows were described as the old-style long bows, not three-curve bows like ours, so we have an advantage as long as we stayed at a distance. Long distance is where the fight would be fought and won.

Mikl described the terrain as rolling hills with short grasses. It was unlike the tall grass near our village; this grass was only a foot or so high with little area to hide other than a few stunted trees and scrub brush. He marked the ground where trails led in and out of the village in several directions. He said, "These four trails lead to distant herding areas, far away from the main village. Two other trails lead to other Mongol villages to the east. These villages were over fifty miles distant. There might be more villages beyond them, but we did not track any farther than the two closest."

I assigned two hunters to guard each of the two trails. They were to kill anyone coming or going to this village. If anyone happened to be coming to this village, and saw our attack, they would retreat in silence and bring help, or worse yet, track us down after we left. No one would be allowed to enter, and no one would be allowed to escape.

My plan was not complicated. We would arrive before daybreak and surround the village. Six bowmen would be mounted in case there were early escape attempts. Twenty men would be on foot. I described what we had to do. "We will kill the two guards first." I assigned four men to kill them. I reasoned, with four men, there would be at least two arrows in each guard, and death would come as quickly and quietly as possible. Peter and George would lead the attack. I said, "If the guards make any noise, they will alert the sleeping village. If that happens, we will hold our positions and kill them as they come out of their houses."

The new information about the two scouts Mikl said were probably seen, but not chased, changed my plan. I was sure the sighting was reported. The fact that they were not chased gave me an opening. They had to be very sure of themselves to ignore such a report. If the Botai were slavers, and I was the Khan, I would certainly not ignore such a report. With this new information, I changed the beginning of the battle.

I said, "I will signal the start of the fight by raising my arm, at which point, Bruno and I will approach the village on foot acting as though we are the two Russians looking for their children. We will scream at them, curse them, and challenge them to fight. If they are as overconfident of themselves as I think they are, they will charge after us, expecting an easy kill. Bruno and I will kill the first of them who come out and then pretend to run away. We will run toward you. When we reach your line, we will turn and join you in killing those who chase us. I have no doubt we will destroy the first group before their old-style bows can reach us.

I continued with the plan. "If any of them escape our arrows, they will retreat to their houses and regroup. At that point, we will close the distance and rain our bear hunting arrows through the roofs of their tents. Our heavy arrows will have the same effect as spears, killing anyone they strike. First, we target the main house of the Khan and then attack the houses surrounding his. My guess is that the second and third in command will occupy the houses closest to his. Do not try to help the captives even if they beg for help. They can be helped later.

"Ander, you must be wary of the goat herder who sleeps alone. That one is as dangerous as the rest of them. That area will be yours to guard, so when the noise starts, they will come out to see what is happening. Kill that herder on sight." Ander nodded to me saying that he understood.

"Our horsemen will hunt down those who try to escape. Do not get off your horse and do not get close to any of them. Use your bows to kill runners at a distance. With our arrows dipped in poison, any wound will be fatal over a few hours."

"Be very careful of the long swords Mikl described. If a rider gets too close, he could lose a leg or an arm with one slice of a sword. If I were one of them, I would try to kill your horse. If you lose your horse, the battle would be one on one on the ground. They have an advantage with the sword being a superior weapon to an axe at close fighting. Do not lose your advantage of being mounted. Kill them at a safe distance and most of all, have no mercy. They will have none for you." There were no questions.

CHAPTER 38

Revenge and Rescue

WE ARRIVED AFTER sunset and set up camp several miles downwind of the Mongol village. We could see the glow of fires and smell their animals. Four guards were set to rotate every few hours. The weather was clear and cold with the distinct look of snow in the sky.

The attack was set for the next day at first light. I felt as though I was on my first big horse hunt fifteen years ago, and I had trouble getting to sleep. There was far too much at stake to sleep well. Had I missed anything? Did I cover every detail? How would the Yar men hold up under battle conditions? I had trained every one of them but wondered if they were as disciplined as they once were. Would they panic? I did not want to lose a single man. I finally dozed off thinking of Marc and Ildiko and our soon-to-be second child. I worried about everyone and every detail, but never about myself.

Someone stirred before sunup, and I was awake immediately. I quietly woke the others when it was time, and we ate a meal knowing it might be the only one of the day. Mikl and Peter told me they had no new information other than that two herders returned to camp and two others went out to a distant location. Two guards protected the village. Everything else was the same.

With one hour left before daybreak, we approached the Mongol camp in silence. When everyone was in position, Peter and George and two other hunters silently crept up on the two guards. To Peter's surprise, the guards were sound asleep with their bows on the ground and their swords still in their holders. Peter and George raised their axes, nodded to each other, and slammed their axes into the sleeping guards' heads with killing power. Other than a slight grunt, they made no sound at all. The herder in the goat house did not stir. The first step went according to plan. We waited for daylight.

An hour later, there was enough light for us to see. I raised my hand and waited for each hunter to signal that they were aware the battle was about to begin. Bruno and I walked forward without making a sound. When we were within range for our bows, but not theirs, we yelled and cursed at the camp. We heard voices, and candles were lit in several gers or tents, but no one came out. They were still half asleep and most likely waited for their guards to signal if there was trouble.

After another minute or two, one man came out for a look, and I shot him through his chest. Bruno had his bow ready as I notched my next arrow. Suddenly, more men from two houses came out and saw us taunting them. As expected, they charged at us, screaming something in their language with their swords held over their heads. Bruno shot the second man and I killed the third. Four others chased us. We turned and ran to where our men waited.

Bruno and I ran away from our pursuers, but we did not run very fast. We set the trap as the four short fat Mongols charged with their swords. When they reached our line, they were cut down by arrows. They dropped to the ground, grabbing at their wounds. They twisted and moaned with pain. I signaled with a whistle, and the horsemen came forward. As we advanced on the village, we smashed the heads of those on the ground to be sure they would cause no further problems. We had killed a good portion of the estimated twenty to twenty-five Mongol fighters. Now, I thought, we probably had superior numbers.

Our first wave of heavy arrows rained down on the tent of the Khan, and we heard screams coming from those inside. I signaled for the next closest tent to be attacked. It was hit with the same result. Two men came out of a ger, and Mikl and I killed them with arrows before they got within range. There was confusion everywhere with Mongols running from the outer tents to the inner tents of the Khan and his brothers. I directed the men to attack the next tent before anyone inside had a chance to organize a defense.

Ander held the right side of the line, and sure enough, the old herder came out with a broken sword in hand. Ander and one of his clan leaders hit the herder with arrows. Multiple layers of heavy clothing blocked a killing shot, but both poisoned arrows did strike as the herder retreated inside.

While this was happening, the slaves heard the commotion and called for help. They begged to be released. Ander's men showed the discipline I taught them many years ago and did not respond to the cries. They stayed focused on the battle.

At my signal, the fourth skin tent house or ger was attacked, and then the fifth and sixth. Arrows rained down on them like it was sleet falling from the sky. The village was in chaos. Mongol women were everywhere, running with children in panic, but they were shot down. When they saw us killing their friends and relatives, the survivors retreated to the main house, that of the Khan. We launched another round of heavy arrows. Sunlight was brighter now.

We rained more heavy arrows on one house after another in unison and waited for Mongols to emerge from the front or back. None of our arrows were shot back at us because the old-style standard bows were not strong enough to shoot them back. Horsemen delivered dozens of more arrows from our campsite.

Hasar crawled out of the back of his house and into his younger brother's house, which was next to his. Many of the people inside were dead or wounded. Hasar armed himself with a bow and sword, and his brother Hachun did the same. The Khan ordered them to try to escape and bring help.

For a few brief minutes, the brothers ran unseen, heading east to the next village just as I suspected they would. Mikl, George, and I rode after them. I yelled another warning about their swords. Mikl nodded, he understood what I said. We were on them in a minute. I notched my arrow and, with deadly accuracy, drove it through Hasar's back. He staggered a few more feet and turned toward me in a feeble attempt to shoot me with his bow, but I shot him again through his chest. Hasar moaned in death. He was finished. I yelled, "That one is for the children!" His eyes were glassy, and his body twitched in death.

Hachun saw what happened. He must have been stunned by the sight of three men on horses running him down. With no escape possible, Hachun stopped short and reversed his direction so suddenly that Mikl, with the momentum of his galloping horse, rode right past him. As Mikl passed his enemy, Hachun swung his sword with both hands and hit Gray Boy. The blade sliced across the front of Gray Boy's neck and would have killed the horse if not for Mikl's woven mats hanging from Gray Boy's neck. The horse felt the blow, but the sword did no serious damage.

Mikl turned his horse around to attack Hachun again when I shot the Mongol through his right shoulder, the same arm that held the sword. Hachun cried out in pain and switched the sword to his other hand. Mikl and Gray Boy were on him too fast. Mikl smashed his head so hard, Hachun's head split in half. I heard the crack of the man's skull and saw his brains splatter. It was over. We returned to the battle. George rode his horse over Hachun to be sure.

The remaining Mongols were all hiding in the main ger of the Khan. The wounded moaned and cried out in pain and begged for mercy. We waited for more escape attempts, but none were made. The Khan had already sent his brothers for help, so for now, his best bet would be to stay inside and try to hold out until dark. Despite the chaos of the attack, my men held their positions.

I signaled for another attack. More arrows rained through the roof of the main tent. Death struck with more arrows coming in waves. We killed those who tried to run. After two hours, there was just one tent still occupied and very few Mongol fighters left. Inside his tent, the Khan knew there was little time left. He needed to do something fast.

Ander held the right side of our line, that area nearest the goat herder and the captives. Despite being watched, the old herder made a successful escape undetected because she wore a sheepskin disguise that covered her completely. The herder crawled away with sheep on both sides of her. It was a clever escape. The herder slowly moved in a westerly direction away from the battle, already feeling sick from the poison.

Temuge called his remaining people together in his tent. "The Russians have us surrounded. They have bows more powerful than ours. If we stay in here, they will kill us all. We have one chance left. We have to create a diversion."

Women cried in terror, and children screamed as he barked orders. His men were terrified. They were down to one desperate attempt to avoid total destruction. The Khan had only a few fighters left plus his women and children, all crying for him to save them.

Temuge told the Mongol women, "Take your children and leave by the front door with your hands in the air. They will not kill women and children." They knew Temuge lied, and several women hesitated, so the Khan pushed the first few through the door and swung his sword at the rest to get them moving. They came out of the ger yelling the Russian word for "mercy," but it had no effect on us. It was not the behavior of the Botai to kill women or children, but we had no choice. If one of them survived, they would find the Krasnyi Yar and kill our people, so it had to be this way.

We shot them down and rained more arrows on the main tent. Death came through the roof for the remaining few who refused to leave. The women provided the diversion Temuge needed. He and his remaining men crawled out of the back of the house and ran. In his mind, it was a shame about the children, but women could always be replaced.

I knew the Mongol women were a diversion and yelled to the far areas of our line to watch for runners. I was not fooled by the Khan's desperate escape plan. Ander's men shot them down as they ran past the right side in panic. Not one escaped. The Mongols who preyed on others for generations were being hunted to the last person. Only the Khan remained.

The few who got past Ander and his men dropped their bows and ran in a desperate attempt to escape the mounted horsemen. Not one of these runners fired an arrow in return. They screamed and ran for their lives. Horsemen closed in on them, at four times the speed a man could run, and killed them with arrows. We dismounted and finished them off with axes. The Mongol village was totally annihilated, except for Temuge.

The vicious Khan ran in the opposite direction from his men. That was his mistake. Peter and Janos held that area. With his gold necklace and earrings, they knew the runner was the Mongol leader, and Peter shot an arrow through his leg to slow him down. Temuge fell to the ground but got up using his good leg. Temuge stood with his sword in his hand and motioned for Peter to come and fight him.

Peter was not fooled. He would not play a game with this man who burned farmers alive and enslaved their children. He stayed on his horse and circled his foe at a safe distance. Neither of them understood the other's language. Despite this, Peter yelled at him, "Your death will be a slow one." Peter shot another arrow into the Khan's shoulder, the one that held the sword.

The Khan, badly wounded and facing death, did not beg for mercy. Instead pulled his knife and screamed his defiance, "Remember this day, white man. My people will find you. Your children will be cut to pieces and eaten by my brothers." The Khan spit at Peter.

Peter sent his third arrow through the Mongol's stomach. Temuge was barely breathing, but he was still alive. Janos and Peter dismounted, and Peter kicked the Khan's weapon from his hand. Peter took his ax and smashed the Khan's right knee, talking to him the whole time. Then he smashed the second knee.

Peter asked in his own language, "Do you have any more threats?" The Khan groaned in pain as Peter took his ax and chopped at the Khan's head, missing him on purpose. Peter laughed at his enemy, the man who had killed so many who could not defend themselves. Janos stood close at hand just in case he was needed. The Khan spit blood, and Peter chopped off half his face including his jaw. Peter circled him and waited so the once-feared Khan could feel the agony before he crushed his head with a final blow. I would have killed him the same way, slowly.

By midday, the battle was over, and we had not lost a single man. What disturbed me most was that we could have lost Gray Boy. That was a lesson we would learn from for the future. Mikl's woven horse mats protected his mount so well that we would make similar mats for every horse in case we ever needed them in another battle.

It was over when Bruno gave the order for Mikl and Jon to release the slaves. Mikl was waiting and moved quickly. He was the only one of us who knew any Russian words. As he entered their cagelike, enclosure they screamed in terror. When Mikl spoke a few words in their language, they cried in disbelief. Instead of a Mongol bringing death, it was someone who came to save them.

He said in Russian, "Your uncle Lazar sent me to rescue you... your cousin Marinova has a new home for you!" Their fear turned to surprise and relief as they wept while they were being untied. All of them had given up hope a long time ago and now cried tears of celebration. Each one of them was filled with overwhelming joy and thanked Mikl, thinking he was the head man.

One of the tall men who seemed to be the slave leader named Alex told Mikl, "There are four female slaves in the Khan's house and those houses of his brothers. I found them still hiding under the sleeping platforms. With the rain of arrows coming through the roof, the Mongol occupants ran to the Khan to be saved, but the slaves escaped harm by staying where they were."

In all, we rescued sixteen starved young men and women. I noticed the house slaves were not as malnourished as the field slaves. I also noticed that two of them only hugged each other as they were freed. I suspected some sort of class conflict between house slaves and those that worked the fields. I hoped it was temporary, but I let it go.

As Mikl and Jon released the slaves, they hugged them with what little energy they had left. Mikl said, "I have food and water for you. I will take you to your new home where Marinova lives. She is my wife." They were so overjoyed they would have followed Mikl anywhere. For now, he led them to the edge of camp where we held food supplies and extra horses. We gave them only small portions to eat. Mikl said in Russian, "Eat slowly." We knew from past experience that starving people could become deathly sick if they ate too much too quickly. They ate everything and begged for more.

I gave the order to retrieve the arrows from every Mongol body. There would be no burning of the village and no evidence of our raid. I ordered that the gold necklace of the Khan and his earrings be left on him. Leaving gold behind would remove any suspicion that another people had slaughtered this village. I called Bruno, Jon, Ander, and Janos and four other senior men to help me smash the heads and bodies with hooves to disguise our work.

As we collected our arrows, I looked at the swords and said to Bruno, "We might want to take those magnificent swords. With the bellows, we could melt the handles and remove the Mongol markings so they can never be identified. We could have Tedd and Dann replace the old markings with a horse on the handle or perhaps something else to identify the new owners."

Bruno asked Janos and Ander what they thought about taking the swords. They readily agreed. "We should take them. They are too valuable as weapons to leave behind and will hardly be noticed when the horror of the rest of the camp is found." Bruno took the sword carried by the Khan, and I took the one that belonged to his oldest brother. Peter took one from the guard he killed. Mikl, Janos, Ander, and Jon found their own next to other dead Mongols. We gathered the rest and distributed them to the men as rewards. There were more than enough to go around with extras left over.

Mongol relatives who might come looking for these people next spring would find no evidence other than wild horses taking their revenge. We worked for an hour to finish our grisly task of smashing their heads and bodies with horse hooves. Ander came upon the Khan and took pleasure in smashing his head until no one could possibly recognize him. Ander worked next to me when he said, "I wonder how many people this Khan killed before we ended his miserable life."

Bruno responded, "Too many."

The work was grim, but it had to be done if we were to disguise our attack. We found all of the heavy arrows, but the count was two short. We were missing two lightweight arrows. We searched the entire area another time with different men looking in different areas, still we came up two short. I guessed that the two missing arrows must have missed their target and flew too far to be found. While we searched the houses for the missing arrows, we found metal cooking pots that were better than our own and took them. The pots were made of the same metal as the swords.

I sent a party of eight mounted horsemen after the herders who were out of the main camp when we attacked. They were easily destroyed. Every animal was stripped of collars and bells and released to the wild. Goats were quick to leave, heading in the general direction of the mountains in the distance. It was a new day for them. Some would be taken by wolves, but most would return to the free life they once knew. Sheep must have been tamed for too long because they followed us by the hundreds.

We were anxious to get away from the Mongol village as fast as possible, but we were still missing those two arrows, and it bothered me. While I searched the village one last time, I noticed a fire hearth with a bellows and two metals that were being worked by a Mongol craftsman. These were the same metals as those that the Russian man traded with Mikl: copper and tin. There were piles of three pieces of tin and seventeen pieces of copper. I looked at the carefully laid out piles when it finally dawned on me! It had to be… copper and tin, when combined, made the new metal used for their swords. *Combined* was the word Marie used. Copper and tin combined made what Russians called "bronze."

I called Mikl to show him what I found. Both of us were excited. We knew Tedd would be excited too. We gathered the metals and the Mongol bellows and packed them on the supply horses for the return trip. I called the other leaders and explained what we had. Now I told them, "We could make bronze swords of our own."

I finally gave up looking for the two missing arrows. I knew the count was off, but we had to leave. If they were left behind, it could be the fatal flaw in the plan, but after three searches, I gave up. We left the Mongol camp with horse hoofs marking the ground everywhere. Many of the captives were too weak to walk, so we placed them on the dragging platforms, and our men walked. Two of the house slaves—Katarina and her sister, Jewel—rode on one platform and hardly talked to the others we had rescued. I wondered if they would become a problem.

It was a short time later when Ander saw the old herder crawling on the trail heading west, still holding on to one of her sheep for support. I was shocked and hardly recognized her. She looked old and haggard, and most of her nose was gone; but without any doubt, it was Gertrude. Everyone stopped to look at her. She was wounded in her leg and chest, and there were the two missing arrows. With all the rags she wore, the arrows were partially blocked from killing her, similar to what the woven mats had done to protect Gray Boy.

Bruno felt no mercy for Gertrude and certainly Ander did not either. She was responsible for his father's death. Ander asked, "How could she have gotten this far?" I stopped caring about her several years before she was banned from the Botai. Seeing her again was like looking at someone that I did not know at all. I had no anger or hate for her but no compassion either. Mikl saw her as his birth mother. He knew she had rejected him, but she was still his mother and did what he could to comfort her as the poison did its work.

We never brought medicine women on hunting trips, so there was no one present to administer any kind of medicine. Gertrude was going to die. She was bleeding from two wounds and had no chance. She knew it. Her last words that day were "Daven, how could you do this to me? If not for you, I would not be dying. And you, Bruno, if you did not banish me, I would not be here." She closed her eyes.

We placed Gertrude on the supply platform right next to the bellows and the bronze pots and went on. Three hours later, we stopped to make a camp for the night. This time, we made a fire and ate well, roasting some of the Mongol sheep. The meat was greasy compared to horse meat. I said to Bruno, "No wonder our people gave up mutton years ago. Give me horse meat anytime."

Over the campfire, we talked of the battle. One hunter after another congratulated me on the perfect plan and having covered every detail, even counting the arrows after the battle. I congratulated them on perfect execution. There were many hugs that night.

Ander said, "Daven, my friend, if you are not happy being a Botai, you have a home with me any time you want it."

Bruno heard the invitation and replied with a grunt, "Daven has a home, he is going nowhere." Ander said that it was a joke and laughed it off. Bruno scowled in his direction and finally laughed along with Ander.

I still wondered if we should have left the bronze swords behind, but they were just too impressive not to take with us. We can use them as models to make our own swords. As I went to sleep, I saw Mikl looking at his mother, unconscious on the ground. She did not move. He still longed for that motherly love he never had and never would have. Gertrude was dead the next morning. I removed the two arrows and helped Mikl bury her along the trail in a grave covered with stones, never to be found again. Mikl offered a prayer to the spirits. Other than Mikl and myself, there were few attendees and there was no ceremony.

When we reached Ander's village; it was evening, and a light snow fell. It made me think about the horse hunts we needed to complete before winter set in, and it also made me think that no Mongol relatives would find that village for another six months. By then, the tents would be torn from the wind and crushed by the weight of the snow. Wolves, crows, rats, and other scavengers would be at work all winter, so there would be no evidence to find next year.

Other Mongols would wonder what happened. Was it horses taking revenge, or was it the Russians who came for revenge and rescued their children? They would find no explanations. Maybe other Khans would think twice before attacking farmers and taking slaves. Maybe not.

CHAPTER 39

Home Never Felt so Good

WE REACHED THE Krasnyi Yar village four days later. The entire group of Botai and Krasnyi Yar men who went into battle returned safely. Following us was a huge herd of sheep numbering into the hundreds. Every husband and every son was a hero, and every family was proud. This story would be told and retold many times for many years.

Ander and Peter were seen as the leaders of the Yar village and received much of the praise, as did the Botai who came to their help. Ander made a wise choice when he asked for Peter. At the evening feast of roasted mutton, there was laughter, singing of the traditional songs, and dancing. Wine flowed as did the lightly alcoholic milky beverage, koumiss. Wives and mothers were overjoyed to have their men back in camp unharmed.

Later that night, at the height of the festivities, Ander called for attention and asked Peter to come to the front of the crowd, which he did. Ander cited his heroism and leadership and named Peter as the new head of the Horse Clan. He was presented with his first Cave Bear claw from Ander's own necklace. Prior to Peter, Jon was the youngest known clan leader. His father, Janos, was there to raise Peter's arm in celebration. Janos was proud and wished his wife could be here to see this. Ander was the Oldson, but with Peter taking over the Horse Clan, it was obvious to everyone that he was second in command.

As the evening quieted down, a group of the leading men including me, Bruno, Ander, Janos, Jon, and now Peter, plus the two other Yar clan leaders, met to discuss the rescued slaves. They were aged twelve to fifteen when they were captured and now ranged from fourteen to eighteen. They would be considered adults if age was the only factor.

For them, it was different. They were taken when they were young but old enough to be worked and became of adult age while they were held captive. They endured more than most of us, as far as hardships apply, but in many ways, it was as though they missed the normal experiences of reaching maturity. None of them was married, none had children, and none had living parents. The young men had not achieved hunting skills, and the women missed the usual maturity process.

Many of them were closely related as brothers and sisters or cousins. Some, however, came from distant Russian farms and knew each other only as prisoners. Having each other is what got them through their ordeal of beatings, starvation, and hopelessness. By being adopted into the Yar and Botai villages, they would have more than just each other.

I knew from past experience that starving people had to be fed sparingly until they were ready for larger meals. All of them were skin and bones, but four were in worse condition than the others. These four were the best workers from two years ago and were held for an extra year with one being held for two years. The Mongols had less need for slaves over the winter, so they kept just a few for more than a year. When we rescued them, these were the weakest.

Our discussion tonight was about their future: what to do with them. I asked the question that was on everyone's mind. "Who among the former slaves stay with the Yar, and who of them come with us to our village?" All of them were similar in age and all had the same skills, that of farmers. Four of the new people were Marie's cousins and healthy enough to travel, so it was an easy decision to bring them to the Botai village.

The issue was their health, housing, and food supplies. There were not a lot of unoccupied pit houses available in either village, so no matter where they went, some of them had to be housed with villagers until spring, when new houses could be built. If all sixteen of them stayed at one village, it would be too hard for that village to provide enough food and shelter over the coming winter.

After much discussion, it was decided to leave six men and women at the Yar village with the remaining ten coming with us to the Botai village. The group of six included the oldest among them, but also four of the weakest who could not travel much farther. The remaining ten included the two female house slaves from the Khan's tent. They would join Marie's four cousins and six other former field slaves. The Yar would have forty-four people in all. The Botai with ten new people would have more than double their numbers.

One woman, who married into the Yar at the last summer gathering, volunteered to take in one of the brother-and-sister pair for the winter. Originally, she came from a Russian tribe and spoke the language very well. She would be instrumental in teaching the newcomers the Botai language and helping them adjust to their surroundings. Naturally, there would be some struggle learning the language and customs, but like all other newcomers, they would learn our ways and become part of us.

It was agreed among the clan leaders that all of them would attend the summer gathering next year. If any one of them wished to return with the Russians, they would be free to go back with Lazar. With nothing to return to for now, their future was here with us.

I asked, "Since these new people are farmers and have no hunting skills, do they become hunters, or do we learn their skills and become farmers? They know things we do not know, things that bring value." I said to Bruno and Ander, "A year ago I would have said make them hunters, but now I am seeing the benefits of change."

I continued with my thoughts, "Change can offer better ways of doing things. Without the new three-curve bows and the horses we ride, we may not have won the battle with the Mongols. Those changes were ideas that I once resisted. I look back at when I thought changes were a waste of time. Now, I see things differently."

Ander said, "We know how to hunt, and we have more hunters maturing next year, as do the Botai. By this time next year, with any luck at all, we will have a herd of horses as large as yours, and every man will be mounted. Farming may indeed have a future. If we can grow more food closer to home, we will not have to depend so much on gathering what nature provides. We can still hunt and gather as we need, but with farming, food supplies will increase."

Bruno nodded in agreement. "We have already seen what can be done with our berry patches and the new apple orchard. Marie has shown our senior women how to replant wheat as we gather the ripe kernels. I agree with Ander, farming has a future. Let them learn hunting from us and we will learn to farm from them, but every man among them must be proficient with weapons. It may be another generation before there is permanent peace."

Mikl spoke, "I will see that our new people become part of the gathering teams. Marie, with her Russian language skills, will help them become acquainted with Botai customs."

Ander replied, "I will have these new people lead a farming group in the spring, and Peter can train the men in weapons and hunting. By that time, they will be fully healthy. With a few days of rest and some decent food, they can help with light work, gathering peas, lentils, and berries as best they can. The heavy work of new housing can wait until winter passes."

As we talked, I watched the new people meeting members of the Yar. They had already mastered a few words, thanks to Mikl and the Russian woman. Smiles and gestures were working too. I also noticed two other things. All of them were eating and drinking continuously, and two of the Yar women who I recognized from the summer gathering a few months ago were very interested in these new men. These same two women were the ones that looked for husbands and rejected Flint. I doubted they would lack husbands much longer. With the six newcomers plus Peter and his wife and new babies over the winter, the Krasnyi Yar people were healthy and growing.

The next day, we bid our friends good-bye and headed home. Peter and Ander rode out with us for a few miles to see us off. We promised to come for a visit in the spring once the snows were gone and to see them again at the next gathering. As we left, Ander jokingly said, "I will feed those two big men plenty of horse meat over the winter, and I promise you, the Botai will be in the mud next year." We laughed. With the size of his new broad-shouldered Russian men, he just might be right.

Bruno yelled back, "I have a few of them too. We will see who goes in the muck!" We waved and headed for home with a trail of hundreds of sheep following us.

The last hundred miles back to our village was covered at a slower pace than on the way to the battle. Going out, we were all mounted; coming back, some of us were walking while the weaker captives lay on dragging platforms. From an area of dry air and short grasses, we slowly entered taller grass with scattered trees, and we saw two horse herds off in the distance. We were close to home.

While I walked, Bruno said, "Daven, I have been thinking about the battle and our future needs. I want every hunter to ride a stallion instead of a mare by the end of next year. Stallions are bigger and stronger and can run faster with a man on their back. At some point, we may be challenged by another mounted people. It could mean life and death in a battle to have the best mounts."

I replied, "Good observation, my friend, I will move in that direction starting with the fall horse hunts." I loved riding my horse, Star, but Bruno made a good point. Stallions were bigger and stronger. With an eleven-month pregnancy time, riding a mare was not as practical as riding a stallion.

"Besides," Bruno said, "I am growing fond of that new drink the women call koumiss. I like the milky taste and hint of alcohol and the light buzz it leaves. I think it might catch on one day. With mares left in camp as work horses, there will be plenty of foals, and with them comes a supply of mare's milk for koumiss."

Bruno talked about Diana and how he missed her and his daughters. He complained that he had all those stupid disputes facing him when he got back to the village and resumed his role as the Oldson. He groaned, "May the spirits save me from them!"

I asked him, "Why did you campaign so hard to become the Oldson if not to settle such silly stuff in the first place?" Bruno knew I was kidding. I told him, "The ladies will be waiting at the edge of the village with their problems for 'the Master' to solve." I laughed again.

Bruno groaned, "May the spirits save me from them! I would rather fight ten yellow Mongols with onion breath than face those women. All I want to do right now is spend some time at home with Diana and my daughters. Both of them will need husbands next year, and those two tall Russians, Alex and Nicholas, might be just who they need! Big men like them will make big sons! We will beat Ander in the tug of war contest for the next twenty years!" We both laughed.

After a few miles, we switched places with Bruno walking and me riding Boomer. Bruno told me, "I have another idea." I waited for him to talk, wondering what else he had on his mind when he said, "Daven, your battle plan was brilliant. We did not lose a man or a horse. No one's life was even threatened, yet their numbers were about the same as ours. There is not one other hunter in the Botai or the Hungarians who could have planned that battle as well as you did." I thanked him and listened for what was else he had to say.

Then he spoke, "I need a full-time man who will be second in command. It has to be someone who can step in if anything happened to me or if I was away and an immediate decision was needed. Daven, I am going to promote you to the title of 'Second Oldson' at the feast when we reach home. You will continue to lead our hunts and battles if any more come up.

"For now, you will stay as head of the Horse Clan at least until we agree on someone to take over for you." I was pleased to hear what he said, but I would rather have heard Bruno say that Mikl was taking over my clan. Perhaps that discussion could wait for another day.

Bruno continued, "It will be a new title, and it might need some explaining, so I plan to talk to the elder women first. I do not want to change the traditional path of succession, but I need a second in command, someone with experience and someone that I can trust. The elders will understand my thinking. I will also explain it to Jon, so he does not think he has been bypassed in the long run."

Bruno talked as he walked. "I know my thinking is outside the expected transition from one leader to the next, but it is needed with our increased numbers. Someday when I step down, you may want to step down with me and let the new leader name a second in command. In my opinion, it is best not to force a line of succession, especially when the person to inherit the title is young and might not be ready to move up. Jon will understand, and he will be better prepared when the time comes. Jon, Mikl, and George are the future when you and I are too old to be in charge of anything except maybe our bowel movements!" We howled.

"My plan of naming you as my second in command will give Jon five or more years to learn under us before taking over. We now have eighty-nine people with the ten Russians joining us. When the newcomers marry, our numbers will grow that much more. Soon we may have to think of forming a third village because we are right back to the number of people we had when Ander moved almost three years ago. The problem is that I know of no other good locations for a new village."

Bruno said he had one more thing in mind. "I am going to name a fourth clan called the North Clan with Mikl as its clan leader. It will be made up of all the newcomers plus Mikl and Marie and their child on the way. When these ten new people marry, the North Clan will have over twenty-three members by next year, not counting children, so he will have his hands full. I have one word of caution for Mikl. The Russians must become part of the Botai rather than staying apart from us. That includes our language and customs. It could be a more difficult adjustment than what it appears."

As I walked, I thought of Ildiko, her second pregnancy, and my son, Marc. It would be a great feeling to hug her in just one more day. Mikl talked of Marie and the fact that he would be a father before the winter was over. If he was a father, I would be a grandfather at the ripe old age of thirty.

That evening, we made our last camp before we reached home. Over the evening meal, I told Mikl of Bruno's plans for both of us. I asked Mikl to keep the secret until it was announced. He was excited and proud to be named a clan leader, joining his best friend, Jon, at the same rank. His comment was, "I am pleased to lead a clan and, Father, no one deserves a promotion to a higher rank more than you."

I reminded him. "I need your help with a few fall hunts before you settle in for the winter learning how to be a family man." In practical terms, he and Marie already had a family with her four cousins who will live with them until new pit houses can be built. The rest of his new North Clan would have to use the one spare pit house we had.

Mikl talked about the new swords we took and how anxious he was to make his own sword of bronze. He and Tedd would work through the winter using their new bellows and the right combination of three parts of tin to seventeen parts of copper to make even better swords and new handles for the ones we took from the Mongols.

We reached the Botai village with the huge stone carving of Ildiko riding Gray Boy. Bruno called a halt in front of the carved rock. He said to Mikl and Dann the carver, "I want you men to melt two of those Mongol swords and pour the new metal over the carving. It will let everyone coming this way know that they are in our home. Let it gleam in the sun. That is us, we are the bronze horsemen!"

Mikl replied, "It will be done tomorrow morning, before the feast."

The entire village came out to greet us. Ildiko, holding Marc, was the first to reach me with a welcoming embrace. Marie and her cousins were overjoyed to see each other, as were the other Russians. Many of them were the same cousins she knew from so long ago. Both sides had so much to talk about, interrupted by constant hugs and screams for joy at seeing them alive.

Marie had a new life, the one she wanted, and her friends had escaped a life of horror. I watched her face and noticed that she did not seem pleased when she greeted the two former house slaves, Katarina and Jewel. I thought it might be because she did not know them, but I was not sure. I suspected it was something more.

The feast started early that evening out front of the village near the now-shiny carving of Ildiko on the horse. Tedd and Mikl had applied the new bronze coating earlier that day. It was so beautiful that it almost had to be touched when you looked at it.

An hour later, our bellies were full, and the wine flowed as Bruno announced the changes. I was named as his second in command. If anything happened to Bruno while he was the Oldson, I would succeed him. After five years, Jon would succeed me as the oldest son of Bruno.

Bruno asked for quiet. He had an announcement. When he had everyone's attention he said, "Mikl was promoted to clan leader. He will lead a new group called the North Clan. He and Marie and their coming child would be the first members along with all of the Russian newcomers" Three of these brother-and-sister combinations already had their eyes on possible spouses, two of whom were Bruno's daughters. I expected the North Clan would increase in size very soon.

Jon was relieved when Bruno explained the changes and was truly happy for me. He told me, "Daven, the promotion is well deserved and gives me five years to learn from my father and you before I have to think about taking my father's role. I am honored to learn from a man like you." He hugged me and patted my back. George, Agi, and Sophia were back together, and Marie was proud of Mikl and his promotion. The feast went on all night with many stories of battle repeated by those who took part. Success was beyond our best hopes.

The biggest question was what to do with all those sheep that followed us home. Although half of the herd stayed at the Yar village, just as many came with us. The Russian farmers stepped forward. Alex said, "Russians know something about herding sheep." The crowd gave him his first cheer. The feast was a great time. The old songs were sung well into the night.

I noticed that Jewel sat at Bruno's fire. As the wine took over, she moved closer to him when Diana got up to dance with Janos. She listened to his every word and smiled. She was a true beauty, but I sensed trouble. This celebration ran longer than any in memory. Several people ate lamb for the first time and enjoyed the "new flavor" of mutton stew.

Ildiko looked wonderful. Marc pulled at my tunic to get my attention, and I carried him around most of the night. I was lost in thought, still thinking about taking those bronze swords. Should we have left them? "Let it go," I said. "Battles were a thing of the past." I hugged Marc and Ildiko and felt the swell of her stomach. We joined the singing. It was time to celebrate, not to worry about something that would never happen.

CHAPTER 40

Adventures of the Bronze Horsemen

I WENT TO sleep that night thinking that battles against other tribes were a thing of the past. The village returned to normal activities over the next month. We completed our usual fall hunts and final gathering as in the past and celebrated our monthly winter festivals. Mikl and Tedd made progress with their improved bellows and learned how to work bronze. The biggest problems we had over the winter were with two females from the Russian newcomers, but that was another story, to be told in the future.

On our first horse hunt of the spring, I assigned two hunters to guard the trail coming south on the other side of the Urals while the main body of us were away. We returned from the hunt with a good supply of meat and two more male colts to train. The men who watched the trail waited for me with a tale of what had happened yesterday.

Patrick and Alex, the recently rescued Russian from last year, returned from their guarding duties with two captives. Each man was secured to a pole with their arms tied behind them. Both men were seriously wounded and no threat to escape.

Patrick told me what happened. "We saw two armed men, carrying travel packs and sleeping rolls on their backs. They looked as though they were searching for something. I noticed they wore red armbands on their right arms, up near their shoulders. From the stories I heard at our winter campfires, I knew they were Smolens, the same people from the north who attacked the clans in the old days."

Patrick continued with the story of the capture. "We watched them approach and let them pass by in silence as they walked the trail heading to our village. At first, I was excited to see them. I thought they might be young men taking a journey or an adventure trip, but I knew journeys were taken by younger men. The big man was not my age. He was more the age of you or Bruno. I realized, they were not travelers, they were scouts.

Alex added, "The big man gave the orders, so we assumed he was the leader. He has two deep scars from past battles and two more wounds from yesterday. One scar runs through his scalp, across his face to the point of his chin. The other scar is in his right shoulder, perhaps an old arrow wound." The description of the old wounds gave me a chill.

Patrick was the lead man and had to make a decision without the benefit of a clan leader. He whispered to his fellow guard, "Alex, hold your fire until I take the first shot. I will take out the smaller man. You hit the leader, but try not to kill him. They will give us more information alive than dead."

Patrick told what happened next. "The two Smolens turned to leave after counting our pit houses and the many horses in our village. The lead scout was so excited that he talked in a raised voice and failed to notice that he was being watched, a serious mistake for an experienced fighter. They acted like beginners, like children with a story to tell. I think they found what they thought would be the next place to conquer and plunder. The leader motioned to the smaller man as they headed in the other direction, back where they came from."

Patrick continued, "We waited until they passed directly in front of us. It was then that I shot the small man through his left shoulder. My arrow penetrated the man so hard that it pinned him to the tree he stood in front of. He cried out in pain and asked for help. The leader saw the arrow in his partner who fell forward, holding his injured shoulder.

Alex told his part of the story. "I hit the bigger man with an arrow with such force that it penetrated into his back pack. He tried to pull the arrow out, but it was tangled in the leather pack and would not budge. He looked around in terror to see where the arrow came from, but he saw nothing. The big man stood up tall with his hand on the wound and tried to get a better look when Patrick's next arrow tore through his leg. Neither shot was a killing blow, just as Patrick planned."

Patrick added, "The big man staggered a few feet farther and fell to the ground. He broke off the arrow in his leg and pulled it out. He was too badly wounded to run. He looked up, and we were on him. There was no chance he would get away. We tied their hands behind their backs and placed lariats around their necks. The lariats were attached to our horses. The young man with the shoulder wound walked without falling. The leader fell many times, and we dragged him before we let him stand up again. When we brought the prisoners into the village, the leader was bloodied and in bad condition. The second one is in better shape."

Patrick said, "Daven, they speak another language so we have not learned very much from them. I can tell you, they use the old-style bows and have no bronze weapons. One other thing of interest, the one we assumed was a young man is a mere boy of perhaps ten years of age. They are yours from here." Patrick and Alex walked with me, Bruno, and the clan leaders. Patts, Elizza, and many of the villagers had gathered around the prisoners. I sent for the elder women.

As soon as I saw the big man, I knew exactly who he was, but he did not recognize me. I was a boy of nine years when I gave him the scar in his shoulder. I instructed Patts to remove the arrows and bandage both men. I wanted this enemy, who came to kill us, to think there was some hope that we might spare their lives. If they had hope of being spared, they might talk to save themselves. I was surprised at the age of the second prisoner, he was just a boy. I wondered what he was doing on a scouting trip like this one.

I spoke to Bruno and the other leaders, including Ruth and Emma, both of whom were present when the Smolens raided our village. I told them, "The big man with the scar was the one who killed both of my parents so many years ago. We will question him first."

Ruth and Emma agreed; without doubt, it was the same man. I said, "I saw my father cut him across his face before he killed him. He deserves no mercy and a slow death. The other one is a boy. He will tell what he knows when he sees the other man die."

Bruno said, "I was fighting for my life that day and do not remember him. We need to know what the Smolens are planning and their strength in numbers. Do what you want with him, Daven. If he killed my parents, I would take him apart piece by piece." Bruno asked Ruth and Emma, "Do you speak any of their language?"

Emma was the oldest. She replied, "I speak an older Hungarian dialect which is similar and related to the original language of the people to the north lands, the Finns. They will understand me enough to know what you are asking them." I waited until Patts was done with them before we questioned them.

While we waited, Toth and three of his Hungarian hunters arrived on horseback. They rode a long distance to come to our village. Toth excitedly told us a very similar story to what Patrick and Alex described earlier. Two Smolens men were seen scouting their village. They were run down by the very horses we gave them. Toth dragged them back to his village. He chopped off one scout's feet and then his hands while the second scout screamed in horror. Toth chopped off part of the first man's face and watched him bleed to death. He turned to the second man.

Toth understood their language. He said, "Talk or die." The second man begged for his life. Toth said, "He told all he knew. The Smolens had grown too large in numbers for their village. They ran out of food every winter and needed more territory. The only decision was which village to attack first, the Hungarians or the Botai."

Toth killed the second man with his ax without asking anything more. He learned a lot less than what I wanted to know from our captives.

The big man, the leader with the scar across his face, would be the first to die and the boy would watch. The first man's death would not be easy. He did not deserve easy. I needed all the information I could get from the boy before we could destroy our old enemy, the Smolens.

I spoke to Toth and Bruno and the others. "I have been thinking about this for years. I knew the day would eventually arrive when the Smolens would attack us again." I said with confidence, "If we use the plan I have in mind, we can defeat the Smolens, but it will be a war of attrition and more brutal than what we did to the Mongols."

Bruno deferred to me. He said, "Daven, the captives are yours. Learn all you can and let the others watch and learn. Have Toth and his men watch too." By now, Patts was finished with her work and I returned to the prisoners.

I pulled my bronze sword from its scabbard and heard the frightening twang sound. I pointed at the big man and said, "I will start the questions with him." The boy said something, but I did not understand what he said and paid him no attention.

I told Emma to ask him the big man, "What is your name. Why are you here, and how many hunters do the Smolens have?" He spit at me. I placed my blade on his right hand. I raised my sword above my head and chopped off all the fingers of the hand that killed my father. I let him writhe in pain for some time. The boy screamed in horror.

I pushed the tip of my blade against the scar of the big man's his shoulder, the scar I gave him when I was nine years old and asked, "Do you remember me? I remember you." His face showed fear for the first time. He knew me now. I raised my sword and told Emma, "Repeat the question."

END

Follow the lives of the Botai, their friends, and their enemies in the second book in this series titled Adventures of the Bronze Horsemen. I expect to have the second book to be published in 2013. See the web site titled "The Bronze Horsemen" for more information.

David Mallegol